An Untimely Frost

Books by Ted Morrissey

Men of Winter, a novel
Figures in Blue, a novelette
The Beowulf *Poet and His Real Monsters,* a monograph

An Untimely Frost

or

The Authoress

~

A Novel

Ted Morrissey

Includes

Researching the Rhythms of Voice, by the author
Discussion Questions

Twelve Winters Press

Sherman, Illinois

Published by

Twelve Winters Press, LLC

P. O. Box 414
Sherman, IL 62684-0414

TwelveWinters.com

An Untimely Frost, or *The Authoress*, was first published by Twelve Winters Press in 2014.

"Researching the Rhythms of Voice" first appeared in *Writers Ask #54*, published by Glimmer Train Press. Copyright © 2011 Ted Morrissey.

Cover & Interior Page Design: Ted Morrissey
Cover Photo: copyright © Grant Newland
Author Photo: copyright © Shannon O'Brien

ISBN
978-0-9895151-1-5

Printed in the United States of America

For Michael, Zachary, Ethan, Spenser
& for Melissa

Contents

Acknowledgments

The first chapter of *An Untimely Frost* was published in *The Sleepy Weasel*, edited by Peter Ellertsen, under the title "The Authoress." "Researching the Rhythms of Voice" was first published in *Writers Ask #54*, Glimmer Train Press. For the *Writers Ask* piece and for the text of the novel in general, I drew much inspiration and some details from *Washington Irving and the Storrows: Letters from England and The Continent, 1821-1828*, edited by Stanley T. Williams. I have read so much and studied the biography and work of Mary Shelley for so long that I couldn't possibly cite specific sources that contributed to the novel, but I express my sincere appreciation for all scholars, whose diligence keeps the past and its people available to us. I would like to thank the following in particular: photographer Grant Newland for his generosity in allowing me to use his work for the book cover (visit photographybygrantnewland.com); Shannon O'Brien for her assistance with graphic design on the cover; Dana Whitten for donating her expertise in translating French; John McCarthy for his support of me and Twelve Winters Press; and Pamm Collebrusco for her always reliable editing and proofreading, and also for her support of me and Twelve Winters Press. Furthermore, I thank my sons—Zachary, Ethan and Spenser—for their help, including their help in keeping me humble. Finally, I thank my partner in all things, Melissa, for her unflagging encouragement and optimism.

An Untimely Frost

All this has sunk me in a state of loneliness no other human being ever before, I believe, endured.

—*from the journal of Mary W. Shelley*

I have often repined at my single state and have looked forward with doubt and solicitude to the possibility of an old age solitary, uncherished and unloved.

—*from the letters of Washington Irving*

One

~

THE LONDON STREETS CONFOUNDED ME. I HAD THE ADDRESS OF
her residence, obtained via my London publisher—how difficult
could it be to find, 261½ Wicker's Lane? How difficult indeed! The
cut of my suit was like a giant flame for the moth-like streetpeople,
hawking their wares directly in my face, so that I smelled their rotting
teeth and breakfasts of spoiled turnips and onions. And solicitous
women . . . at ten in the morning? Even Old New Yorkers waited
until after a proper luncheon for such engagements, I would think.

In spite of the distractions I found the inauspicious house on
Wicker's Lane. I stood across from it and gazed somewhat in awe:
here was the residence of Margaret T. Haeley, authoress of so many
of my fretful nights. For months after reading *Dunkelraum*, before
I could settle into sleep, I would check under my bed and in the
wardrobe for Mrs. Haeley's monster—ridiculous, I knew even then,
for a giant to be lurking in such small places. But if it were possible
at all for her monster to exist, my still childish mind must have
reasoned, then it was equally possible for him to break the physical
laws of space.

My wonder at Mrs. Haeley's monster contributed in no mean
part to my wanting to take up the pen myself. (Which reminded
me, I still needed to finish the proof-sheets for *Andersen's Romance*;
Murry—that was Mr. A. B. C. Murry of Claxton House—was, I
imagined, growing impatient as he wanted to capitalize on the
renewed interest in America in *Sunnydale*, my second book and first
full-length novel; there was a stage play in the works, rumored to
be starring none other than Mr. Junius Booth. Murry had had the

proof-sheets delivered to the hotel and the stack was waiting in my room upon my arrival. No rest for the weary, they say.)

The thought of the house's occupant quickened my pulse but the narrow-shouldered structure itself was remarkably unremarkable: brown-stained boards (in need of fresh stain) which led one's eye to black-shuttered windows that were too small for the house's two and a half storeys; the windows gave the impression the old house was squinting. I recalled the boyhood trick of squinting at an object until the act of only partial seeing—of shutting out more and more light—transformed the object into something altogether of another world. I was tempted to narrow my eyes at the old structure. . . .

Church-bells' pealing in the neighborhood broke my reverie. I was readying myself to cross the lane and call on Mrs. Haeley when I noticed a slightly built black fellow approach the house with a leather tote of wood—wood, yes, I realized, but not split logs or kindling as such—rather broken pieces of furniture: a severed table leg protruded conspicuously from the tote, which the fellow balanced quite easily on his narrow shoulder. He bypassed Mrs. Haeley's front steps and instead went to an alternate door to the side, below street level, that I had not observed at all. A moment to fiddle with the lock and the black fellow with his sticks of furniture disappeared from view.

I waited for a dray to pass; the malnourished beast pulling it deposited a fresh dollop of manure in the lane. Then, dodging the droppings, I went to Mrs. Haeley's front door. There was a bell-key positioned beneath a pane of stained glass, glass which was too smudged and greasy for me to make out its figures. I turned the key and heard the rattling chime within. I imagined its echoing in the empty foyer of a haunted and abandoned house. . . . Thinking of Mrs. Haeley's monster had worked its old spell on my fancy.

I waited, listening to the noises of the streetpeople behind me. I did not want to appear rude but I turned the bell-key again. After all, I knew someone was inside. Another long period elapsed. I took my card from my vest pocket (beforehand I had added the name of my hotel, The Saint Georges) and I was intending to slip the card through the postman's slot when I heard footsteps inside, then the bolt . . . bolts (four!) were moved aside, and the door slowly and creakily receded but only about a hand's length. "Yes?" came a man's voice, English but not a Londoner it seemed. It was gloomy inside Mrs. Haeley's house but with the little daylight leaking into the narrow space I realized the gatekeeper (I thought of Macbeth's jocular one) was the slightly built black fellow.

"Hello there; I've come to pay my regards to Mrs. Haeley—a mutual friend recommends me." *Friend* was a bit strong as I wasn't certain that any true ones existed in the book business but I hoped the innocent embellishment would gain me admittance.

"Mrs. Haeley is not receiving callers today, sir. Thank you . . ." and he began to close the door.

"Wait—please—I've come such a long way—" It was true, and my feet were starting to pain me again. "Will you at least present her my card?" I held it in the narrow opening and felt the foyer's draft on my fingers. The fellow's hand came up, perhaps reluctantly, to take it. The realization struck me that there was no proper servant in Mrs. Haeley's house, just this taciturn handyman or whatever he was, who completed the task and shut the door without further word. The bolts were slid back into place.

I stood a moment at Mrs. Haeley's door, nonplussed at being turned away so unceremoniously; then I began my descent of the five steps but halted when I heard the bolts again. The door opened more fully this time and the black fellow stood in its frame. "Jefferson Wheelwright—author of *Sunnydale* and the Old New Yorker stories?"

I had turned and was looking up from the second step. "That's correct, my good fellow—at your service." I put a finger to my hat brim (a high, round-crown affair I was informed was the epitome of London vogue, though I had not seen a one since stepping from the *Chaos*, an old packet whose crew made certain she was aptly named).

"Mrs. Haeley is not taking callers but she would not wish me to turn away a man of letters without some refreshment. Won't you step indoors, sir?"

"Most kind; thank you." I was still disappointed at not meeting Mrs. Haeley, but I was feeling most fagged and some tea and a taste of biscuit sounded quite glorious. I went in and removed my allegedly fashionable hat (it was chocolate brown velveteen made from the same bolt as my coat lapels, vest and cuffs—I was sparing no expense for my tour of England and the Continent). When Mrs. Haeley's man closed the door the foyer was plunged into a profound gloom for which my eyes were ill prepared.

"This way, Mr. Wheelwright."

"Your name, sir?"

"Mrs. Haeley has always called me 'Thursday.'"

"Like Crusoe's Friday."

"Yes—but one better, she says." The pride in Thursday's voice was evident. From the foyer we went into a long narrow hall. The irregularity of the walls made me think they were in sad disrepair; then my adjusting eyes discovered the appearance of irregularity was due to the fact the walls were lined with books, stacks and stacks of books, each reaching close to the fourteen-foot ceiling. Actually it was my nose that helped my eyes to interpret clearly: the wonderful smell of old books permeated Mrs. Haeley's house. There were hundreds of books just in the hall—perhaps thousands!

Thursday paused for a moment and deftly removed a book from the middle of a stack, about eye height, and handed it to me before turning a corner into a room I soon discovered was the parlor. Daylight filtered in through slightly ajar shutters and sheer curtains—enough light to allow me to read the spine of the book: *Sketches of the Old New Yorkers*. The volume, I was happy to see, was well thumbed.

Thursday took my hat. "It's very nice—I've not seen one quite like it."

"So I'm beginning to suspect."

He placed the hat on a coat tree in the corner from which a long woolen scarf and a dark jacket already hung. The room was of good proportions with several couches and armchairs and low seats of the Ottoman style. A large oval table occupied the more or less center of the room. It all gave the impression, however, that though it was a place to welcome guests, none had been welcomed there for some time.

Thursday invited me to sit while he fetched "a nuncheon of tea and crackers." I took a couch opposite one of the room's three windows. I smelled the dust that was unsettled by my sitting. There were no pictures on the walls, though there were darkened rectangular spaces where ones had been hanging for years. The motif of the book continued as there were stacks here and there in the parlor, none as prodigious, though, as those that stood in the hall.

My eyes had adapted totally and I perused the volume of *Sketches* Thursday had handed me. I opened the cover and there was the India-ink portrait of me rendered by young Melissa Blackwood, my neighbor's daughter during my Albany days (the Blackwoods had moved to Brussels and I planned to visit them on my tour). Little Miss had done a remarkable job on the portrait for such a youthful artist but the likeness was not perfect. Her affection for her "Uncle Jeff" had caused her to widen the space between my eyes and to thin my lips and to tuck in my ears (the ears which had acquired for me the grammar-school nickname of "Chimp"). I realized that the inclusion of my portrait rendered by such a juvenile hand was apropos in so much as the sketches themselves were unpracticed in their way, too—though at the time I considered them the masterpieces of the age. Only two years elapsed between *Sketches* and *Sunnydale,* yet they were worlds apart in craft. I trusted that my new work demonstrated a similar advancement in my technique, but I wasn't so certain: I'd often felt in something of an artistic rut.

The musing reminded me of one of my chief reasons for calling upon Mrs. Haeley. Like the rest of the literary world, I wondered if the authoress was at work on something new. Other than the posthumous volume of her husband's verse that she had edited and for which had written a touching introduction, nothing had come from her pen, save, I supposed, for letters to family and friends (I held out hope of becoming one of the latter).

Thursday returned with a silver tray and pot, both slightly tarnished, two delicate-looking cups, and a plate of crackers. I wondered then if Mrs. Haeley would be receiving me after all. But Thursday, after pouring my tea and adding a spot of cream at my request, fixed himself a cup and sat in a chair adjacent to my couch. I was not used to such behavior from a domestic, and it occurred to me that maybe Thursday was more than that to Mrs. Haeley. When did Haeley drown? It'd been more than ten years. Sipping at my tea, I tried to examine Thursday's features more acutely in the parlor's poor light: his nose was somewhat broad and his lips thick, but his hair, which was brushed straight back, was more Italian in appearance than African; so he seemed of mixed parentage.

"The tea is very good. Thank you for it." I took a cracker from the plate. It proved stale but was tolerable (and welcome) with the tea. "When might Mrs. Haeley be receiving?"

Thursday lowered the cup from his lips. "It is difficult to say. She does not see many visitors so there is no regularity to it."

I would imagine journalists were a constant bother to the household. She had been, after all, notorious in her youth, before Haeley's yachting accident. I recalled the headline in the *Post*: CELEBRATED ENGLISH POET DEAD! / STEPHEN HÆLEY'S YACHT CAPSIZES DURING STORM. A romantic teenager at the time, I immediately fantasized courting and wooing Haeley's young widow, of taking his place at her side, a new King with the Queen of English literati. I had not thought of all that for years but perhaps the notion lay on the underside of my mind when I made my plans for the tour.

We sat in silence for a time with our tea and crackers. I was trying to think of something to say when there was a creaking overhead as if someone were walking about upstairs. I looked to Thursday, perhaps to confirm it was the lady herself.

"Old houses and their rheumatic joints." Thursday smiled, his teeth as white as alabaster in the gloomy parlor.

"Indeed." Then I had the crazy thought that Mrs. Haeley was not there at all . . . that Thursday was an invader of her home, had murdered the famous (infamous?) authoress and buried her in the yard. There were instances of actresses and opera dancers having overzealous supporters who would not leave them be and who sometimes broke into their rooms—even a case or two wherein the worshipper did harm to their chosen idol because of their twisted devotion. To my knowledge, authoresses did not generate such a following (nor authors for that matter), but there is always a first case. "How is Mrs. Haeley?"

"Oh Mrs. Haeley is fine. I make certain she gets her meals and her rest." There was more of that pride in Thursday's voice, though it sounded as if he were referring to a prized equine and not the lady of the house. On the one hand, I had no reason to doubt Thursday's assertion but on the other my first impression of Mrs. Haeley's house

was not of its being a place of sound health. It seemed like a home
from her fiction, a birthplace for a monster. Perhaps her upstairs
apartment was all light and cheerfulness, a place she could revel in
the sort of vitality Thursday implied. After all, Mrs. Haeley was still
a young woman, only some eight years my senior. It was just that
she achieved literary fame at such a young age, her novel the buzz
of New York City, London, Paris, Brussels, all coinciding with her
twentieth birthday. Quite remarkable really.

I finished my tea and crackers, feeling somewhat refreshed,
which was good as I would likely have to hike up to Fullham Road on
aching feet to find a cab. I had been dropped there, wishing to walk
the remaining blocks, to take in the sights and sounds of the Old City.
My head was filled with London stories—of the strolling gentlemen
and ladies, of the fancy carriages, of the gay chimneysweeps. This
idealized tableau was not the London I found. Perhaps it was
somewhere else, in another district. I wondered at the impression
of Old New York my book created and whether visitors were taken
aback by the genuine thing. I was no doubt giving myself and my
pen too much credit.

"Well," I said, placing my cup upon the tray, "thank you, Thursday,
for the refreshment; it worked wonderfully and I feel quite able to
return to the hotel."

"I'm sorry, sir, you did not see Mrs. Haeley, but I will tell her of
your visit and present your card." We both had risen and Thursday
was crossing the room to retrieve my hat.

I appreciated Thursday's politeness but it wasn't the same thing
as insuring me a future audience with Mrs. Haeley.

He handed me my hat. "One thing more, sir, if you would." He
went to a small writing desk in the corner of the parlor and returned
with a pen and ink-bottle. I understood, and sat on the edge of the
couch to autograph the volume of *Sketches*. It took me a moment to
decide what to write but after turning to the cover page I inscribed:
"To Mrs. Haeley and her 'inmates,' Best Regards, J. Wheelwright."
The "inmates" remark, of course, was meant as an allusion to her
novel, where the childhood Hans mistakes the word *intimates* for
inmates, and it proves ominous foreshadowing. I wondered though
if my cleverness—my wanting to illustrate my level of familiarity

with Mrs. Haeley's work—would be grasped . . . and appreciated. It
was done now. I used the ink-bottle to hold open the front cover and
first pages until my inscription would dry, and I lay the pen besides.

A moment later I was on the stoop listening to Thursday
quadruple bolt the door. And the sounds and smells of Wicker's
Lane were instantly upon me. I began making my way—sore feet and
all—toward the hotel, resolving to hail the first cab I saw. I felt the
old melancholia beginning to stir. I hadn't a clue what a visit to Mrs.
Haeley's home would yield, but my experience was a disappointment
of the first order.

Two

~

MY ROOM AT THE SAINT GEORGES WAS NICELY APPOINTED: silk upholstered furniture whose wooden arms and legs were painted golden-green; an ornately carved writing desk with a legend running its border depicting some sort of boar hunt; a spacious mahogany wardrobe; and a high, canopied bed, so high it took a two-step to climb into it. It was in the bed that I had become accustomed to enacting my authorial duties since arriving. I would perform my toilette precisely at six—the sun crackling on the Thames beyond my window—then the hotel porter would deliver coffee and toasted bread with gooseberry jam at six-and-twenty. I would carefully ascend to my bed with the breakfast tray, the portable secrétaire (stocked with ink, pen and paper the previous evening) next to me as well. After finishing my toast and taking a few swallows of the good hot coffee, I'd place the secrétaire across my lap and begin the day's work. In transit I'd been writing a history of the Dutch in New York, focusing especially on Peter Stuyvesant and New Netherland, but the Old City had altered my mood—or perhaps it was my proximity to Mrs. Haeley—and I had had something more fanciful in mind. My inspiration was an ancient Indian tale about an avenging spirit who brings harm to evil-doers. In the original, the spirit takes the form of various animals (bear, elk, bobcat, &c.) to bring the evil-doers to poetical justice; I, on the other hand, was having the avenging spirit overtake the minds and bodies of the evil-doer's friends and family, a sort of enveloping shadow. In *my* mind I was thinking of the story as "Makadewa," the Algonquin name for the spirit, but I knew ultimately that wouldn't do for a title.

So far I was having a splendid time lounging in the gigantic bed at The Saint Georges, drinking the black-black Italian coffee, and scribbling my tale. I even felt a brief—brief, mind you—pang of guilt at the idea that this is what I did to earn my keep in the world. Like many of the Wheelwright men, I'd tried my hand at business, but to dismal results. I simply do not have a head for numbers and inventories and so on—I can conjure whole worlds with my pen, yet adding a column of numbers and arriving at the correct result seemed beyond me (I believe because midway I would lose interest and begin daydreaming of haunted castles on lonely, wind-swept cliffs). Fortunately, my older brother, Peter, agreed to take over the family business enterprises—mainly a copper mine, and a company exporting furs—and allow me to follow my Muse. My literary efforts had been profitable but it was my shares in the family businesses that allowed me such frivolities as traveling abroad. Good luck had been mine in this world, and I tried never to forget it.

I wrote for three uninterrupted hours; the pages lay around me to dry on the spread of plushest qiviut wool. By then it was time for the surgeon's visit, Dr. Carter, whom I found on recommendation of the hotel. His surgery was just down the street from The Saint Georges, and he routinely attended to its guests' medical needs, from fractured bones to flatulent bowels. Carter was an amiable fortyish fellow. My second morning in London I summoned him to my room, via an hotel footman (no irony intended), because of my inflamed feet. The good doctor came at once. Carter had a little whitening beard of the vandyke style, and probing blue eyes that were often behind pince-nez tethered by a silver chain to his vest. His brown suit was simple but dignified and well kept. After his first visit we arranged for his coming each day at the same time; Carter proved quite punctual.

There was a knock at the door and I called for Carter to enter, which he did along with an hotel porter bearing a small metal tub of hot water. The porter placed the tub in front of an overstuffed armchair and laid a folded towel on the small table next to the chair. The doctor and I exchanged pleasantries. Whilst I climbed down from bed, careful not to disturb my pages, Carter added mineral salts and other medicines to the water (from small packages he had brought in his red-leather valise), stirring them with a painter's stick.

I half expected the fine fellow to begin intoning secret incantations, like those black hags upon Macbeth's midnight heath. Leaning against the bed, I removed my stockings; then I went to the chair and eased my feet into the hot bath. At first the water seemed nearly too hot but within seconds its soothing powers took effect. I closed my eyes and sank deeper into the big chair.

Though it had been but a few days, Carter and I had quite an air-tight ritual. While my poor feet soaked, he would stand at the bed and read my morning's work, page by page. This was unusual. I normally let no one see my stories in progress, but Carter was of such an easy nature and asked so childlike on his first visit if he may "take a glance," I felt at ease to say yes. I closed my eyes and listened while Carter read my words and every so often emitted little, audible reactions to the story—a "hym" (more breath than word) at something unexpected, or a chuckle, as light as a blushing maiden's, now and again. I would imagine where he was in the story, noting the picking up and replacing of pages too. Meanwhile, my ailing feet luxuriated in the bath Carter had prepared.

On the first morning, he listened to my complaint while touching and gently kneading my feet and toes, which were blotchy red, except around the toenails where the skin was a vibrant purple. Spots on my feet were pained to the touch while my toes were dead numb. Carter's hands were as soft as those of a wealthy man's favorite daughter. The good doctor said it was a circulation problem; he said that even though exercise irritated my feet, rest was counterproductive, that we must increase blood flow to nourish the nerve fibers. He sounded quite confident in his diagnosis, without being boastful.

After the twenty-minute bath, I dried my feet thoroughly. Then Carter sat upon a chair opposite me and had me place my feet in his lap. It seemed undignified to me, and the intimacy was awkward at first, but I supposed men of medicine were used to such intercourse with their patients. Carter put a pungent balm on his hands and thoroughly massaged my feet, which were a vivid scarlet after the medicinal bath; the good doctor even worked the oily substance between my benumbed toes. Presently my feet were tingling and heated. Carter loosely wrapped my feet in the towel and had me rest them on the chair from which he had just risen. My feet became exceedingly hot, near combustible, but it was not unpleasant. The doctor left me as such for some time while he cleaned his hands in the room's wash basin, then went to the window and surveyed the Old City.

Carter wanted me to take a thirty-minute stroll each day, to encourage blood flow and exercise the nerve fibers. He was in the habit of suggesting destinations and supplying directions while he stood at the window. He was out of view behind me, so I would listen and respond in ways that seemed appropriate. In truth, I paid only half attention as the penetrating balm on my feet seemed to act as something of an opiate on my brain. Perhaps I was merely relaxed and a little sleepy.

On this morning, Dr. Carter said, "Why don't you come to my club, at about two, for a late lunch. I've told my chaps of the famous writer I've been attending and they would be quite thrilled to have you honor our humble society."

I'd been rather enjoying the solitude of my London stay and in fact had no great desire for intercourse with my fellow man. Indeed, there was the well-known "American Circle" of poets and artists into whose concentric (and eccentric) interior I was expected to enter but had avoided thus far. However, the doctor had been so kind and was charging me a pittance. . . . "That would be lovely. Thank you, Carter."

He was pleased. He scribbled the address on a slip of paper before he left me. On his way out, as was our practice, he summoned the porter to remove the tub of water, &c. My feet felt so worked over after these treatments it was hard to say if they were improving but they clearly were not worse overall. It seemed to me that with the physicians of America one had to be prepared for a certain amount of "back sliding" along the path to eventual improvement.

I had done some informal sightseeing since arriving; mainly though I'd been dawdling. The pace I'd kept at home was so hectic that I'd taken full advantage of my holiday abroad. I had kept up my writing, yes, but otherwise was quite the man of leisure. Even the proof-sheets Murry was awaiting lay untouched in my carriage trunk. My disappointing call upon Mrs. Haeley seemed to take the nor'easter out of my sail. But I knew my low lying should not persist.

I had a list of obligations and errands as long as Van Winkle's beard that I must get to while in the Old City.

I decided there was no sense in plunging into the deep end of the pond, so to speak; I would start small (and pleasantly enough) with a visit to Bookman & Sons on Printers Row. Bookman was said to be the best shop in all of London for both rare finds from the Continent and the newly imprinted. The general public was only allowed admittance but one day per week; otherwise it was by invitation only—a decidedly undemocratic way to sell books but it had worked for nearly two centuries. And besides which: I had a letter to recommend me in my portmanteau.

I dressed in my suit of dark blue and dove gray . . . with a complementary hat of the same design as the brown one. I had been so convinced by my hatter's pitch regarding London headwear that I'd had him fashion three in various colors. In fact, other than a beaver-fur affair for cold weather, they were the only hats I'd brought with me, fool that 1 am.

Fully attired then, with my feet feeling none the worse for their wearing once I'd donned my stockings and shoes, I left The Saint Georges. It was a sunny day, though a bit hazy, and warm for the season. That storied English rain had not assailed me since arriving. Maybe it was something of a traveler's tale. The way to Bookman & Sons, according to reliable Carter, was along the Thames about an eighth of a mile to Crescent Street; then turn right, following to Printers Row. A blindman couldn't miss it, he said.

The Thames was the color of lead, like the Atlantic during a winter storm, but not so rough as that of course. The current, moving back out to sea with the tide's receding, was distinct on the surface. There were a few poor folk with lines acast in the river and I wondered what sort of miserable catch the odorous river would give up. A few days' run of sun and warmer weather had intensified the Thames' fetidness; summer's so-called dog days must have been ghastly here about, especially when the winds were still. Before reaching Crescent, a fisherman pulled something dark and appropriately finned from the river. The hand-sized creature danced in the unaccustomed air before the fellow snipped the line and it dropped with a lonely *splunk* in his rusty pail.

Crescent was a pleasant enough street and I soon found myself on Printers Row, an old quarter of the Old City known for its several bookshops and still a few printing houses—though the larger houses, like Murry's, were in the Markham district, a good cab ride away. I easily found the shingle of Bookman & Sons, scarlet letters painted on an ebon background, and entered the establishment. A small, flat-noted bell signaled my arrival. Immediately the delicious smell of books old and new wafted over me. The musky scent of aged paper, the tartness of inks, the rich tanning of leather-bound tomes . . . I took in a robust breath as I gladly shut the door on the world-not-of-the-printed-word.

Books filled the room, which had an arched ceiling, and they were all crisply arranged. Tall shelves lined the walls of the long and seemingly narrow room, and volumes of varying hues set touching one to the next with almost martial order. Either a very, very long table or several of the exact height set end to end ran through the center of the room, creating uniform aisles on either side, and these tables were covered with books as well, each precisely set. Daylight filtered in through a series of narrow windows running above the shelves and along the ceiling just before the walls began to curve in service of the arch. It was an impressive display, in quantity and arrangement—more so even than Manhattan's venerable Nightingale & Co.

I was still taking it all in when from a room to the side a door opened and a gentleman with a bald head so shiny it appeared polished and with impressive white muttonchops shuffled toward me: "We are not open to the public this day, sir, if you please." He wore the dark gray pants and vest of a well-tailored suit but without the coat to match so that his white shirt sleeves stood out like curious spirits come to assess the new arrival. If not for the deep red cravat he would have given a decidedly ministerial impression.

"Yes, I know your policy..." I reached into my coat and produced the letter from Mr. Murry. I unfolded the sheet and handed it over.

He found just the correct angle for glancing through the letter; his lips moved ever so slightly on his pinkishly clean-shaven face. I anticipated a sort of revelation to sweep over the old gentleman's features but he merely refolded the letter and said, handing it back,

"Feel free to peruse, Mr. Wheelwright. I shall be in the office should you need any assistance"; and he shuffled away in his ghostly sleeves.

So, hat in hand and a bit deflated, I began to look about in earnest. I was interested in various sorts of books for various reasons. As inspiration to my own writing, I wanted to find some continental folk and fairytales, especially German, Hungarian, Prussian, and so on. Also histories; for some time I had been interested in doing a detailed biography of Christopher Columbus, so books regarding him or his voyages, or even Genoa or Spain of his day were on my list. Besides these older volumes, I wanted to find the newest writers of Britain and France. We American authors were still held as second class to our European brethren and I wanted to see if it were true, or simply Old World snobbery (easy enough to dismiss as snobbery but deep down I feared its veracity). And, I must say it, vanity made me curious if Bookman & Sons carried either of my books.

I began my reconnaissance trying to discern the method to Bookman's madness when it came to arrangement. It seemed that general subject was one method at least as I ran across a series of books on the revolution in France, including Dunburry's esteemed eighteen-volume study *The French Citizens' War. Its Causes and Its Costs.* Dunburry was beautifully bound in crimson cloth with gilt-edged pages. I saw no price for the set—or for anything for that matter—which was generally not the sign of a bargain. There was a nice leather-bound brace of biographies on Louis XVI and Marie Antoinette, a book each, though hers was notably thicker. These books were all on a shelf along the wall, about eye-level. I scanned the next case, looking nearer the floor, and spied a small volume of Italian folktales—knowing enough Italian to discern the title, *Storia Folcloristica il Sovrannaturale.* I flipped through the pages, which smelled something like good strong cheese, and the typeface was inviting. True to the supernatural promise of the title, the words fantasma and streghetta ("phantom" and "little witch") stood out during my brief perusal. I kept the book in hand.

I continued on, losing myself among the wonderful inventory. At one point Mr. Ghostsleeves shuffled out of his office and watched me from a distance, probably to make certain I was not stuffing my coat pockets with rare books. I looked up from the pages I was studying and smiled angelically at him, and old Mr. Ghostsleeves returned himself and his incandescent dome to his den.

Just then I discovered an entire section of bookcase devoted to the Haeleys. Bookman had Stephen Haeley's first collection, *Schooldays*, the one that had put him on England's literary chart while still an adolescent; it had a green mortarboard cover, identical to the copy in my library at home. And they had several copies of *Verse Composed in Germany*. I was familiar with the poems of course, but I picked it up and thumbed through its pages nonetheless. These were the poems, largely, that Haeley wrote while he and Margaret Townsend were eloping across Europe, he leaving his wife and child; Margaret, just a child of sixteen herself, leaving her father and icy-hearted stepmother. They were in love and brilliant and penniless. What boldness to tramp across the Continent with little more than the clothes on their backs, their only significant possession a box of books, stolen mainly from William Townsend, who missed them more profoundly perhaps than the only-child who had absconded in the night with them. She and her married lover! It was a notorious story.

Then, of course, Haeley's young wife drowned—a suicide?—and the lovers came home to England, Haeley to retrieve his child and, he hoped, an allowance from his family; Margaret to give birth to Haeley's second child. The crossing was difficult and perhaps that contributed to it, but in any event Margaret had barely set foot on her native soil when she miscarried. She nearly died too. Once sufficiently recovered, she and Haeley married, and Margaret set about finishing the novel famously begun on a dare. Haeley probably encouraged his child-bride's writing to occupy her mind and hinder her from dwelling overmuch on the image of her lost child (a little girl, if I recall rightly). No one could have guessed at the immense popularity of Mrs. Haeley's debut work, whose first edition was published anonymously in hopes that no name on the book would be a better selling point than a feminine one. Her novel was the talk of London *and* New York City before a second edition appeared, confirming the rumor that a teenage girl had written it. In spite of the name on the new cover page, Margaret Townsend Haeley, there were plenty of skeptics who suspected that Haeley himself had penned *Dunkelraum* and it was just another outrageous stunt by the overbold couple; that, and the publication of a mere novel would not sully Haeley's image as one of England's premier poets.

One wonders if it strained their marriage for Haeley to be relegated to second seat after his novice wife's meteoric ascent in the English literary heavens. At least Mrs. Haeley was not a poet—she just a novelist—so Haeley remained the true artist in the household. This perhaps was the life-preserving ring of cork tossed to his self-image . . . I realized the perverse morbidness of my metaphor, given Haeley's eventual fate.

The shrill little bell on the shop door attracted my attention, and a regal-looking noblewoman entered Bookman & Sons, one of her carriage's footmen following close behind. She was all lavender silks and lace, an enormous lavender hat attached fashionably askew on her head of white ringlets. Even before the gray-clad and powdered-wigged footman could shut the door, Mr. Ghostsleeves had shuffled to attention: "Lady Penelope, it is a pleasure to see you." He gave a little bow—a wonder his head did not momentarily blind her ladyship.

I was pretending to be engaged in my book while Lady Penelope cast a curious eye in my direction, wondering no doubt if I were of her class, measuring the cost of my apparel, yes, but also sizing up my physical attributes—the idea being that nobility was cut from the same cloth, and inferior *fabric* stood out accordingly. I tried to stand a bit straighter, to adjust the fit of my coat; in sum, to bear myself more nobly. I was dubious of my success as I returned my fuller attention to the books, my lifelong nonjudgmental companions.

There were several copies of Mrs. Haeley's novel of course. Next to these, however, were three thin volumes in black mortarboard. The books were so thin there was no space on the spine for title or author. I slid one from its place and was quite surprised by its cover: DESERT ISLE & OTHER POEMS. BY MARGARET T. HÆLEY. Poems? By Mrs. Haeley? I only knew Mrs. Haeley as novelist, not as poet. I opened the booklette to the first piece, which was the title poem:

> Millions tend to this populace isle
> And factories fill its water-bound 'scape.

Countless capital clerks its deeds they do file,
Countless criminals its maids they do rape.
A thousand machines belch pois'nous black smoke.
A thousand breadless souls swallow only hope.
Yet for me 'tis a desert isle alone
In an empty sea, a solitary home.

Like Crusoe, mine is infinite labour
And not for escape to equal barrens,
But merely to be alive and no more.
My wilds are Eden-naught—but fetid fens.
Blooms are not parti-colour'd roses gay;
All ashen soot of black and dungeon grey.
I both long for and fear finding one morn
An alien footprint on the beach alone.

Would Friday the slayer of blackness be,
A white-white knight of Arthurian lore,
Or dread cannibal sent to consume me?
His chain-mail'd mount trampling me the more.
Best then to avoid that long stretch of beach
And stay in my cave void of sun and leech.
For hope is the labour most infinite—
Golden love the treasure most beyond my sight.

I glanced at other poems and they were of similar theme. They were obviously composed after Haeley's drowning. I recalled, too, another baby that was stillborn, and that Mrs. Haeley's half-sister died in premature childbirth, uncertain, gossip had it, who the father was. All of this happened within a year or two. No wonder Mrs. Haeley felt as abandoned and alone as Crusoe, having only her books for solace and company.

Lady Penelope browsed among the books, her man two steps behind. She was obviously quite pretty in her youth—even still there was an attractive radiance to her features. Mr. Ghostsleeves brought a silver tray with a single china teacup for her ladyship's refreshment. She took up the tiny cup and sipped as she looked at the various volumes, rarely even opening one—but being content with her perusal of title and author. Or perhaps it was color and weight, or texture that amused her attention. I had taken Mrs. Haeley's book of poetry and the Italian folkstories thus far. I came to a shelf of American authors and found biographies of Ben Franklin and my namesake, Thomas Jefferson. I looked for my books but there was neither. I wished that I had not had to introduce myself, for then I would have surely posed as eager enthusiast and asked after my titles, making something of a spectacle for Lady Penelope's benefit. I was not above that, I am ashamed to acknowledge.

I was suddenly out of the mood for book-shopping. On the far end of the store, Lady Penelope finished her tea and had her man return the miniature cup to the silver tray—which must have been some sort of cue for Old Ghostsleeves, who instantly materialized from his den with a stack of books, a half dozen or so, all the same. He spoke quietly but I heard the author's name, Edmund Holland. Lady Penelope indicated she did not require the full order after all, only five, and Mr. Ghostsleeves deftly wrapped the quintet in brown paper and string, after which her ladyship's footman took the bundle and followed his mistress from Bookman & Sons, the little bell humbly heralding their departure. No money was exchanged, which must have meant Lady Penelope had an account. I wondered if it was like so many accounts of the aristocracy and was left perpetually in arrears so that shopkeepers had to put the pinch on commonfolk to keep their business solvent.

I went to the front with my two thin books and found the remainder of her ladyship's order: VERSES & VIGNETTES. BY EDMUND HOLLAND. A quick study taught me that A. B. C. Murry was his publisher as well, and that he had penned two other books, *A Case of Calamity* and *Things in Mist*. I added Holland's book to my modest stack and called Mr. Ghostsleeves to settle the bill—not a handsome sum and Mr. G. was duly unimpressed but did bestow upon me a perfunctory "thank you." He agreed to bundle the trio and have them sent to the The Saint Georges, as I did not want to be burdened with them at Carter's club. I retrieved my hat and emerged from the bookshop into the hazy light of Old London, the shouts and scents of fishmongery in the close air.

Three

~

IT REQUIRED ONLY A COUPLE OF FALSE TURNS BEFORE LOCATING
the King James Club, or simply The James, established apparently
during James I's reign—the name being its only royal connection:
the placard outside the door revealed the former by design, and the
latter by omission. I presumed too it was an open club, that is, open
to professional men and gentlemen alike. It was useful for members
of the aristocracy to sometimes mix with the likes of barristers and
physicians, as one never knew when he may require a suit filed or a
bowel unblocked. I availed myself of the large brass knocker, in the
shape of a lion's head and in need of polishing, and a moment later a
black-suited servant opened up. I stepped into the foyer, the floor of
which was an impressive Italian marble with a gray-green hue. The
servant shut the door then stood taciturnly at a ninety-degree angle
to me. I was not sure what to do, other than remove my hat, and the
door-man was not inclined to volunteer any instructions.

We stood there dumb, in a stand-off of the Mexican style, for
an uncomfortably long time. At last a fellow came from a side
room that looked like a greeting parlor and introduced himself as
Chamberlain; I did not know if it were his name or his title but I
introduced myself as Dr. Carter's invited guest. Chamberlain
adopted a puzzled air. "Carter is not arrived today. Henderson, is
Dr. Carter arrived?" Chamberlain had a neatly trimmed beard with
full brush mustaches that moved wavily as he spoke. The door-man,
Henderson apparently, confirmed Carter's absence and volunteered
that no word had been received.

I could see that Chamberlain, in his black suit and gray tie, was at prodigious labor sizing me up—perhaps Henderson was too. I thought of brandishing my publisher's letter—as if I had come about a position, club librarian or something—when the bell chimed and Henderson promptly received the caller; Chamberlain and I stood by like groundlings at a show. It was a messenger-boy, red-capped and all, just like in the stories. Henderson sent him off with a sixpence for his effort and handed the note to Chamberlain. "Ah, it's from Carter. . . ." He read the note in a single glance and looked up at me in surprise. "Mr. Wheelwright, my humblest apologies. . . ." He offered me his hand. "It seems Dr. Carter is unavoidably detained—in fact, he shall miss lunch altogether—but desires us to make you quite at home."

With that I was ushered into the cozy environs of the club and was treated as the visiting dignitary. It went far in restoring my self-image after my inauspicious welcoming at Bookman & Sons. The club had been a family home at one time, and it retained much of that aura, with red floral paper on walls and portraiture everywhere—distinguished club members perhaps, or phantoms of the family gone-by. I was served quite a lovely lunch of mutton, shellfish, wax beans in some sort of buttery sauce, and sweet potatoes; then ilberry pie with cream and good coffee for dessert. There were a half dozen men at the club's dining table. The conversation was congenial but other than being introduced around as Mr. Jefferson Wheelwright, "the famous American author," no one spoke of my writing and I began to wonder if they had any familiarity with my books at all. I was thinking of politely making my exit when Chamberlain turned to me, "If your afternoon is open, Mr. Wheelwright, you must accompany me to my home for tea. My Penny is a great admirer and would be unhappy if I did not bring you round . . . and, to be completely above the gunwale, I have a daughter at home, Hilary, who has a talent for the pen . . . the next Mrs. Austen perhaps . . . something to pursue one day after her own family is well established." Chamberlain, for all his City importance, looked at me like a skittish suitor who has just asked the apple of his eye for a turn on the dancefloor.

I wanted to politely decline but well-to-do friends in London could not hurt my sales. If Murry learned of the snub, I suspected he would have a word or two on the subject. "That would be lovely.

Thank you indeed." I anticipated an afternoon of listening to a ten-year-old's rhymes regarding peacocks, puppies and parrots but I tried not to let my pique show as I said my farewells and thank-yous all around; meanwhile Chamberlain summoned his carriage, which was a fine ebon rig of the brougham style with perfectly matched four-in-hand Welsh ponies. Chamberlain seemed a wealthy man indeed.

We wound our way through the City streets while Chamberlain shared banal intelligences about this club member, who was already foggy in my recollection, and regarding that building or bridge. I nodded, smiled and asked a question every so often to feign interest. Normally I would have been eager to hear local history and color but the impending recital of Miss Hilary clouded my mood—I hoped imperceptibly. The carriage traveled farther than I anticipated and we came to Haslow Park—"a bit of the country-life in the City," Chamberlain called it, proud, as if he were responsible for creating the rustic refuge, as if he had turned the first spade for God. He peered out the carriage, beaming at the wooded lane down which the horses now clopped. Through the trees I saw a pond or lake and just as I was looking a loon took long-winged flight from its surface, which was as pristinely green as art glass. It was all quite perfect, and I thought of Mr. Wordsworth's lines near Tintern Abbey.

> While with an eye made quiet by the power
> Of harmony, and the deep power of joy,
> We see into the life of things.

My spontaneous romantic reverie was so powerful for a moment that I missed the approach to Chamberlain's house and the horses were suddenly reined to a stop. "Arbor-in-the-Glen," announced Chamberlain. "Welcome to my home, Mr. Wheelwright." It was a fine country house of gray stone and ivy, two and a half floors and many windowed, each framed in vivid green shutters.

"It's beautiful," I said, meaning it, as I stepped from the carriage.

Soon we were inside and Chamberlain was alerting everyone of my arrival; his mustaches were rolling like the ocean. I was nearly embarrassed at the fuss, nearly. Arbor-in-the-Glen's rooms were numerous but small, typical of the country style, so that whole sections could be shut off in the height of winter or summer. Today all the rooms were open and a handful of servants were scurrying about in the wake of their master's arrival. After being given a few minutes to freshen myself, I was ushered into the house's central sitting room, where Chamberlain, country squire now changed into a jacket of blue silk, directed me to a seat of honor near the slate fireplace, which of course was not in use on this hazy summer day.

Chamberlain told me some of the history of the house, knowing, I supposed, that its age would impress an American, even one from Old New York. He also told me his wife was in the stables and would be along presently. Then a door on the opposite end of the room opened and in walked one of the loveliest young women I have ever seen, darkly tressed and in a yellow silk dress. She must have been seventeen or eighteen.

"Ah, my dear," said Chamberlain, both of us rising. "Mr. Wheelwright, may I introduce my daughter Hilary. Hilary, this is Mr. Wheelwright, the American author."

She nodded demurely and lowered her brown orbs, perhaps to prevent injuring me with their piercing radiance. I took the hand that she offered. "Miss Chamberlain, it is my pleasure." I had to fight against dissolving into the old awkward schoolboy. "I understand you are a writer too."

A blush overtook her finely boned features. "Father is biased in that regard."

"Allow me to be judge of that."

We each found our seat while a servant brought tea and tiny cakes. Chamberlain had the servant begin to prepare the repast. I said, "Shall we wait for your wife, sir?"

"When Penny is with her horses, she becomes so involved it is difficult to say when she may return. More than once someone has had to fetch her with a lamp." Chamberlain smiled at his daughter, who returned the confederate gesture.

The tea was quite excellent, as were the small cakes—black raspberry from Chamberlain's own gardens, he volunteered—and we ate them with our fingers from octagonal china plates with a pastoral scene en rouge, a shepherd boy and his charges afield.

Chamberlain spoke of Arbor-in-the-Glen and asked me of my home in America. There was something about the way he said "in America" that gave it an ethereal air, as if it were something of legend and not of fact; an abstraction, like the world of a play where people lived and died and loved but ultimately none of it was real. Though I had been born and raised in the American fairyland and had stepped solidly upon it only weeks before, it was beginning to seem unreal to me too: the creation of an author, or authoress, to be progressively minded, and we were all protagonists and antagonists and foils at his bidding. Or at hers. Actors upon a stage, said Macbeth.

While these thoughts tumbled in my brainpan like loose articles in a wave-tossed seaman's chest, Chamberlain continued talking about his home and grounds, and I risked glances at the lovely Hilary. Risked, I say, for it seemed that her beauty might kill me, might burst my heart if I took in too much all at once. She appeared rapt by her father's exposition, though the information could hardly be new to her.

The old servant who had brought the tea and cakes entered with a bowl of grapes. Chamberlain inquired of his wife and was told she was come from the stables and was dressing. Chamberlain encouraged me to take a sprig of grapes, which I did most gladly.

Hilary, feeling more comfortable with me perhaps, asked of my home: "What sorts of things do you grow there, Mr. Wheelwright?"

"The typical things, I suppose, beans and lettuces. I very much enjoy tinkering in the tomato vines and have quite a variety . . . my housekeeper, Miss Marie, can whip them into any number of delectable sauces and stews. She works miracles."

"Tomatoes; I'll be," said Chamberlain. "We must increase our efforts in this area." My host's earnestness was comical—as if we were discussing the nation's foreign relations—and Hilary sensed it also. We two shared the moment.

"My favorite, I must admit, though not for gastrological reasons, is the pumpkin patch. It's childish I know but all year I look forward to carving jack-o'-lanterns. I fill my porches with them. I could fabricate and say it is my nephews and niece who become overzealous in the carving . . . but it is I who leaps overboard."

Chamberlain and Hilary laughed. She said, "I am sorry, Mr.

Wheelwright, but the mental picture of you, sleeves rolled, carving pumpkins like a mad surgeon is too much. I shall treasure the image forever."

I smiled at the idea too. "Yes, I will miss the season due to my traveling."

"Father, we must make certain that Mr. Wheelwright has a cartload of pumpkins to sculpt when their time arrives. We must."

"I quite agree, my dear. It wouldn't do to rob him of his fondest pleasures."

The door opened and Mrs. Chamberlain entered the room. She wore a simple but attractive lavender smock. She was clearly her daughter's mother. Lady Penelope and I recognized each other immediately.

Chamberlain and I rose. "Mr. Wheelwright, may I present my wife, Penelope. Penny, Mr. Jefferson Wheelwright."

She offered her hand. "Did you enjoy your shopping, Mr. Wheelwright?"

"Yes indeed, and thanks to you, Lady Penelope, I added a new author to my interests." I explained to Chamberlain, "Your wife and I were visitors to Bookman and Sons today."

"First," she said, "we can dispense with the lord and lady rubbish with guests in our home, but tell me, whom do you mean?"

We had taken our seats. The old servant was preparing his mistress's cup.

"Edmund Holland. I am ashamed of my ignorance but I had not heard of Mr. Holland."

"Too few people have, Mr. Wheelwright, but Dick and I are his great admirers." She smiled and reached out to her husband, close enough to take his hand for a moment. "Mr. Holland is something of an enigma, however. Few people have read him but it seems no one has met him—his lovely books appear as if written by a ghost."

"Really? He never gives public readings? No wonder then his reputation is slow to spread."

"Yes, Dick and I fancy ourselves as being somewhat connected in literary society, yet we can find out nothing about the man. . . ."

"Assuming he is a man." Hilary smiled at her white-ringletted mother.

"Yes, quite; perhaps 'Edmund Holland' is a nom de plume." Lady Penelope sipped her tea.

I was taking it all in: Chamberlain and his wife were aristocrats, Lord and Lady Chamberlain, and great supporters of the arts, of writers especially it seemed. I removed a grape seed from my tongue and placed it discreetly in my napkin.

Chamberlain said to his daughter, "My dear, we cannot keep Mr. Wheelwright our captive indefinitely. Go retrieve one of your stories."

"Father, Mr. Wheelwright does not want to be tortured with one of my amateurish tales."

"On the contrary, Miss Chamberlain, I would be most indebted to you if you would share the fruits of your pen."

Chamberlain and his wife were pleased, and Hilary knew it was not to be eluded. I watched her cross the room like sunlight.

"Thank you, Mr. Wheelwright." Chamberlain's mustaches rippled.

"Not at all—truly my pleasure."

She returned in a moment, some papers in hand and two books, which she handed to her father conspiratorially. I of course recognized them as my own. Hilary took her previous seat but perched on its edge. "This is really nothing, I must tell you, Mr. Wheelwright, just a sketch of my aged nanny, Nana Mary I called her. I apologize . . ."

"Hilary," her father cautioned her against excessive humility as a stratagem of delay.

"Yes . . . 'Nana Mary'":

In springtime there were adventures to the field. Operations, you called them. Great operations to collect butterflies and moths, wildflowers and other wild things. Once even a little green snake. I was afraid but you held its coiled body so lovingly, as if a baby sparrow fallen from its nest, that I soon overcame my fear and held it, too. God's creature just the same, you said. God's creature just the same. In autumn the operations were for mushrooms, for apples, for leaves of crimson and gold. My favorite though was winter, warm in your kitchen, big fire blazing. We made hats and headpieces and other adornments for my hair, which you said belonged to a princess in a fairytale.

(Hilary blushed.)

Golden threads and peacock feathers, pretty things prettier still in the fire's glow. I loved those times so, but would have cherished them even more had I known how few they would be, how short the years, how fleet-footed Time, how like Achilles hastening to his own demise.

Hilary looked up from her manuscript, her brown eyes amist. Awe and loss stuck in my throat, making it hard to speak, to breathe. "Wonderful," I managed. "Truly, wonderful."

Though they must have heard it before, the Chamberlains were awestruck by their beautiful daughter too.

I regained more of my voice. "You must keep writing, Miss Chamberlain. You owe it to the world."

"And to yourself," said Lady Penelope.

"Yes . . . to yourself." I cleared my throat.

There was little to say then, so in a bit Chamberlain ordered the carriage to be brought round. They prevailed upon me to sign my books, which I did happily. Then I said farewell to Lady Penelope and Hilary, promising to come to dinner in the near future; and Chamberlain saw me outside to the ebon rig.

"Thank you, Lord Chamberlain, for your generous hospitality."

"No, thank you, Mr. Wheelwright." He paused for a moment. "At the risk of seeming eccentric, I have an odd request." His mustaches hopped about.

"Anything, please . . ."

"I was wondering if I might hold onto your hat . . ."

"My hat . . ."

"Yes, the American fashion is really quite something, and I was wondering that I might take it to my fellow so that he may copy it. I know—vanity shall be my undoing."

I took the hat off. "It is an honor." And a shock.

"I'll have it returned to you promptly . . . at The Saint Georges, was it?"

"Quite." We shook hands and bowed, and in a moment I was seated by myself in the fine carriage, on my way back to the heart of the Old City. I must say I was more than a touch intoxicated with Miss Chamberlain's radiance and it made the natural wonders of Haslow Park become pale in comparison. Instead of Mr. Wordsworth, I thought of Byron and of Hilary's walking in beauty, though not at all like the night—rather, very much day's refulgent splendor. I looked toward the lake but nothing there stirred.

Four

~

I KNEW IT WAS A MISTAKE EVEN AS I DID IT BUT ON MY WAY TO MY
room I requested a bottle of port be sent up. My feet were sore and
all I wanted to do was have a glass of wine and look at my new books,
especially the enigmatic Mr. Holland's. Yet I knew one glass of port
would not suffice. One would lead to a second, a second to a third,
and so on until I was summoning the hotel boy to bring another
bottle. It was my father's inheritance; that, and little else.

I had enjoyed my time with the Chamberlains and hoped to
see them again, especially Miss Chamberlain, but Hilary's presence
had stirred up things in my brain and heart, things I preferred to
let lay, like dozing Cerberus. The old melancholia was descending
upon my soul just as night closed over the City. I lighted the lamps
in my room, changed out of my suit, unwrapped the bundle from
Bookman & Sons, settled into a comfortable chair . . . and poured
myself a glass of port.

I glanced at the book of folkstories but my brain was not up to
translating Italian. I read a few of Mrs. Haeley's poems. The language
was engaging but they were so rife with loneliness and despair I
couldn't read further; her mood was fueling my melancholy. I didn't
need to conclude the evening by dropping into the Thames, books
jammed in my pockets in lieu of leaden weights.

I swallowed some port and took up *Verses & Vignettes*. There
was an inscription in the author's own hand, presumably: "Dear
Reader, With sincere appreciation — E. H." I must confess I was
curious about Edmund Holland but I was also somewhat jealous.
Lady Penelope said that she and her husband were "great admirers"

of Mr. Holland. My writing and I were esteemed, I knew, in certain
circles . . . but admired greatly . . . I wasn't sure. Perhaps I needed
to become an enigma too—stage a disappearance, imply I had been
taken by pirates, sold into foreign bondage. Murry could claim the
small pieces he was publishing came to him via sailors who would,
every so often, pluck a manuscript rolled inside a bottle from the
Barbary seas. Sales of my books would burst the roof. Poor Jefferson
Wheelwright, enslaved somewhere, by a Turk perhaps, or a Chinese
warlord, but risking his life to pursue his art and speak to the world.
My readers could almost hear the clink of chains in my woeful words.

I finished my first glass of port.

True to its title, I discovered the first half of Mr. Holland's book
was poetry, followed by a series of short sketches. The opening piece
was a sort of ode to the sea. A common topic. I wanted to not like
it but a couple of phrases caught my mind's ear: "brine-buttoned
isles in the solitary sea" and "sea-green locks lovely to behold." Not
terrible, I thought. I noted contentedly that Mr. Holland could not
hold his meter, and the lines moved irregularly, to and fro, on the
page.

I read the next poem, "Set," which created a metaphor between
viewing an island from a distance and the backdrop of a theatrical
stage. Both seem real and unreal simultaneously. "Great space
settles the mind into belief." All right; I moved on. The third poem,
"Fisherman," was aptly titled; and the fourth, "Catch."

I continued reading and drinking. The port was having its
desired effect. I was into the third vignette, about a cabby waiting in
front of an opera-house, when I realized something was happening
in Mr. Holland's book I was not expecting. I glanced back at early
poems and raced ahead to other vignettes. Yes, of course; it was
dawning on me: this was not a collection of random pieces. The
poems and sketches all worked together. This was a single story, but
the story of a theme or of a concept. The concept was born in the
sea, primordially, and it came ashore . . . to England, yes, no, yes and
no . . . the shore was not *place* precisely, it was humankind . . . or the
human mind . . . or the human mind's capacity to conceive abstract
thought. . . .

I was understanding but not totally. Edmund Holland required further study . . . and further wine. I read on. There was a vignette about two lovers who can hear the sea but cannot observe it. It is nighttime (perhaps) and they can hear the breakers and sense the ocean breeze but they disagree as to its location. They argue. There is hurt in the argument and it cannot simply be about the ocean.

I was frustrated; I couldn't quite find the vignette's meaning. I was frustrated like the lovers. *Like the lovers.* I was the lovers, and they I. We were grasping for the sea, for that original concept, yet could not find it in spite of its tantalizing closeness. And our lover seems to be thwarting our effort to "find the ocean." Is Mr. Holland saying the only way to locate "the ocean" is through a *solitary* search?

I drank and wondered. It is a lonely journey back to the original concept (whatever *that* is)?

The final vignette was about a young maiden who is fetching water for her elderly father when she slips and falls to her death in the family well. Once her body is recovered, she is cast into her beloved sea, where her "sea-green locks are lovely to behold even in death." I recognized the image from an earlier poem. In fact, all sorts of images and phrases were knocking to and fro in Mr. Holland's book, connecting it all together, driving it all apart. They were moving like the meter in the opening poem, to and fro, they were moving like the ocean itself moves, regular in its irregularity, to and fro. . . .

Before I closed the book I noticed a spot of something on the final page; then another appeared. They were teardrops. I was weeping, my salt tears mixing with the sea and the dead maiden, connecting the real and the unreal . . . and revealing it to be all the same anyway.

I wiped my face with the sleeve of my dressing gown. Grief lay on my chest like a malignant goblin come to possess me. It was leaden there, suffocating me, forcing me down into despair. Yet I knew for all its emotional girth, it was but one word. A word I had promised to never say again as if never uttering it in the world would keep it from being a part of the world; it would reside in the past with all its pricking, piercing barbs, its crown-of-thorns-ness potential unrealized.

(Done with the pretence of the glass, I drank directly from the bottle.)

I fought to keep from uttering the word but my survival

demanded it: it was the ponderous goblin crushing the life from me,
and the only way to expel him and his malignancy was to say the
terrible word.

(The lamps in my room still glowed, I knew, but I was in a darker
place. My eyes were insensible to the light.)

Kathy

(

)

Had I spoken it, or merely thought it, merely acknowledged it?
Acknowledged her? Yes she was real, a real person in the world. I
even knew her place, generally, or thought I knew, which was the
same. The American West, Kansas or Nebraska.

Kathy.

The goblin was gone from my chest—but he had split into a
million forms, a billion, and was attacking every fiber of my being.
The pain of Grief dissected and multiplied, like the worm (the
Worm), with each new grief as potent as the whole.

(I tipped the bottle until every drop trickled down my throat, a
poisonous gathering in my soul. I turned and threw the bottle at the
fireplace but my aim was so pitiful it hit the pillow on my bed and
rolled to its center, perfectly, maddeningly intact.)

"Kathy."

This time I knew I said it aloud and I sat in the dark room of my
heart. Weeping. For how long I sat as such I knew not. My grief
made me insensible to the movement of the clock. I wanted more
wine but even in my despair a tiny voice of reason reminded me how
destructive that could be. Yet I must not stay in the room, which was
filling with grief like seawater and I would surely drown if I stayed
put.

I exchanged my dressing gown for my gray coat and thought I
looked all right. I descended the stairs in record time, missing one
or two steps along the way. In the lobby of The Saint Georges I went
to touch the brim of my hat to the night proprietor and hotel boy
who were lounging at the desk, but I realized I was bare-headed.
Unperturbed, I pulled a lock of hair at them instead; bloody hell on
them . . . they could believe it meant something in America.

I sensed that the night was cool but my port was still burning inside of me. I perspired in the breeze. My feet tingled but I didn't know—or care at the time—if this were good or bad. I looked to the sky like a sea captain reckoning a course. I could discern no stars, however, so set off on a path unedified. My cheeks were still wet and I was thankful the London streets were mostly black. Lamplight was intermittent and weak. I imagined the lead article in tomorrow's *Times*: AMERICAN AUTHOR TEARFULLY WANDERS STREETS. INSANITY SUSPECTED. Lead article? With whom was I tom-fooling? Jefferson Wheelwright would be buried deep in the edition, along with the fire-dog run down in the gutter and the theft from the day-old bread market.

I had no idea of the time but knew it was increasingly the hour of the ruffians on the streets. Every figure I passed was a dark one, coat collar drawn up, hat or bonnet pulled down. At times we exchanged glances and there was a flash of eyeball whites in the darkness. I sensed no humanity, however, as if these figures were extensions of the night or of the City, temporary things that occupied the streets till dawn; then they would fold back into the machinery of the place—figures in a Swiss clock who showed themselves on the hour then receded into the mysterious pulleys and flywheels, beyond sight and comprehension . . . all that masterwork just to signal the passage of Time, an operation of the universe to which only drunkards were oblivious.

My philosophizing was interrupted by the realization there were three men behind me who seemed to be matching my course. I turned at the next corner, willy-nilly, and they indeed followed. I turned at the next corner and the next, making a large rectangle that would bring me back to my starting point, or making a broken shape of some sort that would bring me to an unknown part of the City . . . I knew not which.

My heart raced, pumping the port-laced blood through my veins, and I sweated profoundly. I made a quick turn to my right and knew instantly I was in a narrow alley and not a street at all. Blood pounded in my temples. I stopped near some crates or boxes and waited for the brutes to complete their business with me. But they seemed to pass by the alley's opening; it was difficult to see in the dark. I stood still, my heart slowing a bit. Sweat ran into my eyes or perhaps I was still weeping. Someone brushed past me in the alley; the oaf stepped upon my foot and said nothing as he stumbled along toward the street.

I sensed there was someone else in the dark. "Your turn, gov?" said a female voice. I felt her fingers searching for and finding my trouser buttons. I took a step back against the rough bricks of some unknown building—perhaps the headquarters of the district constabulary . . . who could say? I stood dumb, my fingers clutching the mortar spaces between bricks, sweat and tears streaking my face while the woman worked her craft. Still I had no sense of time . . . I thought of Hilary reading aloud her sketch . . . and of an embellished Kathy gingham-clad in the West . . . and at the critical moment, while the woman was completing her task, my thoughts were of the infuriatingly brilliant Edmund Holland. I fished a handful of coins from my coat pocket. It probably was too much as she said nothing of its being too little. Then she was gone and I was fumbling to re-button myself.

I returned to the street, both overheated and chilled, too exhausted for despair. I was so disoriented in the strange metropolis I knew not where The Saint Georges was, right or left or some queer-angled way. But I didn't care yet. A sort of wanderlust filled my heart, in lieu of love, and I was just letting it run its own course. Shortly I came to a section that was oddly desolate. No one at all was about. My shoes echoed noisily on the bricks. In fact the rhythm of my walking—the sound of it, mind you—put me into a kind of stupor. I recall reading that during the Revolution, on the long trek to cut off Cornwallis, Washington's men actually slept while they marched; and this is how I felt, clattering along only half lucid. I came to an especially narrow street and the popping of my shoe-heels reverberated off the tall buildings so energetically it sounded as if Washington's army was on the move.

My dulled brains listened to the *pop-pop-pops*, and it occurred to me that if this street led all the way to the coast, I would mindlessly walk right into the sea, not even noticing until the saltwater washed the echoes from my ears.

Such were my half-waking fantasies when I thought I detected a slightly higher pitched footfall than my own, and quicker too. I slowed to experiment with the sounds . . . yes, there it was: someone was all but running along the dark street. That someone was behind me but gaining ground rapidly. I could either run too, or halt completely.

I halted, and stood by some steps leading to a home or a small business. The footsteps echoing in the dark were such that it had to be a woman or child, and accordingly I felt no fear (well, little fear). I turned to face the night traveler . . . and she ran into me headlong. She was of so slight a build she was repelled a step or two by the impact.

"Madam, are you all right?" Or so my brain tried to say but my ears heard something more muddied and slurred.

She stepped up and put her child-size hands on my chest. She was dressed so completely in black, the woman was all but invisible. "Sir—*he* is behind me. . . ." She glanced over her shoulder. ". . . you must save yourself . . . go at once. . . ." And she hurried away resuming her course.

"Who . . ."

She looked back at me, I imagined imploringly, but kept her pace. The street was so dark I couldn't say if she were fifteen or fifty, pretty or plain.

Now I *was* afraid. Who . . . what was coming? But I did not heed her advice, or could not. Whichever the case, I stood stock still. I listened for the sound of his approach and heard only the woman's retreating footfalls. If he were coming along the street, he was as stealth as a shadow, as formless as a phantom . . . and not one of those English phantoms who is forever ejecting books from shelves and taking a turn in the squeaky rocking-chair.

I strained to hear and I waited . . . but no one—man, woman, child, beast . . . *or* phantom—came. At least, however, the excitement had sobered me, and I thought the street seemed familiar. I tested my theory by strolling a couple of blocks (as it happened along the path of the running woman) and I was correct: I was in Wicker's Lane, the neighborhood of Mrs. Haeley's house. So the good news was that I knew precisely how to return to The Saint Georges; the bad news was that it was far and my feet were tired and sore. I doubted any cabby was working at this hour. Besides, after my indecorous transaction in the alley—which was already taking on the aspects of an unsettling dream—I was penniless.

Thus, there was no help for it. I turned in the direction of the hotel and began my solitary march. The night felt cold now; I buttoned my coat and turned up its collar. I still kept a chary eye for the woman's pursuer . . . but met none.

Five

~

SLAVISH TO ROUTINE, I ROSE THE NEXT MORNING ON SCHEDULE
though my head ached as if I had in fact been a victim of ruffians
the previous evening. I drank my coffee greedily but had no appetite
for the toasted bread, suffering as I was from a dully bilious complaint.
I managed to nibble some crust; I feared any more than that would
effect a second coming by mid morning.

Carter arrived as punctually as ever, apologetic for having stood
me up the day before. I assured him it was fine and gave him a synopsis
of my time at the club and with Lord and Lady Chamberlain. In
addition to the foot treatment, I asked for some remedy for my head.
Carter, donning his pince-nez, took an envelope from his red case,
poured a white powder in a glass of water and had me sip it while my
feet were soaking. My morning's writing had suffered from my wild
night both in quantity and in tone. My tale of the avenging spirit
had been darkly humorous at times but the most recent addition
was simply dark. In short, the spirit had caused a young maiden
who had been unfaithful to her promised one to take her own life in
a most gruesome fashion: she thrust her hand that bore the ring of
engagement into a machine at the factory where she was employed;
the hand was severed and she bled to death, her promised one's name
upon her pallid lips.

Carter seemed stunned as he read; perhaps the section would
require a rewrite.

The good doctor massaged my feet then I dozed for a bit. The
next I knew the treatment was complete and Carter was preparing
to leave.

"So," he said, "shall I call after lunch?"

"After lunch?" I was dazed from my dozing.

"Yes . . . for the carnival."

Ah, the carnival . . . he had been saying something about it. "Ah, the carnival . . . yes come round after lunch."

"In the meantime, get some rest, Jefferson; you could stand it."

"Quite. Thank you . . . Carter." I didn't recall his Christian name, if I ever knew.

I broke from my morning routine in order to follow my physician's advice. As soon as the porter cleared my room of the footbath and breakfast tray, I returned to my tall bed. The elixir Carter prepared had helped my head but only sleep would make the throbbing cease entirely. I buried myself in the covers and nodded off instantly. I'm not one to recall my dreams, normally, but the moment I fell asleep a most vivid dreaming commenced . . . perhaps encouraged by Carter's white powder.

it is a vast and wild place . the american west i presume . dark shapes lurk every where . bears indians alligators . just beyond my seeing but not my knowing . i wear a ridiculously large hat . high crowned . and as wide brimmed as a mariners wheel . it attracts the attention of bears indians and gators . i hurry after something . or someone . no something . i fear not finding it . in my peripheral vision beneath the wide wide brim i watch anxiously for danger . i am in a meadow now . tall tall grass and wildflowers . indigo blue red yellow . forest trees surround me like the walls of an arena . something white flashes before me scuttled by the wind . it is windy . it is the something i was seeking . i hurry after it thinking this is one of those dreams of frustration and the white thing will keep tumbling just out of my reach . it is a leaf of paper . it tumbles on the wind just atop the grass and flower heads . i reach out and take hold of the paper . surprised . i try to read the words . written in red ink . or blood . i cannot grasp their meaning . as if written in an unfamiliar language . or as if the words swim before my eyes . dancing on the page like live things affected by the wind . i cannot come to the truth before i see another sheet skipping along the grass blades . i chase after it . retrieve it . spy another . as the process continues i amass a sizable manuscript . unreadable manuscript . i think i should be nearing the forest . on the far side of the meadow . but the trees continue to stay precisely in the distance . like the backdrop of a play . something black ahead catches my attention . a bear . no a woman in mourning gown . rushing and dropping these blood written pages . i try to call to her to tell her she is losing her story . yes it is a story written in blood . fresh blood . red red blood . yet it does not smear on the pages . it continues to live . that is why the words seem to swim . they are alive and change as the story changes . a sort of continuous self initiated revision . beyond the authoress control . but not contrary to it either . the mourning woman has stopped and is turned to face me . the meadow is now a field freshly shorn by the scythewielders . only the space . the fifty paces . between the mourningwoman and me is green grass . all the rest of the field is white . white sheets of paper . moving here and there . there is no wind . i want to see the mourningwomans face . to identify her . but dark hair moves across her features . like blown by the wind . there is no wind . i try to speak to Mourningwoman . to question Her . but the instant i open my mouth . the pages . every page in the field . is drawn to Her . like iron filings to a magnetic rod . and She is instantly mummified by Her story . the precise shape of Mourningwoman . now in white pages . a puddle begins to form beneath Her . a puddle of bloodwords . running red from Her story and pooling around Her . a tiny sea . and white white Mourningwoman its only island continent . . . .

When Carter called, my head was much improved but the mood of the dream lingered, like the leaden knowledge of a near-death experience. It was an effort to be cheerful; I knew, however, he didn't want to go to a carnival with a somber companion. En route Carter explained it was a festival in honor of the Heiress Presumptive. How medieval, I thought, but liking the idea of it.

A hazy white sun made the day warm and I perspired. Or perhaps it was still the after effects of my private . . . revelry. I paused to remove my hat and wipe my brow with a handkerchief. Carter said the streets were so busy because of the carnival, that many laborers and domestics had been let go for the bank day to join in the Heiress's celebration. I took the good doctor's word but the streets seemed just as busy as they had since my arrival. Busy and noisy. My New Yorkers were known for their boisterousness but they had nothing on the Londoners, whose street voices, anyway, always seemed to be at a fevered pitch.

Carter and I left the walk to cross a street. I tried to avoid stepping in the manure but would have had to suddenly master the art of levitation to avoid it completely. Carter, perhaps used to city life, appeared indifferent as to his path and the consequences for his boots. I, meanwhile, resolved to have my shoes cleaned and the cuffs of my trousers brushed at the earliest opportunity. I knew just the hotel boy for the job.

The music of a hurdy-gurdy was added to the noise of the street as we came to the section of London designated for the Heiress Presumptive's festival. It was closed to all traffic except that of human foot. Dozens of tents and temporary stands had been erected. Maybe hundreds. The scene stretched for blocks. It was impossible to say how many as the busy multitude obscured its terminus.

The music, I discovered, was coming from a hurdy-gurdy and two stringed instruments, almost like ancient lyres. The musicians, in disheveled brown suits, were plucking and strumming their instruments for all they were worth. Indeed, I expected a string—or finger!—to come flying loose at any moment. A small group had formed around the trio, and several folks were kicking up their heels in a folksy jig. Who's to say how the women dancers earned their keep, but by night they could have been hay-penny prostitutes … out now in daylight to enjoy the carnival and a different sort of masculine company.

A smile lighted Carter's benevolent features as he watched the revelers. "Come," he said, "let's see what other sport there is."

We walked among the throng, the jocular music fading behind. Soon we came to a stand selling ale and Carter insisted on purchasing two pints. The standkeeper was uneasy about his cups so we sat there on haybales and drank the warm ale. I probably didn't need the spirits but the brief rest was most welcome. The Londoners filed past, young and old, children either running wild or being pulled along by their sweating parents. In fact, a goodly crowd of children was assembling nearby at a puppeteer's stage. The performance was due to begin and I found it difficult to resist a story; so Carter and I assured the ale-man we would only be a few yards distant watching the puppet-show and we would return our cups shortly. Some coinage passed between Carter and the ale-man, in soiled apron, to make him easier.

A sizable midday crowd had gathered. Children were seated or kneeling pressed close to the puppet stage while adults were behind pretending not to be equally interested in the pending performance. The puppet stage was concealed behind a curtain of purple and white vertical stripes. The puppeteer's assistant, a tow-headed girl of perhaps fifteen or sixteen, sat in a wooden chair adjacent the small stage. She wore an odd get-up that was a cross between a fairy ballerina and a highwayman. The girl sat placidly ignoring all, even the forward children who tried to engage her. I wondered if she were the puppeteer's daughter pressed into service against her preference, or some street waif he collected during his theatrical travels.

I drank my ale and awaited the performance. Carter seemed quite content, the ale mellowing even further his naturally mellow disposition. The children were noticing some change on the stage . . . a white-haired woman puppet wearing a "golden" crown had moved aside the curtain stage-left and was trying to get the waif assistant's attention; the girl was performing admirably at being quite oblivious. Children began helping the puppet queen, who moved her arms to encourage their rowdy calls: "Hey!" "Miss!" "Girl!" "The Queen!" "You!" Even some adults joined in.

Finally the waif's reverie was broken and she rose from her chair, unhurried, entering in private consultation with the puppet queen. The children hushed themselves but the waif and the queen's conversation was all inarticulate whispers. Then the queen addressed the audience: "Pardon our rudeness, please, as it is not becoming of royalty." The puppeteer had effected a passable dowager's voice. "My assistant Miss Organdy and I are having a bit of a disagreement.

Miss Organdy believes our story 'The Tale of the Lost Prince' is too scary and too sad with so many children in attendance. She is afraid it will cause you a sleepless night—you and your poor parents—especially the part with the wolves and the other part with the black-hearted knight and the cave as dark as midnight." A theatrically timed chill ran through the waif at the mention of the wolves and the black-hearted knight. "Miss Organdy feels a better choice would be 'The Tale of the Tooth Fairy and the Aching Incisor.' It does have an important moral regarding the necessity of cleaning your teeth." Miss Organdy vigorously nodded her tow head to persuade the children, who were already hissing and booing at her.

"What do you think, children?" asked the queen. "'The Tale of the Lost Prince' or 'The Tale of the Tooth Fairy and the Aching Incisor'?"

"Lost Prince . . . Lost Prince . . ." rumbled the children, and some of the adults. Other adults played Satan's advocate and shouted for the Tooth Fairy.

"Very well," said the cockney waif, "but don't blame me for your night terrors." She reached next to her chair and brought up a placard: THE TALE OF THE LOST PRINCE. Children cheered. The waif, dramatically defeated, plopped down in her chair, while the queen raised her wooden arms in victory to the children and vanished behind the striped curtain.

The Tale of the Lost Prince

(Stage curtain still closed. We hear the Queen's voice.)

Queen's voice

It's good to be royalty. There is the palace after all, and the palace guard to do your bidding. And the lovely clothes and the golden crown, and those beautiful balls to preside over. When I was a girl, I could dance and twirl all night. Only the light of morning could convince me to slip out of my dancing shoes. Yes, it's good to be royalty . . . except for one drawback—a very large drawback indeed, especially for a royal girl. . . .

(Curtain opens to reveal a beautiful Princess puppet—lustrous chestnut hair and blue eyes as large as shillings—and the Princess's little dog puppet . . . leaping about and yapping playfully at his mistress. The painted backdrop is a courtyard of stonewalls and potted flowers.)

Queen's voice

And that drawback is . . . the arranged marriage.

King's voice

Daughter! Daughter! Where are you keeping yourself?

(The Princess tries to get her little dog to stop yapping. She doesn't want to be found. She shushes the dog. She turns to the audience and encourages their assistance. [Children begin shhhh-ing.] The King enters stage-right in a purple robe and golden crown; he is dark-bearded and handsome.)

King

Here you are. I should have known you'd be with your little rat. *(The dog growls at the King but not too menacingly. The King growls back.)* Grrrrr. You should be getting ready. You know what today is, Daughter.

Princess

Yes, Father, how could I forget? You or some court advisor has reminded me every day since my fifth birthday: "Upon your fifteenth year, you shall marry the Prince of Leland and unite your two kingdoms forever—forever allies to be strong against invaders from the Black Lands." Yes, Father, I know.

King

(Pauses.) Yes, well, by the way . . . happy birthday, Daughter. The

Prince of Leland will arrive anytime now. If nothing else, you should wash the smell of rat from your hands.

Dog

Grrrr.

King

Grrrr.

Princess

Yes, Father . . . *(She turns away.)*

King

This is an historic event—for two peoples—you should be pleased to be such an important part of it. What is the problem, Daughter?

Princess

I don't wish to marry the Prince.

King

Not wish to marry the Prince?! Why on earth not? Leland is a most civilized and respectable country—smells a bit like Paris in the summertime, but we can't have everything . . .

Princess

The Prince is an old man.

King

Old man?! He's twenty-two . . . I should be so elderly.

(The Princess is silent, still turned away from her father.)

King

(Softening his tone.) Daughter, do you love another?

Princess

(Turns.) Love another? I've been locked up here in the palace for fifteen years taking etiquette lessons and learning to play the harpsichord. I couldn't even meet another boy, leave be fall in love with one.

King

Then I don't see the problem, Daughter. Your heart is obviously ready . . . you shall love the Prince of Leland. It's perfect. And he shall love you. How could he not? You're beautiful . . . and very well mannered. It's perfect.

Princess

Would Mother have wanted this for me?

King

Your mother? I'm certain she would. She and I were arranged—didn't say "Boo!" to each other till our wedding day.

Princess

Did you love each other?

King

Love? Well . . . I'm quite certain we would have learned to . . .

Princess

If she'd lived.

King

Yes . . . if she'd lived.

(The Princess looks down at her dog, who whimpers sympathetically.)

King

Come now, Daughter, no more talk. It's time to get ready for the Prince.

(Curtain closes to the sound of the dog growling and whining.)

The waif calls out from her chair, "Later that morning, the Princess awaits her groom in the royal receiving chamber . . ."

(Curtain opens to the Princess, now in a purple gown and wearing a small tiara in her lustrous hair. The backdrop is a stone wall with a portrait of the King hanging on it and with a window open to a blue sky. The Princess is holding some papers.)

Miss Organdy

She takes solace—do you know what "solace" is?—it's something that makes you feel a little better—she takes solace in reading the poems she likes to write. *(The Princess slowly paces studying the poems. She stops and looks up.)*

Princess

"If there be but one moon casting her lovely light?, How then can she hold the wishes of so, Many unhappy souls on a lonesome moonlit night?, She cannot, surely, so there must be many, many moons, And each soul is blind but to her own . . ."

King's voice

Daughter, dear?! *(He enters stage-left.)* Oh no. *(Stopping.)* You're not planning on reading one of your poems to the Prince, are you?

Princess

(She turns to face her father.) And if I am?

King

Then I must have the crocodiles removed from the moat, for the Prince will become so depressed by your poetry he will leap from the window. *(The King motions toward the open window.)*

Princess

Don't go to the trouble, Father. My poems are for me. They make me feel better when I'm sad.

King

(Sighs.) Yes, well, none of that. You'll be meeting your husband-to-be in just moments. You don't want him to think he's getting a lugubrious bride, do you?

Princess

No, Father. *(She holds the paper down to her side.)*

Miss Organdy stands and heralds the Prince's arrival with a sort of recorder or ocarina—doot-do-da-doo!

King

He's here. *(He stands beside the Princess as they anticipate the Prince's entrance stage-left. Dramatic pause, then the Prince enters dressed in a green and gold uniform. He is boyish and handsome.)*

Prince

(Bowing.) Your Majesty . . . Princess . . . I am most happy to finally meet you both.

King

And we you, young Prince. *(He waits for the Princess to say something, clears his throat to encourage her. She has been looking down since before the Prince's entrance.)*

Princess

(Slowly looking up as she speaks; her tone changes.) Yes, Prince . . . we are . . . most happy . . . too.

King

(Sensing the Princess is pleasantly surprised by the Prince's youthful handsomeness.) Well . . . a special brunch is being prepared. I should see to it. You two should . . . chat . . . you know, become acquainted. I'll call for you momentarily. *(He exits jauntily. The Prince and Princess stand there uncomfortably for a moment.)*

Prince

(Finally.) It's a lovely palace. It must've been quite . . . lovely growing up here . . .

Princess

Thank you. Yes, it's a nice palace . . . a little lonely at times . . . I mean—

Prince

Oh yes, I recall you didn't know your mother . . . and no brother or sister either. That must've been difficult, to say the least.

Princess

Yes, difficult, but my father is a good man, a bit intense at times . . .

Prince

Yes, I sensed that—both, I mean . . . the King can be intense, but he's a good man . . .

Princess

(Her voice a little cheerful.) It's all right. I won't let him know you think him intense. *(Pauses.)* Tell me of Leland.

Prince

(Eager.) It is quite beautiful . . . well, parts of it are quite beautiful. I think . . . I hope you will come to see it as I do. There is a great, green mountain where I love to go walking with my dog—

Princess

You have a dog?

Prince

Yes, my proverbial best friend, I must confess. I even brought her with me. One of the palace guard is walking her—not too pleased with the assignment, I daresay.

Princess

(Giggles.) I'm sure he'll get over it . . . and will be able to take on a dragon or something equally menacing soon enough.

Prince

(Laughs.) No doubt.

Princess

What is your dog's name?

Prince

(Pauses; shy again.) I'm embarrassed to say . . . *(He looks away.)*

Princess

Don't be embarrassed. I promise not to laugh; I don't like to be laughed at either.

Prince

Oh, I'm not afraid of your laughing. . . .

Princess

What then? I suppose it wouldn't do for us to have secrets from one another.

Prince

No, I suppose not—that'd be a bad way to begin. *(Pauses, but looks up at the Princess.)* Well . . . her name is "Princess" . . . she is the finest of her breed, most beautiful . . . for a dog, I mean. . . .

Princess

(Stopping him, gently.) It's all right, really. *(Pauses.)* I think it's sweet.

The waif sighs loudly, "Ahhhhhh . . ." and encourages the audience to do the same, which it does, even some grown men.

(The Prince and Princess are awkwardly quiet again; then the Prince speaks.)

Prince

What's in your hand? Plans for the wedding?

Princess

(Moving her hand with the poems somewhat behind her.) No . . . now it's my turn to be embarrassed.

Prince

Then it must be my turn to promise not to laugh—and I do.

"Practice that line . . . for the ceremony!" hectors Miss Organdy. Some children laugh, but mostly they shush the waif.

Princess

They're not plans for the wedding . . . they're poems. *(More assertively.)* I like to write poetry.

Prince

Poems? Really? I was told your talents were playing the harpsichord and knowing just the right thing to say. I love poetry.

Princess

I thought we were going to be honest with one another. You're just saying that . . .

Prince

No, it's absolutely true. *(He pauses, clears his throat, recites.)* "By all the gods above, And all that dwell below this solid earth, I've never swerved an instant in my love, From that first moment when it had its birth, Nor ever shall I hold thee at less worth, I can but say, to you I'm ever bound, And truth thereof will in the end be found." I didn't write it mind you—it was some Englishman I think—but I love it and wish I could write poetry like that.

(The Princess relaxes her arm and the poems are naturally at her side.)

Princess

I was told your talents were hunting and horsemanship.

Prince

Well . . . may I read your poems . . . *(Sensing her reluctance.)* sometime I mean?

Princess

Yes, sometime . . . I would like that.

King

(Entering stage-right.) The meal is served. Shall we adjourn to the royal dining hall?

Prince

I would like that. *(He has not taken his eyes from the young Princess. The curtain closes.)*

The waif is sitting in her chair eating a roasted drumstick, turkey or goose. She says with her mouth full, "The royal couple and the King have a lovely meal, with roasted turkey and sweetened parsnips and freshly baked rolls and freshly churned butter . . . and pie, there was ilberry pie, as thick as your arm . . . and cream . . ." Miss Organdy is becoming distracted with the menu and the children are impatient for her to get on with the narration. "Yes, well, the Prince and Princess were taciturn during their meal—do you know what 'taciturn' means? it means the cat'd got their tongues—but the King, who did almost all the talking, knew they were quiet because they like each other after all. The King was most pleased. The alliance would be formed and his only daughter would be happy in love. It was a fine day in the kingdom." The waif takes a final bite from the drumstick and tosses it behind her, to where a stray dog is quickly upon it. "All right then," she says, standing and wiping her fingers on her pink organdy skirt, which she wears over a pair of well-beaten trousers, "two months passed while final preparations was made for the wedding. The young Prince and Princess was unable to see each other, but their guard delivered letters back and forth near every day—and rumor had it that there was even a love sonnet or two amongst the correspondence. But who was the sonneteer? The Prince or the Princess?"

Children caterwauled their choice. "The Princess!" . . . "The Prince!" . . . "The Princess's dog!" . . . "The King!—he liked the cut of that boy's jib, h'did!" (from one young upstart). . . . Dr. Carter, caught up in the show, shouted, "The Princess of course! She's the poetess!" I swallowed the warm ale.

The waif raises her small hands to quiet the mob. "As I said, it's been two months—and the wedding day is arrived. All the preparations are completed. It's the morning of and the Princess waits anxiously for the arrival of her groom . . ."

(The Princess's dog is yapping as the curtain opens to the royal receiving chamber. The Princess is wearing a silver white gown with pearly

beading. On her head is a refulgent tiara, a white veil hanging down behind, but not totally covering her lustrous chestnut hair. Her dog is hopping about yapping.)

Princess

I know, I know . . . I feel the same, like I can barely hold still. *(She looks to the blue-sky window.)* When will he arrive? He should have been here by now.

(The dog stops yapping and growls, but not too menacingly. The King enters stage-right. He stands looking at the Princess. He is holding a paper and is speechless.)

Princess

What is it, Father? Has the Prince arrived? *(The King says nothing.)* What's wrong? What's that in your hand?

King

(Finally.) We have word . . . the Prince's party was attacked on the road, raiders from the Black Lands . . . his personal guard was overcome . . . they've all been killed. . . .

Princess

And the Prince?

King

We don't know. Perhaps he has been taken for the ransom.

(The Princess immediately begins to exit stage-right.)

King

Daughter, where are you going?

Princess

(Pausing for a moment.) To find the Prince.

King

We have dispatched a company . . . not to mention Leland's entire army is turning over every rock.

Princess

Then it should be perfectly safe for me to join the search. *(She continues on, her dog at her heels.)*

King

But. . . .

(The Princess is gone.)

Miss Organdy rises from her chair, a burlap bag in hand. "Somehow or another the Princess slipped her personal guard and took to the Leland road, a straight-cut path that led right into the dark mountains separating her kingdom from the Prince's." The waif reaches into the bag and removes a large cloth, rolled scroll-fashion. She undoes the string holding it and turns her back to the audience. It is a backdrop for the stage and she hangs it over the royal receiving chamber. The new backdrop is a wild setting with woods and boulders, just a bit of leaden sky showing here and there beyond the dark-leaved trees.

The waif says to the audience, "There are nicer places in the mountains, beautiful places, but those aren't the sorts of places that raiders from the Black Lands would call home, and the Princess knew to find the lost Prince she must find the raiders who attacked his party . . . *and* she knew the raiders was led by the Black-hearted

Knight hisself. The Princess didn't know him of course, but she knew of his cruelty. She didn't think of the danger she may be in—only of the danger the Prince was surely in . . . if he was alive a'tall."

The waif begins pulling various sized rocks from the bag and setting them here and there on the stage; in the puppet-show world the rocks are boulders. When she finishes she turns again to the audience: "Of course there was other dangers besides the Black-hearted Knight. There was ravens the size of eagles, big enough to carry off the Princess's dog certainly if not the Princess herself." From behind the stage, the puppeteer caws enormous-raven-like, and the sound startles several children (and adults). "And there was snakes, poisonous as asps, lurking everywhere. You as never knew behind what rock." Miss Organdy carefully, slowly lifts up the rocks—children hold their breath, though they have just watched her place each one serpent-free. Satisfied, the waif repositions the final boulder. "But worst of all was . . . can you guess? What was worse than the ravens and the snakes?" Children shout all kinds of guesses, from vampire bats to spiders to dragons. One poor cockney child guesses a "rav'nous oct'pus." I call out, "Wolves! The wolves!"—then to Carter, "It has to be wolves . . . she mentioned them earlier." "Yes!" cries Miss Organdy, pointing to me. "The mountain wolves, some as big as ponies . . . and just as quick and strong, to say true!" A terrible wolfish howl issues from behind the stage. Everyone jumps. Everyone.

And that's when it happened: "The Tale of the Lost Prince" stopped being a play (a puppet-play at that), and the Prince of Leland was truly lost, and the brave and lovely Princess had truly put herself in peril to find him—a young man she loved though she barely knew....

Six

~

KATHERINE WAS DETERMINED TO KEEP TO THE ROAD, THEN SHE was determined to keep to the path; but the farther she climbed, the less discernible it was. The worn path faded then reappeared then vanished altogether, without her knowing for certain it was gone until it had been for some time. The hem of her silver white gown was black with mud and torn in two places that trailed behind on the ground, reminding her of the train she should have worn as she gracefully marched up the central aisle of the cathedral, escorted by her father, King William II, in full military regalia for the first time since his wife's funeral fifteen years earlier—here in this same cathedral, with its impossibly high ceiling, the spires thrusting toward God, and the stained-glass windows of the saints and Christ's bloody crucifixion. Katherine should have marched up the aisle as graceful as a daydream to meet her fiancé Prince Edmund of Leland, handsome yes, and regal himself in red-breasted uniform, shiny saber at his side, but better than all that (and the pomp of the ceremony): Edmund loved her, and she him. Their love was so unexpected and so true, it thrilled Katherine, and frightened her. At fifteen, she didn't understand loving a man, and had no mother or sister to watch, to ask. Yet she was on this mountain, woods and nighttime drawing in around her, searching for Edmund, so filled with fear for his safety there was no space to be fearful for herself.

Katherine's little terrier Archibald kept to his mistress's side. When they first set out he was inclined to chase rabbits and weasels, and catch up with Katherine when it suited him—but his animal senses now compelled him to remain close, perhaps smelling danger or feeling it in his canine bones. Katherine noticed the change in behavior and was both heartened and disheartened by it. She breathed the air and only detected aspen and wild clover, the scents shifting on the wind as it swirled up against the mountain.

The sky was barely light where it could be seen between the forest limbs as the sun had slipped to the other side of the mountain. Katherine assumed the world seemed just as dark to the Lelanders, minus their beloved prince. Soon the moon would be up but Katherine knew it would only be a sliver away from new: she had been moongazing for many nights, unable to sleep thinking about her wedding and her prince and wondering more and more what her mother would have told her as her wedding day (and night) approached. When she did sleep, a woman came to her in her dreams but Katherine couldn't be certain it was her dead mother, the queen. Why not some long-gone cook or scullery maid, mind-embellished in purple satin, or an image totally fabricated by her overactive fancy? The dream-woman, her face framed in white ringlets, talked to Katherine of tragedy and strength—platitudes, Katherine considered the woman's words, both during the dreamtime and the next morning when she recalled them over a bowl of porridge and berries.

Now the dream-woman's adages about courage and determination and faith rang true, or at least useful, on this darkening mountain, Archie silent as dumb death at her side, the only sound her torn wedding gown passing over the cold earth . . . and something else, a twig snapping cliché in the forest gloom . . . unnatural movement between the trees . . . a dark shape slipping from one black trunk to another, as stealth and as clever as imagination.

Katherine's own animal instinct spoke to her from the ancient past: we're being stalked. The whispering, androgynous voice from some glandular part of her brain was calm and quiet; all reportage, no offer of advice, none expected. Archie must have been listening to a similar voice. They continued their pace, on two legs and four, unhastened but with all the false trappings of purpose, of destination.

Then the dark shape bounded from the dark forest, separating into three shapes, three mountain wolves, all black except their yellow eyes and teeth, each humanoid in size, like men costumed as wolves in a poorly timed malicious prank. The giant wolves surrounded Katherine and Archie, who stood his ground snarling and baring his own teeth though he stood only at one's wolfish sinewy shoulder. Katherine scanned the ground for a stick or rock. Nothing—just her hands and wits, and sad defenses they seemed.

The wolves closed in, like projections of the night and the forest, like the malignant part of the world become animated. Katherine could smell their breaths, aspen and wild clover and something putrid that must have been the stench of a thousand deaths trapped there in their black maws.

Without warning Archie lashed out at one wolf, his terrier teeth slashing for throat where the attack would count regardless of size. The wolf reared back and brought his own teeth to bear in the deadly game, catching Archie in the shoulder. Even in the twilight gloom Katherine saw a patch of red show on Archie's fur. Katherine was about to attack or be attacked, some ancient mechanism of the world ready to be advanced, when a sixth figure flew into the clockwork gears. It fell upon a wolf like misfortune, and the wolf tumbled into the dust, locked rolling with the new thing, snappings and snarlings emitting from the suddenly conjoined creatures in a dance as ancient as coupling. Such was the action center stage in the universe until just as suddenly one leapt up from the dust. It was the wolf who lay motionless, a broken black figure on the cold ground. Katherine saw that the other thing was a wolf*hound*, larger even than the enormous mountain wolves. The remaining wolves, understanding the turn of the tumblers, absconded into the forest as quickly and as quietly as they had arrived. The wolfhound, taut as a viola string, stood watching the wolves vanish, then it turned to Katherine and Archie.

Wind stirred Katherine's hair, which clung wetly to her face. "Princess?" tried Katherine, and the great hound wagged its tail and trotted to her. The dog panted in Katherine's ear and tolerated a hug around the neck. Katherine smelled the wolf blood fresh in the hound's mouth. "Good girl. Good beautiful girl."

Katherine released Princess and the hound immediately scampered in the direction from which she had come. Katherine and Archie did their best to keep up as dusk evaporated toward black mountain night.

As adrenaline subsided, Katherine felt the exhaustion that threatened to overtake her. Yet she must keep going. The ground was uneven and footing was difficult in the thickening dark. Princess became more and more invisible, her haunches a gray moving mass against a blacker one. Katherine noticed that Archie was having difficulty keeping pace. With his injured shoulder there was a limp in his gait. In spite of her exhaustion Katherine picked up the little terrier, who seemed to go limp the moment he was in his mistress's arms.

Katherine was wondering how much longer she could go when she realized Princess had disappeared entirely. She halted, the mountain fully engulfed in ebon night now. She strained to see, causing a tear to drip from her right eye, the first she had shed today. A single deep-throated bark came from in front of her. She walked toward it, and in what little light the moon offered Katherine saw Princess at the mouth of some sort of depression or cave. Katherine patted the wolfhound between her ears. The dog thumped its tail on the ground then turned and went farther into the black recess. The teenage girl thought of bats and snakes but knew that Princess had protected her from wolves—surely there was nothing to fear here.

Archie still in her arms, she stepped inside. Katherine heard Princess's padding for a moment then the sound stopped. Her heart raced as she moved cautiously forward; she wondered how high the cave's ceiling was—that is, if there were bats, how far did they hang mouth-down from her scalp? Archie wiggled in her grip and she realized she was crushing her little companion against her chest. "Sorry, Archie," she whispered, mainly to hear something human inside the black cave. With her free hand, Katherine groped forward like a blindwoman. In a moment her fingers touched what she knew instantly was Princess's wiry fur. "Hey girl."

She stood a moment, her eyes becoming accustomed to the near total dark. She listened to Princess's panting and felt it in rhythm with the hound's moving ribcage. Concentrating on the sound for a minute or longer, Katherine realized the dog's heavy breathing was almost perfectly in synch with something or someone else's breathing. She thought at first it was a trick of sound in the echophonous cave, or just her imagination—but no, there was a fourth living creature inside, and near too. . . .

"Hello . . . is someone here?" Katherine explored with her slippered foot and discovered something lay just inches from Princess. She knelt and reached out, slowly, with her hand. She felt a coarse material and drew back for a moment, her breath catching in her throat. Then, bolder, she learned it was a pant leg. She felt a human shin bone. "Hello?" she tried again. A kneecap. Above the kneecap the pants became damp and sticky on the thigh. Blood, her instincts told her: here lay an injured person. She felt farther: Here lay an injured man. The scents of blood and sweat mixed with the cave's mineral stench.

Katherine set Archie on his own feet and

Miss Organdy

'the bloody hell . . .

Seven

~

A TURNIP OR POTATO SMASHED INTO THE PUPPET STAGE: THE Princess and her little dog danced madly on their bouncing strings. Another projectile collided with the chair where the waif had sat only a moment before. "The bloody hell," she repeated. At first it seemed the audience was displeased with the performance but suddenly a wave of discord passed through the crowd and I knew it was something more than rowdy patrons. Children began crying out for their parents and moved like wasps abandoning a smoked nest.

Carter touched my arm: "A riot of some sort, best get—" A rotten turnip sent his ale cup flying toward the puppet stage, which Miss Organdy and her master were hastily tearing down to move from harm's way. The puppeteer was obscured behind the purple and white curtain so I couldn't make him out. It must've been the Prince that she found in the cave . . . of course it was—wasn't it? The question seemed important to me even with havoc breaking out on the street.

Carter pulled on my sleeve and we ran in a direction that seemed opposite the disturbance, though it was impossible to be certain. I glanced back to see how the waif and her master were making out, thinking we should have assisted, but they were already gone, stage, puppets, props and all, even Miss Organdy's rickety chair. Just then a pair of constables (gray suits and heavy mustaches) rushed past us on horseback and though he was not swinging at me per se, one's brandished cudgel knocked off my high-crowned hat. I reached down for it but someone's foot kicked it away. A second and third foot of someone fleeing willy-nilly kicked my hat before I was able to retrieve it, dirty and a trifle bent. Meanwhile I'd been hanging on to my ale cup as if a precious thing, sloshing its remaining contents on my coat and trousers. I tossed the cup toward a gutter and ale burst into a crown pattern on the street. It could not have been the black-hearted Knight "hisself" in the cave . . . why would Princess've been standing guard over him . . . or had she attacked the Knight and was keeping him prisoner, so to speak?

Carter led me through alleys between tall buildings and by the time we emerged on a street—busy but orderly by comparison—the mayhem was far behind us.

"What was . . . all that?" I managed between gulps of air, one hand resting on my hip the other holding my battered hat.

"I'm not sure," said the doctor, equally winded, "a protest timed for the Heiress Presumptive's celebration perhaps . . . something certain to make the papers. Sorry, Jefferson," he puffed. I could sense Carter was embarrassed; like a guest invited home to dine had witnessed an unseemly family squabble. I felt that I should say something to ease his mind but knew not what—so much for the man of letters. I was still trying to concoct a turn of phrase when Carter said, "There no doubt are injuries. I'm on notice at Huntington Hospital. I shall get you in a cab for The Saint Georges and myself across to Huntington, where my services may be in demand."

I thought a moment while Carter began looking up and down the street for a cab. "In truth," I said, "I would prefer to accompany you, if it would not be too great an inconvenience: a storyteller's curiosity, I am ashamed to admit."

Carter seemed at first surprised then pleased—perhaps envisioning himself the hero of some future tale—then again perhaps I should keep my vanity in check. "I cannot promise that all will find your presence welcome, nor can I promise you that the experience will be productive or, for that matter, pleasing . . . but I don't object, my friend."

In a moment a cab was hired and we were clattering across brick streets toward Huntington Hospital, a medical institution of which I had not heard until Carter's reference. The good doctor was distantly taciturn, perhaps steeling himself for whatever challenges he may face. I thought of the great difference between merely describing a victim and attempting to treat him, between godlike authorial omniscience and godlike powers to heal and bestow life. I thought of Mrs. Haeley's infamous protagonist whose fantastic medical abilities make him believe he *is* a god. I looked at the throngs of Londoners as we passed, half expecting to see Mrs. Haeley's monster hulking about in broad daylight. The surge of adrenaline and the potent ale were affecting my perceptions; everything had a gauzy dreamlike quality. A cab-wheel hit an especially nasty bump and we were jostled about for a moment but the teeth-rattling jolt did not clear my head.

At a cross-street the cab slowed to allow a dray to pass in front. A half dozen men and women were packed sitting or lying in the wagon, some visibly bloody, all as somber as the ashes of a spent fire; the dray was headed, it seemed, to Huntington. I wondered how many had been hurt in the—what do the French call it?—the mêlée. I felt the guilty thrill of a witness at a scene of bloodshed. I recalled a schoolyard fight in which one boy pummeled the face of a classmate until blood ran freely from his nostrils and lips. I stood with the others who neither helped the boy being beaten nor turned away—but rather gazed enthralled at the violence, as if a scene of the mind evoked from a storybook, or a painting of some biblical or mythological bloodiness: John the Baptist's beheading or Efigenia's throat-slitting. Is the witnessing made nobler when the observations are turned into art? Is the violence itself transformed into art, like lead into gold? For that matter, is all bloodshed potential fodder for artistic rendering? What if, instead of a saint's decapitation due to the caprices of a princess, the victim is simply an old drunkard trampled in a filthy street by an equally filthy mob—is the old drunk's agonizing death worthy of a painting or a poem? A symphony or a sculpture? And who decides its merits, the artist . . . the artist's audience . . . the artist's patron/publisher? Such were my thoughts as we clopped along at a quicker than customary pace.

Then the cabby was reining his horse to a halt. We had arrived at Huntington Hospital, an unwelcoming brick two-storey building that just as easily could have been a bootblacking factory. We stepped down to the uneven street and Carter handed the cabby a few coins; he seemed pleased with his gratuity as he got his horse moving with a shake of the reins. Once the horse was away I smelled the hospital, as if someone had mixed a vat of excrement and lemon juice . . . using rotten lemons. Carter was without his red leather case, left at his surgery no doubt, and he appeared uncertain what to do with his hands in its absence—trying them in various pockets as we hurried along the crowded walk . . . his coat, his trousers, his vest.

The main entrance to Huntington Hospital was a set of heavy oaken doors but we bypassed them and Carter led me to the side of the building, where patients were dropped (and, I supposed, cadavers hauled away). The dray that had brought the riot victims was pulling off as we approached, the injured taken inside already. The side door was propped open by a broken three-legged chair, probably kept at all for this single purpose. Inside was a long tiled hall; the tiles were most likely white once, now shades of brown. Here and there were chairs and benches along the cracked plaster walls, all occupied, and in between men, women and children sat or lay on the discolored floor. It was strangely quiet and calm, save for a low moan from someone in the hall and an exhausted sob somewhere more distant in the hospital.

Carter was looking over the people, quickly but professionally, beginning to catalogue and assess their medical needs. I wondered if the sick and injured assumed I was a doctor too; I realized I was mimicking Carter's behavior and starting to assume the air of a man of medicine. I liked the notion that some thought I was Dr. Wheelwright, the consulting surgeon from America, and began playing the part more fully—pretending to look about me with a probing, scientific eye, trying to project even that I was drawing some sage conclusions. I noted that the ratio of the horrendous odor had shifted: now more rotten-lemony than excremental but nauseating all the same.

As I was "examining" a woman of about thirty who leaned in a spindly chair holding her shoulder, her arm oddly askew in her lap, I noticed some movement in the hall to my left. I looked more closely: a puddle of blood or bile or both had begun spreading across the tile floor, its source not immediately apparent. I felt myself becoming sick, which would end the charade I'd been coaxing. From nowhere it seemed a woman in an ankle-length gray skirt whisked by and dropped a filthy rag on the advancing liquid—a rag apparently designated for that purpose, by the looks of it, some foul, unlaundered relic of the plague years perhaps. The ghastly rag at least covered the mess for now and I began to gain control over my sickness.

Someone touched my coat sleeve, a boy of nine or ten who had been leaning against the wall. "Can you help me mum?" he said, so cockney it took a moment to translate. I began to respond—something about doing our best and all things in good time—when I saw that the child had a long nail, rusted and bent, protruding from his left shoulder blade through a heavy duck-jacket; around the twisted nail was a nimbus of dark blood.

"Good God," I blurted, not especially consulting-surgeon-like.

The boy looked at me searchingly.

"Just a moment, lad, someone will be with you . . . and your mum," I added turning from him.

From behind, Carter said, "This way," touching my elbow and guiding me elsewhere. We went through a set of doors and were in a large, low-ceilinged room. Wooden pallets ran the length of the plank floor in three long rows, and each pallet was occupied by someone injured or ill. "Do you have a kerchief, Jefferson?" Carter had removed a pale blue one from his vest pocket and he began tying it bandit-fashion over his nose and mouth. I had a white silk kerchief in my coat's breast pocket; I tied it around my face similarly. We had left our hats on so all that showed was our eyes.

"For the odor," I said, part statement part inquiry.

"It may assist in that," said Carter, his words muffled by the mask, which fluttered a bit as he spoke, "but more for our health: some French chemists have been working with a theory that diseases are caused by tiny insects—too tiny for the human eye to see—in the air, and these insects or bugs enter the body through the mouth and nose."

I thought it absurd—tiny bugs too small to see! Leave it to the crazy French! But on the other hand I'd developed a great respect for Carter, so if he believed there may be something to it. . . . I tightened the kerchief knot at the base of my skull. Carter removed his coat and hung it on a peg by the door and rolled up his shirt sleeves to the elbow. He encouraged me to do the same. We began walking down a row of pallets.

"Obviously not everyone here is a victim of the riot," I managed to say through my mask.

"True—those victims are here and there, wherever there was space. I'm simply looking for anyone to whom I may be of service, from the riot or not."

Tending to all these sick and injured were about a half dozen men and women—the only way to tell them from the patients was that they were upright, walking to and fro with a bucket or a cloth. On the far side of the sick room was another man in a suit who must've been a physician as well. Two doctors and six or seven hospital staff to deal with these fifty or sixty people in need—it was a wonder anyone survived. I realized I was among the fortunate, that my doctor had always come to my home—or hotel—when I needed him. I knew of course that the poor had to seek medical care en masse, as it were, from the church or some other charitable institution, but had no true sense of the reality of it.

As I had gathered wool, Carter found a man who was bleeding from his left shoulder. I watched as Carter tore away the man's sleeve to expose the injury. He used the sleeve to soak up the blood and achieve a better view. It was a jagged gash, four or five inches long, and deep. Carter questioned the man about the wound, to determine the nature of it, but he was only semiconscious and his responses were largely unintelligible.

Carter felt along the wound, inside and out, trying to determine if there were any objects to be removed, a shard of glass or a piece of metal. Satisfied there was not, Carter pressed his hand to the wound. "We must stop his bleeding or he will perish from that, never having to worry about a possible infection." A woman was passing nearby. "Mary . . . Mary . . . is there a surgery available?"

The woman, her gray hair pinned in a loose bun, slowed long enough to respond, "I'm sorry, doctor, no—they's all in use." She had a heavy Irish brogue, and seemed as though Carter's and my robber-like appearance were perfectly natural, though no one else was similarly masked. Before Carter could make the request, Mary said, "I'll bring you the surgery box, doctor," and she hurried off.

It seemed to take a long time but eventually a basin of water and a reasonably clean rag were brought to cleanse the gaping wound; then Carter selected a needle from the surgery box and threaded it with "silk," he called it. Mary had rushed elsewhere, leaving no one to assist Carter but me, so he had me steady the man's arm, which felt cold to the touch. The doctor said through his blue mask, "He's too listless to be much trouble, but be prepared to exert more force if need be—I've seen men fight like panthers on the surgical table with little more than their dying breath left in their lungs."

Even though bright daylight shone through the windows, Carter had placed a lamp on a low stool as near to the bleeding man as possible. It was a trick to hold the arm securely and avoid blocking the light and stay out of Carter's way too. I felt a bit like a circus contortionist—the grown man who can fold himself into a carved Cantonese box or some such—yet I managed one way or another.

I assumed Carter would simply sew up the man's skin like a torn trouser knee. First, however, he located the primary source of the bleeding inside the shoulder and dealt with it, which proved to be painstaking work and did not go quickly. My back and neck began to ache from the awkward way I was holding the fellow; I knew though that I had nothing about which to register complaint. The poor man was near dead and Carter was doing the truly difficult labor, Herculean Labor to be sure. Ultimately Carter focused his attention on the man's outer flesh, working steadily with his needle and black silk. In all, the procedure lasted more than an hour. At this rate, I thought, Carter may be in the hospital for days just tending to these "new" arrivals.

Afternoon waned: Carter and I moved about as he worked on more lacerations and punctures and fractured bones, dislocated shoulders and hips, brains suffering from concussion, and so on. In one case, a man's teeth had been shattered, and Carter had to remove the splintered bits of bone where they had become lodged inside his mouth. He had me hold the fellow's head back by placing my index fingers in his nostrils; meanwhile, Carter used a rag to hold open his lower jaw while he plucked out the bits of teeth with his free hand. In another instance, a young girl of fifteen or sixteen had had her foot crushed, and Carter was left no choice but to amputate it above the ankle bone. I had no stomach for the procedure, so

I loitered about outside the surgery room while he received other assistance. The poor girl's agonized shrieks were all but unbearable to me—yet I forced myself to stay just outside the door as a point of honor … or self-image; after a time, the girl's shrieking ceased when she no doubt fainted from the agony. With some patients Carter did nothing because there was nothing to do. His kerchief mask became soiled with other people's blood and his own perspiration. At one point we took a brief break to eat hard little apples and drink coffee from metal cups. We were both too fagged to talk during our repast. I felt myself somewhat in shock too.

Evening came, more lamps were lighted in the hospital. The worst of the cases were seen to and Carter and I cleaned ourselves as best we could, removed our masks, and retrieved our coats. We walked down the long tiled hall, which was not totally vacant yet. I wondered about the boy with the rusted nail in his back; I had not seen him again. Even if someone removed the nail successfully, lockjaw was likely to set in.

My feet were sore, save for the toes which were stone numb inside my shoes. I just wanted to return to The Saint Georges and have the hotel boys bring me a hot-water tub. I wasn't even interested in supper. From a room off the hall with the discolored tile, someone called my name: "Mr. Wheelwright? Is that you, sir?"

Carter and I glanced to each other then entered the little room, where a dark-skinned man lay on a soiled sheet on the floor. "Praise to heaven, it is you, Mr. Wheelwright." The man was propped on his elbows to speak to me, his left leg wrapped in a dirty-white cloth; I saw no blood, however. It took me a moment; it was his voice I recognized first: "Thursday? What has happened to you, man?"

"It is, sir." He lay back, exhausted and … relieved, it seemed.

"What has happened, Thursday?"

"My leg is broken, the tibia," said Thursday.

I wasn't certain in what way to introduce Thursday to Carter. "I met Thursday in Margaret Haeley's home; this is Dr. Carter," I said, aware the introduction was unsatisfactory.

Carter knelt next to Thursday and carefully unwrapped his leg. Someone had cut off Thursday's pant leg at the knee. The lamplight was poor in the confining room but one could see that Thursday's lower leg was badly swollen, and the fracture in the shin bone was obvious. Carter felt about Thursday's knee and leg. He was gentle, yet I watched as Thursday winced nevertheless.

"A clean break it seems," said Carter, "and no bleeding, which is fortunate—but we should get your leg in a plaster cast before the swelling becomes any greater. The hospital has nothing of the sort but I have the materials at my surgery."

It was decided that we would transport Thursday to Mrs. Haeley's house, where I would stay with him until Carter returned from his surgery with the necessary materials. I knew how exhausted Carter must be but he had no intention of leaving Thursday at Huntington Hospital, where he may lay for several more hours before being tended to. Even then, it would surely be a crude splint and he would be sent on his way, loaded in a wagon and dropped at his home. The broken bone would knit poorly if at all, and Thursday could easily lose his leg or his life to bone infection. From my short time at the hospital, I understood the likelihood of all these possible scenarios.

Carter rewrapped Thursday's leg. I went outside to summon a cab while Carter located some assistants to help with Thursday. I secured a single-horse hansom with little difficulty—though cabbies were not as plentiful in this district, especially at this late hour—and in a moment Carter came out of the hospital's side entrance. Two men were carrying Thursday on a long plank of wood; as they drew nearer I saw that hand-holds had been cut out at each corner of the plank. No doubt it was used to carry the dead as often as the quick.

With Thursday balancing on his good leg, we managed to get him into the cab and were on our way to Wicker's Lane. I had mentioned Mrs. Haeley's home so matter-of-factly to Carter, the good doctor perhaps assumed my being there was a natural occurrence (perhaps I wanted it to seem so) but in truth I was nervous at the prospect of finally meeting the great authoress—and in such an awkward way, delivering to her her injured manservant, or whatever Thursday was; and I was in such a state: spattered with blood and Lord knows what, and most certainly reeking like the hospital itself reeked: not the dignified introduction I had envisioned a hundred times.

At any rate, I had wanted fodder for storytelling and gotten my wish.

The cab bumped along and Thursday winced at each jarring jolt—but he did not complain and bore his pain bravely. I feared I would not be so well composed in a similar circumstance; then again perhaps I sold my own cloth short.

We traveled through a section of London with which I was not familiar. In spite of a lantern here and there, the streets were very dark. People were out but they were vague shapes; I imagined them to be women of the street and their male associates. My old New England core of morality flared for a moment but I knew I was not at liberty to be judgmental. I was not, to be sure, Cotton Mather—though we did share at some level a belief in the supernatural. The old Puritan saw witches on every corner of the village green, and I half expected Mrs. Haeley's monster to loom up from the shadows and menace our cab ride.

I dozed a bit in the cab in spite of my anxiety over meeting Margaret Haeley—a testimonial to my utter exhaustion. In dozing, my mind returned to Princess Katherine in the black cave, and the stranger who lay there occupying his own private dark space. In the bouncing cab, my head must have wobbled on my shoulders as if I were the victim of a botched guillotining.

We arrived at Mrs. Haeley's and Carter and I assisted Thursday up the front steps. He produced a ring of keys from his jacket—appearing like someone's gailor—and unlocked the door, bolt by bolt. Just inside the foyer was a candle on a small table. Thursday had me light it and carry it via a heavy iron holder while we made our way, the three of us, to the parlor where I'd been served tea and stale crackers. I wondered if Carter marveled at the stacks and stacks of books lining the tall walls as I had, assuming he could make them out at all.

Once Thursday was situated comfortably on a sofa, Carter went out to the cab, assuring me he would be back within the hour. I took my watch from my vest pocket; angling it in the candlelight I saw that that would put Carter's return at nearly midnight. So far there had been no sign of Mrs. Haeley.

I asked Thursday if he needed anything, and he told me how there would be a pitcher of water in the kitchen and some drinking glasses on a tray. I took the candle, after having lit a lamp in the parlor, and cautiously made my way through the hall to the kitchen. Otherwise the house was pitchy black, and the candlelight cast weird shadows on the literature-lined walls, almost as if the books' characters were trying to free themselves of their narrative shackles: my overtired brain was becoming somewhat hallucinatory. The kitchen proved to be relatively large, with an oval table in the center and a typical iron stove to one side. I hoped to find some dirty dishes on the table, the remains of one of Mrs. Haeley's meals, but it was totally clear, not even a diminutive teacup—and I thought again of the wild notion that Margaret Haeley was dead and I'd been aiding her deranged murderer.

I returned to the parlor with the water pitcher and three glasses, all on the tray with the coruscating candle. I poured water for us both. It had been sitting all day and evening but tasted good on our thirsty tongues. I was becoming used to the brackish London water. Thursday and I placed our empty glasses on a short table in front of the sofa where he lay. I sat in an adjacent chair, and I believe we both fell into a state of demisleep awaiting Carter's return. My mind went back to the interrupted puppet-show except now it was Mrs. Haeley's fictional monster who lurked in the mountain blackness.

In no time it seemed Carter was tapping at the door and I met him with the tallow candle, which had burned low. He carried a wooden box under one arm and his red leather case in the opposite hand. Before shutting the door I noticed that he had the cabby wait. Carter must've promised him a small fortune; perhaps he assumed Mrs. Haeley would eventually pay him for his services to her fellow. I was set on the idea that Carter would get something deserving, from myself if need be.

We went to the parlor, and I lighted a second lamp and placed it on the small table in front of Thursday. I blew out the candle to conserve the wick. The pair of oil lamps provided sufficient light without revealing too much of the parlor's shabbiness. I realized I was glad of this, as if it were my parlor, my house. Carter began to unpack the box. He'd thought of everything—even a canvas sheet to place on the table to preserve it from the messy procedure. He placed the lamps on each end of the canvas to hold it in place, and everything else in between—the wrapping gauze, the powdery plaster mix, the metal bowl for the mixing, &c.

He removed his coat and placed it on the corner tree along with his hat, and my coat and hat; then rolled up his sleeves. Carter positioned a chair next to Thursday's sofa and sat: "The first order of business is the least pleasant—"

"I know," said Thursday, "you must set the break. I'm ready." His fingers tightened on the back of the sofa.

Not certain what to do, I went behind the sofa and placed my hands on Thursday's narrow shoulders, as if to hold him steady; but it was as much for my nerves as for his.

Carter had been unwrapping Thursday's leg, which he then took hold of and carefully but quickly worked into the proper position. I had broken my forearm as a boy, and I winced at the recollection of my similar ordeal. Carter had the two pieces of the tibia in place and used a strip of clean gauze to expertly wrap the leg, securely tucking the ends together where they met at Thursday's ankle bone.

"There," said the doctor, "the worst of it is finished." Carter needed water to mix the plaster, and I handed him the pitcher. He thought it sufficient. After preparing the plaster, he placed a gauzy strip into the bowl, thoroughly coated it, and pulled it between his index and middle fingers to squeeze off the excess plaster paste, which dropped goopily back into the bowl. Then he went about mummy wrapping Thursday's lower leg. I could see by the more pacific look on Thursday's face that the good doctor had already eased his pain a great deal. Carter repeated the process with several more strips, which he'd cut with scissors from his red case. I obviously wasn't needed so I returned to my chair and dozed a bit, with the not unpleasant scent of wet plaster in my nostrils.

After a time Carter was finished and gathering his supplies. I enlivened myself as best I could. Carter had propped Thursday's foot on a pillow placed on the table. "I'm afraid," said Carter, looking at his own vest watch in the lamplight, "that you must stay in this position until morning to allow the cast to harden properly. Do you have any crutches?"

"No, sir," said Thursday groggily.

"I'll come around mid morning to check my work and I shall bring some crutches then."

"Thank you much, doctor." Thursday was already nodding off.

Carter looked to me and I said, "I'll stay here in case I'm needed. Perhaps when you come around in the morning I'll have you drop me at the hotel."

"Very good, Jefferson." Carter smiled at my beneficence—though it be nothing compared to his own—as he retrieved his coat and hat. In truth, I did want to assist Thursday, but I also retained the selfish motive of meeting Margaret Haeley, though the authoress still seemed more part of some fantasyworld than the real one.

In a moment Carter was gone.

Thursday was sound asleep and breathing snorily. I blew out the lamps, went to another sofa near at hand, and was instantly dead to the world as well.

Eight

I DREAMT AGAIN OF MOURNINGWOMAN. THE DETAILS HOWEVER became oblique as I slowly awakened, filtered daylight in my eyes. I wondered why the hotel valet had not roused me with my usual breakfast—I was profoundly famished. Then it came back to me: I was not in my oversized bed at The Saint Georges; I was in fact on a too-small sofa in Margaret Haeley's parlor. I glanced over at Thursday, who appeared to still be sleeping, his leg propped awkwardly on the pillow, which Carter had wrapped in the canvas.

I was reluctant to rise, though my back, neck and shoulders were as stiff as age-cured oak. I pulled myself to a sitting position and placed my feet on the floor—or more accurately on the worn Oriental rug that lay thinly upon the hardwood, which could stand a good cleaning and waxing. I'd removed my shoes sometime in the night, and that recollection sparked another: the sounds of someone moving through the creaky old house. Was it real, or simply a fragment of the Mourningwoman dream?

Thursday emitted a little moan and moved his leg enough that his foot slid off the pillow and the cast knocked loudly on the table. I went to him, padding in my stocking feet. "How do you do this morning, my good fellow?"

He blinked at me. "Mr. Wheelwright, it is you—thought maybe I'd dreamed that part."

"No—'tis I, flesh and bone," then regretted my word choice. I checked Thursday's cast, which was a tad tacky to the touch but otherwise firm as stone. If doctoring falls through, I thought, Carter could become a housebuilder. I helped Thursday to the privé, which was in the rear of the house, and then into the kitchen, where I put him in one chair, his leg propped in another. I performed my own morning toilette, retrieved my shoes from the parlor, and rejoined Thursday. In full daylight the kitchen appeared a typical working-class English one, with a butcher's table on the wall adjacent the stove, several dark walnut cabinets with tarnished brass pulls, and a decorative paper on the walls with a red diamond pattern—faded, and peeling away at the corners.

Domesticity was not my long suit but with Thursday's patient instructions I started a fire in the stove, pumped water in the washroom—and in fairly short order we were having hot tea with honey, and pan-fried bread dripping with ilberry jam. I'd never been so pleased with a meal, partly due my hunger but mostly due my preparing it myself.

I had been wanting to ask, and after filling our cups a third time, I said: "Does Mrs. Haeley require her breakfast this morning?" I was returning the teapot to the stove, mainly my back to Thursday. I held my breath waiting for his reply.

Thursday seemed to hesitate. "Mrs. Haeley's hours are irregular. It would be good if she could wake to a fresh pitcher of water. If she wakes to see you, Mr. Wheelwright,—no offense, sir—she could become quite startled; she is not used to visitors in the house." He considered a moment, while I returned to the table and stood with my hands on the back of an empty chair. "There is a desk in the hall, just outside Mrs. Haeley's door. And an extra pitcher in the cabinet. If she finds her own pitcher empty, she will come into the hall and discover that one." Thursday measured his words as if he were laying bare the details of a criminal undertaking to which I was accessory.

He seemed satisfied with his solution; I however was dubious . . . and even more suspicious. Nevertheless I retrieved the pitcher, filled it with water, and carried it upstairs. Thursday told me Mrs. Haeley's room was the last on the left, the only door with a small secretarial desk next to it. There were four rooms on the second floor, all with closed doors. There was a long Oriental rug running the length of the hall but my footsteps reported like pistol-shots on the aged floorboards. Hung in the hall was a large landscape painting, which I recognized as a tableau of the Rhine though I'd only seen it in illustrations. I recollected the absent paintings from the parlor, and their darkly phantasmal shapes upon the walls.

I placed the water on the narrow desk and my task was complete. Still, there I was, separated by a single door from Margaret T. Haeley, authoress of *Dunkelraum*, and more nightmares than anyone could tally. I listened intently, wanting to hear her move, to mumble in her sleep, simply to breathe. But there was nothing—and I've always had exceptional hearing, thanks in no small measure to these "chimp" ears. Curiosity and suspicion were roiling in my belly: What if she weren't in there at all? What if Thursday really had buried her bones in the cellar? Irrationally, I glanced over my shoulder, as if Thursday could have ascended the stairs. I had to know if Margaret Haeley were behind that door. I wrapped my fingers around the cold glass knob, my heart racing, my lungs catching. What if she is awake? In a state of undress? What shall I do then?

None of it mattered: I turned the knob: Locked! Locked? No! I bent and peered in the keyhole and it was indeed black. Why would Mrs. Haeley lock her door if it were just she and Thursday in the house? Perhaps there was something to fear in soft-spoken Thursday after all. I turned and went downstairs, more apprehensive than ever.

It was time to speak frankly to Thursday on matters of practicality. He was in the kitchen yet but had stood and managed his way to the stove, where he was rearranging the fire, no doubt attempting to conserve the coal. I watched him poke the fire until he was finished and closed the stove. He turned to me on his good leg, apparently aware I was there all the while.

"My good fellow," I began, "we must speak of arrangements. It is clear you will be unable to wait upon Mrs. Haeley as you have; you will need some assistance yourself in fact."

Thursday, looking thinner than ever, leaned against the warm stove. "I have been thinking of it. My sister works in Warwick, she is overdue for a visit. Perhaps she's able to lend assistance for a time."

"I am happy to offer a hand as well. I am on no fixed itinerary—and frankly would consider it an honor to pay Mrs. Haeley some small service."

"That is very generous of you, Mr. Wheelwright, but your

obligations must be many."

"Hardly the case," I said in such a way that may have implied humility.

Perhaps it was my apprehension sneaking in but Thursday seemed uneasy at the idea that I may be about the house—perhaps jealous of his station with the great authoress, not wanting to be usurped in significance . . . or he was indeed up to mischief. "Dr. Carter will be here within an hour or two, and I will go to my hotel. But this afternoon I shall return, and we will post a letter to your sister and make our specific arrangements—I will not hear another syllable to the contrary."

Thursday thanked me, though his pensive manner remained. His room was on the main floor and he had me help him to it. With curtains drawn it was a dim space. I did note a sizable writing desk with a sheaf of papers and pen and ink, and medium-height bookcases on either side of the bed's headboard with each shelf at capacity. He lay on the bed and pulled a woolen blanket over his thin legs. I kept the door slightly ajar and heard him snoring while still in the hall.

I wanted to snoop about the place but knew it was out of the question. I took a book from the stacks in the hall as I went to the parlor, where I would await Carter's arrival. I settled in a chair, resting my pained feet on an Ottoman piece, and perused the crimson-covered book. Tales from the North Country. Scotland & Wales. I opened at random to a story about a Pictish princess lost in the Highlands with her favorite dog. My curiosity was aroused but it could not displace my exhaustion. I awoke to Carter's knocking, the old book open on my chest.

In short order, the doctor checked Thursday's leg, left him a pair of sturdy crutches, and I was in the cab on my way to The Saint Georges. Joyful at the prospects of a big bed, warm meal and hot bath . . . and most of all I missed my manuscripts and implements of inditement. Carter had the cabby drop me at the hotel then he continued to his surgery. I thanked him and made my way through The Saint Georges' lobby and up the stairs—all in a dense fog of half-sleep, almost as if a somnambulist. Hotel employees greeted me and I replied in some semi-lucid fashion: the American author returned from another drunken excursion perhaps. I entered my room and began sloughing garments like a serpent does his skin, caring not where the articles lighted. All I could think of was the big soft bed.

I did notice that on the small side table the valet had placed two letters which arrived in my absence. Despite my drowsiness I had to at least glance at the envelopes. I immediately recognized the hurried, square-cornered script of A. B. C. Murry, my English publisher; the other was by a floridly feminine hand. I could divine the gist of Murry's correspondence: *Where in blazes are my proof-sheets?* The other letter piqued my curiosity—it didn't appear the penmanship (penwomanship) of Mrs. or Miss Blackwood, nor my sister, nor sister-in-law—but not enough to open it at the moment. Instead I crawled beneath the covers and gave in to my utter exhaustion.

I must have fallen into a corpse-like slumber for I awoke in the same position, not having so much as twitched a little finger, it seemed. If I dreamed, the images were lost to the depths of Morpheus' dim halls. I looked toward the window where a narrow gap betwixt the muslin curtains revealed a strip of daylight whose character told me that I'd slept longer than intended and the afternoon was much advanced. I threw back the covers and climbed out, discovering that I was sore from scalp to toenail—as if I'd spent the previous day chopping wood or hauling fieldstone, or some such physical labor as I imagined its effects (having in truth no actual experience on which to base the simile).

I summoned the valet with a tug of the bell cord. To The Saint Georges' credit, in almost no time I was bathed, shaved, dressed, and sitting down to a repast of poached eggs, ham, and good Italian coffee. The valet also took my clothing of the previous day's adventure to be laundered, and my shoes to be cleaned and lacquered. I poured myself a second cup of coffee from the refulgent silver pot—the aroma doing as much as the food to restore me—and set about reading the letters that had arrived. I was mindful of not lingering too long before returning to Wicker's Lane but felt I'd earned a brief respite.

I opened Murry's letter first. Yes, yes . . . he was looking for the corrected proofs of *Andersen's Romance*: "Time," he wrote, "resides in the purse." He wanted to bring out the book by autumn and perhaps run a special Christmas number. True to his nature, Murry did not hold back on any of his jabs and scolded me for snubbing the "American Circle" of writers and artists living in London. Their support could only help my sales; in fact, Murry had taken the liberty of enlisting the Boston-born poet Biron Swinford to introduce me into the Circle and arrange a reading—"a chapter or two from *AR* to get some tongues wagging round town." He'd given Swinford my local address and I could anticipate a visit by week's end. Lovely.

I put Murry's letter aside and went to the medium trunk in the corner of the room next to the mahogany wardrobe, and retrieved the stack of proof-sheets for *Andersen's Romance*. I placed the weighty sheaf of pages atop the writing desk—in sight, in mind, I hoped—and returned to my coffee and the remaining letter.

"Our Dearest Mr. Wheelwright," it began . . . I was delighted to see it was from Miss Hilary Chamberlain, thanking me on behalf of herself and her parents for the recent visit and the "generously kind words you bestowed upon my own humble authorial efforts." She closed the letter by inviting me to dine at Arbor-in-the-Glen at my earliest convenience. Did I imagine it, or was the stationery subtly perfumed? I thought of the umber-eyed Miss Chamberlain in her yellow gown moving across the room like sunlight.

I took a few minutes to compose a brief note to Miss Chamberlain and her parents thanking them for their hospitality and gracious invitation. I would be in touch soon, I said. I gulped down the remainder of the coffee, now grown tepid, and finished dressing. I was down to a single city hat, the one of mourning black, so I donned the matching suit, with the cravat of black and gray diagonal stripes, then called the valet to post the reply to the Chamberlains and to hail me a cab.

It had seemed so far from the hotel to Wicker's Lane the first time or two but now the route was traversed with relative speed. That was the way of it of course: Familiarity shrank distances. It seemed to me though that this "law" was only certainly true of places. Familiarity between people many times made them more remote from one another. I wasn't sure as to why I was waxing philosophic. Perhaps because I'd been thrown from my routine, or because I had witnessed so much misfortune and suffering at Huntington

Hospital. Whatever the cause, I was feeling introspective—more in the mood for a solitary stroll by the river, or better still a lakeside seat near Arbor-in-the-Glen. Somewhere quiet and contemplative; somewhere . . . Wordsworthian.

Instead I was at Wicker's Lane to assist Thursday in sorting out his domestic arrangements. He seemed a capable fellow—wherever and however Mrs. Haeley found him—and even with his fractured leg my sense was he didn't require much help. Yes, there was no question of his capableness, yet that mysteriousness remained in his make-up too. I felt sure I didn't just imagine it: Thursday was a concealer, an obfuscator. I could only hope he wasn't disguising something sinister.

Even under these unusual circumstances it appeared inappropriate to simply walk into Mrs. Haeley's house, unannounced, as it were—though forcing Thursday to answer the door was a poor idea as well. I erred toward convention and used the bell-key. Immediately I heard footfalls—as in two feet—in the foyer, cutting a quickened pace, and the heavily bolted door was pulled back. I was still thinking it all through when I was suddenly standing before a petite woman in a white blouse and patterned black skirt. Her face was fine-boned—as if it had been fashioned by the same God who created birdwings— and her chestnut hair was silvering a touch at the temples. Could it be? . . . It must be: *the authoress herself!*

"Thank Providence," she said, taking me by the arm and pulling me inside. "My Thursday has fallen down the cellar steps and needs help." Mrs. Haeley was leading me down the hall, virtually in a dead run.

The cellar door was just inside the kitchen entrance and it stood ajar. I had lost my voice for a moment but regained it to call out, "Thursday, are you all right, man?" I descended the steep cellar stairs, holding firm to the railing. The only illumination in the cellar was provided by a lamp placed upon the floor and feeble daylight from the small, street-level windows. I saw Thursday's crumpled form at the foot of the stairs. His broken leg lay on the last stair-step, thus I had to step over to reach the floor and kneel at Thursday's side. There was blood running freely from a gash above his left eye but he was moving slightly and making a low moaning sound. "Can you hear me, Thursday?"

He blinked in my direction and tried to speak but produced merely an inarticulate gurgle. I hoped he was just dazed from the fall. I felt his arms and legs and ribs trying to detect broken bones, as I had seen Carter do countless times at the hospital the day previous. My unpracticed hands seemed to find all in order. I realized that Mrs. Haeley was at my side, kneeling and patting Thursday's shoulder, in an effort to comfort him.

"He may only be stunned from the blow to his head. I would like to get him upstairs in better light," I said, assuming the air of the consulting physician again. I was thinking that I needed Carter's aid and wondering how best to summon him . . . when Mrs. Haeley went to Thursday's other side. Apparently she intended that the two of us would manage Thursday, dazed and one-good-legged though he be, up the steps. Who was I to argue? We worked at it for a minute or two, trying to get Thursday sitting upright first of all, but he spilled back and forth between us as if he were made of Cantonese noodles. It would've been comical no doubt had it not been so serious.

"Just a moment," said Mrs. Haeley, before bounding up the steps as spry as a housecat. In her brief absence (and with my eyes adjusting) I noticed that the cellar was orderly, tidy in fact as cellars went—Thursday's doing, I suspected. Even still, it smelled musty and damp, with a hint of something metallic or inky in the air; not unlike the scent of a cavern. I looked overhead, ludicrously, for a dripping stalactite.

Before my mind wandered further afield, fortunately, Mrs. Haeley was there and she reclaimed her post on Thursday's opposite side. In her hand she had a small brown bottle which I knew to be volatile salts. She uncorked the bottle and waved it beneath Thursday's nostrils. The potent vapors reached my nose as well. "Thursday?" said Mrs. Haeley. "Eddie? Can you hear me?"

Eddie? So Thursday had a real name after all . . . but I had no time to ponder it as the salts instantly worked their magic and "Eddie" was coming about. His head snapped to and fro for a moment as his eyes fluttered open. "Mrs. . . ." was the first articulate noise he'd uttered since my providential arrival.

"Yes, my poor fellow," said Mrs. Haeley. "Let's get you upstairs, shall we." That was my cue, and we commenced to get Thursday sitting, then standing. He was somewhat alert now and able to assist in the process, or at least not hinder it too severely. Somehow or another, with Mrs. Haeley's leading and Thursday's one-legged hopping and my exerting force from the rear of the procession, we managed the tricky ascent, and Thursday was soon reclining on a sofa in the parlor.

Mrs. Haeley arranged a chair next to him and spoke to her man soothingly while I fetched a basin of water and clean rags. Mrs. Haeley seemed to think nothing of my familiarity with her home. Perhaps she and Thursday had spoken of me and the role I'd played in his recovery—prior to his accident on the stairs—and the authoress was half expecting me when she opened the door. Hence, not Providence that I'd come *at all*, but rather *when* I had.

Such were my scattered thoughts as I gathered the things and brought them to the parlor. Mrs. Haeley accepted them and began washing Thursday's wound. Once much of the blood was cleaned away, the cut didn't look so severe, just an inch or so long and slightly curved over his left eyebrow. Thursday was still groggy but able to speak, asking us what had happened.

"You took a nasty spill, my fellow," I volunteered. "Lucky not to have broken your neck."

"Indeed," said Mrs. Haeley, continuing to dab at the gash, "I daresay the cellar will be out of bounds to you until your leg is properly knitted."

"I don't know that the cut will close of its own accord," I said. "I am going to send for a surgeon."

Mrs. Haeley made no reply, merely attended to the wound, rinsing and wringing the rag periodically while I went to the desk, hung my hat on the tree, and composed a brief note to Carter. I used the same pen and ink with which I'd autographed my book before. I requested that Carter return to Wicker's Lane as soon as possible and suggested he bring needle and silk thread. Blowing on the ink to hasten its drying, I went out to the street and soon retained a reliable-looking boy to hand deliver the note, giving the lad cab-fare and something for his efforts. It was conceivable of course that the scamp would simply pocket my money and that would be that—a genuine possibility in Old New York certainly and I suspected every large city in the large world. I figured if Carter did not make his appearance or at least send word within an hour or two, then I would perhaps be forced to retrieve him in person.

I went inside and back to the parlor. In just these few minutes I could see that Thursday was more alert, that there was a more vivid gleam in his eye. Mrs. Haeley noticed it too and took the opportunity to have Thursday hold the rag in place himself. "Just like that," she instructed, positioning his hand; then she stood and stepped toward me, her arms open wide for a hug. Which she did, and kissed me on the cheek as well. My face must've glowed crimson, or so it felt.

"What timing," she said. "Perhaps my luck is turning after all. Let me look at you." She stepped away and surveyed me from head to toe. "Italy was good for you—you've put on weight, Monday, but it suits you. You were always too thin." She stood there beaming up at me; somehow her smile was out of place, and had the opposite effect on her features compared to other pretty women: her smile made her appear older . . . tired. Italy? Monday? Always too thin? She obviously thought me to be someone else—did she call her entire circle by days of the week? Perhaps she had only seven acquaintances and it was an efficient way to keep them in mind.

I opened my mouth to set things straight but first I looked to Thursday and his eyes stayed my tongue. I did not fully understand what was taking place but knew to keep quiet for the moment. "Thank you," I said simply.

Mrs. Haeley walked across the room to the coat-tree and took my hat. "Is this what they're wearing in Venice these days? *Very* smart"; and she placed it on her head at a jaunty angle—she turned briskly, the brim of my hat tipped to cover one eye: "What do you think?" She smiled coquettishly, and I must say the look favored her. I had a sense of what bewitched the poet Stephen Haeley—the playfulness, the riskiness of Margaret Townsend. Then in an instant it was all gone. She placed my hat on a peg and resumed the manner of a woman for whom mourning had become part of her character, not merely an unfortunate period in her life.

She took my arm familiarly. "Why so taciturn? Have you been away so long that you've become a stranger to me?" She didn't wait for a response. "You must be tired from your journey, and Thursday could stand some refreshment too. I will make us tea. "Sit, Monday, sit," as she urged me toward a wingback chair.

I wanted to ask Thursday what was taking place here but he appeared to be dozing—whether it was genuine or effected to avoid my queries was unclear, though my mistrustful nature was inclined toward a ruse. The book of Irish and Welsh tales was there where I had left it, so I opened it up and pretended to read. Was this the extent of Thursday's (of Eddie's!) concealment—that his mistress's wits were sometimes muddled? While it was not to be expected of a woman so young—only . . . thirty-seven or thirty-eight—it hardly accounted for his guardedness—and perhaps subterfuge: I strongly suspected Mrs. Haeley was in fact at home on my first visit but Thursday deliberately kept me from her. The idea of it made me a bit agitated . . . until I looked over at the poor fellow with his broken leg and split-open forehead: if his injuries were celestial recompense for his deception of me, his account had been paid in fullest measure!

I went and took the rag from Thursday's blood-stained fingers and rinsed it for him. The water in the basin had become quite foul, so I took it to exchange for fresh in the washroom. In the kitchen there was a kettle on the stove, near to boiling according to the hissing sound, but Mrs. Haeley was not about. I looked out the window to the enclosed yard at the rear of the house, and there was the authoress seated on a stone bench, perfectly idle with her hands folded serenely in her lap. Like the rest of the property, the yard needed some tending—weeds had sprouted in the beds, and the hedges had grown unshapely—yet there were still colorful flowers in abundance, and it would not've been an unpleasant spot in which to while away an hour or two.

I quickly pumped new water and took the last of the clean rags, delivered it all to the parlor, and was back in the kitchen to catch the kettle just as it was starting its shrill whistling. Mrs. Haeley was seated as before, with no thought, I figured, of the tea she had begun to prepare. Thus I assumed the task myself and in a moment placed the pot, cups and saucers, jar of honey, and dipper on the tray; and carried it to the table in front of Thursday's sofa. I realized that I half hoped Mrs. Haeley would not rejoin our little party—I was uncomfortable with the charade thrust upon me and wished to play at it no further.

I prepared Thursday's and my cups, helped him to sit more erect, and handed him his tea. He couldn't feign to doze now but I was not going to take advantage. We sipped our tea quietly while the clean rag on Thursday's brow slowly but steadily collected his blood. We stayed thus for some time; meanwhile my mind swam with myriad thoughts: Mrs. Haeley of course . but "Eddie" too . and Murry's untouched proof-sheets . Biron Swinford's American Circle . Kathy . the Princess in the cave . Hilary Chamberlain . her parents too . Edmund Holland . the avenging Algonquin spirit . Mrs. Haeley's monster . the family Wheelwright back home . Monday? . the waif . Carter . where was he anyway? . the boy with the rusty nail in his back . my aching feet . . . .

Thursday broke the silence: "Is Mrs. Haeley in her yard?"

"Yes, sitting quite at peace when last I saw her." I hoped this was prologue to Thursday's explanation; instead he said,

"She enjoys a cup of tea in the yard."

"I see." I rose and poured a third cup.

"Just a touch of honey . . . yes, like that," he said.

I took the cup and saucer through the house and out of the washroom door. Mrs. Haeley sat as before. A patch of uneven brick led to her bench. I proffered the tea without a word and she accepted it in a like manner, smiling wanly up at me for a moment before taking a sip. It was a pleasant day, a bit warm, but due to the trees and tall houses built close on either side, the yard was already in shade; a finch sang golden from a nearby hedge.

I returned to the parlor and my own drink. I felt renewed enough to read from the book of northcountry tales, which I did for a while, then made another cup of tea for Thursday and myself.

He said, "Mr. Wheelwright, may I trouble you for some paper and pen. I should write to my sister. The postman will be making his final round soon."

I brought the things and Thursday used the back of the book I'd been reading to compose his letter. I thought at first he may need assistance with the composition but his words seemed to come quite fluidly. There was a pained expression on his countenance but I assumed it was from a pounding headache. Meanwhile I rinsed the rag and replaced it to his head, which still wept a trickle of blood. Shortly the letter was finished, sealed and addressed—to a Miss Edith Hill in Warwickshire—and I placed it in the letterbox, tipping up the little white rusted flag to catch the postman's attention. Just as I was about to go inside a cab stopped in Wicker's Lane and it was Carter who stepped onto the curb, red case in hand. He spotted me instantly and called out, "What has happened, my friend, are you all right?"

"Yes, quite—it's poor Thursday again," I reported as Carter approached the steps. In short order I related the circumstances. I did not include Mrs. Haeley in the abridged tale. The wound on Thursday's head was child's play for Carter and the good doctor had it sewn closed in no time. He also checked Thursday's eyes by using a mirror to bounce lamplight back and forth between them, noting aloud that the pupils appeared to behave properly. He instructed Thursday to count back from one hundred, which he did effortlessly. "You are quite fortunate, my good fellow—a fall like that could've been fatal, and you came through with a mere flesh wound. I will remove the stitches in a few days; in the meantime rinse the area gently with clean water each day. If there is any sort of discharge, any sort of fluid seeping from the wound, send for me at once." Thursday nodded his understanding and thanked Carter sincerely.

As the doctor was finishing with Thursday and putting his supplies back in the case, Mrs. Haeley appeared in the parlor doorway. Her face was as white and as lifeless as that of an alabaster bust. "Good," she said without expression, "you've been seen to, Thursday. I am quite, quite tired and am going to my room to rest." She turned and was gone.

Carter looked to me as if to say, *Was that she?* I nodded but offered no more than simple confirmation. Carter and I assisted Thursday to his room and settled him in; then I saw Carter to the door. He asked, "How are you holding up, Jefferson?"

"It's been a taxing brace of days but I suppose I am none the worse for the wearing—certainly better off than poor Thursday."

"Are arrangements in order? It will be some time before the fellow is able to take care of his mistress—this most recent incident makes the fact abundantly clear."

"Quite so—and yes, arrangements are in the works." It must've struck Carter as curiously as it did me that England's most famous authoress had but one manservant attending her. No cook, it seemed, no housemaid nor washerwoman. And the house and yard showed plainly that one manservant was not enough: age and nature were encroaching to be sure. I wondered if it were a pecuniary issue—if there were simply no funds with which to hire more help. Perhaps I could be of use in that regard . . . which reminded me: I reached into my vest pocket and removed a five-pound note. "Here, Carter, you've been a godsend, my friend."

"No, Jefferson, it isn't necessary—"

"I insist. I do not give away my little stories for free—your skills are of certainly greater worth than mine. Now please. . . ."

Carter accepted the note reluctantly. "A sincere thanks," and he tipped his hat.

We walked together up Wicker's Lane until he was able to secure a cab, which he did presently. I returned to Mrs. Haeley's house and its resting occupants. It would be the dinner hour before long, and everyone of us would need sustenance. Both Mrs. Haeley and Thursday were remarkably thin. I felt obliged to fatten them up, to replace Mrs. Haeley's pallor with a rosy healthfulness.

I shut and bolted the door, but only one of the four, which seemed ample to me. I wished that I had brought the *Andersen's Romance* proof-sheets: it seemed I had some time on my hands. I went about tidying the parlor and kitchen. The house was profoundly quiet. The book of northcountry tales wasn't holding my interest so I scouted the stacks in the hall while daylight still came through the windows. Perusing the spines, I heard the postman pick up Thursday's letter to his sister; he left none. No one in London—in the world—had anything to say to Margaret T. Haeley? More than astonished, I was saddened.

I noticed a familiar plain black spine: Mrs. Haeley's book of verse. I had not read all of the poems in my copy that I'd purchased at Bookman & Sons, and I felt a longing to connect with Mrs. Haeley in some way. Strangely, after meeting her, one of my idols, I felt more distant from her than when I was an ocean away—I a too-impressionable boy, and she the talk of whole metropolises . . . cities, mainly, she never visited, even after her literary fame preceded her.

I carried her book to the parlor and settled in. I read again the title poem, "Desert Isle," which took on new significance now that I'd witnessed the authoress's isolation. Was it self-imposed or imposed upon her? Which was sadder? Flipping the pages at random I lit upon the dedication page, which I had not read previously:

> *To all my beloved shades—especially my Hæley, England's greatest poet. . . .*
>
> *& to my dear friend who still waits with me on this side, A. Mundie.*

A. Mundie? Mrs. Haeley wasn't calling me by a day of the week—she thought I was this Mundie fellow. I recalled all I knew of the Haeleys' newspaper-printed history, and nothing regarding an A. Mundie came to me.

Nevertheless, I felt a little mystery had been solved—or at least somewhat elucidated—and I took some comfort in this as I read from Mrs. Haeley's book . . . and waited for the occupants of 261½ Wicker's Lane to rouse from their incubic slumbers.

Nine

~

I DECIDED TO ASSESS THE FOOD SITUATION. IN THE SCULLERY closet there were dry soup beans, rice, flour, a tin of lard (nearly empty), baking powder, soda, salt, something that looked like dried peas, raisins, a small amount of coffee, and a fairly ample supply of black tea leaves. It was a start, I supposed. Vermin had been about, of course, but had not caused too much mischief with the meager stores. I went to the cellar to see if there was more to be had there. I took a lamp as the cellar had already become quite dim. At the bottom of the steps there was the dark outline of Thursday's blood where it had soaked into the earthen floor. The black patch looked vaguely like a silhouette of England itself.

I stepped over merry old England and snooped about for more food. There were several large tables in the cellar, all free of clutter; and two wide cabinets. One contained clothes, men's clothing it appeared. I wondered if these were Haeley's old things—articles to which Mrs. Haeley was too attached to discard. In the other cabinet were two blocks of cheese, some small potatoes, a ham, and a bottle of port. One of the blocks of cheese had an ample wedge removed already, and on the shelf was the knife for cutting. I put the cheese on one of the tables, cut another sizable wedge—then proceeded to carry the cheddar-wedge, smoked ham, new potatoes, and the bottle of port upstairs.

Nosing about in the kitchen I found a rusted corkscrew and a dusty glass, and so poured out a tumbler of the port—warning myself that I must go easy on the wine: I did not need a drunken spectacle here in Margaret Haeley's home.

I only half knew what I was doing but set out to make biscuits. I had seen various cooks do it often enough, so I understood the basic principles. It wasn't a pretty process—I was wearing as much flour as I'd used to mix the dough—but presently I had a pan of biscuits in the oven, whose temperature was a challenge to keep consistent, but I maintained a vigilant watch on the fire and did my best with it.

Meanwhile I sliced several pieces of ham and placed them in a pan to fry, along with the potatoes, which I had cut into cubes. Everything, I must say, smelled amazing; and the port was excellent: I was having a splendid time playing domestic to Mrs. Haeley's little household.

Before long I proudly had our evening meal on the kitchen table: ham and potatoes, cheddar cheese, biscuits with the remaining ilberry jam, and glasses of port. I roused Thursday and told him the food was ready. I made sure he had his crutches then I went up to summon Mrs. Haeley. I tapped on her door with the news. She did not respond, so I figured she probably wouldn't be joining us. On the one hand, I had no burning desire to revive the role of A. Mundie, but I also felt a cook's disappointment at my chef-d'oeuvre going untasted by the guest of honor.

Downstairs Thursday was still en route. I assisted him the remainder of the way and prepared his plate. The poor fellow looked as if he'd just survived a week-long bacchanalia but otherwise not too bad, all things under consideration. He set to his meal without hesitation, especially the glass of port, which he nearly emptied in one long drink; I refilled his glass.

I was about to take my first bite when Mrs. Haeley appeared at the kitchen doorway. She looked perhaps a little improved—less ashen—than before her rest. "It smells wonderful," she said. I got up from the table and escorted Mrs. Haeley to her place, then prepared her plate as if she too had a fractured leg and wounded head. She didn't seem to mind the attention. She took her silverware in hand and went about eating with no ado.

Well, the ham was a bit overdone, the potatoes a bit under—nor were the biscuits a culinary triumph, as I must've stumbled upon the standing army's formula for "hard tack." However, everyone's hunger proved an ambrosial sauce, and we ate and drank rapaciously, leaving not even a tittle of cheese. Here I was, at table with the great authoress—a scene I had envisaged countless times—and no one uttered a syllable during the meal.

When Mrs. Haeley swallowed the last of her wine, she said, "That was lovely, Mundie. Thank you. It seems like old times, except Elena did the cooking then. You remember Elena."

"Somewhat . . ." I said uncertainly.

Mrs. Haeley smiled faintly. "Somewhat? I recall you fancied her, all bird bones and raven tresses. I wonder what became of the waif."

I was at a loss in the conversation. I had lit a candle on the table before we ate. It was dusk now so the single flame provided our only light—our faces then were half shadow and sallow glow, moving mercurially with a draft that could only be detected via the candle, playing not upon our skin.

"Do you know what would make the reminiscence complete?" Mrs. Haeley was suddenly more animated, as if the nighttime enlivened her. "Let's have our coffee in the music-room and, Mundie, you must play the pianoforte for us as you used to do."

"I am . . . out of practice." It was not a lie: I had not played in years, and even at the pinnacle of my talents I was only passable.

"We can forgive a botched fingering or two—can we not, Thursday? After all, we ate your dinner." There was a touch of mischief in her smile.

"Touché." There was no avoiding it.

Mrs. Haeley helped Thursday to the music-room while I prepared the coffee. I held out a feeble hope that if I dawdled long enough, she would lose interest. I piled the dinner plates in the washroom while the water boiled. I ground the beans with a mortar and pestle I found earlier in one of the cabinets. In a few minutes the water was hissing and I poured it into the metal pot, then pressed the grounds. I set the pot and cups on the tray and took it down the shadowy hall.

The music-room, I discovered, was across from the parlor. Mrs. Haeley had lighted several lamps and the room had an almost cheerful radiance. The furniture was of the same style as in the parlor, except until this evening it must have been covered—the white sheets lay in piles on the floor where Mrs. Haeley had just put them: the smell of dust was plain in the stale air. The pianoforte, a medium Broadwood of unpolished ebony, was in the corner, and Mrs. Haeley had placed a tri-candelabra so that I could read the music sheets—which was a relief; otherwise Mrs. Haeley and Thursday would've been treated to a recital regarding little Mary's tenacious lamb—for that was the only song I seemed to recollect.

Mrs. Haeley, delighted as if it were her birthday, poured everyone coffee. I took a couple of careful sips before assuming the piano-bench. I fingered an E-flat and even my metallic ear could tell the wires were badly out of tune, a condition which could in no way detract from my performance. I stared at the sheet of music on top—something by a German composer I did not know, Werner Schlözer, titled "Junges Deutschland" (Young Germany, I translated absentmindedly, virtually exhausting my knowledge of the language). The composition at a glance had some challenging chord changes but all in all was not impossible. I felt that I should offer a heartfelt apology as introduction but decided to just dive into the pond as it were.

I began . . . and noticed that the opening notes echoed in the high-ceilinged space. I soldiered onward, my fingers feeling as nimble as a stone-cutter's. Following a particularly clumsy turn of musical phrase, I glanced at Mrs. Haeley expecting to witness a pained expression—but she appeared enraptured, seated in an embroidered chair, her floral cup held delicately in her lap. I exaltedly achieved mediocrity for a few measures and risked another glance at my hostess, who still looked to be listening to an angelic quintet casting spells with their celestial harps. . . .

And it occurred to me that Mrs. Haeley wasn't hearing my idiotic playing at all: she was awash in a private reverie, listening to a phantom pianoforteist, enjoying a spectral sonata, perhaps reliving another night in this very music-room—with Stephen Haeley and Mundie . . . a happier time, the world at their feet, the possibilities infinite. Maybe it was unkind, but I experimented and interjected a couple of bars about Mary's lamb—only Thursday seemed to notice, and he was but half awake reclining on a sofa. I went back to Schlözer and finished the piece with a juvenile flourish. The final notes lingered in the room unforgivingly.

In spite of my lackluster performance I anticipated the customary applause from my audience but they sat there as quiet and meditative as Quakers. I went to the chair between Mrs. Haeley and Thursday, and freshened my coffee. Mrs. Haeley continued to stare at the pianoforte, her head moving slightly, still in time to the music that only she heard. We sat for some time. I noticed that, as in the parlor, pictures had been removed from the walls—to be sold, I now realized—and only their squarish shadows remained. I suspected that after a time the furniture would go; then extraneous clothes and such; and finally the books . . . no, the walls and roof would be sold off before the books, the stacks of which would remain like the skeleton of the great authoress's house-life, to be picked over by the scavenger birds of curiosity.

The coffee was still hot but had turned bitter.

After a while Mrs. Haeley's expression drained: her private concert must've ceased. She took a sip of coffee. I offered her more and she looked at me searchingly. She studied my face as if she intended to render it with oil and brush. A full minute or more passed.

She said, "You are not Agamemnon Mundie." Not accusation; merely simple statement of fact.

"No, madam. My name is Jefferson Wheelwright."

"Mundie died of typhus," she said without expression; "they cremated him in Venice; I read one of Haeley's poems—'Ode to the Eastern Light'—at his memorial; they played 'Junges Deutschland,' his favorite composition. What sort of parents name a child Agamemnon?"

I said nothing. What was there to say?

She looked at me further. "There is an American author by the name of Jefferson Wheelwright." Mrs. Haeley was still making declarative statements. She put down her cup and left the room with purpose. I heard her in the hall then she returned with a book in hand—my book, *Sketches of the Old New Yorkers*. She sat and flipped to my portrait, the generous one by Miss Blackwood; then she read what I had autographed. Mrs. Haeley smiled, but it was of discomfort, of embarrassment.

She offered me her hand. "Mr. Wheelwright, it is good of you to call."

Her small hand was chiseled from Polar ice. "It is an honor, truly, Mrs. Haeley." I relinquished her thin fingers. "Would you like more coffee, madam?"

She looked at the cup on the side table as if it had just materialized there, the trick of a Turkish magician. "No thank you, Mr. Wheelwright. I . . . I must apologize. I haven't been feeling myself and must retire early. Won't you call again? . . . Tomorrow if you like. I'm certain I will be better on the morrow."

"Yes, madam. Thank you." I stood as she did, and I watched her leave the room. I thought that the contrast of her white blouse and black skirt was apropos, as she lived in two worlds, communed with both the living and the dead . . . and perhaps was forgetting how to tell the difference.

I had believed Thursday was dozing but he said, "Mundie loved her, always had, even when the three of them were inseparable . . . wanted to marry her after Haeley's accident. She put him off, still too grief-stricken . . . Mundie left to winter in Italy. Mrs. Haeley never saw him again."

I wanted to ask about Mrs. Haeley's confusion but suddenly felt quite exhausted, and my feet pained me terribly. I had gone too long without Carter's deft treatments. I took the cups and pot to the kitchen and drank the last of the coffee while I scrubbed the dinner dishes. It'd been some time since I had cleaned my own dishes—leave be someone else's too—but I considered it an act of humility, like assisting a blind beggar through a busy cross-street while cabbies hissed at you to move along. In short, I felt that cooking and cleaning for Mrs. Haeley and Thursday were beneficial to my soul. Still, I thought of Thursday's sister and would have no difficulty relinquishing the soul-blanching opportunity to her—another act of generosity, from my soul to hers.

I finished in the washroom and looked in on Thursday, who lay on his bed with a book, unopened, in hand. A candle burned low on his nightstand. He was awake and contemplating the ceiling. I noticed a cobweb in the corner, swaying leisurely in a draft.

"Everything is put away," I said. "I should be getting back to the hotel. Are you and Mrs. Haeley quite battened down for the evening?"

"Yes, thank you, Mr. Wheelwright. You've been most kind and magnanimous with your valuable time."

"I shall call upon you tomorrow. In the meantime, my good fellow, stay away from stairs." I wagged my finger at him. Then I collected my hat and coat, and set out to find a cab to The Saint Georges. For the first time since my arrival there was a chill in the London night air. Had it not been for my suffering feet and my exhaustion, it would've been a pleasant hike to the hotel.

I hoped a cab would be close at hand but I walked for a time without seeing any. I was approached by solicitous women. In the dark they were but abstractions of women, shapes and voices, and smells—perspiration and alcohol, tobacco and some floral perfum that was both powerful and ineffective. I was not interested and communicated as much by walking past without a word. On a corner a fellow played a violin. When he heard my approach he used his foot to jangle a tin on the sidewalk in which passers-by were encouraged to drop a coin or two as voluntary remuneration. His tune was pleasingly mournful—I thought of ships on a dark sea, so distant that their lonesome crews could only see the lanterns of the other, while the currents conspired to keep them from a more satisfactory communion—and I tossed a bob into the tin. The street violinist, dressed in little better than rags, dipped his head in appreciation and played on.

The moon was nearing full but clouds and the tall buildings prevented its beams from lighting the streets. At the moment I preferred the shadows. My mood was darkening and I sensed a kindred spirit in the London nightworld. The lamps that were lighted here and there were alien things and unwelcome. I was of a mind to snuff them out as I advanced, cutting a swath of unmarred darkness in my wake.

I was seriously thinking of this—of further blackening the black night—when a cabby pulled to the curb and inquired if I wanted his employ. I indicated I did by stepping up into his rig and knocking once on the ceiling; my only words were "The Saint Georges" and we were off. The ride was brief. I paid and entered my hotel, its doors held open by uniformed boys, whom I tipped a hay-penny each for this small and superfluous service. I headed straight for the grand staircase but was stopped when the manager called out to me. He approached, and I noticed his gray suit and red vest and the card he waved in his fingers.

"Mr. Wheelwright, sir, you had a visitor who waited at length but eventually left his card." The manager stood before me as if he'd just delivered news of armistice, or of holy papal ascension. I took the card, not bothering to glance at it: there was no need: it was the poet Biron Swinford, set upon me by Mr. Murry, charged with dragging me into the American Circle for my own good (or at least the good of my book sales—for Murry's good in other words).

I thanked the manager perfunctorily and asked him to send some port to my room, and continued on my way, tucking the card into my vest pocket. By the time I'd changed into my dressing gown and slippers, the port had arrived. The hotel boy poured a glass and left the bottle, per my instructions. I was tired but not feeling as drained as before. I considered retiring straight to bed after a glass (or two) of port, but the calm and quiet of my room were very soothing, so I decided to read a bit from Edmund Holland's book—though the last time its sophistication had unnerved and depressed me so that I'd taken to the streets in a drunken ramble of self-pity. Now I knew what to expect and opened its pages with a reverence, yes, but also with a more analytical eye. I wanted to know not simply *what* Mr. Holland was doing as an artist—but *how* he was doing it. (And could his technique be . . . emulated?)

My intent was to read just a few pages, enough to ruminate on for a time . . . but the narrative drew me in and would not release me. I discovered that I'd taken a few sips of wine—however, by and large I had neglected my drink, which was supplanted by Mr. Holland's intoxicating words. I had a vague sense of what he was up to, the careful repetition of images, sometimes viewed straight-on by the reader, other times almost from an angle . . . so that you didn't know at first they were the same image: the waving sea grasses . the maiden's whipping hair . the wife's waving to her husband, destined to be lost at sea . . . to name but three scattered through the book like gemstones in a crowded jewelry-box, revealing themselves only when the light catches them just so.

And Mr. Holland's sentences: they seemed simple at a glance, slight of punctuation—looking from a distance like a schoolgirl's letter home while visiting her rustic aunt. Yet the sentences cut like diamonds . . . no, like medical scalpels edged in diamonds, and turned with Carter's skillful touch.

I closed *Verses & Vignettes* and looked over at the proof-sheets for *Andersen's Romance* on the writing desk. I rose slowly and approached them as if they were a sullen lover to whom I was compelled to say something, but knew not what. I unwrapped the manuscript tied with simple string and turned back the coarse paper on top, exposing the title leaf, which read like an accusation:

––––––––

ANDERSEN'S ROMANCE

A Novel by
JEFFERSON WHEELWRIGHT

Author of
SKETCHES OF THE OLD NEW YORKERS
& SUNNYDALE

§

A.B.C. Murry & Co. Publisher

London • Edinburgh • Paris • Berlin

––––––––

I began reading Chapter I, "The Peacock in the Pear Tree." I finished Chapter I; then Chapter II; III; IV; then V . . . *it was all wrong!* . . . terribly, terribly wrong! Compared to Edmund Holland's book, mine was that schoolgirl's letter home . . . less than even: at least the schoolgirl's inditement would've been sincere. My novel was simple and mocking—a sort of schoolyard insult hurled unwarranted at my unsuspecting reader. Mr. Holland had done it to me again—I was rattled, verging even on despair.

I told myself I was just tired, that I'd had a very trying set of days. A good night's rest and I wouldn't be so self-critical on the morrow. I used the chamberpot then crawled beneath the covers. Perhaps I slept but more accurately my mind occupied some netherworld between sleeping and waking. The images had the qualities of dreams, yet were not outside my conscious control. Much of my demidreaming concerned Mrs. Haeley of course and her own netherworld of undifferentiated past and present . . . and of practical matters, of how the authoress would make do with Thursday impaired as he was. I imagined Thursday's sister, Miss Edith Hill of Warwick; I saw her as all bird-bones and raven tresses. Then my stream of semiconsciousness shifted to my book. What if Andersen's ancestors had not been blacksmiths but rather shipwrights, would that not intensify the maritime metaphors later in the story? And what if Andersen's first love were a ship, a small sailing yacht—the *Kathy*, no the *Cathy* (to obfuscate cleverly)—and not a horse, was there not much more symbolic opportunity in a feminine ship than a sexless equine? I must remember all this for the morning . . . no, I knew better—I would only recall that I'd had revisionary thoughts, not what they'd been. . . .

I rose and donned my gown and slippers, and lit the writing-desk lamp. I was not depressed anymore; I was excited, almost elated. I dipped my pen in ink and began making simple corrections on the proof-sheets. Soon I was composing in the margins—whole new paragraphs that would then continue onto the verso, with arrows and asterisks as guideposts. I thought of Murry's pique at having to set the book anew, but only vaguely as I cared not a jot! My artistic mind was ablaze as it had never been: what did it matter if the old version of *Andersen's Romance* were lost to the conflagration! My pen moved on, as if guided by another's hand . . . Edmund Holland's, or Stephen Haeley's ghost's . . . was Agamemnon Mundie an artist too? Perhaps in naming me, Margaret Haeley possessed me of his soul, a kind of holy black magic in the service of sacred literature. My fingers became blackened with the dark art. . . .

At first my changes were relatively minor but soon they propelled me forward in the story to rework later chapters, which in turn pulled at the plot in earlier sections. I dissected my manuscript into its chapters and laid them on the floor in sequential order. I wrote at the desk but at times I sat upon the floor and tinkered with passages there. Chapter twenty-two, "The Maiden's Voyage of Mirth," would have to be rewritten from scratch, with no maiden, no voyage . . . and probably no mirth: I took some fresh sheets and commenced with zeal. Pages, renumbered (once, twice, thrice in some cases), spread about me everywhere, drying. I thought briefly of my Mourningwoman dream and wondered if the pages would come to me of their own accord, mummifying me in words. I hoped that Murry would peel the sheets from my shrunken corpse and publish this newly conceived story—better a posthumous good book than a bad one to bring embarrassment to the living author.

I was running low on ink, yet my thoughts flowed like the Thames at hightide. I thought I must wake the hotel boy to fetch me more. As if my mind had been read, there was a knock at the door. I looked up from where I was seated on the hard floor and noticed gray day's beginning outside my window. Had I written through the night? "Yes," I called, and the valet entered with my customary breakfast. Needless to say, the fellow was taken aback to find me and my room in such disarray.

"Good day, sir."

"Just set the tray on the side table. I will see to it myself."

"Very good." As he placed the food and coffee, he said, "Begging your pardon, sir, but there's a gentleman here to call upon you."

I pulled myself to a standing posture, realizing for the first time how stiff and sore I was. "At this hour?"

"Yes sir—he says he mustn't chance his missing you again."

That devil Swinford, I thought. "Fine; show him up will you?" In fairness, perhaps Swinford had written on his card that he would come again first thing. I found my vest on the back of a chair and fished the card from the pocket. There was nothing written on the back; then the name on the front surprised me greatly:

Mister Chester Peacock
President & Operator
Peacock & Family
Bank & Mortgage

Baker & Regency Streets London
Est. 1753

Chester Peacock? My head was so beclouded with images from my book, it took a moment to place the name. Mr. Peacock was our London banker of course, whose institution was entrusted with the finances for my grand tour of the Continent, and other Wheelwright family interests in general.

Mr. Peacock, whom I'd never met, appeared in my doorway looking every bit the miser—apropos to his profession I supposed. He was Jack Sprat thin and as bald as a toad. Moreover, his name was ironical given his lead-gray suit. Even his eyes, which peered above wire-frame demi-spectacles, were the color of a pencil's dull tip. Perhaps he did not appear to be the undertaker, but certainly the undertaker's trusted assistant.

"Mr. Wheelwright, please forgive this early intrusion." He came forward, surveying the wreck of my room—and me. He offered his right hand; in the other he held a tall hat of charcoal gray. "It's good to finally meet you."

I invited him to sit, and we navigated between the sheets of paper on the floor. Once seated, he removed a large brown envelope from his hat, where he'd been stowing it temporarily.

"I am afraid, Mr. Wheelwright, that I am the bearer of unfortunate news."

I felt a sudden chill and pulled my dressing gown around me more tightly. "Well, what is it, man?"

From inside the large envelope he produced a smaller one, which he handed to me without benefit of gloss. It was addressed simply to Mr. Jefferson Wheelwright—obviously it had been part of a whole package. I recognized my brother's practiced hand as I broke the seals and unfolded the letter:

Dearest Brother—
I trust this correspondence finds you well. Your curiosity is no doubt enflamed so I shall get right to it. . . . This letter brings bad news but first let me say that no family member or dear friend has come to harm—the news is not as calamitous

as all that, and for this fact we must be thankful indeed.

If you have been reading the papers—of course you haven't . . . you've been spinning tales of ogres and Indians in haunted forests (<u>wink</u>)—you would be aware that copper has plummeted. At present mining it, even with a skeletal crew, is a losing endeavor : it costs far more to dig it up and process it than it can fetch on the markets. Hence I have been forced to suspend the mine's operations indefinitely. This was a blow but not a crippling one. Then on the Seventeenth of July a fire broke out at the Bridge Street warehouse. We were about ready to ship the furs in full, so were near capacity. All was lost, Jefferson! Not only the furs, worth $10,000s, but the warehouse and docks too. Everything turned to cinders!

We will rebuild, starting small as Grandfather Patterson had in the beginning; and copper prices will rebound eventually. The meantime will be assuredly mean. The Wheelwrights are not paupers but I'm afraid your grand tour will not be so grand after all. Our other modest enterprises are still afloat of course—though at this time I must underscore their <u>modesty</u>.

I have communicated the particulars to our English banker, Mr. Peacock, who will continue to oversee your interests while abroad. His hands will be full now—for as Grandfather liked to comment, it is easier to manage a lot than a little! I have augmented your coffers to the best of my ability for the time being : it must see you through til your return home. I have taken the liberty of writing the Blackwoods in Brussels, as you may wish to visit our old friends sooner than you had planned (and stay longer than intended).

Do not trouble about all this, Brother. We are well; and hard work keeps body & soul fit. Write your tales and see your sights : a beautiful view still costs nothing!

Affectionately,

Your Brother,

P. W.

I was in shock as I refolded the letter and set it aside. My fingers had smudged the paper with dark magic.

"My sincerest sympathy, Mr. Wheelwright. The vicissitudes of business can be cruel indeed," said Chester Peacock, beginning to unpack his large envelope further. "I have gone over your account carefully, and with your brother's recent deposit, you have just shy of fifteen-hundred pounds." He handed me a ledger sheet with the precise figure: £1,487 . 26½d. "Not a princely sum but no small amount either. We must look toward economy, and I humbly suggest the first order of business is to procure more frugal lodging while in the City. I have discreetly made inquiries and have the addresses of a half dozen respectable establishments." Mr. Peacock handed me a piece of paper with the addresses neatly penned. "We have some lads who do errands for the office—I would be happy to put them at your disposal to transport your trunks and such; Peacock and Family will gladly absorb the negligible gratuity."

I was overwhelmed with the turn of events. If Mr. Peacock looked the part of undertaker's assistant, I no doubt appeared a proper client.

"I have interrupted your breakfast, Mr. Wheelwright, with this unsavory intelligence—which has not, I sense, fully settled just yet. You should eat and gather your thoughts. The situation is not emergent; we have time to plan things with care." He waited for a reaction of some sort but was left wanting. "You have my business address—here too is the address of my home. . . ." He proffered another card, which he placed on the silver breakfast tray when it became clear I was not going to receive it manually. "Feel free to call night or day when Peacock and Family can be of service." He saw himself out of my den of chaos, shutting the door—perhaps thankfully—behind.

I sat for a long while, thinking about my sudden reversal of fortune, yes, but also about my book. I was not finished revising yet. Murry had already advanced half for *Andersen's Romance*—perhaps I could renegotiate the remainder on the grounds of the novel's improvements. Renegotiate—it was an ugly word. Artists should not be about renegotiating, or negotiating in the first place, the terms of their art—considerations of coin could have nothing but ill effect on art *and* artist.

But such was the way of the world.

And I must uproot myself from The Saint Georges. Won't the *Ledger* love that: AMERICAN AUTHOR FALLS ON DIFFICULT TIMES / BOOTED FROM FIRST-RATE HOTEL. No doubt the scandal would make a record transatlantic crossing and get New Yorkers' tongues wagging too—something my brother did not need in his heroic efforts to resurrect the family's fortunes. I could leave the City immediately, perhaps projecting the image of the impetuous traveler; spend a quiet fortnight in Paris; then make my way to Brussels, where I could remain the houseguest of the Blackwoods indefinitely—not precisely what I had in mind for my Continental tour. Not to mention, the charade was thin and most likely would fool no one.

I spread gooseberry jam on cold toast and nibbled at it a long while. I poured myself a cup of coffee. It was strong and tasted ambrosial after a sleepless night and the shock of my brother's letter, which I looked at again, to make certain it was real and not some lingering detail of a vivid nightmare. There it lay, of course, wickedly corporeal and ink-stained.

Carter would be arriving in a few hours for my foot treatment, which was—punning aside—sorely needed. I had a bit more toast and coffee before climbing into the big bed. The long night of revision and the shocking news were too much for my constitution and I instantly succumbed to a dreamless sleep.

Ten

~

I MAY HAVE SLEPT AWAY THE DAY—OR THE REMAINDER OF MY days, like a fairytale princess who's eaten of a poisonous apple (I recalled just such an Hungarian tale)—if not for Carter and the hotel boy's arrival and their rapping on my door. I wobbled my way to the door, not careful enough and a proof-page attached itself to my heel. I unlatched the door and Carter and the boy entered the chaotic wreck of my room (my life!). I made my way back to the tall bed, more pages sticking to my bare feet—yet I felt too fagged to reach down and detach them. In fact I had the odd thought that if I attempted it, I would lose my balance and carom to the floor, and as I fought to regain my equilibrium—isn't that what the scientists of physics call it?—the pages would adhere to my forearms and calves and face, papering me willy-nilly.

Carter, perhaps surprised to find me thus, directed the boy to place the tub of hot water in the usual spot, though Carter had to move some of the proof-pages away. I watched from the edge of the bed as silent as Brother Benedict. The good doctor dismissed the boy and immediately began preparing the footbath. I eventually summoned the energy to shake the pages of *Andersen's Romance* from my feet, and I sat in the chair, easing my sore and discolored extremities into the medicinal water.

Carter, used to reading my work during this time, began busying himself with organizing the pages, which spread across the carpeted floor seemingly haphazardly. There must've been some order to them however: though I paid little attention, my sense was that Carter discovered a pattern in the madness, and he had them in proper order tout de suite. It seemed too that I was waiting for him to finish the task, for the moment he did I said:

"I shall be moving from The Saint Georges. . . ."

"Indeed?"

"Yes—I shall be moving in with Mrs. Haeley and Thursday."

"That's very magnanimous of you, Jefferson. Cannot other arrangements be made so that your tour is not interrupted? I thought Thursday had a sister that was going to lend a hand."

"Quite right, but it seems Mrs. Haeley has a book manuscript that she's been working on and is nearly finished with—and she has requested my humble assistance in its final touches." The fabrications came to me so naturally they almost seemed true.

"Sounds very exciting—"

"Yes, but mum's the word, my good fellow—the newspapers and all . . . you understand."

"Of course, of course."

We were quiet for a time and perhaps I dozed with the glorious heat from the footbath radiating upward—heavenward!—through my whole body until even my brain seemed to float in a hot fog. I also felt the lightness of relief, with the plot hatched for avoiding the ignominy of vacating the fine hotel because the Wheelwrights had suddenly fallen upon hard times. I recalled veterans of the Revolution who, in my youth, had to depend on the generosities of their fellow townsmen for the most basic necessities as they were unable to hold steady employ. They appeared by and large of able body but it was as if their minds had been wounded—and not because of a blow to the head: the experience itself had maimed them. The townsmen paid them in food and in reasonably comfortable places to bed, &c., not out of sympathy or appreciation for their services in Washington's great army but more a sense of obligation, a debt that must be paid so they paid it. One such veteran, known simply as Old Tom, staggered through the streets of Albany, "whiskey walking" though supposedly he never touched a drop of anything harder than ale or cider, and muttered to the ghosts of his past. He was not a danger, the War relieving him of all his violence along with his sound mind. . . .

While I dozed and wool-gathered about the veterans, Carter had completed my treatment. "When will you be moving to Wicker's

Lane?" he asked.

I blinked at Carter as if emerging from a thick dream. "Immediately . . . today I should think."

"You should rest, Jefferson. Avoid wearing yourself down."

"Yes, yes . . . thank you, my friend. I shall heed your warning."

Carter had packed up his red case, so he donned his coat and hat and bid me adieu. The hotel boy came and went, taking with him the tepid bathwater; I asked him to send up the manager at the gentleman's earliest convenience. I had just finished buttoning my shirt, its tail still hanging outside my trousers, when the manager, a dark-haired fellow with impressive mustaches and a bit of stoop about his shoulders, knocked and entered my room (what already felt to be *former* room).

I informed him of my having a change of plans, and I instructed him to forward my bill to Peacock and Family in Bankers Row. A letter to the hotel from Mr. Peacock before my arrival had secured my credit. I requested too that the manager include in the bill the services of a hotel employee or two to assist in my relocation. I surely was vacating The Saint Georges much more expediently than Chester Peacock had presumed—thus it wouldn't be necessary to accept his offer of feeless movers.

I had a large satchel in which I carried my instruments of inditement and manuscripts, &c., while traveling. I retrieved it from the wardrobe and placed my pens and ink bottles (tightly corked) into an interior leather pouch, then stuffed the satchel full of the proof-sheets. I was suddenly of a mind that all this should be carried with me as if as precious as a newborn babe—not to be left in the rough grip of some Saint Georges lackey. No doubt the warehouse fire reported by my brother's letter had affected my mind and subsequently the worth I placed on the revised proof-sheets. I buckled the satchel securely and finished dressing.

I wrote a brief note of instruction, including Mrs. Haeley's address (however not mentioning the authoress by name). With luck the move would be quickly forgettable to the movers and no tongue-wagging would alert the gossips of a potentially scandalous story— scandalous, I supposed, on several fronts. When I descended to the hotel lobby, I gave the note to the manager, who received it without a word. Then I had the doorman hail me a cab. The lobby area, furnished chiefly in green and gold silks, was busy with midmorning comings and goings—I knew that The Saint Georges would miss my business not at all. No doubt the hotel boys would no longer have to draw lots to determine the honor of lugging the tub of hot water upstairs to my room.

I stepped almost directly from the hotel doors and into a waiting cab. My satchel was heavy on my shoulder but I would not leave it behind in the hands of strangers. My other things I cared little for (though I suppose I should have, as they could not have been cheaply replaced). As I stepped into the cab, I called out the destination's address—"Two sixty one and a half Wicker's Lane!"—and it did not sound like a real place to my ears, as if I had called out Shangdu or Valhalla or the banks of the River Styx . . . or the periphery of my own conscious mind, the shadowland between waking and dreaming.

The horse and cabby had difficulty navigating the congested street, coming to full stop more than once. But I was patient; in fact I felt no rush at all: I needed time to concoct a story that would facilitate my becoming a houseguest of Margaret Haeley. The cab's well-worn leather upholstery was pungent, like perspiration and wilted ambition. Street noises came into the cab dissociated from their sources, and may have been emitting from the unconscious: voices and horse hooves and rattles and bangs spilled forth from the shadowland like dice from a gambler's box. For a moment I closed my eyes and the sounds transported me to the crowded streets of Old New York—I may have been there or any bustling street in the wide world. Perhaps I lapsed into dream for a moment because I had the odd thought that I might open my eyes and see my Kathy walking along the street, jostled by the other frenetic pedestrians. And she was no longer wearing the pioneer-style gingham dress of my imagination but rather a smart city-suit—skirt and jacket of fine summer-weight wool, a fancy brimless hat pinned to her lustrous hair, the length of which bounced between her shoulder blades like a schoolgirl's as Kathy hurried along.

I turned my face toward the city walk and opened my eyes half believing I would see her there—half believing I would call out her name and she would hear me in spite of the clamorous street and she would catch my eye . . . smile and wave. . . .

I opened my eyes:

For a moment she was there as I envisioned her, then she dissolved from the world like a Bedouin's mirage of life-giving water. I blinked hard, as if the act might blink the sudden sense of loss from my heart.

As my vision cleared, I did see a familiar form among the throng of Londoners. It took a moment to place her, but it was the puppet-show waif—Miss Organdy—yes, surely it was, but no longer in her theatrical get-up—instead a simple jacket and skirt which hung loosely on her avian frame. I was of a mind to call out to her, though I knew not what, when the cabby turned a corner and the waif was gone . . . more efficiently than a dreamt girl from a vaporous dream.

Before I had time to take it all in the cab was stopping before Mrs. Haeley's house. I stepped to the curb and paid the fellow, still feeling half in a fog. The weight of the satchel on my shoulder seemed the only thing keeping me at anchor in the physical world. Mrs. Haeley's street was not a main thoroughfare but was busy enough nevertheless. I felt some trepidation as I knew not how I was to install myself in the eccentric Haeley household but I was already waist deep in the Rubicon, having instructed the hotel to transport my things here. It would no doubt take some time but I had no wish for their beginning to arrive before I made way for them. Logically, it was Mrs. Haeley who should approve my installation, yet I felt it was Thursday's approval that was requisite.

I thought of the first time I approached this house—then with similar trepidation—and it seemed much longer ago. I adjusted the strap of my satchel so that it was more secure on my shoulder, and advanced toward the door. I was about to turn the bell-key when I heard something mournful coming from inside the authoress's house; then I realized the weeping sort of sound came from the pianoforte in the music-room. I listened for a moment, holding my breath so that my lungs would not interfere with my hearing . . . yes, I suspected so: it was "Junges Deutschland," the song of my bizarre recital. The composition was naturally lugubrious—laden with bittersweet nostalgia—but with Margaret Haeley's touch (I assumed it was she who played) the notes absorbed a more melancholy tone, a kind of widow's lament. The sad melody affected the actual air, making it difficult to breathe. This must be what miners experience when trapped by a cave-in and their precious good air is running low. I turned the bell-key, perhaps a bit frantically, to regain my breath, to save my life. The moment the chiming bell began echoing in the foyer, adding its tinny dissonance to Mrs. Haeley's somber tune, the pianoforte went silent, and in a moment I heard hard heels on the wood floor. The bolts were released and the door swung open.

I was quite certain it would be Mrs. Haeley who greeted me but whom precisely she would greet—me or my doppelganger, Mundie—was anyone's guess. Mrs. Haeley, dressed as before save for the addition of a plaid shawl around her shoulders, stood studying my face for a moment. Perhaps I was somewhat silhouetted by the bright street scene. At last her eyes glanced at my hat, and she said, "Mr. Wheelwright—please come inside."

I followed Mrs. Haeley into the house, shutting the door as I entered. "Eddie has told me of all that you've done for him, and I am grateful." She was standing in the foyer, facing me. Stacks of books surrounded her like primitively hewn pillars of stone in a pagan shrine, and it struck me that she was a sort of priestess—raising the dead in her famous book and worshipping a brazen idol in the memory of Haeley, gone these many years. What of Mundie then?—a kind of bishop of this strange religion, but dead now too. And Thursday?—an acolyte perhaps. And myself?

Hat in hand, I said, "It has been no trouble. I am honored to be of service to. . . ." I nearly finished *the manservant of Margaret Haeley* but his place in her house still confounded me, plus I did not care to sound the star-struck adolescent, agape at the famous authoress.

She smiled at my modest reply, and perhaps, too, at my awkwardness—again the gesture seemed unnatural on the face of someone who'd known so much loss and sadness. "Please, your bag must be heavy—place it in the parlor then join me in the music-room for tea. I was just making a pot. . . ." Then as if on cue the kettle began whistling shrilly in the kitchen.

Once in the parlor I set my satchel near the wall, where no one would stumble over it in the shuttered half-light. I hung my hat upon the tree and went to the music-room. I kept an eye out for

Thursday but he wasn't about. I had an odd reversal of perverse imagination and wondered if Mrs. Haeley took advantage of the fellow's vulnerable state by bludgeoning him with a spare table leg— recompense for an accidental insult long forgot by the perpetrator, or perhaps a case of mistaken identity, the authoress forgetting her man's familiarity and taking him for a common burglar.

It was pure fantasy . . . and profoundly unchristian of me. Since reworking the proof-sheets my imagination had been hyper- energized. Now that I thought of it, I'd felt like my creative mind was a run-away horse, a wild mustang, since first standing in front of Mrs. Haeley's house. It was as if the authoress radiated waves of creativity and one merely had to soak them in.

I had taken my familiar chair in the music-room, and I looked at the pianoforte; I thought I could hear remnants of "Junges Deutschland" lingering along the room's high ceiling, perhaps caught in cobwebs and struggling to free themselves like wingéd creatures suddenly imperiled. The phantasmal melody was discordant and a touch unsettling. Around the room the dust covers still lay in heaps like ghosts in repose.

In a moment Mrs. Haeley was there with the tea, setting the tray on the small table between our chairs. There was no lemon or cream or sugar, so we took our tea with honey, which dissolved instantly in the steaming china cups. Both cups were chipped but Mrs. Haeley gave me the one that was less so. "Thank you," I said, one set of finger and thumb holding the light-as-air saucer, the other the miniature handle of the cup.

We sat there for a moment pretending to be engrossed in the steam from our drinks. Then Mrs. Haeley began, "Thursday tells me you're on a tour of the Continent—" she had the air of a theatergoer who's arrived after the first act— "What cities do you plan to visit, Mr. Wheelwright?"

"My itinerary is ill-defined I'm afraid . . . it has more the feeling of tramping than of touring." My tone must've communicated a hint of embarrassment, for she replied:

"There is much about tramping to recommend it as the superior approach, much indeed."

I recollected her and Haeley's tramping across Europe in their infamous youths. It had been an accidental allusion, and I quickly moved on: "The only destination I know for certain is Brussels as there are old friends who now live there." I sipped at my still-steaming tea.

"Ah Brussels, a beautiful city but I made little more than a stopover there. I recollect being overwhelmed by the Cathedral of Saint Michael and Saint Gadula—the breathtaking stained glass especially. I'd say the city is worthy of your interest, with or without the attraction of old friends."

There was something about the way she said "old friends" which made it sound like a foreign phrase, foreign to her at least. Perhaps for the authoress *old friend* had become synonymous with *dearly departed* or *achingly recollected*. No phrase seemed safe then as if my every iteration would be a pinprick to her heart.

She continued, "When might you be leaving England, Mr. Wheelwright, speaking in general terms?"

"At the risk of sounding mysterious, I truly cannot make such a prediction. It could be within a few days or I may be in merry old England for some time yet." The word "merry" fell flat in the music-room air as if the house were too accustomed to mourning to allow jocularity even if only by sterile denotation.

Mrs. Haeley sipped her tea then placed the cup and saucer on the side table as if suddenly resolved in some matter. "Mr. Wheelwright, I've had an odd thought—not just now but ever since I awoke (perhaps I dreamt it)—would you consider staying here, in my house, for a few days, well, for as long as you like? I know that I am not good company for Thursday much of the time—he's never made such a remark, but I know . . ."

I was slow to respond, a bit stunned by Mrs. Haeley's serendipitous offer, and she went on before I could speak.

". . . and I must say your arrival here, now, at this time I mean, strikes me as a good omen. Haeley always encouraged me to be receptive to omens but I'm afraid over the years I've become rather calloused against such beliefs—such receptivity does, after all, leave one vulnerable—"

Determined not to be too slow again, I cut Mrs. Haeley off just a hair: "Your suggestion is most gracious, and I humbly and gratefully accept."

She smiled—a smile of gratitude—and it seemed more natural.

"I suppose there is no moment like the present one—if you will excuse me, I'll send a note to the hotel regarding my things." My eagerness was graceless, to say the least, but the serendipity of her offer had momentarily set me off-balance. I went to the parlor and pretended to compose a note, then empty-handed I slipped out of the house to pretend to find an errand-boy to deliver the pretend note. I walked around the corner, out of view of the house's forward windows—in case Mrs. Haeley or Thursday were spying me, which seemed highly improbable but there was no purpose in risking it.

I waited a few minutes then re-entered the house and the music-room. Mrs. Haeley sat as before. "Done," I announced. "My things shall arrive later today . . . if my directions are followed accordingly." I took my chair.

Mrs. Haeley smiled at me benignly and I feared for a moment that she'd forgotten the invitation—that she'd forgotten *me* for that matter! But she said, "Do you not wish to oversee the packing, Mr. Wheelwright? You mustn't feel rushed on our behalf."

"The hotel men seem to do a careful job—they seem a first-rate lot." The lie implied that I'd perhaps spent a few evenings "pulling a pint with the lads," as it were.

"You are most trusting, sir."

I did not feel like lying further on the subject so I said nothing at all—which could have been read falsely as humility but so be it. The awkward silence was mercifully broken when Thursday hobbled into the room on his crutches. Mrs. Haeley sprang from her seat: "The most wonderful news, Thursday—Mr. Wheelwright has generously agreed to stay with us for a time. Until everything is set right again." She had put her hand on his shoulder and gently urged him toward a chair.

Perhaps Thursday were merely in pain but when he said, "That is most kind indeed," there was something forbidding in his voice, as if my installation were the last thing he would want. I recalled then my feeling that it was his approval that was necessary somehow. Perhaps I should have evaded answering Mrs. Haeley until consulting Thursday, but there was no helping it now.

I busied myself with reheating tea for the fellow. While I was in the kitchen, the pianoforte was struck up again, and this time it was a less leaden composition. Badly out of tune, however, the instrument was only capable of so much lightness. I returned shortly with the freshened tea to find that Mrs. Haeley had installed Thursday quite comfortably in his chair, his leg propped on an Ottoman stool. I prepared the cups and we three were settled into an easy posture. I wondered how we would occupy ourselves but only for a moment. Mrs. Haeley began interrogating me about my home and about America in general—an almost mythical land she had always intended to visit. She was quite passionate on this point: she had never entertained the notion of living in the States, but seeing their natural wonders appealed to her very much.

Once she got me talking about myself and my country the time passed quickly. Thursday would join in now and again with a question or comment, but for the most part it was the authoress who directed their inquiries. More tea was poured. Mrs. Haeley seemed insatiably curious. She wanted to know about my boyhood, about Albany, and of course about Old New York. Some of her inquiries, like about the Original Mayor and his shrewish wife, were clearly inspired by her reading of my *Sketches*, and I was quite flattered by the thought of the great authoress perusing my book—no doubt here in this house, perhaps in her beloved yard even. Had Thursday attended her then, or was he a newer arrival?

I excused myself to use the privé and when I returned I noticed how tired-looking Mrs. Haeley was, as if the conversation had quite worn her down. Thursday too had dark patches about his eyes, so that he appeared a watcher after several days' vigil. I should not have gone on so. I was about to apologize for my inconsiderate ramblings when the bell-key chimed. I offered to answer the door and there were no objections. As I surmised, the hotel men had arrived with my things. One attended them at a cart on the street, and the other stood on Mrs. Haeley's top step. I doubted that either would recognize Mrs. Haeley by sight, in spite of her persistent infamy, but there was no reason to call her to ask about where to put my belongings. I directed the fellow to place my things in the parlor, as I knew not where else. In short order my trunks and bags were deposited there.

I tipped the fellows a halfcrown each from my vest pocket, and they returned to their cart and the gray mare who stood stock still except for swishing her ratty tail at flies.

I returned to the music-room and said that my things had arrived. I anticipated Mrs. Haeley's commenting on the efficiency of the hotel men but she made no mention of it. Instead she said, "I'm sorry, gentlemen, but I am still not quite myself. Mr. Wheelwright, allow me to show you the spare room at the top of the stairs. You are quite welcome to call it your own for as long as you like." She rose slowly from the chair, as if a much older woman than she was, and I followed her through the hall and up the stairway. At the room she had in mind, she turned the knob and pushed the door so that it swung open. The hinges were badly in need of an oiling. The effort seemed to be almost too much for her, and without a word she went to her bedroom, two doors down, and disappeared inside.

I stepped into my new room and looked about; it was sparely furnished with its main features being a singleton bed, secretary desk, bureau, and small wardrobe. I recalled then that Mrs. Haeley's half-sister, Fanny I believe she was called, was a companion to the literary couple during the heady days of *Dunkelraum*'s meteoric rise. I also recalled that Fanny died in childbirth, along with the child, only a few months before Haeley's yachting accident. There was a smell of dust in the stale air, and the wood floor could stand a vigorous scrubbing and waxing—but all in all it would serve quite nicely . . . and Chester Peacock & Family could not object to the price.

I returned to the music-room but Thursday must have gone to his room. I took the tray with pot, cups, &c., to the kitchen, straightened things up a bit, then I set about the business of settling in. I took my bags to the spare room, trying to be as quiet as possible. When partially emptied, I was able to move one of my smaller trunks to the room—however the remainder of the trunks would require more than one man (well, one man of letters) to haul up the stairs. So I arranged the trunks along a wall in the parlor, out of the way. Then I went to my room and unpacked. Every now and then I would stop and listen for a sound from Mrs. Haeley or Thursday, but the old house was as quiet as a crypt. The bedroom window looked out over the small enclosed yard, so not even any street noises disturbed the solemn quiet.

My homes had always been abustle with family and servants; thus the quiet struck me as singularly odd. It may have been the ideal environment for finishing my reworking of *Andersen's*, however. I looked to the small secretary desk in the corner of the room, and it seemed to be begging for the composition of something great. Perhaps I could oblige it.

Not at the moment though: the exertions had taken their toll, and I was suddenly utterly exhausted. I removed my shoes and lay upon the singleton bed, which seemed especially diminutive after the giant bed of The Saint Georges. The horsehair mattress was stiff from want of use but otherwise tolerably comfortable. Of course a bed of nails would've seemed a Turk's silken luxuriance at the moment. I thought I would only nap for a few minutes. . . . .

Eleven

~

. DARK SHAPE UPON DARK SHAPE MOVE FROM SILHOUETTED
treetrunk to silhouetted treetrunk . blackness absorbed into
blackness . then released again to grayinbetween . like hate into
the world . lupine shapes . lupine shapes moving with stealth
and darkpurpose . three darkworldwalkers in the gathering
gloom . aching for the metallic taste of blood on their teeth . for
the bellygnawing to cease for a blessed moment . darkshape
upon darkshape upon darkshape . darkworldwalkers . like
hate into the world . the grayinbetween . scent of fear .
oldbeckoningfriend . reckless to wander into wolfpaths in the
gathering gloom . darkworldwalkers . oldbeckoningfriend .
bellygnawing . scent of fear . darkshapes drawing closed the
snare . aching for the metallic taste of blood on their teeth .
scent of fear . lup

I was awakened by the sound of footsteps. The room was perfectly
dark and it took me a moment to find my bearings. I recalled that
I was in Mrs. Haeley's house, though my being there did not seem
quite real. The foreboding feeling of my dream lay heavily upon me.
I realized I was cold and had been for some time. I had pulled a
corner of quilt on top of myself as I slept but it was insufficient. I had
no idea of the hour other than it was nighttime.

There was the stub of a candle on a small table next to the bed but
no matches at hand. I had a half-empty box in my coat pocket—the
coat I had hung on the back of the desk chair in the corner. The bed
and floorboards creaked as I rose and stepped carefully in the dark,

unfamiliar place. I located the matches and soon lighted the candle, which sat in a badly chipped saucer, a saucer of the set from which I had drunk earlier. The tallow was old and dry, and it released a sour smell into the air. I checked my pocketwatch only to find that it had stopped before ten o'clock. I slipped on my shoes and carefully opened the bedroom door.

The hall was dark. I moved as quietly as I was able toward Mrs. Haeley's room and discovered that the door was slightly ajar. I wanted to enter and satisfy my curiosity as to whether the authoress was abed or not—but I did not want to be caught as some sort of midnight creeper, sneaking uninvited into ladies' bedchambers. I stood there for some time, with sallow candlelight falling upon the authoress's partly open door, just listening. My sense was that Mrs. Haeley was not inside, that the footfalls I'd heard were indeed hers, leaving her room.

Downstairs I could not find her. An upright pendulum clock in the parlor indicated it was ten minutes after midnight. I reset my pocketwatch and wound the stem. The noise of the tightening spring was remarkably pronounced in the quiet house. I went to the kitchen and peered through the window into the yard. It was too dark to say for certain but Mrs. Haeley didn't seem to be on her accustomed bench. I walked through the house, pausing for an instant at Thursday's door—could Mrs. Haeley be . . . surely not— and came to the frontdoor. It was quadruply secure, which suggested that Mrs. Haeley had not exited by that means, unless she carried the keyring of a gaoler. Still, my curiosity was piqued. I placed the saucer and candle on a small table near the door, unlatched it, and stepped outside, careful not to let the door shut behind me. I descended the stairs to Wicker's Lane. The street was dark and still, though an avenue or two distant I heard the rattle of a cart; the sound faded as it rattled farther away, then the sound was absent altogether. The street was perfectly quiet then, and it was difficult to accept that I was truly in Old London, teeming heart of empire. At that moment I may have been standing on the quiet green of any quiet town in New England . . . or on a lonely mountain trail while black lupine shapes moved through the forest like ravenous lunarshadows. There was a slight breeze and I realized how long it'd been since I'd felt the wind on my face. I longed then for a bracing sort of wind; this breeze was warm and damp.

I went back inside and shut the door.

In the foyer I faced the stacks of books. The candlelight was absorbed so thoroughly by the dark that I could barely see them, each of which stood taller than me, their acmes disappearing in the gloom. Only the books' dun-colored edges stood out to view. Selecting at random, I carefully slid one volume from its place, careful not to upset the stack. I located a lamp in the parlor and used my candle, which was nearly spent, to light its wick. With the improved illumination, I returned to my room to read and hopefully fall back asleep. I had a taste for some port but knew of no more in the house. I would have to stock the larder to a degree, presumably from my own funds, diminished though they be, on the morrow.

Back in my room, I placed the lamp on the side table, settled myself into bed, and looked at the book. The lamp oil was cheap and smoked with impurities. *Fantasmagorie* . . . the title rang a bell . . . I looked further: it was a collection of German ghost stories translated into French. *Fantasmagorie*: *Phantasmagoria* in English. Yes, it must be! The book of legend, the one that inspired Mrs. Haeley to write *Dunkelraum*. Everyone—well, every bibliophile—knew the story: how Haeley and she were staying with poet friends in Geneva, passing back and forth *Fantasmagorie*, and discussing it each stormy evening, then finally challenging each other to write a supernatural tale of his (or her) own. One fitful night—one fateful night—the character of Dunkelraum came to Mrs. Haeley (eighteen-year-old Margaret Townsend then) in a disquieting dream. The rest, as we say, is history.

My French was a bit out of practice but I was able to read with relative ease. The opening story, "La hache du bûcheron"—"The Woodsman's or Woodcutter's Ax"—was about a lonely mountain cabin that is haunted by the spirit of a woodsman who'd died a violent death. The woodsman's ax was left in the cabin, and it was unused by the new woodsman, Götz, who had moved to the cabin with his young wife, Addelaide. One day, however, the helve (?) of Götz's ax cracked—perhaps due to the extreme cold, as it was the proverbial dead of winter (mort de l'hiver)—and Götz took up the

previous woodsman's ax out of necessity. But it seemed the ax was
the keeper (?) of the dead woodsman's soul, and almost at once the
dead woodsman began taking possession of Götz. As long as Götz
was outside felling trees and chopping wood for the cabin stove, all
was well. In fact, Götz felt a vitality he'd not known before, as if he
had the strength of a dozen lumbermen (apparently, I mused, death
had done the previous woodsman's soul good and it was well rested).
When Götz returned to the cabin, he began acting strangely toward
Addelaide, treating her coldly instead of tenderly as he always had.
Götz insisted that the stove was not hot enough and forced Addelaide
to put in more wood. She tried to protest but was shocked when
her beloved raised his hand as if to strike her. Though she tried to
compensate (?) for the over-hot stove, she burned Götz's breakfast of
flat biscuits and pork gravy. Götz, who'd been watching her with the
intensity of a crocodile, became livid and tossed the smoking pan
of biscuits across the cabin, striking the opposite wall, where Götz
had placed the previous woodsman's ax. Then Götz picked up the
pot of boiling . . . no, nearly boiling gravy threatening to pour it on
Addelaide's beautiful young face. He began *ladling* (oh dear) insults
and accusations upon her. Poor Addelaide was totally confused
and, panic-stricken, tried to defend herself against the ludicrous
falsehoods. It seemed that Addelaide reminded the spirit of the
woodsman of his lover, who had not only betrayed him but who also
directed her new lover to murder the woodsman so that they could
steal his life savings and run off to München together. Götz began
demanding the return of his money, the hot gravy rolling violently in
the pot, and Addelaide knew not what to do but play along with her
suddenly insane husband. She assured him the money was there in
the cabin—not stolen, merely hidden! But Addelaide knew that they,
newlyweds, had no money tucked away. Götz, wild-eyed, demanded
that the "whore" take it from her "whorish hiding place" (her "cachette
pute," double entendre for her sex, even more obviously so in French,
the serendipity of translation). Addelaide began rifling through the
cabin's few furnishings, frantic—Götz meanwhile growing more
impatient by the moment, seeming to want any excuse to douse her
with the hot gravy. Addelaide looked under their bed; then she lifted
its heavy mattress—her fear giving her the strength of a man. She

cried that there was no money, that there never had been, and tried once more to reason with her husband. But Götz would not stand for her lies any longer and he hurled the contents of the pot at her. She jerked away at the final second and the hot gravy missed her face, but scalded her shoulder and breast through the simple dress that she wore. Götz, infuriated, came at her with the pot itself. Addelaide rushed for the cabin door but knew she would not reach it in time. Out of the corner of her eye she spied the previous woodsman's old ax, leaning near the door where Götz had left it—

There were footsteps in the hall, quick and light; then I heard Mrs. Haeley's bedroom door open . . . close . . . and latch. The authoress had returned, but where had she been?

—Addelaide grabbed the ax and hefted it over her head. It all happened in a single moment. Götz swung the heavy pot at her— laughing, he was *laughing*—and she brought the ax-blade down on his head, splitting his skull in two, killing him instantly. In shock, it took Addelaide a moment to realize that the handle had broken and that the ax-head remained in Götz's skull. Le manche brisé n'avait aucun poids dans les mains toujours tremblantes d'Addelaide: The broken handle had no weight in Addelaide's still trembling hands.

Reading had cast its spell, and I was feeling quite ready to sleep. I raised myself up enough to blow out the lamp, and I lay back in a comfortable position to nod off. Somewhat on my side, I watched the orange-glowing wick as it gradually faded to black. My consciousness seemed to fade at the same pace. I supposed I would think of the story of the possessed woodsman and poor Addelaide, but instead I found myself virtually obsessed with Mrs. Haeley's whereabouts in the dead of the night. The mystery became bothersome to the point of irritation, and I felt myself re-igniting toward full wakefulness.

Then it struck me, like the proverbial lightning bolt from the blue sky: Mrs. Haeley must've exited and returned via the cellar, or had simply been there all along. I recalled my first seeing Thursday, coming toward Mrs. Haeley's house with an armload of furniture pieces, and how he disappeared to the side of the house, presumably gaining entry through a cellar door. That must have explained the authoress's middle-of-the-night vanishing.

I felt confident my theory was correct; however, instead of being returned to a sleepy state of calm, I was fully inflamed by the notion of knowing for dead certain. I relit the lamp, whose wick had become barely discernible, and exited my room. The house was deathly quiet of course but as I passed through the foyer I thought I heard sounds coming from Wicker's Lane—perhaps it was near enough to sunrise that workmen were beginning to stir. There was light coming from beneath Thursday's door, yet I heard no noise from the fellow, whose room was off the main hall. I hurried past, my own lamp seeming to cast as much gloom as light. I suspected the cellar would be locked for some unearthly reason but my suspicions were unfounded and the door glided open easily. In fact, its hinges may have been the only set in the house that did not cry out for a thorough oiling.

I had the bizarre notion that I would find a sort of pagan shrine in the cellar—which was ludicrous, if only for the mere reason I had already been in the cellar on two occasions and saw no such thing. I was careful on the narrow stairsteps, not wishing to take a tumble as poor Thursday had. My lamplight was swallowed up by the webby dark. The scent of unsettled dust was thicker than I remembered.

At the bottom of the stairs I looked about the cellar gloom. I recalled then my childhood fears of Mrs. Haeley's monster—of his lurking in the dark corners of my bedroom—and some of that irrational terror came back to me now, and I had to force myself to remain calm. Still, my heart and my breathing quickened. I willed myself to take a step farther into the cellar, which was as I recollected: crowded and musty, but also benign.

My eyes were adjusting slowly and shapes began to materialize in the shadows. They tended to be illdefined shapes, however, which invited my overcharged imagination to interpret them as sinister, as Mrs. Haeley's giant monster even, in a crouch ready to spring forth and murder me with unnatural cruelty and malice. No, I scolded myself, the "monster" was merely a stack of old chairs. Then the familiar objects took on the form of wolves in the dark; I could almost see their glittering orbs and smell their bloody breath.

I was about to declare my reconnaissance complete—though I had learned nothing—and retreat up the stairs when I realized that the gloom to my right was unbroken. That is to say, elsewhere in the cellar, thanks to my adjusted vision, there were odd shadow shapes here and there—not to be confidently identified, mind, but discernible enough to suggest a sort of crazyquilt patchwork of dark on dark. On my righthand, however, there was a solid wall of darkness—blackness, to speak truly—and yet too close to be a cellar wall, not to mention too consistently ebon.

Cautiously, I approached the black, my freehand outstretched and my lamphand held high. The dark, dank air of the cellar seemed palpable. Then at last my fingers contacted the black . . . cloth . . . heavy black cloth. Groping along, I searched for the end of it. The lamplight was drawn into the cloth just as a sponge draws in water. By the time I came to the end, I realized it was a theatrical blackout curtain—designed to keep the goings-on behind it completely out of the audience's view, even if bright light was required to set the scene.

I pulled back the curtain, almost expecting to reveal a show of some sort. Instead there was only a large table, here and there covered with stacks of papers, books, journals, and manuscript boxes. There were also pens, quills, bottles of ink, and a white handkerchief neatly folded but bearing the dark marks of finger- and thumbprints. Before the table sat an upholstered chair, richly embroidered and ornately carved, resembling somewhat a queen's throne. An unlit lamp was there too; I touched its font and it was still warm.

It seemed then Mrs. Haeley was at work on something, and this was her writeress's lair. Why she chose to work in such a cheerless place, when she had an entire house at her disposal, was beyond me. I thought of the contrast between us—of my lounging in the giant featherbed at The Saint Georges, sipping Italian coffee, and of her catching a chill in this damp tomb. Perhaps it in some way accounted for our different tones: mine irreverent and a shade farcical, hers morose and brooding. But no—I was placing the cart before the mare. The authoress's work was morose and brooding because her life had been a series of shattering tragedies, starting with the death of her authoress mother when Margaret was but eleven days old. She must've believed for a time that she and Haeley could evade the darkness that had followed her since infancy. Perhaps their tramping across Europe wasn't tramping at all; perhaps it was escaping. To no avail, however—the baby in her womb miscarried, then the other deaths, including her half-sister's in childbirth and

Haeley's drowning.

No, she did not *choose* to write in the cold cellar: its darkness
and isolation beckoned her like old and dear friends.

I wanted to look through the papers, to see precisely what was
there—but it seemed a violation . . . and more than a violation of trust.
Here, I believed, was Margaret Haeley's soul laid bare. The literary
world had not heard from her pen in years. Perhaps in that time she
had constructed a colossal work of self-reflection, or a treatise on
the human condition, or quite possibly something colossal enough
in scope to be both. The authoress, in my eyes, was quite capable of
such a work.

I would not allow myself to read uninvited but I could not resist
a tactile experience, if only to assure myself it was all quite real: the
authoress had been writing and here it lay in all its tangible glory.
Timidly, I reached down and touched the topmost manuscript pages.
For some reason I anticipated their being warm, like the font of the
lamp, but of course they felt as chill as the cellar itself. It was with
great restraint that I prevented my eyes from focusing, even for a
brief instant, on the words on the pages, which I could tell marched
across the paper in a spidery feminine script.

I believed I heard movement in the kitchen, directly overhead,
so I retreated from Mrs. Haeley's lair and returned to the main floor,
which seemed as still as before. I suddenly felt quite exhausted—so
much so that I merely went to the parlor, blew out the lamp, and all
but collapsed on a sofa: dead, as we say, to the world. . . .

ine shapes . darkworldwalkers . drawing closed the snare .
reckless to wander into wolfpaths in the gathering gloom .
aching for the metallic taste of blood on their teeth . sent
of fear . oldbeckoningfriend . one before one behind .
darkworldwalkers . one to scent of fear oldbeckoningfriend
. bellygnawing aching to cease for one blessed moment .
darkshape upon darkshape . like hate into the world . one
before one behind one to scent of fear oldbeckoningfriend .
reckless to wander into wolfpaths . darkworldwalkers . in the
gathering gloom

Twelve

~

THE SHRILL WHISTLE OF THE KETTLE WOKE ME. THE HEAVY curtains on the parlor windows were separated a crack and a beam of sunlight cut through the moted room like a butcher's bone-blade. I lay there a moment, my back feeling as stiff as a landscape painter's palette. It seemed that resourceful Thursday had gotten himself around and was making our breakfast tea. I truly had a taste for good, black coffee—café noir, as the French say—but I had used the last of the beans . . . something else to add to the grocer's list. I listened carefully to the quiet house. There was the pendulum swing of the upright clock, and, when I pulled it from my vest pocket, my own watch's ticking. Then I thought of time itself as a physical thing moving through the halls and rooms. Not alive per se but real nonetheless. If I sensed it as a real thing, could it be turned back someway? Could I return Mrs. Haeley to a period before her great chain of losses? I realized that that would be almost to her birth, as her mother died only eleven days thereafter. What of me? Could I turn back time to before Kathy's going west? And if so, what then? Could circumstances be changed, or would we merely move through the tragic events again? Which would be no less painful for all our foreknowledge, for all our wisdom of experience. Images had merged in my mind and I was seeing time as vaguely lupine, as a sort of loping bringer of death, as bitter destiny's disinterested messenger.

Such useless musings. I realized that someone was singing—not operatically but, rather, low . . . singing to oneself. A pleasant feminine voice. So it was not Thursday who prepared our tea. Mrs. Haeley? No, I could not imagine Margaret Haeley singing anything, except perhaps a funerary dirge.

I had only begun to sort out who the morning singer may be when a striking Negress stepped into the parlor and said, "Good morning, Mr. Wheelwright, breakfast is nearly ready—a lean repast I'm afraid—but do you prefer a tray, or would you care to join Eddie and me in the kitchen?"

I was struck quite dumb, which apparently struck my interlocutor as amusing. She smiled, revealing teeth as white as polished ivory: "I'm Edith—I'm sorry, I thought you knew of my coming."

"Edith," I managed to repeat, pulling myself to a setting position on the sofa. "Of course, of course . . . Thurs—"

She smiled again. She wore a long apron but beneath it was a dress of pearl-gray lace. "It's all right—I may start calling him 'Thursday' too. I believe he is quite taken with the nickname."

I heard Thursday's crutches in the hall, moving toward the kitchen. "I will join you—please give me a moment, my dear." I was not one to use familiar endearments with strangers but there was something about the manner of Thursday's sister that inspired easy affection.

Miss Edith turned on her heel and left me alone in the parlor. I joined them shortly. Mrs. Haeley was not present. Edith had been seated at the table with Thursday when I stepped into the kitchen, but she quickly got to her feet to serve my breakfast. I said good morning to Thursday and sat at the place that had been reserved for me. The meal was simple—a sort of oatmeal with raisins and dried apples, biscuits with butter and boysenberry jam . . . and coffee! I could not hide my delight as the aroma steamed from my cup. "Bless you," I said, which elicited a smile from both Edith and Thursday.

She said, "I'm afraid I'm a farthing unpatriotic when it comes to good ol' English tea. When I lived on the Continent I became quite the devotee of coffee—my day is never quite on course if I must do without."

I sipped the hot brew, which was strong and good. "What took you beyond England's shores, if I may ask?"

"Governess school—I am a governess, Mr. Wheelwright. My family has given me leave to lend you all a hand."

"That is most kind of you," I said.

"Not at all—my brother would do the same for me."

Thursday reached over and squeezed Edith's arm affectionately: "What are elder brothers for? That, and harassing you every moment of the day as we were growing up."

"Perpetual teasing perhaps, not harassment." She turned to me: "And what little girl wouldn't relish the attention she received from her big brother, regardless of its form . . . within bounds of course."

We ate in silence for a moment, except for the clicks of spoons in bowls, then Miss Edith asked, "Do you have siblings, Mr. Wheelwright?"

"I do, an older brother and sister. I am the proverbial baby of the family. My sister, though only two years my senior, has always treated me as her own child—so I must confess I had the double pleasure of being doted upon by two mothers while growing up."

Thursday spoke: "And double the maternal expectations?"

"I cannot claim that burden. My brother, who took charge of the family's businesses while still a teen, has had the singular pleasure of expectation heaped upon him, singularly."

"Have you no interest in the family businesses, Mr. Wheelwright? Please forgive my prying," said Edith as she refilled my cup.

"I'm afraid I have neither the interest in nor the head for business. The Wheelwrights would have been street paupers long ago if business decisions were left to me." The turn in conversation had left me suddenly uneasy, and perhaps my manner showed as much.

Edith said, "But it is the world's gain, as we have been blessed with another great writer." She reached across and touched her brother's hand. Were they both then admirers of belles lettres? I noted the similarities and differences between brother and sister. Edith was darker in complexion. While her brother's skin was the color of sand soaked by an incoming tide; hers was of a shadow cast upon that wet beach. Her hair was curly while Thursday's was wavy, but about their eyes, nose, and mouth they had a similar European cut to their features. Thursday's eyes were blue-gray; hers pure gray, but subtly penetrating like her brother's.

"The world has perhaps gained another great *scribbler*," I protested, though not too ardently. I took in my final spoonful of oatmeal.

"You are too modest," she said. "You will find you have many admirers in England . . . and on the Continent for that matter."

"Well . . ." I was somewhat at a loss for words, ironically. ". . . thank you for saying so—I'm certain my London publisher hopes you are correct."

Thursday asked, "Who is your publisher here, Mr. Wheelwright, may I inquire?" He too had finished his oatmeal, and was nibbling on a biscuit.

"Murry, A. B. C. Murry, of Claxton House—though I don't know for how long—he must be growing quite impatient with me."

"How so?" Thursday sipped his coffee.

"I have the proof-pages for my new work and their return is decidedly overdue. Also—never mind, I don't want to bore you."

"No, please," said Miss Edith. "We quite want to hear, especially about a new work forthcoming from Jefferson Wheelwright—it is exciting to think indeed."

I felt myself reddening—crimsoning in fact—but was elated at the admiration. "Murry is expecting me to make a few corrections, perhaps tinker with a sentence here and there—but I'm afraid I have been inspired to rework the whole book, from stem to stern as it were. I am not quite finished but it will have to be completely reset. I imagine Murry will be apoplectic when he discovers what I have in mind."

"How exciting indeed," said Edith, smiling broadly, and a bit mischievously. "I can hardly wait to read it. May I ask the title?"

"Yes, *Andersen's Romance*—Andersen with an e-n."

"I must be bold and insist on an autographed copy one day."

"I am honored to comply but that day may be long in coming at this rate."

Thursday spoke: "I trust you have the pages here—you must dedicate yourself to the task, Mr. Wheelwright, and not be nursemaiding me and Mrs. Haeley. My leg is much improved and I shall be up and around in no time at all."

"Neither of you need worry. I have taken a fortnight, and I'm certain I can take longer if needed—the Halfords have been quite understanding and generous," said Miss Edith.

"As well they should be. They know they have the finest governess in England in their employ."

I said, "I appreciate your sentiment, Thursday, and I do plan to work on the pages. However, I've never been able to devote more than two to three hours a day to my writing. I find anymore than that to be too taxing. And we can see why I am not fit for productive labor, if a few hours of pushing a nib across a sheet of paper is enough to waste me for the day."

"Not true at all, Mr. Wheelwright," said Edith, sounding genuinely vexed. "Good writing is a labor—granted, a labor of love for those who make their living by it, but difficult work all the same. And as far as productivity, a beautiful story or poem transports us to places, within ourselves, that can be reached through no other means. No, do not denigrate your gift by calling it unproductive, even if only indirectly."

I was surprised by her passion but also moved by it. "Here, here," I said, raising my chipped cup, "to the literary arts."

The three of us touched cups to mark the toast and drank down our coffee.

"That appeared downright conspiratorial."

We looked up in surprise at Mrs. Haeley in the kitchen doorway.

"Do the three musketeers have space for d'Artagnan in the conspiracy?"

No one spoke for a moment, then Thursday said, "You have not met my sister, she arrived first thing this morning—Mrs. Haeley, allow me to introduce Edith. . . ."

The authoress had come to the table, and she extended her hand, which was thin and pale at the end of her ebon sleeve. "How do you do, Miss Edith? Thank you so much for coming to take care of us for a time. Eddie's accident was quite unfortunate, but Providence has sent us Mr. Wheelwright and you in our most needful hour."

Edith took her hand, and—perhaps I only imagined it—a shock seemed to run through the governess, something subtle yet powerful. I was reminded of Mr. Franklin's journal and his description of the sensation he experienced when the lightning came down to his key then dissipated swiftly through the lines he held fast. I studied Miss Edith's face for the briefest moment and Thursday's sister did appear stunned, before she regained her composure, and her smile. She said:

"It is an honor, ma'am."

Mrs. Haeley said, "Coffee—in the morning, how decadent. May I have a cup?"

Edith got to her feet to retrieve another cup and saucer from the cabinet, which, like everything else, needed a good scrubbing. "We have eaten all the cereal but I am happy to make more—it would only be a few minutes. . . ."

"No thank you—the coffee and one of those glorious-looking biscuits will be quite enough." The authoress looked especially wan in the morninglight that made its way through the half-shuttered windows. "I believe I shall breakfast in the music-room—it has the best sun this time of day and I hope to do some reading. I'm afraid I'm quite behind." I recalled Mrs. Haeley's legendary reading, almost mythical for one so young. It was said she read fluently in five languages by the age of eighteen. It was perhaps her and Haeley's mutual love of reading—of languages—that brought them together in the first place.

"I'll bring your breakfast in a moment," I said, "just as soon as the coffee is reheated. Would you like butter and jam with your biscuit?"

"No, as is, if you please. Thank you."

She turned, and I heard her go to the hall and select a book or two from the prodigious stacks: I wondered that she had the strength to manage them, and I half expected to hear their crashing down upon her, crushing her like a sparrow beneath a pile of stones. I thought I should assist her but something prevented me—it must've been akin to the contradictory impulses of parents who want to protect their children but who also want to gift them a sense of independence. Before I could decide what to do, Mrs. Haeley's rummaging ceased and she must've gone to the music-room. Miss Edith had kept the stove hot in case more cooking was required so it took little time to reheat the coffee. Shortly then I went to the authoress, saucer and cup in one hand, plate and biscuit in the other.

Mrs. Haeley had moved a chair near a window and pulled back the heavy drape. Dust was still thick in the sunlit air. She had two books in her lap, neither open. She had to angle her head a bit but she sat staring blankly at the pianoforte. I wondered if she heard spectral music. As I crossed the room it occurred to me that it was my playing of "Young Germany"—awful though it was—that seemed to retrieve her mind from the past, where it had been locked for who knows how long. Thursday, after all, was not shocked by her disorientation—perhaps it was her regular state, and perhaps she had returned there now. Perhaps Margaret T. Haeley would never speak to me again. The thought saddened me as I set her coffee and biscuit on a side-table within her reach. I was anxious that she say something to let me know if she was communing with the living, or if she had, like Eurydice, returned to the realm of the dead.

I recognized the volumes in her lap and said, "Chapman's Homer," hoping to coax a response. Her vacant eyes were the gray-blue of the Alleghenies as they look in blue-gray winter. She said nothing.

I wondered if I should fumble my way through "Junges Deutschland" again, an antidote to her forgetting, but as I crossed the room to leave, Mrs. Haeley said:

"It seems to me, Mr. Wheelwright, I have not been outside this house for some time . . . for longer than I can recall—would you be kind enough to escort me later this fine morning?"

I faced her from almost the doorway. "I would be honored, Mrs. Haeley. Honored and delighted." I was of a sudden a schoolboy doted upon by his most beloved teacher.

She smiled. "I shall have my breakfast and read some Homer, then see about 'pulling myself together,' as they say."

"Very good—I shall be at your service, madam, whenever it is requested." I jocularly tried to sound like the French valet but affected more the image of enamored pupil.

As I stood a moment too long, she took up her saucer and coffee-cup. I exited the music-room. I could hear Thursday and Edith conversing in the kitchen as she tidied up; their words were indistinct. A tad giddy, I knew not what to do with myself. I performed my morning toilette and donned my best suit. It occurred to me that Chamberlain still had one of my hats—I would likely never see it again. No matter, London had hatters aplenty; then I recalled my financial state, and it came upon me like a cold creeping flood that I was no longer the sort of man who could stroll into a shop and order an expensive hat on a whim. I must be the sort of man who watches his pennies. More than watch them: I must pinch them—is that not the expression? A kind of miser-by-necessity, a miser-of-shrunken-means.

It was neither a role I relished nor one for which I was born to play. Indeed, it required a change of character. I thought of a New York green-snake and how effortlessly the reptile sloughed his skin to reveal a glossy new one, and I envied him that. I wore my black suit, which suggested a funerary tone, but I imagined Mrs. Haeley would be in her customary mourning-style dress, so she and I would be kindred dark-spirits. Perhaps her mood would rub off on me, like soot from the fireplace spade, lending my writing a sharper edge, something it had always lacked; and perhaps I in turn would lighten Mrs. Haeley's words in some way.

Now I had only to wait. I took the *Andersen's* proofs from my case and went downstairs to the parlor. I sat at the French-style desk in the corner and began reading through the pages. It was difficult to gain a true feel for the changes without their being set in type. Maybe I should send a chapter or two to Murry and let the proverbial cat from the bag: he must find out sometime.

I read through the changes I'd already made, and, fortunately, they still seemed right. I felt that I was moving in a productive direction. Yet when it came to making further revisions, I didn't feel in the proper frame of mind. I feared driving my book from the new and proper path if I wrote while in the wrong—for lack of a choicer word—*mood*. Perhaps my sudden removal from The Saint Georges to here had unsettled me, literarily and figuratively, and that is why I felt insecure in proceeding with the reworking. Then I recalled that it was reading Edmund Holland's writings that had begun me on this path at all.

I was in luck: the trunk which contained Mr. Holland's book was one that I had left there in the parlor. I went to where it sat along the wall and undid its latches. My newest books were near the top of the layers of the articles I had packed in some haste. They were folded in a heavy fisherman's sweater I had brought. I wore it onboard the ship a few times but otherwise it had gone untouched as the English weather had so far been quite mild—in fact, too warm at times. At any rate, I returned to the desk with *Verses & Vignettes* and began browsing through Edmund Holland, hoping to find my newfound voice.

> The wind howls, wicked only when it ceases for a moment and I am able to hear their arguing. They hurl bare-knuckle insults, hurting one another with a prize-fighter's precision. Their souls bleed in invisible crimson streams. My brother and I are waist-deep in the foul flood, and neither has learned to swim.

I read on and Holland's narrator seemed to be female, which made the violent imagery all the more jarring. Though here of all places— in the parlor of Margaret Haeley—I should not be surprised by the juxtapositioning of the violent and the feminine. Early readers of *Dunkelraum* were shocked at its macabre images and therefore convinced the anonymous author was male, perhaps a serious poet like Stephen Haeley who did not want to sully his reputation as an artist by being known as a writer of novels—and a sensational novel at that. Soon, however, London discovered the truth: that the lurid tale of Professor Dunkelraum and his monster was conceived by a young woman, one Margaret T. Haeley, the poet's teenage mistress then bride (after his original wife drowned herself, presumably in despair at her abandonment). Yes, Mrs. Haeley was notorious in her youth, both romantically and literarily.

I thought of my own heroine, Katherine Halford, and turned to the chapter in which her character is explored. I read it through ... and found Katherine . . . tame. Yes, she was flesh and blood and bone on the page—she "cast a shadow," as it was said. I had done my job as a storyteller in that regard but there was no edge to her, nothing to make her even a shade . . . dangerous. I thought hard about what I could introduce into her character. I stared at the edges of the pages before me. I saw how one sharp edge of the paper ran into a sharper corner, then ran ninety degrees into another sharp edge; my eyes followed the distinct path again and again. I noticed the pen poised in my hand: the slender grip of poplar wood, yellow poplar that showed the darkened pressures of thumb and forefinger; the pointed nib plump with black ink waiting to gush words on my page like a summer melon that is finally wedged. And the bottle of ink, unstoppered and as beautifully round as a sultan's chamber, the liquid tar-black but as glossy as spilled blood.

Still nothing came to me, no bright-ideaed inspiration. I felt as dull-witted as a drunken coolie.

My eyes went back to the paper edge, but this time the lines of script drew in my attention like a hooked fish and I read of the words there. Katherine was at her dressing-table; she'd gone there after a disagreement with her mother over Andersen—Katherine insisted that Andersen and she were merely friends, and that was all either of them wanted. After all, they'd been playmates since childhood, like sister and brother. Katherine studied her image in the mirror on the table and she brushed her chestnut curls.

(Nib touched page.)

Katherine placed the brush on the tabletop, then she slowly slid out the table's bottom drawer. She reached beneath silk hair scarves *for what was she reaching?* and her fingers found the bottle. She glanced in the mirror to be sure no one had entered her bedroom *what sort of bottle?* and she grasped the familiar neck and brought it forth. The bottle was dark-brown glass *I knew then what it contained.* She removed the cork and sniffed its sweet scent of Scotch liquor, then Katherine took a drink, and it both burned and cooled her throat. She took another before corking the bottle and returning it to its secret place.

So Katherine Halford has a weakness for alcohol? Who would've thought it? Like domino bones tipping one another in a row, I immediately saw how this fact would affect so many details of the story, and how those altered details would in turn alter so many others, and they. . . .

I began to think about the word *romance:* in olden days a romance was a very particular kind of story, with a hero and a quest and a villain who was determined to keep the hero and his quest forever parted. There was a lovely lady to inspire the hero, and often supernatural forces in support of the villain's villainous designs. But *romance* has come to be something different—the old formula still thrives but is no longer called a "romance" per se. It has more to do with the hero and lovely lady, perhaps with supernatural forces thrown into the mechanics, and perhaps a villain too. The quest though has changed the most since the darker ages: now it seems the lovely lady and her charms are the quest itself in a modern romance. Thinking of it in this way, one cannot help but feel that the *evolution* (there is a good word) of the romance has been toward simplicity; it has been about flattening the formula, and in so doing, squeezing out much of its most vital stuff.

I looked to Mr. Holland's book, still open on the desktop, motes floating above its pages like sparks of the author's vivid imagination. This was his genius perhaps: driving the romance back toward complexity, by adding layer upon layer of meaning—just as the Bard had done two centuries ago. I then began to think about forms of the word romance: romantic, Roman, romantically, romanticize, Romanesque. What if it is not Andersen's romance—that is, his romantic affections, his *love*, for Miss Halford—but rather his romanticized view of her that is the central conflict? Central but underlying. Yes, this turn in her character—her taste for liquor—could fit nicely with this new view of the book.

I scribbled some brief notes in the margin of the proof-page. I felt on the precipice of something important and didn't want to lose the perspective. This may change everything—again.

"There you are, Mr. Wheelwright." Startled, I turned to Mrs. Haeley, who had entered the parlor with great stealth; no doubt my being lost in the world of imagination aided her craftiness. "I don't mean to interrupt your work. Would you prefer to continue?" Mrs. Haeley had exchanged her simple mourning dress for one with a matching jacket. Her hat was benighted, however, and a demiveil obscured her eyes. Even though I sensed that the ensemble was no longer, as the French say, en vogue, she was smartly dressed for an excursion in the City. I noticed that the jacket, especially, hung loosely on her, implying she had lost a good deal of weight, or the suit was secondhand.

"No," I said, "I'm at an excellent place to quit for now—and am quite ready to see the City."

"Wonderful. I trust you have not visited the Museum of Natural Sciences."

"I have not indeed." I was putting away my pages, &c., as we spoke.

"The Museum's grounds are delightful—I used to enjoy walking there very much."

I stood and took my hat from the tree. "Then by all means, madam." I gestured for her to lead the way.

There was an umbrella stand in the foyer and I began to take one with a "crook'd handle," as the Brits say, but Mrs. Haeley stopped me:

"Let us not be pessimistic, not today, Mr. Wheelwright."

I left the umbrella where it was, and we exited through the front door.

Thirteen

~

O N WICKER'S LANE I TOOK UP THE STREETSIDE POSITION, OF
course, but Mrs. Haeley led our way in the direction of a more
populated street. I tried to see if any of our fellow pedestrians, who
began to cross our paths like drunken bees in search of a well-hid
hive, recognized the authoress, but none seemed to. Not surprising
really. She did wear the black-lace veil that came to her nose, which
was pointedly Anglo-Saxon; and the London throngs were well-
about their own business. Nevertheless, I wondered again if the
world at large had forgotten Margaret Haeley. I was quite certain it
had not forgotten Professor Dunkelraum and his monster. After all,
the phrase "Dunkelraum's monster" had been used in Parliament and
in Congress, and just a few days before my departure, an editorialist
for the *New York Evening Gazette* alluded to the professor's wretched
creation. It had come to mean in the popular vernacular a problem
of our own creation that will not let us out from under its pernicious,
even deadly, effects.

The thought reminded me that I had not seen a newspaper
come to Mrs. Haeley's home, and none were stacked in some corner
somewhere. It was as if the authoress had shut herself off from the
outside world, and had no interest in its whereabouts or its well-
being. Perhaps like her fictional monster at the end of *Dunkelraum*,
she had had her fill of the world. Given her great personal losses,
who could blame her?

I tried to discern Mrs. Haeley's mood as we strolled, quite
like a courting couple, down the street. Her lips were curled in a
Mona Lisa-esque smile, recalling to my mind the Flemish School's

depictions of saints just prior to reaching blessed Martyrdom. Her eyes were obscured by the demiveil, but it occurred to me that their gray was reflected in the sky, which I could see in the narrow space between the rooftops of the city. They were eyes that seemed never quite safe from a sudden storm.

"Is it a far walk to the Museum, madam—shall we hire a cab?"

"In my youth it would have not been far at all, but perhaps we should take a cab." Her words fluttered the delicate edging of the veil ever so slightly.

I raised my hand and called out to a passing cabman, but he already had a fare and passed us by with an apologetic touch of his brim. The next one halted though and we climbed in, stepping over manure collected in the gutter.

"This idea is on the mark," said Mrs. Haeley, turning up her veil to reveal her face fully. "One does not want to be too fagged to enjoy the grounds." She looked pale, but most Londoners appeared to have just emerged from their sickrooms after a tedious confinement.

We amused ourselves for a time observing the busy streets— so much humanity, of every stripe, rushing about like members of Parliament late for a rollcall, or like cardinals tardy to a conclave. Then she said,

"The cab ride is wise but I must say it makes me feel like an old woman. I was a great walker in my youth. I daresay Haeley and I saw half of Europe on foot—the better half."

"I was a great walker in my youth as well—there was a time when I felt as if I knew every tree and stone in the forests and fields around Albany."

"Pish, Mr. Wheelwright, you are still a youth—you will be a great walker again."

"Perhaps you're right." I thought of mentioning my foot ailment but decided I rather liked Mrs. Haeley's opinion of me as youthful; then I realized that my ailment was much improved, the alternating numbness and soreness barely noticeable. Carter's treatments had been working their magic.

Just then the cab's wheel must've hit a dislodged brick in the street, for Mrs. Haeley and I were tossed together rather violently for a moment. She held onto my arm, I to her gloved hand ... perhaps for a bit longer than we might have. The cab settled and so did we, straightening our hats and ourselves. We were quiet again until the cabby stopped at the Museum, a three-storey stone edifice of impressive scale, with Greek columns and statues of gryphons on either side of the steps leading to its entrance. I overpaid the cabby with a shiny sovereign, deliberately, to impress Mrs. Haeley, who didn't take notice anyway, and I chastised myself for my pride and my stupidity.

I'd lost my bearings and had only the vaguest sense of our location in the City. The anachromic sky offered no help. A slight breeze hinted at the direction of the Thames, whose putrid smell was yet distinct in a metropolis of pungent odors. I determined then that we were somewhere east or southeast of the river. I looked again to the great building and the letters carved in stone above its frieze—M • V • S • E • V • M • O • F • H • I • S • T • O • R • Y • & • N • A • T • V • R • A • L • S •C • I • E • N• C • E • S—and wanted very much to venture inside and snoop among its unique holdings. Its Egyptian Room was legendary, as was its collection of medieval manuscripts.

"We'll be sure to visit some of the exhibits, Mr. Wheelwright," said Mrs. Haeley as if reading my thoughts, but no doubt merely interpreting my awestruck countenance.

I smiled at her intuition. "Let us see about the grounds." I offered my arm, and we strolled in the direction of a tall iron gate, the doors of which were open to their full width. The space marked the entrance to the grounds, and I thought of Vergil's Gates of Sleep, of iron and of ivory, that separated the upper and underworlds. The street and walk had been strangely quiet, by the standards of midmorning London, but once we passed through the iron gate I could see that the grounds had attracted many visitors. There were several pairs—couples, yes, but also men with men, and ladies with ladies, and one solitary woman in a raven-black dress pushing an infant carriage over the Museum's well-tended lawn. The wheels of the carriage ran as smoothly as if on polished marble. Most of the visitors, however, kept to the paths that had been lain in crushed white stone. These paths of white ran in curvaceous arcs, and I sensed that if one could view them as a bird does, perhaps from the gondola of a balloon of heated air, then they would form an artistic pattern of geometry, or even a picture of some sort.

I glanced at Mrs. Haeley, who was only half a head shorter than me, and saw that she'd lowered her veil. I noticed too, in the white daylight, that her jacket and dress were not black but very dark blue— not quite a color of mourning but the very first color of *morning*, when Night begins to loosen her grip. Though it be silly over such a triviality, I felt then that we were somewhat mismatched, not quite a pair of visitors of the dead out from a morbid place for some air, but rather . . . I know not what—occupants of separate spheres altogether who have come together, briefly, due to some cataclysmic event?

I listened to the sound of the crushed white stone beneath our heels, and I couldn't help imagining that they were not stones but fragments of bones, taken from the Museum's collections—extra artifacts of long-gone clans, and of forgotten animals that once roamed the English misty moors before they were English at all.

The woman in black had stopped pushing the carriage on the lawn, and she was nervously fussing about the carriage's occupant, who remained out of view due to the contraption's canopy. The woman was not so young, graying curls fell beneath her straw bonnet, and I wondered if she were the mother, or perhaps an experienced nanny out with her charge. No one seemed to take notice of the scene but I—certainly Mrs. Haeley was oblivious—and I thought I should go offer some aid (of a sort I could not imagine) when of a sudden the woman decided all was well (enough?) and returned to pushing the smooth-moving carriage. I was unaccountably relieved.

Mrs. Haeley said, "Please excuse my prying, Mr. Wheelwright, but you seem to be at work on something, in the final stages of writing even, do you mind my asking after it?"

"Not at all—I am honored by your interest. It is a novel, a romance—well, I intended it to be a romance but it is wanting to be something else entirely."

"How fascinating. Yes, we breathe life into our creations and then wonder at their wanting to live on their own."

"Quite."

"A *romance*." She said the word in that way that she had, as if it were from a foreign language. "As long as I'm prying and as long as you're obliging me . . . I notice, sir, that you travel alone. Have you left a wife at home in America, tending your brood?"

It was a natural question but I was startled by it nonetheless and perhaps took a moment too long to respond. "No—no lady has honored me with her hand. . . ." There was no need to go further but I heard myself doing so. "I asked for such an honor once but the young lady had other designs. One failed attempt strikes me as quite enough." I had never articulated my experience with Kathy in that way, not even to myself.

"Now there is a modern *romance*: Brokenhearted author quits America to tour Europe . . . to forget *her*."

"That would be quite a tale. How would it end?"

Mrs. Haeley thought for a moment; a breeze fluttered her half veil. "A true romantic would have him find love in a foreign land and live happily thereafter."

"And a realist, madam, would have him what, eventually return to America, older and, with any luck, wiser?"

"That is still too romantic. A true realist would set him on the road to meet his soul's one companion before having his normally trustworthy steed throw him from the saddle and knocking his head upon a rock."

"So a realist would murder the hapless fellow?"

"Still too romantic. He would lose all rational faculty, so he would be returned to America without even the ability any longer to author his own sad story."

I was left silent by the desolation she described—the delolation that was rooted so deeply in her imagination—but I noticed Mrs. Haeley wore that enigmatic smile again. Perhaps it was a sort of defense against the world, like an apiarist's netted mask shielding him from the worst stings.

We'd been strolling over the white path, taking turns that looped into a sort of figure-eight, and found ourselves near the entrance of a labyrinth made of yew hedges that were just taller than headhigh. A plaque announced it to be BLACKWOOD'S GARDEN. "Let us enter the labyrinth, Mr. Wheelwright," and so we did. The path was of the same white stone except over time bits of dead leaves had mixed among the stone, giving it a dunnish cast in the dove-gray daylight. It was a labyrinth of sharp and sudden turns. At first Mrs. Haeley guided us, though we remained side by side, as if she knew the way. Soon, however, we appeared well into the heart of the maze and had no sense of direction whatsoever. The sunless sky provided no assistance. Now and again we would hear another visitor on the other side of the hedge but saw no one. I must admit to having to keep down a small amount of claustrophobia that began to take shape in some obscure corner of my soul. There was nothing to fear of course—after all, we had not come upon the skeletal remnants of some previous visitor who'd perished in the labyrinth like a luckless prisoner locked in an abandoned garrison.

Nevertheless, I looked to my companion to see if she exhibited any baseless anxiety but her countenance remained as mysterious as ever: she may have been consumed with fear, or having the gayest time of her life. I simply couldn't say.

A moment later I began to hear childish whimpering and I thought for just an instant Mrs. Haeley was discomforted by the unending turns; but the authoress heard the sound too and we understood that the childish whimpering came in fact from a child. We followed the sound and, with only a pair of false turns, we came upon a girl of eight or nine. She was in the path, facing an intersection in the labyrinth. She wore an inexpensive blue frock; unruly chestnut curls fell upon her narrow shoulders. It was easy to suppose she'd become separated from a parent and had wandered in the maze until she came to this perpendicular set of paths. Perhaps the choice, right or left, was the proverbial final straw that crushed the camel's hump. So there she stopped, tears cascading down her ruddy cheeks, dampening the bib of her frock.

"What is the matter, little one, lost your way have you?" Mrs. Haeley knelt in front of the child and she lifted back her veil.

The girl's whimpering slowed but she did not speak. I thought it strange that we heard no father or mother (or elder sibling or nanny at least) calling for the lost child. For that matter, neither did the girl call out for help in finding her way. Perhaps there was a family of deaf-mutes visiting Blackwood's Garden. I produced a handkerchief from my pocket and Mrs. Haeley used it to dry the girl's cheeks and wipe her nose. I took back the hanky, now moist with grief, and folded it into my pocket.

"There now," said Mrs. Haeley, "you must come with Mr. Wheelwright and me until we can locate your mummy."

She acquiesced to the plan, silently. We continued on our way, three abreast with the girl between us. The path was barely wide enough and at times my shoulder brushed against the hedge. Mrs. Haeley held the girl's hand. The girl seemed much calmer now, trusting in us completely. She was right to do so of course, but anyone might've come upon her in the maze—someone whose designs were not so benevolent. One read in the papers of such sickening tragedies with increasing regularity it seemed. The girl was fortunate in that regard.

We walked for a minute or two, encountering no one, not even someone remotely, on the opposite side of the hedge. Perhaps the parent, desperate, had gone to fetch a constable for assistance. I was about to ask our charge her name—to make conversation, yes, but also to satisfy my curiosity as to whether she could speak—when we came upon another T-shaped interchange (or perhaps the same one!) and Mrs. Haeley said, "Let us try this way, Fanny," and we turned left, as unified as a military band.

Fanny? Had Mrs. Haeley and our sudden charge had a dialogue and I'd missed it? No . . . Fanny was the name of Mrs. Haeley's half-sister, the only companion of her otherwise lonely childhood. Was she using "Fanny" as a sort of pet-name? Did she name every nameless child Fanny? I didn't care to reflect on the other alternative: that Mrs. Haeley was receding into her past again, like a new-moon tide that'd been ashore too long.

Now I had something else to fret about (mildly, like a forgotten debt suddenly remembered) besides finding someone who was responsible for the girl. Is there no end to this labyrinth? Whose idea had it been to enter the Garden? Mrs. Haeley's . . . yes—no . . . mine. . . . I was even confused on this point. We were, I concluded, mutually to blame for this predicament, though I would have preferred to scoot the majority onto Mrs. Haeley's side of the scale. Fortunately I had no time to ponder my lack of magnaminity as we suddenly turned, with Mrs. Haeley's silent encouragement, and found ourselves outside the labyrinth, at a different side than the one on which we'd entered. I daresay we all felt a little relief, even the urchin who'd trusted herself to our care. Though the sky overhead was unchanged, it seemed less oppressive on this side of the yew maze.

We followed the outside of the labyrinth, the girl still betwixt us, to the main entrance. No one appeared to be waiting there, anxiously. I began to wonder what we would do if no one presented themselves on "Fanny's" behalf—it'd certainly cut short Mrs. Haeley's and my excursion. We stood at the entrance for a moment, as if we were a family awaiting a carriage to whisk us off to Sunday service, or some such family place where families go. I wondered if I should offer to find the nearest constabulary . . . or orphanage (I was becoming a mite irritable) when we heard someone calling out—"Mary! Mary! There you are, child!" It was a middle-aged man in a dark suit—good quality, I could see as he approached, but very well worn. Beneath his tall black hat sprouted blond hair graying yellow at the ends.

"Papa!" and the girl pulled herself easily from Mrs. Haeley's grip. In a moment he was picking up his child; both were visibly relieved. Mary clinging to him as an octopus must its prey, the father spoke to us: "Thank you for keeping her track . . . I was distracted for only a moment and I looked to her and she was vanished, quick as a sprite." He had a City dialect but one whose long vowels had been flattened by a solid education.

"It was no trouble," said Mrs. Haeley, who, I realized, had a similar dialect. "We were simply worried for her sake."

"We are quite glad," I added, "that you are reunited." I knew my gladness to be equal parts altruism and self-interest. We watched the father depart; he attempted to put little Mary down so that she could walk on her own, but she was resolute in clinging to her papa's neck and he did not object. "Well," I said, "a pinch of drama to spice our morning. Where to next, madam?"

Still watching the father and daughter, Mrs. Haeley took a moment to reply. I wondered still at her calling the child by her dead half-sister's name but could make nothing certain of it. Then Mrs. Haeley said, "There is a lovely fountain, just over there. . . ." She waved her hand in a nebulous direction, indicating someplace out of view.

We set off, staying to the white path. She did not take my arm and I did not make a display of offering it. It no longer seemed a necessary formality. The episode with the little girl had initiated a bond between us. I felt that a true friendship had begun to take root—something more than a shared literary connection. True, there is a special sort of intimacy between an author and an appreciative reader; and when they may meet in the real world sometimes that intimacy transcends the pages of the book and becomes almost palpable. With Mrs. Haeley and me, we had played both parts, one to the other, which could increase the effect in an exponential way.

At first glance the Museum grounds appeared perfectly flat—ideal in fact for a nine-pin tournament—but I discovered that there was considerable slope. The fountain of which Mrs. Haeley spoke materialized gradually, from the top downward, as we neared it. Its pinnacle was a bronze (weathered green) of Orpheus and Eurydice (I came to discover—though at first they were just two figures, one half turned to peer back at the other). Water sprang between them, like the separation of eternity made visible. Orpheus, lyre in hand, watches in horrified agony as Eurydice is drawn back to the underworld, her thin arms outstretched imploringly. Her face is nearly blank with resignation to her fate, perhaps a sad smile beginning to form on her lips. A gown is draped upon her like a disheveled burial shroud, one small young breast uncovered. Orpheus and she stand on separate pedestals, their feet just touching the water's surface, his sandaled, hers bare. The falling water dappled the surface so that it appeared more solid than not, especially with the white sky overhead which spread its muted light evenly. I noted that Mrs. Haeley and I cast no shadow upon the ground, as if shades ourselves, but when I peered directly into the fountain, a dark, irregular shape materialized on the water. Beneath, farthings and halfpennies could be seen, vaguely—perhaps the coins were as indistinct and half-realized as the wishes that were affixed to them when tossed into the fountain: THE ORPHIC FOUNTAIN, a plaque said, sculpted by Louis-François Roubiliac in 1752.

"Many wishes indeed," said Mrs. Haeley, as if reading my thoughts again, but I supposed it was just that we were like-minded fancifiers come upon the same image. I wondered at the wisdom—or cynicism—of the sculptor's figures for a wishing fountain (and what fountain was not?) as Orpheus was perhaps the most brutally disappointed wisher in the classical world.

We were joined then by a young couple who were in the grip of each other so completely they moved as if of one body. To say they joined us is misleading. We did occupy the same area, the four of us, around the Orphic Fountain, but in a more profound sense the young couple were the only occupants of a sphere of their own creation. They were as distant from Mrs. Haeley and me as if they were picnicking on the moon, as if observing the eruption of a lunar volcano. As such, I was able to observe them more directly than one is generally able to do in public. He was blond and smartly dressed in blue tails, an emerald-green waistcoat, crème cravat and tall silk hat. A perfect young English gentleman with an easy athletic build; his only fault: a bit short in the leg and therefore not much taller than his companion, who was dressed more simply but was also elegant in her way. Ebon hair and olive complexion, she wore a dark gray dress with a white ruffled bib, in the center of which was a red and white cameo pin. A long peacock feather was angled stylishly from the band of an otherwise simple black hat. The feather moved in the slight breeze perhaps much as it did when the bird sauntered about his yard.

Though we were only a few feet from them, they did not speak to us; in fact they appeared not to notice us at all—we may have been a pair of phantoms out on a daytime haunt. Then I had the thought, What if *they* were the ghosts, and that is why we seemed to be of different realms? It was ridiculous but I was tempted to accidentally bump into them, to assure myself of their corporeality. I turned to say something about them to Mrs. Haeley but she was in a reverie of her own—or maybe a member of theirs, and I was the only pariah. The authoress stared at the young lovers with a singular intensity. Had Mrs. Haeley been so reclusive that this display of ardent attachment—though common enough in the world among the young—held her gaze as if a novelty of the Far East? As if a rare relic escaped from the Museum's exhibition hall? Then it came to me that my hyperbole may have been closer to the truth than I'd imagined at first. Perhaps Haeley and she came here, to this very spot, when in the throes of their early passion. Even if not this precise place, the amorous couple could easily remind her of Haeley and herself nearly twenty years earlier. In fact, the young gentleman recalled Haeley somewhat, based on the notorious poet's portraiture and the descriptions I'd read. I realized that there were no pictures of Haeley in the authoress's home, the home she'd shared with him for a few years at least, before his drowning. I had the odd image come to me—but an image that struck me as profoundly true: Mrs. Haeley always seemed to be moving with a sort of . . . negative space next to her, as if there'd been a sketch of Haeley and her, and someone (a cruel-hearted child, for instance) had cut the poet from the picture, leaving only an empty outline, a crude void in the shape of a man, next to Margaret Haeley; so when you were with her, you could not help but notice there was emptiness always beside her. And all you could do was to try to occupy that vacant space, but it was an inexact fit and hence temporary, as short for this world as the malformed member of a litter.

Mrs. Haeley seemed quite content to stand by the fountain—perhaps the rhythmic bubbling of its waters entranced her mind. In any event, the expression on her finely boned face was pacific, and I was loath to disturb her in what seemed a rare state. I sensed a quietness about her life but a quiet more of mourning than of repose, a quiet after calamity not accomplishment.

The lovers, still oblivious to us and the world, walked away from the Orphic Fountain, and we could not help watching after them. At some distance they crossed the path of the mother (or mother-figure) in black with the baby carriage. Did they nod to her? Did the gentleman quickly touch the brim of his hat? It seemed so but they were all too far away to be certain.

"What do you say to visiting some of the exhibitions, Mr. Wheelwright?"

Her question startled me but I hoped not too visibly. "That sounds like a fine idea, Mrs. Haeley," and we began strolling toward the Museum itself. The large stone structure had been looming as a backdrop to our little drama the entire time. At a distance, with its dark-brown stone against the white sky, the building was suggestive of an Ancient Wonder. The effect was no doubt some of the architect's intent. We followed the path around a hedge, and the steps to the main entrance came into view; about a half dozen visitors were coming or going up or down them.

"Mr. Wheelwright," began Mrs. Haeley, "I have what may seem a strange request, perhaps even a bit forward—so feel free to decline if it makes you uncomfortable: it seems the whole world calls me 'Mrs. Haeley' and I do not mind at all—to this day I miss my Haeley terribly . . . but sometimes I also miss being called more familiarly, as a family member might or a dear friend."

It took a moment to realize what she was suggesting—I must admit I was a bit thrown off by her sudden intimacy. "You would like me to call you 'Margaret'—" there was nearly a question mark at the end.

"As long as I'm so bold: there was a name that only a few people in the world called me by, and those dear people are all long deceased. They called me 'Mae,' like the month but spelled m-a-e."

"Mae," I repeated, liking the sound—it was a name of bright colors on this colorless day. "All right, I am pleased to call you Mae, but on the condition you will reciprocate by calling me 'Jeff,' a name used only by my siblings and best school chums"—and Kathy but I omitted that detail. As Mrs. Haeley—Mae—suggested, it did feel a bit awkward, but how could I deny such a request? Reject such a gift?

We reached the steps of the Museum, which seemed now absent any visitors save for us, and entered through the massive oaken doors, though they moved with relative ease, having been hung it would seem by expert hands. I anticipated smelling something foul . . . the rot of leather, or the wrappings of ancient mummies, cast off and lying somewhere in a putrid heap . . . but instead I detected the tang of floor-wax and a scent almost like fresh-cut lemons. The authoress stopped and breathed in deeply: "Ah," she said, exhaling, "I'd almost forgot the smell—there's nothing else like it in all the world, or at least in all the world I've traveled to."

I removed my hat and we strolled through the wide, marble hall toward an exhibition room. Windows near the high ceiling brought in diffuse daylight, but the flames of sconces along the walls reflected vividly in the polished floor, like the eyes of cave-dwelling beasts. Our footfalls echoed profoundly. We entered a roughly square room that appeared to be devoted to the geography of the British Isles; or it may have been simply homage to mapmaking, as they were in glass cases and framed on the walls in copious numbers. Here and there were also tools of surveying, charting, and cartographing: chains, levels, transits, compasses, and so on. Hand-printed cards with each map gave a date and cartographer, if known. One map, in a long, glass case, dated to before the Conquest—the coastlines, rendered in a sort of umber "ink" (the color of dried blood), were dangerously jagged, like the jaws of a predatory ocean-creature, and the islands were grossly out of proportion. The map, though under glass and held in a frame, was clearly deteriorating at its edges, and it looked as if a strong breeze would simply blow the coastlines into particles of brown dust. At home, in the maritime museum, there were charts used by Colonial settlers, but even they were centuries younger than this and other wonders in the room.

"I sometimes lose sight," I said, "of just how old your merry old England is."

"Yes," said Mrs. Haeley, "you colonies are still in your infancy—just you see what happens when you grow up." I saw her smile though her face was half in shadow.

We continued to look at maps for a while. I noted how the eastern side of the isles took realistic shape long before the western portion was better known. A similar process was at work at home. Thanks to Captains Lewis and Clark, and the intrepid souls who were following their trail, we had a growing sense of that vast expanse. I sometimes imagined Kathy in the ponderous nothingness of the West, a beautiful soul in a space void of time and physical place. I wanted to go west someday, to Chicago or even St. Louis, but it seemed now the Fates were blowing me in the opposite direction. Perhaps I should keep going, past Persia and Turkey, into the Orient then beyond . . . Japan and another ocean (a more peaceful one, it is said) to California and the other territories, arriving in the West by way of the East—but, no, the Wheelwright family funds would dry up long before reaching such an exotic destination: the wheel would fall off the carriage prior to crossing the Persian deserts, and, ironically, there'd be nothing this Wheelwright could do to fix it.

I followed Mrs. Haeley into the main hall. We seemed, still, to be the only visitors to the Museum—its only inhabitants even. We

were making our way to the next exhibition room when suddenly
there was a swish of movement behind us. I turned to see a little bald
fellow in a gray plaid suit; he carried an ancient-looking tome in both
hands like a religious offering—he had miraculously perfected a way
of moving on the polished marble so that his steps were virtually
silent. The little book-bearer (or great-book bearer) whisked past us
with not so much as a nod in greeting. Mrs. Haeley and I glanced at
one another and knew what the other was thinking: we commenced
to following the fellow.

We attempted to mimic his stealthy locomotion—I was all but
on tiptoe—however, we made the racket of a Dutch battalion by
comparison. Nonetheless the plaid-suited fellow paid us no attention
as we trailed him in the lengthy corridor . . . up a flight of stairs . . .
along another corridor . . . turning into a more modest hallway (this
carpeted)—I was astonished he said nothing to Mrs. Haeley and me
as he must have known we were there. He arrived at a dark-stained
door and only paused for an instant before the door was opened
from inside (how someone knew of his wanting in was unclear, for
he said or did nothing that I could discern). The fellow entered with
the ponderous book still before him; and the door was closed.

"My curiosity is enflamed, Jeff."

"Mine as well. . . ." I couldn't quite call her Mae, seeming too
contrived at the moment.

We walked toward the door, which now projected the solemnity
of an ancient totem, and we approached cautiously as if it may come
to life and riddle us to gain admittance. No such thing happened
of course and we stood before the door, not certain what to do. I
noticed there were words painted on the door but they were greatly
faded from age: I made out READING ROOM just as the door was
opened.

My heart quickened as if it were the door to a ghoul's crypt that
had swung back, seemingly of its own accord. Being a gentleman, I
allowed Mrs. Haeley to enter first. We discovered a large room with
a half dozen or so rectangular tables evenly set apart. At the tables
sat hunch-shouldered men poring over books of every dimension.
A powder-wigged fellow at the door, apparently the porter, cleared
his throat and said, "Credentials, please"—though with his accent

it sounded more like *Credenchoolz*. I was taken aback and thought we were about to be ejected from the premises, when I recalled Mr. Murry's letter of introduction that I'd folded into a square and placed inside my wallet, forever the nesting rat. I removed the letter, carefully unfolded it and handed it to the porter, who stiff-leggedly delivered it to an important-looking chap at a small walnut desk in the corner, most certainly the librarian. A lamp sat on the desk illuminating, what else?, the open pages of a book.

Mrs. Haeley appeared mildly surprised by my response to the porter (I was hoping for more), and we watched as the librarian peered through the small, circular lenses of his spectacles, which shown in the lamplight like diminutive moons, to read Murry's neatly penned introduction. The porter and librarian conferred for a moment, and my sense was that it was more about Mrs. Haeley, the only female in what was in all likelihood a men-only enclave. I imagined myself pitching a gallant fit at her rejection; then I thought I noticed the librarian mouth the name "Haeley" and in a moment the porter returned my letter and motioned that we should enter at our leisure. I replaced the handy paper to my wallet, and we moved away from the door.

The room was lined with tall bookcases, each shelf of which was filled with untold volumes—I was reminded of Mrs. Haeley's foyer, and of Bookman & Sons. Most of the seats were occupied but there were two chairs at a center table, so we went to them and I held Mrs. Haeley's chair before taking one myself. I wasn't quite sure what we were doing in the quiet room, save for the occasional turning of a leaf, or scribbling of a note, clearing of a throat. On the table were several small slips of paper and stubby pencils. Mrs. Haeley took up a pencil and wrote "Robert Byrd Townsend." Immediately the fellow in gray plaid materialized at the authoress's elbow and took from her the paper. Mrs. Haeley and I exchanged glances, perhaps to say we hoped the poor man wouldn't have to go far to retrieve the work. Around us the gentleman scholars seemed to be silently expressing some pique at Mrs. Haeley's presence. I doubted that any besides the librarian knew who she was; even in that regard I wondered if the deference was shown more to her dead poet husband than to her and Professor Dunkelraum.

In a moment Mr. Plaid Suit was returned with a two-volume work, both with covers of scarlet cloth: Ghostly Tales of the Scottish Highlands & Other Assorted Legends, by Robert Byrd Townsend (published, I discovered, 1779). I skimmed the introductory note of volume I, in which the author thanked various Scots for their assistance in gathering the stories. Mrs. Haeley had opened volume II more randomly and was reading a midway chapter. On a slip of paper I wrote, "Your grandfather I presume." She took the pencil from me: "my grand<u>mother</u> Rebecca!—'Robert' her nom de plume."

I recalled that *Dunkelraum* was first issued anonymously; in fact because Stephen Haeley had written the preface, many believed him the author.

Mrs. Haeley whispered, "I've a set at home if you'd like to read her."

I nodded and we got up from our chairs, our curiosity about the room and its workings satisfied. I believed the scholars were relieved at our departure. We nodded thank-you to the librarian and porter. As we were leaving the room, with Mrs. Haeley just before me, I solved the mystery of the prophetic doorman: as the authoress stepped over the threshold, a board demurely squeaked inside the reading room—no doubt a happy accident that circumvented disruptive knocking on the portal.

"We've been having quite an adventure," said Mrs. Haeley as we were retracing our path. "I could stand refreshment; there are some lovely shops on Barrow Street, if my memory serves."

We exited the Museum, filled with so much unviewed treasure, and I discovered that Barrow ran to one side of the Museum grounds. I sensed that the scene was not quite as Mrs. Haeley recollected but nevertheless we soon located a shop with shaded tables and chairs in front. We ordered tea and pastries that Mrs. Haeley called "bishop's buttons" (though she said in some quarters they were known as "bride's bonnets"), then we sat at a vacant table. Londoners rushed before us on the walk, and carts and carriages clopped along the street; thus it was noisy, but otherwise quite a pleasant spot to repose awhile. We sat quietly for a minute or two.

Surprising even myself, I blurted, "It must be difficult. . . ."

Mrs. Haeley fastened her graphitic eyes to me, wondering perhaps what I meant. I wondered too. To have lost her mother before knowing her . to have lost her children one by one . and Haeley . and Fanny and Mundie . to have been alone all this time . to be a woman and authoress . to be known for the book you wrote a lifetime ago . all of it I meant. She seemed to be forming some way to respond, when the shopkeeper brought our refreshments and the sudden topic was suddenly dropped. We went about fixing our cups of tea, cream and sugar for me, just a splash of cream for Mrs. Haeley. A bishop's button I discovered was a more or less circular piece of flakey crust about the size of a man's palm, with a dollop of sweetmeats in its center. It wasn't completely to my liking as each swallow left a somewhat bitter aftertaste but I'd grown hungry from our tramping and the pastry did help to restore me. The tea, on the other hand, was quite good. The English know their tea!

Occupied with our food and drink, we were able to disregard my earlier ejaculation. Besides, what could Mrs. Haeley respond? My statement, though vague, was self-evident. I wondered for how long she would want to continue our outing; perhaps I should hail a passing cabby—but she appeared quite lively as she sipped her tea and stabbed flakes of pastry with her gloved finger and placed the flakes carefully one at a time on her tongue. A castaway rescued from a desert island would not relish his food more than she her bishop's button.

I was feeling a need to initiate some sort of dialogue, regarding I knew not what, when a young woman began calling out from the crowded walk: "Come see the mechanical marvel of Europe, a miracle of machinery . . . the Germans may've i'vented it but we perfected it. . . ."

The voice was familiar, a trifle cockney. Then she came into view among the harried passers-by, and it was Miss Organdy, the puppet-show waif, looking as pale and thin as ever, wearing a scarlet dress and some sort of boyish leather cap.

". . . The Velociquad's the spriest machine on dry-land, faster'an a team of matched blacks, I'll tell you what . . . faster'an one of ol' Bonaparte's balls. . . ." She had a stack of yellow handbills and passed one to whomever looked likely to accept it; the waif set one at our table. ". . . Another demonstration, fit to unhinge your jaw, in precisely—" She checked a watch that she brought fobbed from a pocket of her dress— "precisely twenty-one minutes, mark," and she replaced the watch with dramatic flair. "Test your mettle and take a ride on the Velociquad yourselves. . . ." Her voice was fading on the crowded walk.

Mrs. Haeley took up the handbill as a breeze twisted its corner—I could smell that the ink was still damp. "In Combie Park," she read aloud, "near the Museum," and she handed the paper to me. There was a sketch of the Velociquad, a four-wheeled contraption with pedals as one may find on a weaving machine, and a long board or seat running lengthwise between the wheels. A pair of fashionable daredevils sat astride the seat, one in front (the operator it seemed), one behind (the passenger). The caption read: Dr. Velocitor & an Amazed Fellow.

"We must attend," said Mrs. Haeley, finishing her tea in a single gulp. "Mustn't we?"

"If the lady insists." I folded the handbill and put it in my coat pocket.

I helped Mrs. Haeley with her chair, then we stepped into the flow of the crowded walkway. Even with the din, behind me I heard the shopkeeper already gathering up our dishes, preparing the table for another customer on this busy day—with a white sky still, but perhaps growing warmer. We headed in the opposite direction of Miss Organdy, or whatever name she assumed at the moment, and I felt a twinge of disappointment. I wished to speak to her, I wished to know if it was the young Prince in the cave—the puppet-show narrative was left incomplete and I felt a small part of myself was therefore unfinished too, like a thread left hanging from the cuff of one's shirt: it just wouldn't do to leave it hanging there—it must be finished and tied off properly.

The tea and pastry had quite restored the authoress, and I was at some pains to keep up with her. My feet were a bit sore (I would have to send for Dr. Carter, whose companionship I was missing—we had become fast friends). I tried calling out to Mrs. Haeley, even using "Mae!" to arrest her attention, but she continued her inspired pace through the crowd that'd come out on this pleasant enough London noontime. A fellow in a striped jacket bumped into me and we said our apologies, though I believed mine sounded more sincere, and I realized I'd lost sight of Mrs. Haeley. I continued making my way through the veritable sea of people, angling my shoulders, quickening my step or slackening it as the momentary need arose—all the while looking left, right, forward, my eyes darting from face to face, or the back of each hatted head to each hatted head. But I could not locate the authoress. A bubble of panic began to rise deep within my soul and there was no earthly reason for it. She was not lost, nor was I. I suspected she was penniless but that was no matter. If it came to it, a cabby would give a respectable lady transportation and wait while the fare was gotten from the home. Nonetheless I found myself becoming alarmed at Mrs. Haeley's continued absence. I stopped on the walk and looked behind me into the milling pedestrians. I hoped that the waif Miss Organdy had reversed her course and I would find her approaching me, her waspish form draped in scarlet—I hoped it for no other reason than to see a familiar countenance. I realized that that rising bubble of panic was perhaps no more than a bubble of loneliness, one that had been forming for some time, perhaps since my arrival in England, or my departure from New York Harbor . . . or perhaps since Kathy's leaving me standing in front of the apothecary's in Albany, in an instant further removed from me than the West or anywhere else could possibly take her . . . or since my father's death.... I began to wonder then if Mrs. Haeley had been real at all, as this outing with the great authoress had the trappings of the unreal, or even what the painters call "the extra-real" . . .

"Jeff—" I turned to find Mrs. Haeley smiling at me. "I thought I'd lost you," she said, and I suspected the smile was just a thin veneer over her own panic . . . her own loneliness.

"No—it won't be that simple." She took the arm that I proffered, and we continued along the busy walk toward Combie Park. The bubble I'd been sensing sank back deep into my soul but it did not dissolve and disappear. We picked our way across Barrow Street, and I soon realized we were part of a specialized group: the curious about this new machine, the Velociquad. I glanced down at the manure stains on the cuffs of my trouser legs, and it seemed that a horseless means of travel in the City was sorely needed. Perhaps the good "Dr. Velocitor" was onto something.

Our group passed through the gates into Combie Park. It was not difficult to find our way as yellow handbills were tacked to trees here and there leading us on. I looked up through tree limbs hoping to see some break in the monochromic sky but it was still a perfect dull white, like a canvas, I thought, awaiting the artist's paint. I glanced at Mrs. Haeley and she had lowered the veil over her eyes. Her lips were parted as if she may be trying to catch her breath. The outing must've been taxing—I resolved we would hail a cab just as soon as the demonstration was concluded. It surely would be done, well, quickly.

I truly noted my fellow groupmates for the first time. Mainly we were men, but several women and children too—about thirty in all. A few of the children appeared to be street urchins, so claimed their ragged clothes and besooted faces. Every metropolis in the world has such children of course but London's streetchildren seemed especially beaten-down and desperate.

We took a curve in the path marked by the yellow sheets and we suddenly were looking at a long grassy field, almost absent of trees except at the far end, a few hundreds yards away. Another thirty or more spectators were here and there, including a dozen surrounding (it turned out) Dr. Velocitor and his machine, which was impressive to behold: a metal framework painted an eye-dazzling red, four wagon wheels coated in India-rubber, a long seat upholstered in quality saddle leather, and a mechanical system of pedals with a loop of tight chain from axle to axle. It seemed that the operator was to move the pedals, thus causing the four wheels to turn in unison, meanwhile maneuvering the contraption via metal handles that forked to each wheel in front, presumably to effect a movement to the left or right. It appeared the job of the person behind was to hold onto the operator for dear life—and perhaps he could assist in halting the thing too, by putting to the ground his feet, as I detected no other means for accomplishing the necessary task.

Dr. Velocitor was holding court with a group of admirers. While he spoke he rested a gloved hand on his machine's "saddle" (I overheard him call it such), as if the Velociquad were a prize racehorse. The doctor looked to be in his mid to late thirties but in fine shape with a trim belly and barrel chest. He had a long mustache whose shape imitated the operator's steering handles on his machine. He wore a red plaid jacket, open to a white shirt and red silk scarf; and brown hunting trousers with leather patches at the knees (and seat I assumed). Glossy black riding boots and a leather cap similar to the one Miss Organdy wore completed the look of the well-to-do exotic.

As Mrs. Haeley and I stepped closer I heard him expounding on a German invention that he had resurrected from "utter failure" to "modern-day marvel." Muscular jaws were at work behind the ornamental mustache; his teeth were brilliantly white and straight. I was beginning to think that Dr. Velocitor was something of a marvel himself. I glanced at Mrs. Haeley and she appeared captivated by the dashing inventor.

"...the future," he was saying, sounding to my ear like a Welshman, "that is all, ladies and gentlemen, the mere future—and you are here to diaper and swaddle her." He patted the Velociquad's saddle adoringly. There was gloved applause from some of the gathering, including Mrs. Haeley, who suddenly appeared a mourner in this conversely bright and jovial crowd. I must have as well.

"Now who will be the first to ride boldly into the future?" He patted the saddle again, toward the back where a passenger would perch.

A gentleman in a tall silk hat, angled jauntily to one side, stepped up: "I, good sir!"

"Capital! That's capital," said Dr. Velocitor, who, from his free hand, allowed a belt to unfurl with theatrical flair. I hadn't noticed he was holding anything, though I had noticed the cavalier gloves that reached nearly to his elbows. He fastened the heavy brown belt loosely about his athletic midsection and I understood this was to be used as a handhold for the passenger. The doctor removed a pair of heavy spectacles from his jacket pocket, the sort that blacksmiths sometimes use to keep the sparks from burning their eyes, and he placed them on his face with care. Then Velocitor stepped astraddle his machine with an unnecessarily high, military-looking kick and he took hold of the steering bar. He positioned himself forward in the seat and placed a foot on the high pedal while the other foot remained on terra firma. He indicated with a nod that the gentleman should sit behind him, which he did, a bit awkwardly, and held onto the doctor's belt.

Everyone waited for Dr. Velocitor to shoot off like an arrow but he did not move. After a long pause—no doubt to heighten the drama—he said, "Sir, your hat." Understanding came to us all a bit slowly, then, realizing, the gentleman removed his tall hat and handed it to a lady friend. He re-secured his grip on the belt . . . and they were off—

Velocitor shoved away with his foot and began pumping the pedals. At first the machinery was quite stiff but in just a few yards everything began to move more easily and the Velociquad picked up speed. The slight downhill grade of the field obviously assisted the good doctor.

The small crowd applauded and "oohed" and "aahed" as Velocitor and his passenger rolled onward, their rubbered wheels bumping along the uneven ground, and the two men popping from side to side and at times hopping up from the saddle altogether . . . but somehow staying aboard the mad machine. Dr. Velocitor was fast approaching a copse of birches—from our vantage he appeared to be getting very close—when he pulled on the steering bar and the Velociquad made a sharply angled turn to the left. I saw that the doctor had quit pumping the pedals and was allowing momentum to take the machine through the maneuver. The gentleman held fast to the safety belt, and when they were fully turned back toward us I could see that the passenger was a tad wild-eyed . . . and decidedly pale, in contrast to the ruddy flush of his cheeks.

Dr. Velocitor began pedaling furiously and was able to maintain an impressive speed for a minute, but the, now, uphill grade took its toll and the machine's velocity declined precipitously. In fact the doctor was beginning to be rather crimson-faced himself with his exertion as the Velociquad rolled to an easy stop just before the curious crowd, which reacted in enthusiastic applause. The doctor and his passenger dismounted, both waving triumphantly to their admirers. Velocitor, still somewhat winded, began walking his machine in a tight arc to point it away from the gathering again.

"Now," he said, "would anyone else care to take a ride? My assistant

Miss Felicity will be happy to accept your generous donations."

Miss Felicity (Miss Organdy!) stepped from the crowd, her scarlet dress ablaze, and waved a bird-bone hand at all then touched her leather cap. She came toward the doctor and his speed-machine.

I wondered who would be next but not for long as Mrs. Haeley said in a raised voice, "May I give it a go, sir?"

Everyone turned to her (to us).

Velocitor pushed back his cap a bit; sweat had formed on his wide brow. "I fear it may be a bit too risky for the fairer sex, madam..."

"Fear not, sir, we do not break so easily." There was a brief snatch of applause.

Velocitor thought for a moment. "I don't know that the Velociquad may be ridden side-saddle."

"Fear not again—I had no such intention." A shocked murmur rippled among the onlookers. "What is more," she grew bolder, "I thought my friend may be the operator." She touched my shoulder.

Dr. Velocitor was nonplussed. "It's not a toy, madam. . . ."

"This is the famous American author Jefferson Wheelwright— imagine if he were to write favorably of your machine." She allowed the vague but attractive idea to hang suspended before Velocitor's eyes. (Meanwhile I was gratified to hear someone in the crowd, a feminine voice, mention "Old New Yorkers.")

"Very well then," said the doctor, "but be duly careful, and do not let the Velociquad speed out of control." He patted the saddle as if it were a barely tame beast that required reassurance.

It all happened so quickly that I had no time to consider whether I even wanted to operate the odd contraption. The boldness that allowed a mere girl to run off to the Continent with her married lover, with only a few pounds and a box of stolen books between them, remained in Mrs. Haeley's personality it seemed. Such boldness was foreign to my more cautious sensibilities but I found her brash proposal exciting—and I was glad to be seen by the onlookers in the park as that sort of person: a swift-witted corsair, in possession of a potent pen. . . .

Mrs. Haeley took a scarf that had hung loosely about her neck and put it over her head to secure her hat, knotting it snuggly beneath her sharp chin. Without consideration, I handed my hat to Miss Organdy (Miss Felicity!) as if an acquaintance—she, as if an acquaintance, promptly placed it on over the leather cap, cocking it provocatively above her right eye. I stepped to the machine and Velocitor handed me the belt, which I secured about my waist (I was able to employ the first available hole), then he offered me the safety spectacles. I took them as well and assumed the position of operator—not quite managing the military panache in mounting it that the doctor adroitly affected.

Mrs. Haeley, hiking up her skirt so undemurely that her stockings showed above her shoe tops, got in the saddle behind me, and took hold of the belt about my middle. I slid the spectacles onto my face and noticed immediately that the right lens was severely scratched, separating the scene in that eye somewhat in half. Dr. Velocitor held onto the steering bar as if the reins of a horse that needed to be steadied in anticipation of an unfamiliar rider. "Mind your speed," he said to me, quietly, before letting go.

The machine began to move even before my clumsy feet had found the pedals. I felt Mrs. Haeley's grip tighten on the belt. I began to exert some force with my legs, and the Velociquad lurched forward with a bump-bump as the right-hand wheels rolled over an especially uneven patch of ground. My palms were perspiring and it required some effort to keep hold of the steering bar, particularly when the wheels were bumping about.

I thought of Velecitor's warning but my efforts to contain the machine's speed had no effect whatsoever. It seemed a thing possessed—I knew it to be possessed by gravity and momentum but logic was little comfort. I realized Mrs. Haeley was beginning to flop about something like a ragdoll behind me. Yet I heard a high-pitched peal of mirth: the authoress was enjoying this mad ride. I tried to enjoy it too. The spectacles were heavy and my head must've been narrower than Velocitor's, so they began sliding down my nose, threatening to fly off with the next colossal jolt. But I didn't dare let go of the steering bar with one hand to secure the spectacles for fear that it would be I that would go flying off.

I knew we must be approaching the copse at the extremity of the field. I attempted to dead reckon peering through or above or around the jostling spectacles with the scratched lens. What I saw, then, was a sort of bits-of-broken-mirror portrait, with some elements left out altogether and others reproduced again and again. There was no mistaking that a group of spectators had gathered before the stand of birches—however, was the group there a dozen strong, or half that, or double it? My rattling eyeballs and brain refused to hazard a guess.

The first image that singularly arrested my gaze was a baby-carriage with, I supposed, a woman beside it—the pair we'd encountered earlier? It seemed to me, yes. Perhaps this association unleashed a flood of associations because the other images in the shattered portrait were the little labyrinth girl and her father, the ardent lovers by the fountain, the librarian and his beplaided assistant . . . even the shopkeeper with his tea and bishops' buttons and Miss Organdy in conflagratory crimson—all there at the end of the field toward which Mrs. Haeley and I hurled with ever-quickening velocity . . . and, it seemed, ferocity. I tried to look again, the spectacles wobbling on the tip of my nose, and now I believed I saw other familiar persons: Dr. Carter, and the Chamberlains (Lord and Lady and Miss Hilary in her sunbeam gown), Thursday and Miss Edith, and even the beclouded banker Chester Peacock. Had my clattering senses had more time, they might have detected the whole Wheelwright clan before the copse, and Kathy miraculously returned from the West . . . even Stephen Haeley and Agamemnon Mundie returned, even more miraculously, from the dead. . . .

A voice broke me from my momentary reverie: "Turn, Jefferson, turn—" Mrs. Haeley was shouting in my ear. I instantly pulled on the steering bar with my left hand and pushed with my right. The crowd at the copse, perhaps suddenly realizing the danger, dispersed willy-nilly—or so it appeared in my badly obscured vision. The Velociquad veered to the left. It maneuvered more easily than I'd anticipated and so I'd oversteered it—plus the adrenaline surging through my bloodstream no doubt had an effect too. As such the machine began to tip with its right-hand wheels coming off the ground. The pedals spun wildly of their own accord as my feet paddled only the rushing air.

Nevertheless the Velociquad seemed to be slowing and I believed for the briefest moment I was going to regain control—then the left wheels, the ones still in contact with the earth, were severely jolted and Mrs. Haeley and I were pitched from the saddle, rolling somehow in tandem that positions were reversed and when we came to rest the authoress lay atop me as if I were a poorly stuffed mattress between her and the hard ground. Meanwhile the Velociquad had overturned on its side and its right wheels turned in madcap rhythm with the pedals.

Dr. Velocitor came running to our aid—or, more likely, the aid of his invention—at the head of a pack of curious on-lookers, anxious to see a broken bone or two. "Mr. Wheelwright!" said the doctor. "Are you quite all right?" His words were directed at me but his hand was slowing the rotating wheels of his machine.

I realized Mrs. Haeley was shaking. I felt the convulsions of her ribcage through my own trunk. In fact it felt as if Professor Galvani had attached his electrical battery to a skeleton which lay across me jostling with current. She was not quick to remove herself from me—all of which I took to mean that the poor woman was severely injured . . . then the sound began: a rolling peal of laughter loud enough to tremble the leaves on the trees. Everyone was somewhat in shock, and the strange scene persisted for longer than it might have. I discovered I had an unencumbered view of the pure white sky (that is, Velocitor's safety spectacles had flown off entirely in the final sudden stop). I thought the sky a perfect screen for a magic-lantern show, where stars and Oriental dragon-shapes of red and blue and green might fill the space, as they can fill the mind's eye.

A gentleman assisted Mrs. Haeley to her feet as she still cackled a bit. I got up and dusted myself off. "My apologies, sir; I hope your machine is none the worse," I offered.

The doctor and a couple of volunteers were setting the Velociquad upright. "It appears to have survived relatively unscathed—and yourselves?"

"I'm quite all right," I said. "Mrs. Haeley, are you fit?"

The authoress's name seemed to elicit a reaction from Velocitor and others but no one remarked on it.

"Yes," said Mrs. Haeley, regaining her composure and straightening her hat and scarf, "as a fiddler, thank you."

I took a pound note from my wallet and exchanged it with Miss

Organdy for my hat. I wanted very much to ask the waif about the Princess in the cave and about the identity of the injured man, but remained silent. The authoress and I walked away from the crowd, which for the most part was dispersing too—as Dr. Velocitor lovingly tended to his machine.

Fourteen

~

M RS. HAELEY FELL ASLEEP IN THE CAB RETURNING TO HER HOME.
When we arrived, she was so listless I felt I was supporting
more of her weight than she was herself as I helped her toward the
steps—an observer may have suspected I was escorting a drunken
woman, shamefully intoxicated in the middle of the day. Miss Edith
must have been watching for our return because she came outdoors
and assisted me with the authoress, though assistance was hardly
necessary. Once inside, Edith led Mrs. Haeley upstairs to her room.
I went to the parlor, which was beginning to feel like my place in the
house, more so than the bedroom that had been lent me. There I
sensed the presence of Fanny, the half-sister, or more specifically I
sensed the presence of her death. It seemed to me that on that very
bed she'd suffered the agonies of childbirth—a painful process that
would kill both her and the child. There was no visible evidence
of it in the room yet I felt it just the same—another product of my
overactive imagination.

I removed my coat and hat and loosened my cravat, in preparation
for a brief nap on the sofa . . . when I spotted a folded piece of paper
lying atop Edmund Holland's book which I'd left on the French
writing-desk:

> Dear Jefferson—
> I hope you are well. I dropped in to check on Thursday's
> leg, which appears to be healing nicely, and thought you may
> need another foot treatment. Please feel at liberty to send for
> me if the latter is the case.

Take care &
    be in good health!
        Carter

I lay on the sofa thinking of taking a midday slumber—a siesta as the Spanish call it—and though I was physically quite fagged, my mind was restless in the extreme. I put my arm over my eyes to darken the room but it only helped in that it clarified my mental agitation: I was consumed with thoughts of *Andersen's Romance*, teeming with ideas for its revision. There was no point in trying to sleep. The thick sheaf of proofs stood sentinel on the secrétaire. I went to them as if a neglected lover and immediately found where I'd left off.

Always influencing my revisions now was a sense of Edmund Holland's work, which smoldered in my creative mind like a hot ember buried in a stack of coal, spreading its heat upwards, and soon to ignite the whole lot. I was ruthless in my self-editing, crossing out entire sentences, paragraphs, and at times pages. But I added even more, writing in the margins and on the reverse of pages, or inserting new sheets when need be. It remained the story of Andersen and Katherine and their conflicted romance but it was becoming the story of their culture too, and the story of writing their story. I did not fully grasp what I was up to, not at every level, but that was all right. Edmund Holland brought me somehow to that understanding: that a book could contain mysteries which were mysterious even to its author. This precept may sound simple enough but it was revelatory to me. Writing *Sketches of the Old New Yorkers* had been like constructing a frame house (or so I imagined). I developed a plan then went about building the narrative precisely as called for—tinkering with no dimensions, substituting no materials, not believing myself at liberty to improvise even my own design. I had approached writing *Sunnydale* and *Andersen's Romance* in the same careful manner. Now, with my fancy unshackled from a preset plan, I discovered things about the characters and their worlds I'd, quite literally, never imagined before.

So absorbed was I, I only half-noticed when Miss Edith placed a tray with tea and biscuit on the sofa's side table. At some point thereafter, looking up from the proof-page on which I'd been scribbling with vigor for near a half-hour, I realized I was quite famished. I went to the sofa, prepared myself a cup of tea and munched on a biscuit. I noted that its crumbs were caught in the wet ink on the page but brushing them away would've smeared the words so I left them there to become part of the work, like insects in amber. The writing, which was so essential to my being, combining with the bread of life, so to speak, struck me as perfectly apropos—perhaps only more so if they'd been crumbs of Eucharistic bread, and then a few drops of sanguine wine on the page would've completed the symbolic tableau.

I stayed thus for the remainder of the afternoon, surfacing infrequently from my reverie to hear Thursday or his sister in the hallway or, fainter still, the kitchen. Mrs. Haeley, quite exhausted I presumed, seemed not to stir. The revised and new pages grew around me—on the tea table and end table, on the sofa, on the floor—as if reproducing themselves. Meanwhile my fingers grew black at the novel's rebirth. I thought of the old newspapermen I'd known in Albany and New York City who went to their graves with permanently stained fingers, ashes to ashes, ink to ink.

My neck and back were quite stiff from having remained hunched over my novel for so many hours but I had made great progress with the revision. I should have been more worried about Murry's accepting the changes. After all, he'd paid for the other book—the one in title only, for all practical purposes. It would be costly to compose the pages again. That, however, was not my concern: I was only interested in writing the best book that I could. I cared little if Murry turned it down. I cared little if everyone turned it down as long as it became the book I wanted it to be. This too was a new attitude that I could only trace to Edmund Holland's influence.

I stood and stretched. I heard the front door shut, and in a moment I smelled sausages and cabbage. I went to the kitchen and discovered my assumption was correct: Miss Edith had purchased the steamed food from a street vendor. It sat in a large Dutch oven still wrapped in paraffin-coated paper to keep it warm. The governess, turned maid, cook and housekeeper, had also prepared a broth, which simmered in the pot on the stove.

"Mrs. Haeley requested an early supper," said Edith, almost

apologetically.

It was not quite six o'clock. "That sounds—smells!—wonderful. I'm quite hungry."

Thursday came into the room on his crutches, smiled at his sister, then took his place at the table. I spent a few minutes in the washroom before joining him there. Thursday and I helped ourselves to the sausage and cabbage while Edith ladled broth into three mismatched bowls on the table. Before joining us she prepared a tray and took it to Mrs. Haeley, who apparently preferred to supp in her room. Edith encouraged us to begin eating without her; I followed her brother's lead in doing so. Miss Edith returned to us shortly and prepared her own plate. Meanwhile I'd discovered that the pitcher on the table contained hard cider and I poured three cups.

Thursday inquired about Mrs. Haeley's and my outing, and I related the tale of the run-away Velociquad. I embellished now and then, for the sake of my audience's amusement of course, but even as I told it I imagined ways of making it still better on the next recounting, which perhaps I would do in ink. I asked after their day together and it sounded quite tame by comparison.

The meal was wholesome indeed, especially with the addition of Miss Edith's broth, which seemed to be made with bovine stock. Neither morsel nor drop remained when I'd finished. "Thank you," I said, dabbing with my napkin at the corners of my mouth, "that was most excellent and satisfying." I began to push back my chair, which grated on the well-worn wood floor.

"My sister isn't yet finished with her amazements."

"It's nothing," said the governess, seeming to blush.

"Indeed?"

"Indeed," said Thursday with almost parental pride. "She has managed a gooseberry cobbler for dessert—it is warming on the stove."

I looked and there was a pan there, its top covered by a checkered cloth.

"You mustn't feel obligated to sample it, Mr. Wheelwright—I only play at being a cook."

"Not at all—a portion of cobbler sounds quite lovely."

"Well," said Thursday, "I cannot oblige Edith's delicious cobbler without some good coffee to accompany it. Please, Mr. Wheelwright, relax awhile and we'll let you know when all is quite ready."

I chose a volume at random from the foyer stacks and walked back through the kitchen to get to Mrs. Haeley's small, untended yard. I took up a seat on the authoress's bench. In the narrow space above, the sky was still an uninterrupted white. I wondered how long such a dull sky could persist; perhaps it was quite common in England. I'd chosen, as luck would have it, a volume of verse by Biron Swinford, the poet whom Murry had charged with inserting me into the American Circle in London, but I'd managed to elude that pleasure, and maybe I was entirely safe here in Mrs. Haeley's home, which seemed somewhat separate from the world at large. What troubled me was identifying with whom the idea of separation originated: with Mrs. Haeley or with the world?

Swinford's verse was sophisticated but a bit too sweet for my prolonged taste.

> Hummingbird hover'd about its floral house,
> Hover'd there where bees too had been before,
> Supping nectar and vigorous of wing—
> Enigmatical as creatures of lore.

The image of the hummingbird—*like* the hummingbird—hovered before my eyes as I drifted into a reverie, a sort of waking dream. . . .

Mourningwoman is across a great field from me, a black trunk against a copse of birch. There is nothing except the grass and the birches, and Mourningwoman and me, facing each other across the expanse of field. My vision becomes telescopic, and Mourningwoman seems to draw nearer to me as my eyesight extends out—but there is something not quite right with the field of vision and Mourningwoman remains obscure even once she has been made large to my eye. In her background the white-trunk birches are sharply rendered though Mourningwoman, closer, remains an obfuscation. I strain my sight but to no purpose. Red appears on the periphery of my vision, and at first I am quite certain it is the

bloody-mouthed wolves. I am reluctant to see more directly
and thereby confirm my suspicions . . . but Mourningwoman
is gone entirely and so there is no justification to not seeing.
I look. The waif—or rather, many many embodiments of The
Waif—dance merrily in long lines on either side of the field.
All of The Waif wear the blood-red dress. The Waif smile,
The Waif laugh—and it is the sound of branches breaking in
a storm, branches snapping in a storm. . . .

The kitchen door was opening, and I was surprised to see it was
Mrs. Haeley who was bringing dessert on a tray. I began to stand but
she stayed me: "Relax, Jeff, I am quite capable"—she shut the door
with her foot and continued toward me. She did appear restored;
there was even a faint rosiness in her thin cheeks and I assumed it
was not placed there cosmetically: the authoress did not seem the
sort of woman who would use cosmetics. There was only the one
bench in the yard so Mrs. Haeley placed the tray on the end, and
she and I sat quite close as she passed a small plate with a generous
helping of cobbler, still warm, and a fork.

Mrs. Haeley sampled the dessert. "Mmm . . . quite good—I wish
my Thursday a speedy recovery but I will be sorry to see Edith return
to her situation. She's been a god-send."

"Indeed," I managed with my mouth full.

Mrs. Haeley was in mid-bite when she quickly added, "Your
companionship has been heaven-sent, too, Jefferson."

"Thank you, Mae, but it's been nothing compared to your
hospitality. . . ." I had to check myself, suddenly recalling that Mrs.
Haeley had no idea of the service she was rendering me and the
depleted Wheelwright resources. I felt I should tell her all—should
cleanse my conscience and put our friendship on honest footing—
but instead I traded her my vacant cobbler plate for a cup of coffee,
still steaming; and we sat in the yard enjoying the peace and the
tenacious flora that managed to bloom in the neglected garden plots.

We remained that way—quiet except for our sipping and the
clicking of cup returned for a moment to saucer—until Mrs. Haeley
said, "I'm wondering . . . there is a staging of *Dunkelraum* at the
Orpheum that I've not seen—it's being presented this very evening,

we passed an advertisement in our ramblings—would you be interested in accompanying me to the theater, Jeff?"

"I would be delighted."

"I haven't been out . . . well, I cannot say since when, and I had great fun today—I just want it to last. . . ."

"You do not need to explain. I'm having a splendid time as well." It seemed there was more I should say but Mrs. Haeley, perhaps a touch self-conscious, took my empty cup and saucer, and placed them on the tray:

"Then in two hours' time we shall—what do you Americans say?—'step out onto the town.' I've never understood Yanks' affection for prepositions." She smiled to let me know the ribbing was meant good-naturedly, then she took up the tray and went toward the house. I held the door for her. She stopped at the threshold: "I'm sorry if I'm taking you from your work, Jeff, but I hadn't felt myself for a long while, and I mustn't . . . waste the opportunity. Death has been a stern tutor and has taught me the only moment we can depend upon is the present one."

I did not know what to say, and Mrs. Haeley continued into the house.

I returned to the bench and Biron Swinford. I was, however, distracted again and my thoughts were more of Mourningwoman than of Swinford's sweet verse. I also thought of Mrs. Haeley's writing nook in the cellar and I was more curious than ever to know on what she was working. After a time the backdoor opened and I suspected Mrs. Haeley was returning, but it was Thursday. By the time I realized, it was too late to assist him and he was swinging his way toward me on his crutches.

"You've become quite a proficient," I said, motioning him to join me on the bench.

He smiled in greeting, then sat and propped his crutches on the bench between us.

"How's the leg?"

"There seem to be ants on the march to and fro, but otherwise tolerable. Improving I do think." In spite of his optimistic report Thursday looked to be pained. I thought I recognized the countenance; it seemed Thursday had some unpleasantness to broach.

I elected not to encourage him if that were the case: "Miss Edith's cobbler was exceptional. Perhaps she should abandon her charges and open a bake shop."

"I'm certain your praise means a great deal to her."

I took another stab at small talk: "I'll send a note to Carter on the morrow; perhaps the good doctor can do something about those blasted ants."

"That would be very good," said Thursday, without enthusiasm. Then, "Mr. Wheelwright, I feel I must speak plainly . . ."

"Please do, my fellow . . ."

"In being herself, Mrs. Haeley . . . is not herself. . . ."

"I don't follow."

"I've been with her more than a year now, and before I arrived she'd . . . slipped into that other place, only coming back for brief periods before slipping again . . . periods of only a few hours to a day or two. Before you came, Mr. Wheelwright, she'd been slipped away for so long I began to figure she was never coming back."

"Why hadn't you summoned a physician, sir?"

"I did one time—he thought it was merely the early arrival of old age, of senility—perhaps triggered by all the unhappiness, all the loss, when a young woman."

"That seems an overly simple diagnosis—why didn't you seek another opinion?"

"When Mrs. Haeley understood she'd been seen by a doctor, she made me swear I'd summon no more."

"But why?"

Thursday considered for a moment, perhaps choosing his words carefully, or pondering a riddle he'd never fully solved himself. Finally, "Posterity, to put it simply. Mrs. Haeley, ever since her husband's death and she saw how the press distorted him and their life together—reporting rumors but dressing them up as facts, fabricating things altogether, stories of events that never happened— she became very careful what she fed the press . . . and the most careful thing is to feed them nothing at all."

"That certainly accounts for her reputation as a literary recluse."

"If the public knew of her . . . spells, people would no doubt believe she's become insane—a madwoman holed up here in her old house. . . ."

. . . Living with Stephen Haeley's ghost, I thought, uncharitably wondering if the public wouldn't be half correct. I said, "She seems to want to put to an end her reclusive ways. Tonight—"

"I know, the theater." I was surprised Thursday cut me off; in fact, this was a different Thursday entirely. But I wasn't angry. He clearly cared deeply for his mistress, and the caring had excited his emotion. "It's impossible to say when she will slip away. If it happens in public . . . well, the press is very hungry."

"I shall be careful," I said, realizing that I didn't even quite know what it meant to be careful under the circumstances.

"Yes," said Thursday, reaching inside his shirt jacket and removing a folded newspaper. "This was slipped into the mail-slot." He handed it to me even as he began to gather his crutches. I unfolded the paper to the front page of the *London Evening Illustrated.*

'DUNKELRAUM' AUTHORESS
EMERGES TO TAME
MECHANICAL MONSTER
ACCOMPANIED BY AMERICAN
NOVELIST WHEELWRIGHT

The story had little to do with our riding the Velociquad—apparently our near-death experience was not sufficiently sensational. Instead the writer (I shall employ the term loosely) recounted sordid rumors regarding Stephen Haeley and his bride, and grotesque details of his tragic drowning. There was little about me in the article, except for the implication that Mrs. Haeley and I had been romantically linked for some time.

Of course there was a single-frame illustration: an India-ink drawing of Mrs. Haeley and me on the Velociquad, which was terribly out of proportion and did resemble a mechanical monster; and the couple who were contentedly riding the beast—while on-lookers fled for their lives pell-mell in the background—looked nothing at all like the authoress and me. For one thing I had a full and curvaceous mustache (I've never grown a mustache, leave be a full and curvaceous one), and I wore my hat while taming the monster (astonishingly, of all details to get perfectly right, the illustrator had managed an exact likeness of my hat); and Mrs. Haeley was fashionably dressed in the latest Parisian suit (or so I imagined), and she more resembled a no doubt popular dancehall girl rather than a world-famous novelist (sultry smile on her plump lips and all). We appeared quite oblivious to the danger we were in, and were causing—perhaps we were too thickly in a lovers' fog.

The writer got the title of *Old New Yorkers* wrong, calling it *The Sketchbook of Old New York*—I must confess of all the erroneous details, this hurt me worst.

So it began already, and I was in large part to blame: I'd called the authoress by name in front of the public. Otherwise she would have escaped quite without notice. I might have vowed then and there that no further food would be added to the press's plate by resolving not to allow Mrs. Haeley to be seen in such a public venue, but instead I resolved only to keep her identity unknown while we were out and about. In truth it fed my self-image to be seen with her, even if only I knew it was she, Margaret T. Haeley. And, I must further admit, I enjoyed her company. I sympathized with Stephen Haeley for falling in love with the teenage Margaret Townsend—I understood how he succumbed to the temptation to abandon wife and child to run off with her to the Continent. And that was in her ebullient youth—she must have been something special indeed. An ocean—another world—away I developed a juvenile crush on her authorial persona: a crush that had never fully faded it seemed.

Thursday had made his way back indoors while I sat contemplating the situation.

I should at the very least share the newspaper account with her (I assumed Thursday had not) and let her decide if she wanted to risk another public sighting. I refolded the *Illustrated* and put it in my back pocket. Unsure what to do, I took up Swinford's verse and went inside. Miss Edith was working on the supper dishes in the washroom as I passed through. I was in the hall, just beyond Thursday's room, when the front door bell was turned, and I took it upon myself to answer. I unlatched the heavy door and was quite ill-prepared to find a stunningly beautiful young woman at the entrance.

She wore a jacket and skirt of dove-gray velveteen with pearl buttons, and a fashionable black satin bonnet. A fancy footman in powdered wig stood at attention two steps below.

"Hello again, Mr. Wheelwright. I hope I'm not disturbing you," she said, with a simple bow of her head.

"My word . . . Miss Chamberlain! I'm so sorry—I did not recognize you right off. . . ." I wished that I had put on my coat, feeling quite awkward in just shirt sleeves and vest.

Hilary Chamberlain smiled at my genuine fluster. "Father asked me to return this to you and I discovered you were no longer at The Saint Georges, but the manager was kind enough to give us this address." I realized then that the fancy footman was holding a fancy hatbox tied in blue ribbon. Miss Hilary took it from him and handed it to me. "Father wanted me to be sure to thank you so much and to renew our dinner invitation, for this coming Friday perhaps?"

I held the hatbox in both hands. "Friday," I repeated.

"Yes, or another day if you are previously booked." She paused a moment. "You are welcome to bring your friend."

"My friend. . . ."

"Yes," she smiled, radiant, "your lady friend." Her eyes darted about the shadowed foyer, perhaps looking for a glimpse of the authoress.

I was thinking how quickly news traveled in the Old City. New York was infamous for its lightning gossip but it was an amateur next to London. Miss Hilary interpreted my silence as indecision.

"When you have a moment to check your appointment book," she said pleasantly, still beaming, "just send Father word at the club, if you please."

"Of course. Thank you so much for bringing this round—and thank Lord Chamberlain. I will send him a note on the morrow."

"Good day, Mr. Wheelwright." She bowed, and the footman assisted her down the steps.

"Good day, Miss Chamberlain—thank you again," I said as she departed. I closed the door slowly and she was just stepping into her coach, I saw through the crack, when I shut it completely.

I went to the parlor and untied the hatbox ribbon. I lifted the lid and there was a folded paper along with the gray hat. It was a note from Lord Chamberlain expressing his appreciation for my allowing him to borrow my "fine American hat" and inviting me to visit the King James anytime I wished; he wrote, "Consider yourself an honorary member."

Now I could at least wear a different suit of clothes to the theater with Mrs. Haeley. I thought of the newspaper account and of Thursday's words of caution, and I thought that I should go tap on Mrs. Haeley's door and speak to her about the story and all, but it wasn't a conversation I could envision having. I must think about what I would say, I must rehearse my words. . . .

Meanwhile there were the proof-pages for *Andersen's Romance*, which I sat down to again.

Fifteen

~

THE ORPHEUM THEATRE WAS IN AN ESPECIALLY VENERABLE section of the City, thus precipitating a lengthy cab ride. The sun was all but set, and the lanterneers had not yet completed their work—so the theater district seemed to be beneath a darkened veil, one that likely softened its shabbiest features. I paid the cabby, and Mrs. Haeley and I were deposited on the boardwalk before the playhouse, where an old fellow with white mustache and beard stood swinging a red-light lantern announcing the performance: "Come one, come all, Ladies and Gents . . . witness Professor Dunkelraum's monster come to life . . . see how it menaces the countryside . . . who will stop its murderous rampage? . . . witness the terror if you dare…"

Mrs. Haeley took my arm. "This is not it, Jefferson."

I wasn't certain what she meant, then she pointed to the theater's lamplit marquee—this was the Occidental Theatre.

"The cab dropped us at the wrong spot," she said, "but the Orpheum is only a block or so over." Then she added, "I know *that* story," nodding toward the old fellow with white mustache and beard.

We began strolling along the moderately busy street. The light was exactly right for giving sway to one's imagination. Details were indistinct, so one could fancy that an encountered couple was a fine gentleman and his lady, or an overpainted streetwalker and her sudden client; that a fellow by himself was a tortured poet searching for inspiration in the theater district, or a ne'er-do-well looking for a shallow pocket to pick clean. A sliver of silvery moon, curved like a ring of onion, shown between rooftops and it was a relief to see anything at all in the sky after a day of uninterrupted whiteness. A tall gentleman passed us tipping his hat, and I responded in kind.

It was farther than Mrs. Haeley implied but we at last came to the Orpheum Theatre, and there was a fellow out front kindred to his Occidental brethren trying to attract an audience. In fact in the poor light and with my imagination agallop I thought it was the same white-bearded gent, transported here as if on a Persian carpet, or perhaps Mrs. Haeley and I had managed to circumambulate though we had seemed to walk straight away. At first the Orpheum appeared a similar copy of the Occidental but as I looked more closely I discovered it had the potential to be its twin—twin in ornate splendor—except the Orpheum had grown far shabbier. As a groom may say, the theater had been ridden too hard and put in its stall still wet. The old hawker out front called with a hint of Scottish brogue:

"See the story of Dunkelraum as you've none seen it afore . . . comely maidens driven to madness their selves by the monster's unnatural gifts . . . Who can stop him? And what maiden—or matron!—would want him stopped at that? . . ."

The play was titled "Dunkelraum's Monster and the Maidens' Menace."

"Are we come to the correct show?" I asked the authoress.

"Indeed—unless you'd prefer not to attend, Jeff."

"No," I said. "It sounds . . . intriguing."

We proceeded into the candelabra-lit lobby, with its peeling wallpapers and well-worn Oriental-style carpets, and we purchased our admission. The center-most seats in the auditorium were taken, so Mrs. Haeley preferred the mezzanine. I thought it may be providential as we would be less likely seen up there. We located the stairs. They were carpeted, and there were copious cigar and cigarette burns from years of careless smokers, so many burns that in the dim light it at first appeared that the fabric was deliberately patterned. We emerged at the side of the mezzanine, stage-left, and discovered it was sparsely populated. We found our seats in the front-most row. Mrs. Haeley was on my left and no one occupied the seat to my right, not yet anyway, so I placed my hat there. It still bore the mercurial scent of the hatter's, though it had been generously perfumed before being returned to me.

"It's a good crowd, I should think," said Mrs. Haeley, looking toward the floor-section. She seemed excited to be there.

"Yes." The seats below us were nicely filled with only an open seat or two here and there.

Mrs. Haeley reached into the side pocket of her jacket and produced a silver-handled lorgnette. "I'm happy to share," she said as she positioned the lenses before her eyes. There was nothing to see onstage yet, save for the orange-red curtain, so the authoress surveyed the theater patrons. She seemed to scan them thoroughly—perhaps the writer's penchant for observing human behavior, to be "an insect in the outhouse" as they say in the Appalachian states. After a minute or two she handed the lorgnette to me. In truth I wasn't terribly interested in the theatergoers; I was antsy to get on with the production itself, as I wasn't quite certain what sort of play I was about to witness. Nevertheless, I moved the lorgnette's field of vision across the growing crowd, which seemed, to be frank, a rather motley gathering . . . rather Bohemian if you will. I may have been wearing the best suit of clothes in the house:

Men moved about glad-handing acquaintances or sat finding a light for their cigar. Women gossiped with their near neighbors or adjusted their hats, some of which were inconsiderately adorned with plumage. A fellow played the box-style pianoforte to the side of the stage, a jaunty picaresque tune. I was on the verge of returning the lorgnette to Mrs. Haeley when at the blurry extremity of my field of vision I noticed a fellow standing . . . and, yes, waving—at me! I focused on him, a thin fellow with impressive black muttonchops and long, curving mustache, wearing a blue coat with large brass buttons. He was definitely trying to get my attention, and knew he had gotten it. I raised a hand and returned his wave. There was something familiar about him as he smiled and then took his seat.

Mrs. Haeley had noticed the exchange. "Who is he?" She accepted her lorgnette from me.

"I'm afraid I can't place him."

We sat idly for a minute or two while the final patrons took their seats, only a handful of whom joined us in the mezzanine. The pianoforte player suddenly stopped his jocular melody, paused for a long moment, then began a more ominous selection; boy ushers hastily snuffed most of the houselights, which gave the effect of intensifying the stage's flickering footlights. I envied the dramatist that: that a mere alteration in the atmospheric could prime the audience and set their attention in the proper frame. We story-writers have no such facile tricks up our conjuror's sleeve. It occurred to me then—what if our books came wrapped in a picture of some sort, some illustration that would set the reader's mood before he even opened the front cover? I would have to mention it to Murry—right after I mention that I've totally reconceived *Andersen's Romance*, thus requiring its type to be recomposed, totally. I could share my flash of genius about the illustrated wrapping while dodging a torrent of blows and abuses.

A fellow walked out from stage-left. His coat of tails matched the hue of his painted cheeks: two crimson dots like overlarge punctuated periods upon a field of white face powder. With his bold trousers of yellow and black stripes, he appeared the company's clown. "Good evening, good evening, ladies, gentlemen—and you, my fine fellow. . . ." He pointed to a patron in the front row, causing a subtle expression of mirth from the audience. "Welcome to this evening's performance of 'Professor Dunkelraum's Monster and the Maiden's Menace,' just returned from packed houses across Europe. I daresay the company could've stayed in Paris for the rest of their live-long lives, but we believed it was time to bring the show home ..." A smattering of applause, and a rowdy whistle or two. Mrs. Haeley used her lorgnette to observe the master of ceremonies more plainly. "You know the tale of course—or you know parts of it. When it was first come out, the fancy writers at the time said it was—well, hold on . . ." The clown reached inside a coat pocket and removed oversized red-painted spectacles which he then balanced just on the tip of his nose, the way a dottering schoolmaster might, and from the other pocket he brought out newspaper clippings and held one at arm's length. "Let me see, let me see . . . ah yes, one fancypants called Mrs. Haeley's book 'vile' and 'disgusting.' Another, let me see, said it was 'a tissue of filth'—let's see, one more, 'ungodly' and 'morally rep—' what's this? 'morally rep-re-hensible.' That's to say, the fancypants didn't think much of ol' Professor Dunkelraum. Well . . . you know what me and the company says to all that? Them fancypants, they ha'nt seen nothing yet." Larger applause and louder whistles. "So, ladies and gents—and you, sir—may I present our humble show. . . ."

The clown exited stage-left while the fiery-orange curtain was drawn back on each side to reveal what appeared to be part madman's laboratory and part harlot's boudoir. To one side was a long examination table on which, apparently, lay a body—*apparently* because it was beneath a white covering that resembled a lace tablecloth. There were Parisian-style doors at the rear of the set, and flashes of white light indicated an electrical storm was brewing—the warbling roll of thunder came from off-stage. A loud maniacal laugh also erupted off-stage, and another, this one blending aurally with the thunder. Then from stage-right entered Professor Dunkelraum, presumably; knee-breeches and stockings, dun-colored coat atop them, wild white hair, and a face pinched around a monocle.

[Dunkelraum goes to a table where beakers with various colored liquids boil above overlarge flames. He puts on heavy smithy gloves and begins checking the beakers one at a time, holding them to catch the light and examining them with the monocled eye.]

Bertha: [Off-stage] Hans! Hans!? Where are you, Hans? You're not in that creepy old laboratory, are you? Hanzi!? [She pronounces it like "hands" and "handsy." Bertha enters S-R. A young woman, blond, diaphanous white shift that barely reaches her stockinged thighs. Through the shift, one can see that Bertha has much to recommend her as a companion.]

Bertha: Hanzi, I thought you were on your way to bed.

Dunkelraum: [Still focused on the beakers.] I must check on my work. I know you do not understand, my dear, but my man is nearly complete—then I can finally rest. . . .

Bertha: [To audience, disappointed] Who said anything about resting?

Dunkelraum: [Replaces the final beaker to the flame then turns dramatically to the audience.] This is my lifework, Liebchen—all the years of painstaking study and sacrifice . . . come down to this monumental moment. I shall advance the clockwork of science by a century, and future generations shall know the name Hans Dunkelraum as mankind's greatest benefactor.

Bertha: "Dunkelraum the benefactor"—there *is* a ring to it, Hanzi.

[Dunkelraum has been moving toward his creation on the table; he dramatically lifts the lace-fringed cover enough to reveal a cadaverously white hand.]

Dunkelraum: In a moment I shall throw the lever [points to a red lever on the laboratory wall] and my man shall rise from the dead, a modern-day Lazarus.

Bertha: Throw the lever, Hanzi, so we can go to bed—I'm . . . exhausted [winks to the audience].

[Leaving the cadaverous hand revealed, Dunkelraum goes to the red lever—lightning flashes, thunder rumbles—and he throws the lever. Cacophonous thunder, explosions, smoke appears on stage. The white hand begins to move, clenching and unclenching.]

Dunkelraum: I've done it, I've done it, Liebchen! [Kisses Bertha on the cheek, laughs maniacally, exits S-R.]

Bertha: [Curious, moves closer to the monster, still clenching its hand.] So this is the big deal? [Clenching and unclenching her fist, mocking the monster. Suddenly the covering begins to stir. It is being raised in the middle. Up, up, up . . . until the cover looks like a tent with an impressive pole supporting it.]

(*The audience clapped, hooted and whistled at the tent's fabulous raising.*)

[Bertha goes to the table and, cautiously, lifts the cover to peer beneath at the "pole". She looks up at the audience, wide-eyed.]

Bertha: This *is* a big deal.

Dunkelraum: [O-S] Bertha, dearest, are you coming? Liebchen?

Bertha: [Peeks beneath the cover again.] Not just yet, Hanzi, give me a minute. . . .

[From the pianoforte comes a typical music-hall number.]

Bertha: [Singing, and moving coyly about the stage.]

> A brainy man can open the world
> And no mistake I do love me professor
> But let me tell you truly, girls—
> Old Dunkelraum is a little lesser.
>
> A lady needs a gent to hold'er tight
> When a cold storm blows, but remember
> On those other steamy hot nights
> To join the club you need just the right member.
>
> Old Dunkelraum's man may be a monster
> And show no refinements when we eat
> But the Prof's monster is no imposter
> When a lady wants'im to deliver the meat. . . .

At first it sounded as though the actress was being joined by a chorus, singing off-stage perhaps, a touch dissonantly, but it soon became clear that they sang more than contrapuntally—they sang another song entirely.

> The busy tribes of flesh and blood,
> With all their cares and fears,
> Are carried downward by the flood,
> And lost in following years.

The actress playing Bertha, also confused, tried to go on with the number for a few bars, but then the pianoforte halted altogether, after its player, out of reflex no doubt, struggled to find the proper key to accommodate the chorus' song.

I looked to Mrs. Haeley, who used her lorgnette to survey the mounting confusion. The alien hymn continued—"Time, like an ever rolling stream, bears all its sons away. . ."—louder and clearer, and the audience members in the floor-section began standing or turning round in their seats. The confusion was emanating from the rear of the auditorium. Patrons, a few anyway, began to jeer and catcall at the disrupting choir. The singers came forward, finally in view for us in the mezzanine. They came like a cortège, all in black and at a funeral pace. Six, seven, eight, nine—yes, nine choralists. The leader held forth what I determined to be a silver crucifix and a Bible, the crucifix reflecting the stagelights, the Bible absorbing them.

The clownish host had joined Bertha on the stage, and he was attempting to stop the singers or calm the house—but it seemed neither was to be accomplished. The chorus, still singing their dirgical hymn and undeterred, continued their slow but steady march, snaking their way down the righthand aisle, up the steps and onto the stage. They passed within an arm's length of the befuddled pianoforte player, who simply stood and watched the benighted procession.

They stopped in a line on the stage like the Lord's holy warriors, embarked on a new, yet age-old, crusade. I realized that all the singers, about half of whom were women, held a book in their hands—the Geneva Bible or a hymnal I figured. Shoulder to shoulder, they continued their song of protest, having to do their best to be heard above the jeering crowd, some of whom tossed wadded newsprint at the chorus, in lieu of stones or at least rotten fruit. They concluded their hymn amidst the missiles—"The flowers beneath the mower's hand lie withering here 'tis night"—and their leader stepped forward, a gray-bearded fellow in a wide-brimmed black hat.

"Friends and neighbors," he began above the din, "while your flesh may protest, we give your eternal soul great service—sparing you from this vile filth, this wretched corruption. . . ."

I assumed he meant specifically the bawdy play, and he must have too—but I came to realize that he was referring to the book in his hands. He'd been waving it back and forth while speaking, in an effort to shield himself from projectiles I thought. With the word "corruption," however, he opened the book's cover and ripped out its title page. Even from the mezzanine I recognized the illustration facing the title page: it was the well-known (famous would not be overstating it) drawing of Professor Dunkelraum fleeing his laboratory just after bringing his monster to life. The protestors were not bearing Bibles or hymnals. Rather, each had a copy of Mrs. Haeley's book, and they proceeded to tear out its pages with a sort of rapturous glee.

"You see," shouted their leader, torn pages of *Dunkelraum* raining down upon the stage, "you see, my friends, what this sort of corruption breeds—even greater corruption!" He motioned toward the cast, who stood together on the side of the stage watching the improvised spectacle. "Dunkelraum" was calmly smoking a cigarette. The actor playing the monster had given up the charade and was seated on the edge of his table, the fancy white cover on his shoulders like a kingly robe, toying with the "tent pole," a wooden club, in his hands. With the pale face paint and darkened eyes he did seem a fantastic ghoul. A torn page of *Dunkelraum* fell too near a footlight and began to burn. The Professor himself sauntered over and stamped out the miniature blaze.

I turned to Mrs. Haeley, who appeared to be taking it all in like any other theatergoer, and said, "At least one audience member appears to know we are here. If knowledge of your presence were to reach the protestors. . . ."

"Yes" is all she said as she folded her lorgnette and returned it to her dress pocket. There was no emotion in the utterance by which to gauge how she felt about the protestor's harsh words. Not that the attacks would have come as any surprise to her—reviewers had been unkind, to put it mildly, when the novel first appeared seventeen years before. But it's one thing to read a scathing review, and quite another to witness the utter disdain in person.

As we made our way toward the mezzanine exit, I sensed that there was added commotion to the drama on the ground floor, though I was unable to determine its nature. Downstairs the lobby was a scene of great tumult as word of the protest must have spread though the district like an unchecked fire, and a throng of the curious descended upon the Orpheum—no doubt many weren't even certain what they were hoping to see. I noted some gray-suited constables in the frenzied crowd, but it was difficult to say if they were attempting to bring order or were merely inquisitive onlookers themselves. In any case there appeared little hope of our fighting the current and making our way back to the street, and it was unlikely that we could do so in total anonymity. I was about to suggest that we return to the mezzanine and wait out the tempest when I noticed a hand raised above the heads of the crowd, and it seemed to be beckoning to Mrs. Haeley and me. I recognized the wave. My eyes followed the slender-fingered hand to a dingy white cuff, a blue coat sleeve with large brass buttons, finally a padded shoulder and satin collar: yes, it was the fellow who'd caught my lorgnetted gaze before the performance began. There were the unruly hair, long mustache and impressive muttonchops. He was smiling reassuringly and motioning us toward himself, at the far side of the lobby, away from the congested entrance.

Mrs. Haeley did not seem to notice him. I said to her, "This way," but she didn't hear above the uproar. So I took her by the elbow and directed her toward the beckoning fellow, and she didn't resist.

When we reached him, he did not bother to introduce himself above the racket but rather indicated we should follow him, which we did with little hesitation. He was tall and slender, at least a head taller than me, a point that was exaggerated when he donned a silk tophat. He wasn't quite as youthful as I had imagined. From behind I'd noted a balding spot, and his black hair was generously salted in spite of the distinct scent of hair dye. His clothes were well worn, and his boots could have stood a new heeling. His stride however was vigorous and we soon exited the theater via a rear door and were in a suddenly peaceful alleyway.

The alley was quiet but gloomy, illuminated by only a street lantern at a far end and a few candles burning in the upper windows of the building across from the Orpheum. The three of us stood looking at each other in the poor light, seemingly waiting for someone to initiate the dialogue. The tall stranger smiled amidst his muttonchopped face, a gold tooth glinted wanly.

At last I broke the silence: "Your assistance is much appreciated, Mr.—"

He came to animated attention, perhaps even clicking his worn-out heels together. "My apologies—I shouldn't have assumed: Biron Swinford, at your service." The poet bowed.

"Ahh ... Mr. Swinford—no, sir, *my* humblest apologies: I thought I recognized your countenance from the New York literary papers and from your book, which I was just re-reading this very afternoon. Quite lovely." I marveled at the coincidence and mused that such an occurrence would cheapen a literary plot.

"The portraits of which you speak are all quite dated I'm afraid. This is the seventh year of my expatriation on your fair shores." He had turned his attention to the authoress.

"I apologize again. May I present Mrs. Margaret Haeley. . . ."

"It is an honor, madam." He was nearly luminescent with joy in the dim alley.

Mrs. Haeley offered her hand and the poet accepted it gladly, but Mrs. Haeley was silent and I feared that something was amiss. I began to concoct possible excuses, then the authoress spoke:

> "Hummingbird hover'd about its floral house,
> Hover'd there where bees too had been before,
> Supping nectar and vigorous of wing—
> Enigmatical as creatures of lore.

> "Wild bird humming in sweet souled stanzas;
> In aerial flights of fancy fairing
> The scarlet heart plainly for all to see:
> Like the humming bird's soul born for baring."

Mrs. Haeley lingered in her reverie of recitation for a moment, then smiled at Biron Swinford. "Haeley was a great admirer, Mr. Swinford. Had he lived, you no doubt would've had a champion on this side of the Atlantic."

The poet was rendered speechless for a moment. "Thank you,

Mrs. Haeley. I . . . thank you. . . ."

The sound of commotion not far away broke the moment.

"We must get together, Mr. Wheelwright. Mr. Murry is quite insistent on the point."

"Yes, I've lain low long enough I suppose." I thought about the best way for Swinford to contact me. "Send word to the King James Club on Baker Street, sir, let me know how to get in touch with you."

"Splendid," said the poet, still aglow with Stephen Haeley's posthumous admiration. "My horse is liveried a few blocks over, but if you head in the opposite direction of the Orpheum, you should catch a cab in short order."

I must admit it was pleasant to hear an American accent, a Boston accent at that—perhaps entering the American Circle would do me good after all.

We thanked Biron Swinford and watched as his long form departed the darkened alley like an elongated shadow. In fact, with some coaxing, one's fancy might well have seen him as Mrs. Haeley's monster haunting about the shadows. Then we set out on the vague course he'd outlined for us.

"A fortuitous meeting," said Mrs. Haeley. "I have the sense you've been avoiding Mr. Swinford."

"Well, let us say, not eagerly seeking."

In a moment she said, "I understand about tunneling underground and staying put, but I suppose every hare must eventually leave his warren—if only for a few moments in the daylight. . . ."

It seemed there was more she wanted to say but thought better of it, or she lost her train of thought. We'd taken a turn or two in the wickerwork of alleyways, not too concerned about our bearings as long as the tumult of the theater fell astern, but we failed to emerge onto a well-traveled thoroughfare, and in fact the surroundings appeared to grow seedier. I looked to Mrs. Haeley but it was too dark to see if she'd begun to worry. She said nothing and at times was so quiet I wasn't certain she was there beside me at all.

Broken glass and the grit of the City were underfoot.

We at last came to the rear of a building that was fully enlivened. A set of barn-style doors were open to the alley, and lamplight and the sounds of a boisterous crowd spilled generously onto the alleyway bricks. My instinct was to avoid the place but Mrs. Haeley was once again more adventurous. Before we had a chance to exchange a word, she led us into the hullabaloo. The place was quite populated, and it was a motley gathering indeed, with citizens of every stripe represented: common laborers and professional men, rustics and soldiers—and many women too, though they mainly appeared working class. It looked to be an ancient warehouse. In one crowded corner a makeshift bar had been erected with stone blocks and two-by-fours, and "barmaids" were busily distributing drinks in cups and jars and flagons, in whatever could be appropriated for the merriment.

We slowly made our way through the noisy crowd. I wondered at the point of the gathering. Was there to be a spectacle of some sort, a musical performance or a bare-knuckle bout? Or was it simply merrymaking for its own sake? I scanned the room as best I could but only saw a sea of people, laughing, drinking, smoking, trying to make conversation above the clamor. We just about walked headlong into a woman carrying a pint jar, holding it tight in both hands as she attempted to prevent its contents from spilling. "A hay-penny to make hay, darlins?" She cackled at her bit of poetry, revealing a pair of blackened front teeth. She was redheaded but balding as a man would.

I did not understand but Mrs. Haeley reached into her pocket and presented the woman with a halfpenny in exchange for the jar. The woman dropped the copper in an apron pouch, which I could see was bulging heavily with coinage, then she pushed past us, no doubt to resupply herself at the bar.

Mrs. Haeley held the jar to her lips and took a brief swallow. "Gin," she said, handing it to me.

It was a poor idea for me to drink hard liquor but I couldn't resist sharing the moment with the authoress. The gin was green to be sure and burned my gullet on the way down. I was about to return the drink to Mrs. Haeley when there was a bit of rumpus to my right. My first thought was that fisticuffs had broken out but I soon realized there was a stairway, and the hubbub was caused by a large group descending the steps and suddenly mixing in with the already overcrowded throng. A derby-hatted fellow stopped midway on the stairs and called out that the next game would begin in a quarter hour. A new group began pushing toward the stairway. It is difficult to say if we were prodded by the crowd or if Mrs. Haeley deliberately moved us in that direction, but in any case we were about to witness the next game, whatever sport it may be.

I had thought the air of the main floor to be oppressively ripe but we had not quite achieved the upper floor when its unique fetidness assailed our nostrils. Mrs. Haeley batted her hand before her nose as if to shoo away the stench like a noisome gnat. The second storey was less crowded but not by much. It continued the tableau of the lower floor in terms of the mixture of classes and professions; however, the population appeared more heavily male, and the barmaids who circulated gin were younger and handsomer. Grimy lanterns hung from nails on the walls, and I thought how the old building was a perfect firetrap—no doubt the Wheelwright family's unfortunate warehouse fire fueled my observation. The fellow in the derby hat who'd called from the stair now stood up on a box or some such and said to the second-floor party, "Lord Birkdale is a champ to be certain, and I know many of yous come special to see his lordship in action, but sadly Birky's taken ill in the foot . . ."

Some began hissing their disapproval.

". . . I know, I know—trust me, enthus'asts, I share your dis'ppointment. But, the happy news is we've a splendid replacement, do we not, Mr. Cox?"

A burly fellow in a begrimed fisherman's cap stepped from the obscurity of the crowd carrying something in his arms. When he was standing next to the master of ceremonies, Mr. Cox raised up a white and brown terrier holding it mainly by the scruff of its scrawny neck. The wiry little dog was glass-eyed with excitement or anxiety.

The M. C. said, "I give you Herr Dunkelraum, who we believe will earn the stripe of champion every bit as much as Lord Birky—do we not, Mr. Cox?"

Mr. Cox, a fellow of few words apparently, affirmed by raising Herr Dunkelraum above his head and shaking him for theatrical flair.

"Now place your wagers, gentlemen, then on with the match."

A trio of scruffy lads, the eldest of whom was no more than twelve, began circulating through the crowd collecting coins and notes and exchanging them for slips of colored paper, either green or pink. I'd been to enough two-pony races back home to know that the gamers were betting on the terrier (green) to win or his opponent (pink)— perhaps another dog? I looked to Mrs. Haeley and her expression was serenely enigmatic. I offered her the jar of gin and she took it without a word. I had no interest in betting but must admit that my curiosity was piqued.

We moved forward through the crowd and discovered that the M. C. had been standing on the edge of a small oval arena, perhaps twenty feet by ten feet. The walls of the arena rose only about three feet off the badly stained wooden floor but were angled inward so that the terrier or what have you would be hard pressed to climb out. As we watched, the M. C. tossed fresh straw onto the oval's floor, and two men came from the back of the room bearing wooden cages. They set the cages at one end of the oval. It was too dim to see inside the cages, especially from our vantage, but their contents were quite agitated and rattled the cages ominously from within.

Excited anticipation was palpable in the fetid air.

I looked across the oval and immediately noticed, of all things, my hat, or in fact one just like it—the first I'd seen in London other than on my own head. I began to wonder if my hatter was correct about its popularity here, then I realized that it was Lord Chamberlain who was wearing the hat, a dark-gray version thereof, which he'd no doubt gotten from his own hatter using mine as a model. Our eyes suddenly met. He smiled, though he seemed a bit embarrassed to be discovered, and put his finger to the brim of his new headwear in salutation. I returned the gesture. His lordship seemed to have a companion, an older fellow, distinguished enough looking, with a bald pate and metal spectacles with rectangular lenses. On the other hand, he may have been standing near Lord Chamberlain by mere chance.

"I swear, Jeff," said Mrs. Haeley, "you know more people in London than I."

"Mere coincidence," but I fancied the idea of being a well-known man about town in the Old City, a true member of the literati.

"Wager up 'n up," said the M. C.—the trio of young bet-takers had evaporated from the crowd. "Dunkel, if you please, Mr. Cox." The dog's taciturn handler placed him in the oval, opposite from the cages, which now rattled with increased vigor. The little terrier instantly assumed an aggressive posture, the fur on his back raising a bit like a dorsal fin. "Gentlemen, on three," said the M. C. to the lackeys who stood by the cages each had brought to the oval. They undid heavy leather straps that secured the cage doors. "One . . . two . . . three," and the lackeys lifted the doors with military precision:

The rowdy crowd whooped and cheered and whistled as rats, each nearly as large as the terrier, scurried forth from their captivity, four from each cage. Immediately Herr Dunkelraum attacked a rat, clamping his jaws on its neck and giving it a lightning-quick jerk. The other rats meanwhile had run about the little arena in search of a ready exit. Dunkel dispatched a second rat as efficiently as the first and in like manner. Both brown-furred rodents lay on their sides with their tails curled into S shapes and blood trickling from their open mouths—mouths that held teeth sharp enough to remove a man's finger with little trouble.

The remaining half dozen rats, having determined there was no passage out, instinctively switched to another mode of survival and turned their full attention on Herr Dunkel, whose bared teeth and darting eyes searched for the next target. It was a terrible spectacle, but too terrible to turn away from. The rats began weaving in and out of each other's path like a maneuver in which they'd been trained, a maneuver intelligently designed to confuse their attacker. The terrier's head swiveled to and fro as he tried to fix on a single adversary to bring down. One rat, as if sacrificing himself for the greater good, passed close to Dunkel's bloody jaws and the terrier obliged him with his instant death—but in that blink of a moment, two rats attacked the dog's shanks, understanding they must immobilize him to have any chance of killing him.

This set of assaults initiated all out warfare, with the terrier twisting and snapping, and the rats lunging and clawing and scurrying, squeals emanating, rodent and canine alike, blood flowing . . . and when all was said and done in less than a half minute all the rats lay dead and Herr Dunkelraum hopped about on three usable legs, bleeding from at least a dozen deep wounds and holding one eye but partly open.

Though they were mere vermin, the destruction of the rats made me aware of the specter of death that had arrived so easily, evaporating the lives of the rodents as quickly and completely as alcohol disappears from the skin. The simile was true too in that alcohol leaves behind a sensation of cold, as does the visitation of death. Standing next to the authoress I felt the cold shadow of death. Of Death, personified. Earlier I'd said that Haeley's absence accompanied the authoress like a negative space my own self was attempting to occupy—and not wholly successfully—but now I understood it was not negative space at all: it was a space held by Death, as if Mrs. Haeley's silent escort, and I stood in Death's place feeling his cold breath on my shoulders, wearing his gloom like unwanted apparel.

Mr. Cox had taken up the bleeding Herr Dunkelraum in a bloodstained towel, and the lackeys were already at work scooping the dead rats into coal shovels. Mrs. Haeley took a sip of the toxic gin. "I believe one match is quite my limit, Jeff, if you don't mind terribly," and she handed the jar to me.

"I quite agree." I put the jar to my mouth but did little more than moisten my lips. My stomach was turning already and the drink would do nothing to settle its bilious eruption.

The master of ceremonies was calling out the next game as we made our way to the stair. I knew the lanterns were stable on their rusted nails but before my eyes they seemed to dance as if in the hold of a wave-tossed ship. The illusion befuddled my sense of up and down, and even though I recalled that we were on the second storey, I had the feeling that we were *down* already and the staircase would lead us to some subterranean place, to an underworld. I sweated with irrational fear and my knees threatened to buckle as we descended. I held fast to the shaky railing with my free hand to prevent myself from falling altogether. Someone coming up jostled me and I dropped the jar. However it did not break as the rancid gin slopped out. It was no matter as Mrs. Haeley had had her fill of that too.

Finally on the main floor I felt more secure, though the mismatched gathering struck me as a Dante-esque assemblage of lost souls. We hurried from the old edifice, and the alley seemed to possess the freshness of a new-mown field. Clouds had gathered while we were inside and raindrops were falling between the buildings as if from a careful gardener's watering ladle. The drips were warm and heavy but I don't believe either of us minded.

Sixteen

~

W E WALKED IN SILENCE FOR A TIME AND SHORTLY CAME TO a street that had a fair amount of human traffic, though no cabbies were in view. I had no idea where we were in relation to, well, anything. I tried to find a landmark of some sort but the buildings were too tall and the sky too beclouded. I wanted to believe that Mrs. Haeley possessed some native sense of direction so I followed her lead, though she herself appeared to be in an even more distant place. I suspected she was a trifle numbed by the cheap gin. My tongue and throat still seemed coated with the awful stuff.

I was curious if the exhibition we just witnessed was commonplace in London, but I doubted if the authoress had any idea. More and more I sensed that Margaret Haeley neé Townsend had spent her whole life cut off from society—not *uppercrust society*, mind you, but rather society as the normal everyday workings of the world. Perhaps that is why her book had always seemed so otherworldly: it was in fact of her world and not ours. She could have no more written about London and Londoners as I could have written about Tibet and Tibetans.

As if she knew I was thinking of her, she suddenly took my arm as we continued our, seemingly, aimless ramble.

I heard a rig coming along behind us and I turned even though it was too large of a team to be a simple cab. As it halted on the street I instantly recognized the fancy brougham rig and perfectly matched Welsh ponies. The carriage window slid open and Lord Chamberlain's face, mostly in shadow, appeared: "Mr. Wheelwright, may I have the honor of giving you and your companion a ride?"

The rain had increased a degree—and for all practical purpose we were lost—so I said, "It would be most appreciated, your lordship."

Mrs. Haeley said nothing and did not resist as I encouraged her toward the door that had been opened, and the step-up extended. There was another occupant who moved across to sit next to Lord Chamberlain, leaving the authoress and me an open bench. As soon as we were seated, the step was retracted, the door secured, and Lord Chamberlain inquired as to our destination. "Wicker's Lane," I said, which his lordship called out to his driver, and we were off. I was not certain of protocol but assumed the lead:

"Lord Chamberlain, may I introduce Mrs. Margaret Haeley."

"It is an honor, madam." He tipped his hat (my hat, so to speak).

Mrs. Haeley, perhaps a touch too slowly, offered her hand.

Lord Chamberlain turned to his companion: "I believe that you two are already acquainted." It was an ambiguous remark but I believed he meant his companion and I were acquainted.

Lanternlight shone into the carriage for a brief instant reflecting off the rectangular lenses of his spectacles—it was the old fellow who'd been at the rat fight—yet I was sure I'd never seen him before then.

He put out his hand. "A. B. C. Murry, at your service." By his voice I could tell my London publisher was delighted to shock me.

"Mr. Murry," I said, shaking his hand, "at long last."

"Indeed, Mr. Wheelwright."

Perhaps I was merely feeling guilty, but the way he said *indeed* seemed to allude to the overdue proof-pages I owed him. I considered explaining their tardiness but thought better of it, as it was neither the place nor the time. Instead I said, "This has been quite an evening for chance encounters. Earlier I bumped into Mr. Swinford."

Murry said, "How have you been enjoying your English holiday, Mr. Wheelwright?"

"It's been, well, eventful, to be sure."

"He has been a godsend," said the authoress. "I'm afraid I've kept him from his work as I've been a needful hostess."

"Not at all . . ." I wasn't certain how his lordship and Mr. Murry would take Mrs. Haeley's characterization of our time together. As a gentleman I felt obliged to clarify the remark, but I doubted that

Mrs. Haeley wanted her financial woes to be public knowledge. I certainly did not want mine to be: so best to let it lay.

"In truth," said Lord Chamberlain, "our running across you tonight is quite serendipitous. Murry and I were saying at dinner that we need to arrange a reading—perhaps have Mr. Swinford recite some of his newest poems, and, Mr. Wheelwright, you could regale us with a passage or two from your forthcoming book—I'm sorry, what's the title?"

Murry beat me to the punch: "*Andersen's Romance.*"

"Quite . . . a passage or two from *Andersen's Romance*. What do you say?"

What could I say?, but "Yes, that sounds a terrific idea; I'd be delighted."

All was silent a moment, save for the rattling of the carriage and the clopping of the four ponies, then I blurted out, nearly surprising myself, "On one condition though—"

Eyes were difficult to see but I felt three pairs suddenly fixed on me—perhaps even the driver's ears were perked, as were the eight ears of the ponies.

"I would like Mrs. Haeley to read as well, in fact to be our featured reader." I turned to her and said, almost privately, "I'm sorry, Mae, to put you on the spot but I know you've been writing."

"Yes, yes," said Lord Chamberlain, "that'd be quite wonderful . . . Mrs. Haeley, if you would do us the honor. . . ."

Mrs. Haeley was silent for a long moment—I wondered if she were angry, or, worse, if she'd lost her hold on the world—then she said, "I'm sorry, gentlemen, but I am unused to being asked such things. I would be profoundly happy to oblige in joining Mr. Swinford and Mr. Wheelwright in a reading . . . but I do have one unbendable stipulation, and that is that Mr. Wheelwright must have the main spotlight. I won't hear of any other arrangement."

"It's agreed then," said Murry, no doubt salivating at the thought of a new work from the authoress, whose pen had been all but silent seventeen years. "We need to set a date and find a proper venue."

"Regarding the latter," offered Lord Chamberlain, "may I suggest the King James? As club secretary, speaking on behalf of the members, we would be honored to host the event."

The fine carriage rumbled and bumped along the largely empty streets of the Old City, and I felt Mrs. Haeley growing slack at my side. It seemed the adventurous day and evening, not to mention the harsh liquor, had of a sudden overtaken her.

After our agreement regarding the reading, we had all become quiet for a time. It was peaceful and pleasant, with the interior of the carriage smelling of burnishing oil and wax, the way only fine leather upholstery does. I was beginning to feel sleepy too, in spite of the night's invigorating surprises, yet I also felt the need to say something, so I broke the spell of quiet: "Mr. Murry, I want you to know I've been at work on the proof-pages of the book; I've not been disregarding my obligation. . . ."

"That's very good, Mr. Wheelwright," said my publisher, perhaps surprised that I broached the topic directly. I felt I'd made myself into a schoolboy who'd been caught at playing hooky by his master. Nevetheless I felt I should further confess that I'd totally reconceived the book, that I was in the throes of transforming it into an altogether different story from the one he'd purchased more than a year before.

I opened my mouth to speak the words of confession, as if to the village priest, and Mrs. Haeley slumped over onto my shoulder. It was unseemly public behavior for an unmarried man and woman to be sure, and I imagined Lord Chamberlain and Mr. Murry were somewhat taken aback—though they said nothing and the facial expressions I caught in the erratic patches of lanternlight revealed no such reaction. Before I could entertain the notion of coming clean about the book again, we were stopping on Wicker's Lane and I was assisting the authoress from the carriage. Heavy, warm drops of rain continued to fall.

We thanked our benefactors and found our way inside. Miss Edith was immediately there in the foyer lighting a candle and taking Mrs. Haeley by the arm as the lady of the house seemed quite listless with exhaustion. She did manage to tell me goodnight before Edith began helping her upstairs. I figured I would let her get Mrs. Haeley settled before retiring myself to the spare bedroom, so I went to the parlor and lighted a lamp. I shed my coat and hat and unbuttoned my vest.

In spite of my fatigue, meeting Mr. Murry at last and the talk of a reading made me think seriously about my novel revisions. I did not delude myself that I could accomplish much work at the moment—I needed sleep more than anything—but I was inclined to at least look at the sheaf of proof-pages, to commune on some level with my characters and the world I'd created for them, to assure them that I'd not forgotten them and would be returning to them very soon. I took the lamp to the secrétaire; immediately my senses informed me something was altered on the desktop. A tiny bubble of panic emerged as I at first suspected the proof-sheets had been handled and mislain, but quickly, and with no small relief, I discerned that was not the case. What then?

And it came to me: I had left but one book on the desk—Edmund Holland's remarkable *Verses & Vignettes*—and now there were . . . three books in a stack. I examined the two new volumes and they were Mr. Holland's as well, *Things in Mist* and *A Case of Calamity*. How in the world had the other books by the mysterious author been added to the first? I had been meaning to eventually hunt them down, at Bookman & Sons or elsewhere. I randomly flipped through *Things in Mist* and something about the title page caught my attention. I flipped back to it. . . .

It was inscribed—generically, I wondered, like my copy of *Verses & Vignettes*?

I brought the book closer to the lamp and strained to focus my tired eyes:

> *To Mr Wheelwright,*
> *With warmest regards ~*
> *E.H.*

Astonished, I opened to the title page of *A Case of Calamity*:

> *Dear Mr Wheelwright,*
> *With great admiration ~*
> *E.H.*

And *Verses & Vignettes* . . . a postscript had been added to the original generic inscription:

Dear Reader,
With sincere appreciation ~
E.H.

P.S. ~ It is a genuine honor, Mr Wheelwright,
to count you among my readers.

I looked around me at the dark corners of the parlor expecting perhaps Edmund Holland to leap out at me. He had been in this house! Likely in this very room! It was possible that the other two books had been delivered, but he had to have amended the inscription of *Verses & Vignettes*. And then, as if the lamplight were being intensified, I realized that I must surely know "Edmund Holland" already—but who was writing under the nom de plume? Someone in the house? The authoress was the logical choice except she was with me when the books were placed on the desk . . . unless she had a confederate do it, like Thursday. But no, *Verses & Vignettes* was altered, unless that had been done another time and I simply hadn't noticed. Had there been such an opportunity? I could not think of one, but I was having difficulty thinking at all. Who else then? Thursday of course—Mrs. Haeley called him "Eddie" at times, as did his sister. Yet Thursday did not strike me as a writer, though I would have been pressed hard to define how it was that someone *seemed like* a writer. Edmund and Edward were common enough names; maybe it was simple coincidence that Thursday's given name was the same, or nearly the same, as the mysterious author's—who now was even more mysterious! Then someone outside the house? Someone who delivered the books and added the postscript while Mrs. Haeley and I were out. . . . Lord Chamberlain? Carter? More preposterously: Lady Penelope—a "great admirer of Edmund Holland"; or Miss Hilary—perhaps her innocent memoir about her "Nana Mary," the epitome of naïveté, was but a ruse to throw me off Edmund Holland's trail. . . . Or it could have been someone else altogether. After all, The Saint Georges could have given my new address to anybody. . . .

I reread the inscriptions to assure myself I was not hallucinating them, being, after all, in need of sleep. The personalized remarks indeed existed. I wanted to confront Miss Edith or Thursday and get to the bottom of the enigma—in fact I felt my bosom swelling with a sort of mad impatience to know what was what. The lamplight flickered in an unfelt draft, and the wavering light, for some reason, brought me back toward reason: Whoever was Edmund Holland had his (or her) reasons for anonymity, and I must respect those reasons even if I had no means of grasping them. At the same time, I conjectured, the mere detail that the mysterious author(ess) had troubled to present me with autographed books implied that the writer wants to be known, at least to me—and quite possibly to the whole world, having grown tired perhaps of creating art in the gloom of personal obscurity. All artists long to be embraced by their admirers, for their true person to be known and acknowledged as creator of the beloved art, whatever its form.

So it seemed to me, anyway, standing there in Margaret T. Haeley's dim parlor.

I heard someone light of foot descend the old stairs, Miss Edith I presumed, and I let her pass through the foyer and hall unaccosted. The desire *to know* still had hold of me, but sounder reason kept my impassioned query in check. Appropriately, I still had T*hings in Mist* in hand, so I took the slim volume and the lamp upstairs to my room. I wasn't quite sure why I felt the need to keep possession of Mr. Holland's book, almost as if a sort of amulet. In spite of my exhaustion, I suspected that sound sleep may not come easily this night: too much had happened of late, too many strong images had inserted themselves in my imagination—the slaughter of the rats, to name but one—and reading Mr. Holland's subtly powerful prose may just be the necessary antidote to those potent pictures. I hoped of course that such wouldn't be the case.

I readied myself for bed, donning my sleeping-shirt and jacquard robe, and lay atop the covers. The lamp was turned low, too low to read by comfortably, but it was very peaceful to recline there, holding Edmund Holland's book to my breast as if I may open it any second—and it was a possibility. I felt a pang of guilt at wasting the lamp oil but lay thus nevertheless. After a time it came to me that the position of *Things in Mist* was apropos; something was in fact weighing on my heart, the book literally so but something else metaphorically. I considered the feeling: it was akin to loneliness, a sort of homesickness, though that was not it per se. It was like sadness or mourning, yet I was not stricken with grief as it were. I considered further . . . there was a familiarity about the sensation. Stupidly, I removed the book from my breastbone as if it may relieve my heart of the weight it was bearing—again ascribing a sort of magical power to Mr. Holland's words—but of course the physical act had no bearing on the figurative sensation.

Then understanding began to dawn on me, slowly, like a winter sun. The feeling was akin to that which I felt upon Kathy's leaving me, there in front of the apothecary's in Albany. I watched her walk away toward her father's carriage, and each step she took was a brass weight added to the scale of my soul: the further she removed, the heaiver of heart I became. Standing there, while noontime Albanites busily rushed to and fro, I thought that when she went west, as she intended, the physical distance would surely kill me, would surely crush my heart with the ponderous weight of her traveling hundreds of miles into the wilderness.

I obviously survived, and time heals as they say, but deep wounds don't always heal entirely. Scar tissue forms—even disfiguring scar tissue—but the original wound can still seep. I recalled veterans of the Revolution who, twenty years afterward, still bled from musketball holes and saber slashes. Some, too, wore the haunted expression of a wounded soul.

Kathy's carriage rolled away, and I was so deaf with sudden grief I couldn't hear the clop of the horses or the squeaking rattle of the wheels.

This feeling, however, was different: it was more like a phantom sense of loss. It was, I realized, the anticipation of bereavement. My heart had kindled an affection for Mrs. Haeley—a genuine love, not the mere adolescent crush of idol worship—and my head knew there was only one destination for such an attachment: I would be deposited, heavy-hearted, on some path, utterly alone, more solitary than the final summer sunflower faded and bent toward a darkening autumnal sky.

I must have dozed. The scent of smoke from the extinguished lamp, having exhausted the oil, brought me partly round. A sound in the hallway brought me further. I suspected it was Mrs. Haeley on a mid-night writing haunt. I wanted to seek her out but resisted: the authoress deserved her space to create, both her physical space and temporal. I turned on my side in an effort to drift fully to sleep—but a sudden bang startled me . . . Mr. Holland's book, of which I'd forgotten, slid off the bed and struck the floor with surprising force, as if it were more than the paper and ink, cloth cover and binding materials, but the weight of the author's meaning, too, that resounded in the dark, words quite literally laden with meaning.

It was fruitless. I was fully awake now. I listened to the corner of my mind in which the revision of *Andersen's Romance* resided—there was always a sort of burbling from that corner, like a restless child at church whispering in his pew, and I needed simply to turn my inner ear to it for the progression of the story to be distinct. (Of course there were other children, further distant, more discreet, but those stories must wait their turn—paying them all heed serviced none.)

I found my calfskin slippers in the dark and recalled that I had no means of light; the one stubby candle I'd left in the parlor. I took the lamp, with its empty font, and began my way downstairs. I discovered I was becoming quite accustomed to Mrs. Haeley's house and was navigating it with little trouble in pitch blackness. In spite of my best efforts to the contrary, the old stairs wheezed and moaned beneath me, sounding like a laboring giantess in the quiet night.

Downstairs, a bit of light crept into the house, almost as if through the walls, and I located the candle. With its aid I was able to refill the lamp and trim its wick in the kitchen, and thus provided myself with better light by which to work on my novel. While in the kitchen I was watchful of the cellar door, envisioning Mrs. Haeley at work down there. I well knew the configuration of the cellar of course, and that the authoress sat beyond the theatrical curtain in her ornate chair toiling by lamplight at the large table, but I couldn't keep from imagining her in a more fanciful place down there, a sort of fantastic underworld, created and projected by her fertile mind. I also thought of the upcoming reading and was eager to know what the authoress had been writing, perhaps for years. How would one follow a novel like *Dunkelraum*, instantly famous on at least three continents? Perhaps it was that very question that kept her pen silent all this time.

I returned to the parlor with my lamplight, the new oil burning a tad pungently. At the secrétaire I put aside Edmund Holland's books and set the sheaf of proof-pages front and center. I had to gain my bearings so I read my most recent revisions, revising some further, but successfully picking up the scent of the narrative and its new course. Mixing my metaphors, I thought of the plot like that at times—as a ship that must be navigated to the correct destination. I had already completed the sail, nearly two years earlier, but now I'd become dissatisfied with the port city and felt the need to try again, though I was still unsure of the new destination. I thought of Admiral Columbus, who intended to arrive in the West Indies but tripped upon a new world instead.

I took up my favorite pen, its poplar wood worn especially smooth in the familiar places of my thumb and fingers, and dipped the nib into the glass bottle of ink, and continued the revisions. I felt strangely confident of where I was taking the story—or where it was taking me—in spite of the obscurity of the ending.

I had written a good long while when my thoughts were interrupted by hearing Mrs. Haeley emerge from her subterranean den and pass through the hall, as quiet as a rush of air. I thought she might stop in—she surely saw the light in the parlor and knew I was at work—but then I heard her tread up the stairs. I felt a pang of disappointment—and, stupidly, rejection—until I reasoned that she wanted to leave me to my work just as I'd left her.

Having been brought back to the real world by the brief incident, I realized how tired I'd become. Outside I heard the earliest harbingers of the London day, so I finished the thought in which I was midstroke, blew out the lamp, and lay upon the parlor sofa. It had grown cool in the room, but curled inside my jacquard robe I was sufficiently comfortable. My stomach rumbled and my final voluntary thought before sleeping was wondering what fare Miss Edith would produce for our breakfasts.

It was a cadaverous sleep and in the proverbial blink of an eye I awoke to someone's turning the bell-key. . . for a second time, I realized, and further realized it was fully day beyond the parlor's shuttered windows. It seemed no one was going to answer the caller at the door besides me so I got my rusty bones moving and went to the foyer. I straightened my robe and raked my fingers through my hair, as if to make myself presentable. I undid the locks and pulled back the heavy door . . . and was delighted to see Dr. Carter on Mrs. Haeley's stoop.

"Carter—what a wonderful surprise."

"I trust I'm not calling too early. . . ."

"Not a'tall, not a'tall; please come in." He had his red case in hand.

"I thought I should check on my patients."

I shut the door behind him and led him toward the parlor. "That's most kind of you, most kind."

"How's your complaint, Jefferson?" We were in the parlor so I took his hat and placed it on the tree next to mine.

"My feet are much improved. Your prescription of exercise has been on the mark. I've been most active of late, and my feet have bothered me very little—they are more tired than sore."

"Do you feel you would benefit from a bath treatment? I've brought the materials." Carter patted his case.

I was really in no mood. I was hungry and a little impatient feeling, but I said, "You be the judge." So I sat in a wingback chair— the smell of disturbed dust recalled the house's general disuse, at least before my arrival—and I removed my slippers. Carter bent on one knee and examined my feet, poking and kneading as he did on the day of our meeting, and just as then he would glance at my face to see my reaction to each specific prodding.

He was very thorough and finally said, "I quite agree—your ailment is much improved, and I believe we can forego the treatment, unless you feel you'd like—"

"No, no," I said removing my foot from his leg that he was using as an examination table, "I believe we should let well enough be, for now anyway. Thank you."

Carter stood, with a bit of a creaking moan that attested to his middle age, as I reslippered my feet.

At that moment Miss Edith swept into the room, wearing a lavender dress I had not seen previously. "I'm sorry," she said the instant she saw Carter, "I didn't realize a visitor had come. . . ."

"It's quite all right. Dr. Carter, may I present Miss Edith Hill, Thursday's sister."

Carter bowed and said he was pleased to meet her.

Miss Edith was reverent: "Dr. Carter—my brother has told me of your kindness and of your generosity with your expertise. We are both most grateful." She lowered her eyes of storm-gray as she bowed her head.

"Not at all—I am happy to be of service." He smiled within his neatly trimmed beard. "I wanted to check on your brother while I'm here."

"Yes, please—he is in the yard with Mrs. Haeley. Mr. Wheelwright, you slept so soundly we decided not to wake you for breakfast—you must be starving. . . ."

My stomach growled in affirmation, as if a cued thespian, and we all shared a good chuckle at the timing.

She continued, "We have a raspberry tart and tea, and if you like I can fry some eggs. Dr. Carter, won't you join us?"

"I've only had some weak tea at the hotel, so if you're certain it'd be no trouble—"

"None at all," I volunteered, my impatience rearing up a bit. "Please, if you all would excuse me a moment to properly dress."

"Perhaps I may examine Thursday in the meantime," said Carter.

"That sounds perfect," said Miss Edith. "Please, have a seat, doctor, and I will have him come to you while I prepare the tea and eggs."

I went to my room and quickly exchanged my sleeping attire for my gray suit. I chose a purple tie—nearly the same shade as Miss Edith's dress I realized—but forewent a vest in the interest of expediency. Carter and Thursday were just emerging from the parlor as I returned.

"The leg seems to be healing splendidly," said Carter, sounding quite pleased, "a bit of swelling and dermal irritation, but all that is quite expected when a break has been cast. The cut above the eye is coming along too."

We three went to the kitchen, Thursday ahead of us, on crutches of course. The smell of the heated lard for fried eggs was pleasantly strong in the hall, making me recall many a happy Albany morning.

Carter and Thursday went directly to the table, while I walked to the window to spy on Mrs. Haeley in her enclosed yard. My heart fluttered adolescently to see her there, looking composed on her bench of stone, a green-covered book open in hand, a cup and saucer within easy reach. She wore a dove-gray dress beneath the tartan shawl. On the one hand, the authoress was the very picture of serenity, yet there remained an aura of unhappiness—or it may be more accurately described as a highly tenuous happiness. If a dragonfly were to have the complexities of emotion, it would surely feel thus in the awareness that it had but a single day to experience the wonders of living in this world. A single day to know silver ripples upon water, a single day to lift its wings on a pleasing summer breeze, to have the pleasure of kindred companionship. . . .

I joined Carter and Thursday. The raspberry tart, partly served, was in the center of the table. When I was seated, Thursday cut pieces for the good doctor and me, and served them on Mrs. Haeley's chipped china. In a moment, Miss Edith filled our cups with good hot tea, which we sweetened with honey and let cool while she cracked eggs into the iron skillet on the stove. The eggs sizzled and popped in the fat. No one spoke while she deftly managed the eggs by holding onto the skillet handle with the aid of a checkered towel. In no time Edith spooned perfectly cooked eggs, two each, onto Carter's and my plates.

The governess returned the hot skillet to the stove-top then joined us with her own cup of tea.

"Everything looks and smells quite wonderful," said Carter as he sliced into the tart with his fork. Red juice trickled from the tart and pinked some egg white.

It was an understatement; I was suddenly so hungry I had to resist the urge to wolf down the delicious-smelling repast.

Brother and sister, perhaps sensing my appetite, gave us some time to begin eating before initiating a conversation. Edith eventually said, "We've heard of the upcoming reading, and it sounds like a marvelous event."

"Reading?" inquired Carter, a bit of egg yolk dripping from his fork.

"Yes," I said, "by a queer turn of chances, Mrs. Haeley and I met up last night with Lord Chamberlain and my publisher, Mr. Murry—and the punchline of the story is that they are arranging for Mrs. Haeley and me to give a private reading, along with the poet Biron Swinford." I thought of mentioning that we'd met him too, but that would only serve to complicate the tale.

"That *is* marvelous," said Carter. "Where will this reading take place, and when?"

"At your club, as a matter of fact; the exact time is to be determined."

An odd look passed over Carter's face with the news, something like a loss of enthusiasm, like the luster had suddenly worn off the event. Thursday and his sister remained quiet, and I was at a loss to account for the sudden change of tenor. What had I said? Then it came to me—I'm so dimwitted at times: the King James was no doubt a typical club in that it admitted only men, and moreover men of clearly European stock. An exception would be made for the authoress, of course, but it seemed unlikely that Thursday and Edith would be welcome to attend. My feelings about the reading were suddenly dulled too.

I recalled the invitation extended to Mrs. Haeley and me to dine at Arbor-in-the-Glen. Would the proposed reading supersede the dinner, or was it still in force as well? I continued to eat, but mechanically, and I was not enjoying the wholesome breakfast as I should.

The quiet at the table was becoming awkward, and I was certain this was not the desired effect of Miss Edith's comment, so I said, "The tart is most delicious."

She smiled. "Thank you. Would you care for more, Mr. Wheelwright? Doctor?"

Before we could respond, we heard Mrs. Haeley entering through the washroom door. She looked pleased to find us all at the table, though I sensed that her eyes fell unsurely upon Carter, whom she had met but perhaps could not place. I did not want to embarrass either of them by performing an introduction that proved superfluous, so I merely greeted the authoress with a "Good morning," as did Carter.

She prepared herself another cup of tea then joined us by sitting in the remaining chair. Meanwhile Carter and I had finished our eggs and pastry, and we were both, I believe, quite satisfied.

Mrs. Haeley brought the book she'd been reading to the table, as it had been in the pocket of her dress and she removed it while taking her seat. I had to pretend to stretch my neck as if to relieve a crick but I managed to see the title on the narrow binding; it was Stephen Haeley's collection of verse composed in Germany, when he and his young mistress were tramping through Europe. I felt a stab of foolish jealousy but at what precisely I couldn't state. At what she and Haeley shared in their impetuous youth? At her unflagging devotion to Haeley? Or simply at the fact she was reading Haeley's poetry—which she undoubtedly knew by heart—and not my *Sketches*? I assured myself of my silliness and drank from my teacup, whose contents had grown cool.

Dr. Carter spoke up: "I am pleased to report that Thursday appears to be mending with avidity."

"That is quite wonderful news," said the authoress, smiling briefly toward Thursday before taking a careful sip of tea. She seemed distracted, and I wondered that perhaps she were still occupied with whatever thought she'd entertained in the solitude of her yard. Perhaps reading Haeley's familiar poetry had started her slipping into the ghostworld of the past. I felt again that pang of phantom loss, a sort of premonition of bereavement.

We were all quiet for a moment or two before Mrs. Haeley said, "I have been thinking about the proposed reading, and I wonder at its location. I have no doubt the King James is a fine old club and would be an elegant setting, but. . . ." She looked to me as if it were due to my feelings that she was treading hesitantly.

"But you have reservations?" I offered.

"Not precisely. . . ." She placed her hand on Haeley's book, absentmindedly it seemed. "This house, you see, used to be a gathering place for poets and writers, artists and philosophers, really intellectuals of all stripes; it was a buzzing hive of creativity, of creative minds. I know it may be difficult to picture now, but there was a brief time. . . ." She patted the clothbound book—it appeared that she must have been attempting to connect with Haeley's spirit, or even to summon the dead poet. The authoress continued, "I've been thinking, I would like for this old house to perform that role again, if only in pale mimicry of its former self."

I felt I should say something but sat there dumbly for too long, and Mrs. Haeley went on, "It is really your evening though, Jefferson, and I don't want to capture your king as it were."

"No, no—that's not at issue at all." I thought for a moment but knew not how to articulate what I was feeling.

Mrs. Haeley said, "I know, I know—I am not blind to the fact that the place has grown shabby, but maybe we can put things a bit more in order." She was addressing Miss Edith in particular.

"Absolutely," said the governess.

"What do you think, Jefferson? Would it offend Lord Chamberlain, do you think? Or put-off your publisher? We would be sure to make it clear that the club members are most welcome here."

I looked to Carter, who knew his lordship far better than I, and he seemed to express no objections. The change of venue would also afford Thursday and Edith an opportunity to attend the reading— which I suspected was Mrs. Haeley's true design. "It sounds quite ideal. Thank you for opening your home." Nevertheless I thought of the dusty furniture and the unwaxed floors, and of the walls' dark rectangles of sold-off paintings; and I pondered how much order could be brought to the chaos. "I will see about contacting Lord Chamberlain and Mr. Murry," I said, and the authoress seemed pleased, which was becoming increasingly important to me.

Seventeen

~

A T FIRST EVERYONE PITCHED IN TO READY MRS. HAELEY'S house for the reading. Luckily Miss Edith possessed a keen sense of organization and quickly authored a masterplan. It soon became clear, however, that the lion's share of the labor was going to fall to Miss Edith herself. Thursday of course was of limited use due to his leg; the authoress was too frail in general to do much in the way of scrubbing, dusting and waxing; and I was so unused to such occupations my efforts tended to be more hindrance than help. Besides, Mrs. Haeley and I still had much to do to prepare for the private reading—a private reading that would be presented for the most part to perfect strangers . . . and perfect *influential* strangers at that. Moreover, I had even yet to decide what portion of *Andersen's Romance* I would read.

Miss Edith, who was beginning to show signs of stress at having to make ready the old house, in essence singlehandedly, had sat her brother to the tedious task of polishing silverware in the kitchen, while I had been directed to carry rugs to the yard to be beaten. I was beginning to perspire at the exertion and quite frankly I longed to return to work on my rewriting. Further frankness: I was mildly annoyed at having to disrupt the physical space of my rework of *Andersen's*. That is to say, I'd overtaken the parlor for my own writer's den—first the secrétaire, then the sofa and café table, and the floor space throughout—with stacks of proof-pages laid systematically hither and yon, though granted it was a system only I could decipher with ease (relative ease). Now, however, the parlor would be cleaned and I would be forced to uproot my working area. To me it represented more than an inconvenience: the lay of the revised pages in the room was tied to the narrative's shifting landscape in my mind. Hence disturbing the stacks of pages, shuffling their arrangement somehow or other, was tantamount to someone's striking me in the head with a plank and thus jumbling my wits. I knew that I could reestablish a system of work elsewhere (or else*when*)—after all, I'd begun the process in the well-appointed room of The Saint Georges—but whether I could recreate the precise system (that is, carry through with the reworkings as I had begun to envision them)—well, that was another matter entirely.

As such I felt a twinge of envy at Mrs. Haeley's having an undisturbed den, dank and dark though it was.

I had deposited a rug in the yard (to be beaten by whom it wasn't precisely clear) and was returning to the music-room for another when the bell-key chimed in the foyer. I was available to answer so I did, and found three women of varying ages and physiognomies. Their leader, a fortyish woman who introduced herself as Marie, explained that they'd been hired to assist with the housework at this address. Their services had been paid in advance, said Marie. It had to be Carter, I thought. After our late breakfast, the good doctor had kindly volunteered to take a note to Lord Chamberlain at their club regarding the change in venue for the reading. Patient Carter had waited in the parlor while I composed the delicate missive.

I showed in the trio of charwomen and took them to Miss Edith, who was in the washroom preparing to heat a tub of water. Miss Edith considered the dynamics of the new workforce for a moment, then gave each of them directions. I stood by the washroom door, and I sensed that the women would have preferred taking the instructions from me, but (fresh coins in their purses) they set to work tout de suite.

I meanwhile gathered my proof-pages and instruments of inditement and went to the spare bedroom upstairs. There was the room's small desk, smaller even than the parlor's secrétaire, and I attempted to work there for a time but soon found the bed to be a more productive site. I missed my enormous bed at The Saint Georges and I wondered briefly if I would ever know such luxury again. I pushed the unproductive thought from my mind and forced myself to concentrate on the proof-pages. I had reworked about two thirds of the novel but it was the final third that was the most challenging: bringing the various threads of the story together in a way that not only made sense but also pleased the reader emotionally. I realized my sense of readerly pleasure had also been altered by Edmund Holland. Before reading him I believed that there were two possible endings for a story: happy or sad (a wedding or a funeral, as it were)—and I was a great believer in the happy ending. However, Edmund Holland's writing introduced me to a third possibility, which in fact could be an infinite multitude: that is, an ending that is ambiguous—a conclusion that is neither happy nor sad; rather a conclusion in which happiness or sadness is no longer the point. True, I had only read *Verses & Vignettes* in its entirety, but all of Mr. Holland's language walked this saber's edge of emotional truth. That's not to say that his prose was muddy, not at all. His language itself was always crystalline in its clarity, but beneath the precision lay myriad competing emotional subtleties for the reader.

I worked for some time on my revisions, though by work I often mean simply thinking about the story and its characters, and toying with words. In fact, one thought in particular began imposing itself on my conscious mind—it was that tune, the one I'd gracelessly played on Mrs. Haeley's out-of-tune pianoforte: the Schlözer piece, "Junges Deutschland" . . . the mournful notes sounded again and again in my brain. I tried to blot out the spectral melody but could not. My fingers recalled each chord as it was struck, thus palseying them from writing.

This torment went on some time . . . until I realized the music was not a memory that continually replayed in my skull, but rather someone was actually playing "Young Germany" in the music-room, and the song's sad melody was reverberating and twisting through the wooden bones of the old house. There was no way to blot it out, and I had to accept I was finished revising for the time being.

I organized the proof-pages then went downstairs, where a miraculous transformation had occurred, or rather was still occurring. The three charwomen, together with Miss Edith's hands-on management, had brought the house from something like a place abandoned to a tidy and even cheerful home. Refreshing scents like lavender-infused soap and lemony wax replaced the stale dust and mildew to which I'd become accustomed. I poked my head in the music-room, where Mrs. Haeley sat at the pianoforte playing "Junges Deutschland" almost absentmindedly, over and over it seemed. The tempo was so slowed in her reverie, however, an only semi-alert listener might not have even realized he was hearing the same melody repeated.

The authoress appeared quite oblivious to the dusting and window-washing going on in the room, which I presumed would be the precise site of the reading.

I was beginning to wonder what to do with myself, and was even considering a solitary stroll, when the bell-key was rang. I made myself of use and answered the caller. Once again I was surprised to see Miss Hilary Chamberlain there.

"Mr. Wheelwright, does no one porter the door here but you, sir?" Miss Hilary smiled like sunshine.

"It is my special talent, m'lady. Won't you come inside." I noticed in the street a second rig behind the fine carriage of the Chamberlains.

"I am on a special errand myself," said Miss Hilary, still smiling beneath a fashionable lavender bonnet.

"Yes?"

"I understand there may be some walls that are a bit bare. We have several beautiful pieces in storage—my parents are such rabid collectors—it's a shame that the art spends most of its time undercover in a dark cabinet. Do you think Mrs. Haeley would mind displaying some of the pieces for us?"

I thought of the authoress's far-away expression as she sat at the pianoforte—she may never even realize pictures had been hung. "I suspect she wouldn't mind at all. Please," I said, inviting Miss Hilary and her men inside with a wave of my hand.

Thus began a parade of workers carrying paintings of various shapes and dimensions, plus some bronze statuary and the like. I introduced Miss Hilary to Thursday's sister, who was quite content to have the new arrival orchestrate the distribution of art. The walls had been wiped clean but there'd been no time to scrub them with the vigor they required, so dark rectangles remained. Miss Hilary chose pieces that would hide the unseemly patches, also giving thought to the subject and composition of the paintings. At times she would ask my opinion—"Venetian port at sunset, or Hungarian peasant woman with dog? What do you think, Mr. Wheelwright?"—and the men holding the art would position each in its turn to facilitate the decision. Once a choice had been made (more often than not she kindly went with my recommendation), a pair of fellows with hammers and nails and wire and such would secure the piece to the wall so that it was perfectly positioned. I had never considered the craftsmanship of picture-hanging; in my family home, paintings appeared on the walls as if by magic, or so it seemed to disinterested me.

As we moved about the house placing artwork it occurred to me that I should ask Miss Hilary to read her "Nana Marie" vignette or some other ditty at the literary reading—the gesture would no doubt be well received by Lord and Lady Chamberlain—but an idea that was forming prevented me. I had a vague notion that I wanted to leave space in the program for Edmund Holland—that by leaving room for him, he would be drawn out and become known to us. I felt a bit like a spiritualist who planned to call forth someone's dearly departed through an occult practice. Yes, should Edmund Holland actually appear it would be akin to an act of witchery.

The paintings were hung and various statuettes placed here and there; and I must say the works of art did bring the old house back from the dead, or at least they served as the undertaker's cosmetics to make the cadaver appear less cadaverous. At some point Mrs. Haeley had quitted the pianoforte and disappeared. After Miss Hilary's departure, I learned from Thursday that the authoress had gone to the cellar (to work on her manuscript presumably). An afternoon writing session? It seemed out of character. Yet Mrs. Haeley's underground den was so morose, in a sense it always cast the impression of darkest midnight.

Thursday and I sat in the now cheerful music-room and read—I the collection of Scottish and Welsh folktales, he a biography of Flemish painters—while Edith and the charwomen completed their work in the house. Eventually I heard Miss Edith let them out the front door, giving them her sincere thank-you, then she too disappeared. Edith was no doubt exhausted and wanted to rest before supper. There was a small dayroom, intended for hired help but likely unused for years, which one accessed from the washroom, and Miss Edith had taken it for her own upon arrival. Upstairs there were two other rooms in addition to Mrs. Haeley's and the one I was occupying, but I had no idea what condition they were in; and, besides, in the dayroom Miss Edith was close to her brother should he need anything in the night.

After a while the bell-key rang, and it was a messenger with a note from Lord Chamberlain fixing Friday evening—two days hence—as the time of the reading. I doubted I would complete my revisions in the interval, but I must at least decide what to read from *Andersen's Romance*; also I must give some thought to smoking out Edmund Holland, who had acquired a kind of mythic aspect in my imagination. Should he materialize the effect would be as if I'd conjured the Bard himself from his holy crypt. In the foyer, I noticed that the stacks and stacks of books were still against the walls, but they had been dusted and straightened so that they had an almost military precision. They truly looked like columns that were supporting the very frame of the house, as if slipping one volume out of order might threaten to bury us occupants in the ruins of Mrs. Haeley's home.

Eighteen

⁓

THE NEXT DAY IT WAS DECIDED THAT I SHOULD ACCOMPANY Thursday and Miss Edith on an outing in the City. Thursday was feeling fit enough that his confinement was beginning to weigh upon him; and Edith, too, needed a holiday from domestic responsibilities. Mrs. Haeley meanwhile was a woman possessed: she suddenly seemed determined to complete whatever she'd been writing. Perhaps the opportunity to read for Murry and other literary enthusiasts made real for her the possibility of publishing another book, whereas her publication of *Dunkelraum* must have become something like the memory of a long-ago dream, its reception by the public was so varied, and its absorption into the very fiber of English culture so complete—almost as if the island nation itself spawned it—it was perhaps easy for her to lose sight of the fact that she, Margaret T. Haeley, was indeed the story's authoress, that it had sprung forth from her own inspired fancy. Whatever the explanation, Mrs. Haeley remained sequestered in her den most of the night, not even ascending for a wholesome supper of bean soup and bread pudding; rather, Miss Edith took the determined authoress some of the sustenance along with tea when it became clear she would not be joining us. We assumed she stopped long enough to eat.

About mid-morning Thursday, Edith and I outfitted ourselves for an excursion into the City. Edith wore her dove-gray dress with black lace trim, and a coordinating bonnet. Thursday appeared to own only workaday clothing. He had on the pair of trousers that had had one leg cut off at the knee to accommodate the plaster-of-Paris cast, and they had not been even moderately laundered since their re-tailoring. He also wore a European-style cotton shirt and a jacket of heavy "duck" cloth similar to what seafaring men wear and can therefore be seen by the hundreds on any wharf in the world. I in my fine fawn-brown suit with the matching hat which had been slightly battered in the Heiress Presumptive's celebration riot—well, I daresay we made an odd trio.

I had Thursday and Miss Edith wait in front of Mrs. Haeley's house while I walked up to a busier street and secured us a cab. In no time we were headed to the heart of the Old City. I was planning on having the Hills act as guides and direct our excursion, but I soon learnt that London was just as strange to them as it was to me. Thursday had been in the City more than a year, he explained, but had confined himself mainly to Mrs. Haeley's immediate neighborhood—my sense of his relationship to the authoress was forever changing but never clarifying. Miss Edith knew the City even less so. Hence I directed the cabby to the Museum of Natural History, an area I at least knew a little.

It was a strangely clear day, and in fact the air was even a touch autumnal—I must say it caused in me a subtle pang of homesickness for my New England. The feeling soon passed, and I was looking forward to showing off the Museum grounds to Thursday and his sister, just as if I were an Old Londoner. We spoke very little during the ride, each I think enjoying the hum and bustle of the ancient City. It occurred to me that almost every time I'd ventured out in the City I'd encountered the waif, "Miss Organdy," and I wondered if she would appear somewhere today. I recalled the half-told tales I'd come to associate with the waif—even Mrs. Haeley's and my ride on the Velociquad ended prematurely, now that I thought of it—and I wondered if their tellings would ever be complete.

We were deposited at the very spot where Mrs. Haeley and I had been just two days before. Miss Edith and I assisted her brother from the cab, and then Miss Edith paid the cabby, in spite of my insistences to the contrary. We looked to the grounds of the Museum, and it seemed about as busy as on my previous visit. Yet, due to the radiant day, the place had a quite different aspect. Sunshine made the lawn more verdant, the path of crushed stone more brilliantly white—the difference between a pale water-color rendering and one done in bold oils.

"Are you feeling up to a stroll?" I asked Thursday, but both brother and sister answered "Quite so" and in such perfect unison that it made us laugh.

With Thursday between us on his crutches, of which he'd become an extreme proficient, we entered the grounds through the tall iron gates. Immediately I was handed an advertisement by a gentleman in a brown suitcoat and beige trousers:

~ Demonstration ~

Of Mr. Watson's Amazing

House-Sized

CAMERA OBSCURA

'See the Past through the Future – in the Present'

. . .

The device was located on the grounds near the Orphic Fountain, it said as I read aloud to my companions, strolling with our leisurely gait. There was an artist's rendering of a hexagonal structure.

"Sounds fascinating," said Thursday. I had not seen him looking so, well, alive. It was as if his many months spent in Mrs. Haeley's house of mourning had taken him toward the grave, and now, from under the place's influence, his vitality was returning. I wondered if I too were being drained in some similar manner . . . no, if anything my encounter with the great authoress and my staying under her roof had energized my creativity. I realized then that I feared to some degree that when I separated from Mrs. Haeley her influence would be lost forever, and I would return to my old self, with my sad wit of mediocrity by comparison.

We followed the path toward the fountain and saw the gathering for the camera obscura long before we reached it. Twenty or thirty people, mostly men, a few women and children, stood in a straight line receding from a hexagonal structure the size of a garden house.

Flanking the camera obscura were tall framed curtains, so that one could not see around the sides of the structure; that is to say, whatever was going on in the focal front of the camera obscura was hidden from view until we were actually inside the dark chamber. I knew the principle of the device from my schooldays: it had a lens in one side, and whatever the scene was before the lens was projected, upside down I recollected, on the opposite side. I'd read of camera obscurae that were large enough to enter but I had never experienced such a device, not even in New York City, a place where seemingly a man could experience anything he wished.

As we took our places in the line, directed by a pair of adolescent assistants who made sure we were in a single file, I saw that the door to enter the camera obscura was on a side of the hexagon not directly opposite the focal lens, apparently. Besides opening a narrow door to enter, one had to pull aside a blackout curtain as well. I realized too that the visitors to the camera obscura must have been exiting via another door on the other side of the flanking curtains. The line moved with some vigor as each group of visitors was only allowed two or three minutes inside.

It would be interesting to be inside the device—the promoters wisely *obscured* the subject of the *camera* so, if nothing else, one's curiosity was piqued as to what exactly one would see—but beyond that the camera obscura held little fascination for me. Throughout the centuries it'd been used chiefly by artists, to aid in their achieving realistic detail in their drawings and so forth. I recalled that a sheet of paper could be secured on the side opposite the lens, and the artist could then trace the projected image with precision on the paper, upside down of course, but then the drawing could be righted and ... voila!

A few more visitors entered the camera obscura, and the line crept forward. Another dozen or so people had come behind us, including a pair of towheaded children, brother and sister presumably, who were in a gleeful dither about entering the chamber. Their mother or nanny had her task cut out to keep her charges reasonably quiet and calm while they waited, with their proverbial pants filled with ants. I might have offered to let them go ahead of us, but there was poor Thursday on his crutches and one sound leg—I needn't prolong his time in the line. It was a lovely day, but out in the open the sun was bright and a touch overwarm. Miss Edith had had the presence of mind to bring a parasol, and she kept it raised altruistically above her brother, in spite of his insistence to the contrary.

I continued to muse while I waited. Perhaps my brains were beginning a slow simmer beneath my sun-heated hat, and I thought that the camera obscura may not just be a useful device to the artist of line and ink . . . I mused especially about the small lens that amplified the focal image. Was this not the "trick" of Edmund Holland? Did the author not direct the reader's attention to specific and fine details that in turn amplified some larger picture of character or scene or setting? My mind raced through a catalogue of examples from Mr. Holland's work—the seahorse that "flitted and flirted" through the blades of seagrass, the bed of which was the final resting place for the lover's drowned corpse; the strand of waist-long flaxen hair that caught in the eyelash of the bereaved bride-to-be; the "copperheaded" worm that poked from the skin of the poisoned pear—yes, these images were revealed via a carefully cut lens that in turn projected them larger than life to the mind's eye, transforming the reader's skull, I concluded, into the darkened chamber of the camera obscura.

My imagination wandered further: What if a playwright could perform the same sort of narrative trickery? What if he could somehow direct the audience's attention to some minute detail on the stage and transform that impish grin, that signet ring, that blood-splashed sash into a grand image before the audience's collective eye? It was pure fantasy of course, and fortunately our turn in the camera obscura arrived before I could make myself totally ridiculous.

We were ushered into the wooden structure, which smelled of pine and pitch, and for a moment there was enough daylight to discern its simple walls and plain planked floor. A pair of middle-aged gentlemen, men of business it would seem, entered the camera obscura too, and the five of us were instructed by a young assistant to "move round the center of the chamber." His point became clear the instant the curtain and door were closed: on the floor, at the exact center, was painted a white circle onto which a scene appeared. As my eyes adjusted and I positioned myself properly, I could tell that it was two young actors performing a drama—but how in the world did it materialize *on the floor* of the device? One of the businessmen inadvertently stepped into the beam of light that streamed into the chamber and the scene was interrupted for a second or two until he realized his faux pas and moved aside with general apologies to the group. At the rear of the chamber the stream of light encountered a mirror that was angled heavenward . . . I would not have sufficient time to figure the workings of this camera obscura fully. . . .

Hence I turned my attention to the true wonder: the moving scene that appeared, almost it seemed, by magic at our feet. The clarity of the picture was remarkable. There were two young actors dressed in the trappings of Elizabeth's England—a teenage boy and girl, he in doublet and ruff, she in conical cap with trailing gossamer veil; he spoke imploringly from bended knee, she was somewhat elevated on a platform draped in green velvet—but there were no words to be heard, it was a dumbshow. She peered down from her slight perch with amorous gaze. . . . Of course! How could I be such a dimwit? It was Romeo and Juliet, in the Capulet garden. Just as it came to me I heard Miss Edith whisper to her brother, "What man art thou that, thus bescreened in night, so stumblest on my counsel?" to which Thursday replied, "By a name I know not how to tell thee who I am." Brother and sister were conspiratorially delighted at recalling the dramatic exchange.

One of the businessmen placed his clenched hand above the circle, disrupting the scene with an exact shadow of his fist and sleeve, and Romeo's face flashed briefly on the man's white cuff; indeed, there seemed something familiar about the angle of the actor's jawline, and the cocksure way he held his head when delivering a line. Before I could contemplate further, however, the exiting door was opened and we were shown out into bright sunlight. It was good to be in the fresh air as the chamber had quickly become oppressive. I shaded my eyes beyond the brim of my hat and attempted to achieve a better view of the young thespians as we were directed away from the camera obscura. I thought my bedazzled eyes were playing a hoax: Could it really be? The "actor" portraying Romeo was the waif, Miss Organdy. When I saw her face three-quarters on and not solely in profile, I knew it to be true: what an appropriate twist on the Bard's life and times on the London stage—a boyish girl playing a moonstruck boy. I tried to see if Juliet were perhaps a boy acting as a girl—true to Shakespeare's day—but I only spied her-him from behind now and couldn't determine one way or the other.

As we removed from the area of the camera obscura our pace was slowed with distinction—Thursday must have been growing weary on his crutches. After all, though he'd mastered them, the poor fellow had only used them to travel from room to room in Mrs. Haeley's house. For that matter, I was a bit fagged myself, now that I thought of it. As fair fortune would arrange it, not far from the Orphic Fountain we happened upon some tents and tables that had been set up, and peddlers with pushcarts were selling their wares. We sat Thursday upon a bench, and he immediately began fanning himself with his hat. I told Miss Edith to rest herself as well, and went to a pushcart vendor for some refreshments. In a moment I returned with three steins of cider, a wedge of cheddar that the peddler had divided into thirds, and a large sprig of grapes that were so purple they almost appeared ebon.

Thursday and his sister were most appreciative. Miss Edith at first insisted that she pay for their share from her small beaded purse, but I wouldn't hear of it. I was unused to pecuniary worries and had difficulty grasping their full weight. We took a moment to enjoy the repast in silence. All three of us were more than content to watch the many visitors coming and going at the tents. After a time, though, I felt compelled to take advantage of our leisure to gain further intelligence regarding the authoress and her situation. I said, "I've been curious, Thursday, about how Mrs. Haeley has been sustaining herself; clearly the house, for example, has been neglected for some time."

I anticipated that Thursday would be somewhat surprised by the inquiry, but he didn't appear to be; maybe he'd been expecting such a line. "It has been a struggle since her husband's death," he began, watching the cider in his cup. "After several petitions, the Haeley family granted her a small allowance, in exchange for her having no contact with her stepson, and in recognition of her desire to keep Stephen Haeley's poetry in the public's awareness. She had been writing reviews, anonymously, for the literary papers that provided some income. But, because of her . . . condition, she has been unable to write for many months." When Thursday had looked up from his drink, his face made it clear that what he was telling me was in strictest confidence. I let him know that I understood.

The moment was concluded when we all three noticed a young juggler in a red and white striped shirt as he kept three, then four, then five pins turning through the air; he'd placed his hat on the ground, and grateful passers-by would deposit a coin or two with a resounding *clink*.

Perhaps because I was deep in the throes of revising *Andersen's Romance*, but whatever the reason, nearly everything seemed to me a metaphor for writing, and the juggler was certainly no exception. The juggler's task and the storyteller's were similar in that the spinning pins were like pieces of the plot that must be kept in motion at all times, and their movement must appear effortless to the reader; and if the juggler were to miss one, likely they would all come tumbling to God's green earth. At the very least, the audience would become aware of the pins' movements and be so focused on them they couldn't enjoy the juggler's trickery. I was thinking of milking the metaphor further when, without forewarning, the juggler tossed a pin toward the crowd that had gathered to watch his performance. A fellow in a brown corduroy jacket caught the pin on reflex and stood gazing at it in a most surprised manner—to the general delight of the audience, who applauded and whistled at his feline reaction. The young juggler, now down to four pins, threw another at the same fellow, who caught it with his other hand—now the crowd cheered heartily. The fellow in brown corduroy, who seemed to be in his thirties and who wore a slouch hat tilted somewhat dandily, appeared dumbfounded for a moment.

We spectators, staring from either the tents or from a group standing in loose formation near our tent, were eager to know what would happen next. I must admit I was quite surprised when the fellow in brown tossed a pin toward the juggler, who managed to absorb it into the orbit of his routine, but awkwardly for a moment before regaining his rhythm. The fellow suddenly sprouted a mischievous grin on his countenance. He looked round to his fellow spectators for approval and was quick to receive it: he underhanded the fifth pin at the juggler, who'd been wearing a face of worry, but the young man handled the returned pin with aplomb. Miss Edith and Thursday applauded his feat.

Then the juggler again tossed a pin to the fellow in the crowd, who immediately threw it back . . . then there was another exchange . . . and another . . . then it became clear and I heard Thursday say it aloud: "Accomplices." The fellow in brown corduroy and slouch hat was a trained juggler too. He maneuvered himself away from the crowd so that the two of them were now the center of our attention as they juggled the pins back and forth with awesome speed. Another accomplice stepped from the crowd, a mere boy in green plaid jacket and knee-length breeches, and joined the juggling duo. The boy carried a pair of pins in each hand, and he went about adding these one at a time to the five already in elliptical flight. The jugglers had to move farther and farther apart, and toss the pins in higher and higher arcs to accommodate the growing number of projectiles. The zeniths of the arcs were such that we could not see them from our vantage inside the tent.

The mounting intensity of the routine wore on the tricksters, one could tell, but they persisted. Meanwhile, their boy assistant had picked up the first juggler's hat and was circulating amongst the crowd for further remunerations. In addition to coins, I saw that gentlemen were beginning to deposit notes as well, pound-notes I presumed. The lad came into our tent, and Miss Edith took three pennies from her purse and dropped them one by one into the hat, which had become bulky with people's generosity. I was loath to give the boy a note as he passed by me but the only coinage I had were a pair of haypennies—not wishing to be seen as a joyless spendthrift, I put a folded pound-note in the kitty after all. I looked to see if Thursday or his sister had noticed my magnanimity but their attentions had returned to the jugglers, who now would've had to raise their voices to one another to have a conversation. I felt some envy toward the boy and his cumbersome hat: perhaps I could learn some circus trick and line my pockets but good as a journeyman performer: perhaps I could learn to swallow a sword, or to contort my body into a Bavarian pretzel. . . .

Something had happened and the crowd was showing its wonderstruck approval. The second juggler—the accomplice in the brown corduroy jacket—was taking on more and more of the burden of keeping the pins aloft. He juggled three with his right hand while continuing to exchange pins with his partner in red and white stripes. Now, in a lightning flash, he added a fourth pin to his one-handed routine; now a fifth . . . then in a shift almost too subtle to notice, the accomplice stopped returning the pins to his partner, the original juggler, but rather added them as they arrived to the set he was now juggling with his left hand, until he quickly had all nine pins in his possession, apparently tossing them at a great height above his head to maintain his rhythm. It was truly amazing, almost beyond belief if I were not witnessing it with my own eyes.

So, I thought, the accomplice, who appeared a mere stranger in the curious crowd, is in fact the master; and the garish-shirted fellow is the protégé.

The master-juggler, who must have been near exhaustion, concluded his routine by tossing off the pins one at a time to the protégé, now standing a few feet in front of him. Soon the master was down to the original three pins, which he caught himself to bring the incredible routine to its conclusion. He bowed deeply as the crowd erupted into applause and ecstatic shouts. Those of us seated in the tents got to our feet in ovation. Thursday's sister helped him to stand so he could show his full appreciation as well.

The jugglers and their assistant absconded with their well-earned booty, and the three of us returned our attentions to the simple repast. Thursday appeared much improved but there was no point in tiring him further. I had an idea how we might continue our City ramble without overtaxing his slight and mending frame. We exchanged a few remarks about the juggling act and various pedestrians that happened into our field of view while we finished the cheese and grapes; then I led our contented band to the street to find a cab, which we managed with little trouble. While Miss Edith and Thursday took their seats, I spoke to the cabby for I was unsure of my desired destination. He said he knew the way I described, so I joined the siblings and we were off.

"To where are you kidnapping us, Mr. Wheelwright?" said Miss Edith, obviously delighted at the mystery.

"You shall see, dear lady."

"Let us not spoil Mr. Wheelwright's fun," said Thursday, happy also to be sharing the puzzle.

The cabby took several turns through the congested London streets, and I began to wonder if he truly knew the way . . . but soon he was entering the edenic setting of Haslow Park, and my companions were as thrilled and surprised as I had hoped. I tapped on the cab's top so that the driver would slow his mare's gait—our objective after all was not to rush through this oasis of natural wonder. Thursday and Miss Edith were captivated by the park's sylvan beauty. They looked with wonder at the verdant forest, at the wildflowers that carpeted the forest floor, and they must have been in awe too of the vibrant birdsong. At the cab's slow pace its wheels barely interfered with the avian chorus. When one is in the City too long, one can grow forgetful of this other world, this older world. One can begin to believe that life is constructed entirely of bricks and planks, is held together with mortar and rusted nails. I thought of Margaret Townsend and her reckless poet, Haeley, escaping the mortared conventions of City society and flying into the wilds of Europe, freeing their imaginations perhaps as much as their impassioned souls.

But then I wondered if my thesis were in error, as coming to the Old City had enlivened my Muse—no, it was not the City at all but rather my proximity to the authoress and my reading of Edmund Holland. Perhaps this also accounted for Mrs. Haeley's taking refuge in her house and staying put since Haeley's death; it was as if she had quarantined herself against the malaise of the City, guarding her creative soul against corruption. And she wrote in her darkened cellar as if she feared the old house itself weren't adequate protection: she had to burrow into the very earth, like a combatant engaged in trench warfare.

We were approaching an especially scenic spot in the drive that intersected a worn footpath leading to the pond. I called to the cabby to halt there. I did not know if we definitely wanted to take the path to the water's edge—given Thursday's situation—but the spot afforded our best view of the pond thus far, hence if nothing else we could take a long moment to gaze at its sparkling surface. As soon as the cab stopped its motion, however, Miss Edith made ready to

disembark (I suppose it was the natural conclusion). I glanced to
Thursday . . .

"Please," he said, "take a stroll—I am perfectly content where I
am."

So I stepped down from the cab and assisted Miss Edith. I offered
the governess my arm, and we began walking toward the pond, some
one-hundred or more paces distant. We had only advanced a few
yards, though, when I heard a horse's trotting gait and at almost the
same moment a feminine voice called out my name. I turned to see
Miss Hilary Chamberlain riding ladylike on a pure white Arabian.

"Miss Hilary," I returned as she reined in her mount.

Her young face was beaming. Adding to the aesthetic were a
deep-red riding gown and a feminine top-hat with ostrich plume—
she was the quintessence of British leisure class, and I had no idea
why there were not carriages aligned along Haslow Park filled with
young gentleman callers, near fisticuffs among themselves for a few
minutes' audience with Lord Chamberlain's only daughter.

Of course Miss Edith too had turned, and I believe Miss Hilary
was taken aback for a moment, no doubt convinced that the lady
on my arm was the authoress herself. But the well-bred young
woman recovered instantly and veneered a pleasant smile over
her momentary expression of surprise. "Hello, Miss Edith, is that
correct?"

"Yes, good day to you, Miss Chamberlain."

I realized then that I had not informed my companions that
these spectacular woods were on the property of Lord Chamberlain.
Edith was likely wondering how Miss Hilary suddenly appeared
here, and on horseback.

"You must come up to the house," said Miss Hilary, now fully
rebounded from her surprise. She glanced toward the cab and saw
Thursday peering from its window. "All three of you," she added.
"Father is away but Mummy is about somewhere. You must come up
for some tea—I shan't accept any answer but 'yes.'"

"Well then yes," I said on our behaves.

Miss Hilary began to turn her horse, but stopped and said,
"Actually this is most fortuitous, Mr. Wheelwright—we have prepared
a surprise for you but were not quite certain how best to deliver it.

Now you are here." She smiled most delightfully and cantered off before I could respond.

"A surprise," repeated Miss Edith, who was also intrigued by the notion.

"Apparently," I said, "but I haven't a clue. Do you mind taking tea with the young lady?"

"Not at all."

We were returning to the cab. "We won't stay long," I assured Thursday, who'd been privy to our exchange.

"Don't curtail your plans on my account," he said as I assisted his sister with the step up into the cab. "I feel quite well."

He did appear less weary, but I told myself we mustn't overdo it nevertheless. We followed the drive to Arbor-in-the-Glen, where Miss Hilary already had a manservant standing by to receive us. The fellow assisted us from the cab, then he spoke to the cabman and handed him a stack of coins, dismissing him from our service—much to his gain, it appeared. Thursday and his sister were taking in the simple splendor of Lord Chamberlain's home while the transaction proceeded. Arbor-in-the-Glen was far from opulent, with its whitewashed brick exterior and copper shutters of weathered green, but it was grand in its way. The servant showed us in and invited us to freshen ourselves; he said that Miss Chamberlain would receive us in the main salon. We each took our turn—I insisted on mine being last—and thus I was just seating myself on a floral sofa in the salon when Miss Hilary entered. She wore a silk and lace gown of the deepest purple. If the light had not been so abundant from the salon's southern windows, the gown may have appeared to be one of mourning. However, there was nothing mournful about the young Miss Chamberlain's air: her smiling countenance and sapphiric eyes were charmingly festal.

She swept in and placed her hand on Thursday's shoulder, not wanting him to trouble to stand. I however stood and took the same hand when she offered it. She had me sit as she claimed the opposite end of my sofa. She inquired of our day and appeared most enchanted by the details of our outing, coaxing them from us with her ardent questioning. To the young lady's further credit, she made certain it was a lively four-way conversation, and not simply a tête-à-

tête between her and me to which Miss Edith and Thursday had the
honor of being witnesses. In fact, I sensed a bond beginning to form
between Miss Hilary and Miss Edith, though the latter was several
years her senior, perhaps as many as ten, not to mention their other
obvious differences, like their stations in society. Their exchanges
revealed them to be clever young women with similar intellectual
bents, both loving literature, it would seem, and they had a fascination
with European languages beyond the obligatory French. They traded
volleys of salutations in several tongues, including German, Spanish,
and, of all things, Serbian. For a time, in fact, Thursday and I were
the odd-fellows-out as it were.

Meanwhile, the manservant had brought in tea and those
little raspberry cakes—those cakes of which Lord Chamberlain
was so proud. Like an anxious schoolboy, I found myself growing
impatient for my surprise and began to wonder if Miss Hilary had
forgotten. How best to drop a hint without appearing that that was
precisely what I was up to? I had but a few minutes to ponder this
age-old question before a maid came to the rear door of the salon
and immediately Miss Hilary, spying her peripherally, turned and
asked if all were in order. The maid, a girl not much older than her
mistress, indicated in the affirmative and exited.

"Well, Mr. Wheelwright," began Miss Hilary, beaming again, "as
you may imagine, your surprise is ready." She turned to Thursday
and Miss Edith, and said as if in confidence: "The splendid thing is,
we can partake of Mr. Wheelwright's surprise as well."

I was most intrigued.

"If you would all follow me, please," and our young hostess rose
and began leading us toward the salon's rear door. We hesitated a
moment while Thursday got set with his crutches, then we were off.
Normally Miss Edith would follow immediately behind Miss Hilary,
but under the circumstances I took her place. We passed through a
long hall with only a few pieces of furniture; it was adjacent to the
kitchen, so I presumed the hall could be used for dining when his
lordship's guest roster ranneth over.

Miss Hilary, in her gown of deepest lavender, led us outdoors to a
dooryard shaded by ancient chestnut trees. A long table was standing
parallel with the hall, and there were a maid and manservant at each

end. Instantly one realized their role was to remove a white sheet that had been draped over whatever lay on the tabletop: a length of irregular lumps. My mind jumped to the ridiculous notion of a series of decapitated heads beneath the covering, but I was also reminded of the burlesque version of *Dunkelraum* Mrs. Haeley and I had attended. . . .

My wandering mind needed to wander no further once Miss Hilary had us before the table and she signaled her people to theatrically rip back the sheet:

At least a dozen orange pumpkins . . .

. . . and it came to me: I had told the Chamberlains how much I relished carving jack-o'-lanterns and that I would miss doing so due to my traveling abroad. Miss Hilary stood there beaming, of course, waiting for my verbal reaction; Thursday and Miss Edith were most likely perplexed.

"You should not have troubled, Miss Hilary—truly, this is too much," and I revealed the backstory to brother and sister. "Where on earth did you obtain ripened pumpkins at this time of year? I should think in this climate especially they would be late bloomers indeed."

"I'm not certain where Father found them. I implored him to do so for your sake, Mr. Wheelwright, and, well . . . here they are."

Ah, yes: the power of an only daughter's wish to her doting—and wealthy!—father. Mountains could be moved, mighty rivers tamed.

A third servant had arrived with a basket of knives and large serving spoons, and the like. Miss Hilary motioned toward the implements: "Shall we?"

"I would not wish to disappoint," I said, "after Lord Chamberlain has gone to such trouble." I removed my coat, loosened my cuffs, and began pulling up my sleeves. Thursday did likewise. Miss Hilary thought of everything, and one of the servants tied a white towel around my neck like an overlarge bib; Thursday, Miss Edith, and Miss Hilary herself received just such bibs as well. We looked a team of ill-equipt surgeons about to perform an elaborate procedure.

I felt an odd pressure of expectation, being cast as the expert in the field. I selected a medium pumpkin, more oval than round. I weighed it in my hands as if I could tell something significant about the fruit by doing so; then I set it firmly on a corner of the long

table and poised a knife-blade over its stemmed crown. Everyone
waited expectantly for me to pierce the flaming skin as if it were a
momentous event, a warship's christening or bride's unveiling. I
hesitated, allowing the anticipation to rise ... then finally thrust the
blade in several inches. I proceeded to make a star-shaped incision
around the stem, just as my brother had taught me to do so many
years before. I was still under scrutiny: "Please, feel at liberty to dig
in," I said, and they each did.

At first I was quite aware of the pumpkins my companions chose,
and of their carving progress, but soon I was engrossed in my own
effort and paid little attention to theirs. I used a large serving spoon
to scoop out the seeds and fibrous mush. I then used the knife to
scrape the interior walls of the pumpkin to remove every last seed.
Butcher paper had been spread on the ground to receive the fruity
effluvia.

I was ready to sculpt the jack-o'-lantern. I sat in one of the
spindle-back chairs that had been brought outdoors for the occasion.
A tad out of practice, I elected to render a classically ghoulish face,
and began the first angular cut that would eventually be a pair of
*tri*angular eyes. I added a devilish grin and felt the masterpiece to be
finished. It was simple but nicely symmetrical. I looked to my fellow
artisans. It seemed Miss Hilary was trying to follow my example, but
her novice's hand was botching the face rather badly; I complimented
her effort nonetheless. Edith, on the contrary, demonstrated some
carving finesse with oval eyes notched in a way to suggest glancing-
left irises, and a matching mischievous grin sporting a solitary
bottom tooth. She looked up and caught my scrutinizing; I smiled
my approval. Thursday, meanwhile, was another case entirely. He'd
been using a small paring knife to make myriad cuts, serpentining
this way and that, and as I watched he removed a single thread from
the cloth that formed his bib; then with one hand inside the jack-
o'-lantern and the other outside, he used the strand of thread to
saw or shave very fine bits of meat and skin from the incisions he'd
made with the knife. I've returned to using anatomical terminology
because Thursday's method was more akin to a surgeon's than a
woodcarver's. Yet for all his painstaking care I hadn't a clue what he
was making of his patient.

Since there were plenty of pumpkins, we each had a go at a second effort. Feeling "warmed up," as equestrians say regarding their exercised mounts, I attempted a more sophisticated jack-o'-lantern—this one with circular eyes (that, yes, mimicked Miss Edith's design) and (my master's flair!) a lightning-bolt styled mouth. Say what you will, but it required care to render that mouth just so.

Miss Edith, to my surprise, had carved essentially the same design as her first effort. As I examined her two jack-o'-lanterns side by side, however, I came to realize that they were almost perfect opposites: the eyeball-notches glanced right instead of left, and the mouth turned down at the corners into a wicked frown; yet the single tooth remained precisely where it had been. Ahh . . . this was the same face, but now wearing a new mood. I wondered then if Miss Edith were projecting an entire character onto her pumpkin persona; if she were sufficiently supplied, would she render the whole catalogue of human emotions via these simple shifts in two facial elements? I doubted not that she were capable of it. Miss Hilary had carved basically the same simple design as her debut effort, but it was much improved. She was not beaming but was pleased with her marked improvement. I suspected Miss Hilary was a perfectionist and, given the opportunity, she would carve as many pumpkins as it would take until she had produced the paragon of the form.

We three watched while Thursday labored over his second creation, which seemed just as grotesque and formless as his first— though for all of its crazy lines, it did appear singular in design; and Thursday made his minute strokes with great purpose: it was anything but random slashing.

As we watched Thursday make his finishing emendations, Lady Penelope entered the dooryard via a path that ran beside a large vegetable garden then over a hill and toward, I presumed, the stable. My presumption was supported by Lady Penelope's wearing a lavender riding gown, and she was holding a crop in her gloved hands. Her ladyship's white ringlets spilled from beneath a straw bonnet, tied beneath her chin by a lavender scarf. As if I required further clues as to her recent occupation, when she drew near I saw that the skirt of her gown was dotted with brown mud.

"How wonderful, darling," said Lady Penelope, "you have united

Mr. Wheelwright and his pumpkins."

"Yes," said Miss Hilary, "it was quite a stroke of luck to find him and his party in the park."

"It has been quite a treat," I said, beginning to untie the towel from around my neck, self-conscious of my appearance.

"Mummy, these are Mr. Wheelwright's friends, Miss Edith and her brother . . ."

Thursday's familiar-name no doubt threw her, so I quickly volunteered, "Edward, Edward Hill, an acquaintance of Mrs. Haeley," I added the latter to try to enhance Thursday's pedigree in Lady Penelope's eyes, as she may have been a trifle puzzled at our odd crew.

Thursday removed his hat with pumpkin-stained fingers and bowed to Lady Penelope.

"How do you do," responded her ladyship. "Please, do not let me interrupt—finish your interesting carving."

"In truth," said Thursday, "I believe I am all but done."

We all looked at his creation, and I for one had no conception what he'd done—besides make an intricate mess of a perfectly fine pumpkin. A few more parries with the paring knife and twists of thread between his fingers, and Thursday called his creation complete.

"We must see them in their natural setting," said Lady Penelope, and at first I believed she meant the garden but then it came to light that she meant darkness when Miss Hilary suggested the curing-house. "Quite so," agreed her mother, whose eyes had the capacity for beaming like her daughter's; and her ladyship directed the help to retrieve some candles and to transport the jack-o'-lanterns accordingly.

While they were thus engaged, Misses Hilary and Edith, and Thursday and I all tidied ourselves. A servant whom I hadn't before seen brought glasses of cool cider on a tray, and we gladly took the refreshment. Meanwhile, mother and daughter chatted about their horses, especially one who they feared was developing the spavin. Our drinks finished, the Chamberlains led Miss Edith and me (with his leg, Thursday was content to sit in the shade) past the garden, then diverted on a path away from the impressive stable, home to perhaps two dozen of England's finest equine specimens. From their brief conversation I gathered that Lord Chamberlain owned an even larger stable in the north.

Shortly we came to the curing-house, a low brick structure of typical design, with a rusted tin chimney, which presently emitted no smoke. The three servants, having delivered the goods, stood off to the side. Though I was the only gentleman present, I was convinced to dispense with proper etiquette and enter the curing-house first, followed by Lady Penelope, Miss Hilary and at last Miss Edith. It was close quarters inside, and the ceiling was so low I was obliged to remove my hat. It was warm and the air was heavy with the sweet smell of cured meats. The jack-o'-lanterns were arranged on racks of varying heights. One could get a sense of their ghoulish physiognomies while the door remained open, but once Miss Edith closed it, the space was plunged into darkness and the pumpkins burst to life.

I looked immediately to my creations and was pleased with their glowing eyes and mouths, especially the jack with the lightning-bolt grimace. Miss Edith's were placed next to one another so that, I discovered, if I closed and opened each eye at a time, the pumpkin faces seemed to be a single countenance that changed expression to and fro. Of Miss Hilary's creations, clearly her second effort was the superior (one did not require a darkened room and lighted candle to draw that conclusion); however, there was something more engaging about the first. For some reason, its flaws—the errant cut marks, the grossly irregular features—possessed it of a character its near perfect brethren didn't project. I wondered if Miss Hilary had any sense of the superiority of its inferiority.

Last, I turned my attention to Thursday's jack-o'-lanterns. At first, expecting a mess of indecipherable incisions, that is precisely what I saw. But I soon realized a babel of awe coming from my curing-house companions, and that awe was inspired by Thursday's creations. Thus I looked again, and this time I saw them for what they were . . .

More than mere faces, the artist had rendered whole scenes in his fruity medium by manipulating the pumpkin skin and candle-glow as shadow and light. One scene depicted a monstrous figure pursuing a frightened woman, the monster behind her, it seemed. Really to the left of the tableau but as if in the distant background, stood a two-storey house, from which, one imagined, the two figures had come. Without the ability to articulate how I knew, I knew that the figures were Mrs. Haeley and her monster, that is, Dunkelraum's monster. And the house was Mrs. Haeley's house on Wicker's Lane, though in the carved scene it stood quite alone.

The second pumpkin (I presume I have the chronology correct) was even more intricate: it showed three figures: the monster stood upright in the farthest plane of the background—arms at his sides, perfectly still, like an Algonquin totem; in front of him, in the same posture but slightly to his left, was a gentleman, whose hatless head reached only to the monster's shoulder. The third figure was in the foreground: a woman in repose, Mrs. Haeley, I knew it to be. More than in repose, she may have lain on her deathbed.

In spite of the closeness of the curing-house, a chill ran along my spine; I realized too my heart was racing. . . .

I nearly hadn't noticed an especially queer object in the second tableau—to the figures' right and miniature as if in the far distance (yet no perspective gave it sense): a boat, twin-masted but with sails at rest.

We all stared at Thursday's miraculous creations. I believed that everyone interpreted them as I had, but I could not bring myself to remark anything that may have confirmed that belief. We stood there stone-dumb for a few more moments, and it came to me that I was the gentleman figure in the second scene, that it was I standing in front of Dunkelraum's monster as we enacted the authoress's death vigil.

I know not who opened the door, but soon we were outside in blinding daylight, returning to the dooryard. I told myself that my reading of Thursday's jack-o'-lanterns may have been due to my overwrought imagination, and nothing more. Nevertheless, the feeling of profound foreboding was quite real, and clung to me like a pernicious dream. I looked to Miss Edith to see if she were affected so, but her expression was fathomless.

We lingered at Arbor-in-the-Glen only as long as proper etiquette would insist, declining a perfunctory invitation to dine, on the reasoning that Thursday's leg should be taxed no further. I, for one, was anxious to return to Wicker's Lane and look in on Mrs. Haeley. My uneasiness regarding her well-being had been profound since viewing Thursday's bizarre pumpkins. I believe everyone was uneasy and desired our visit to come to a closure, though of course the well-bred Chamberlains would not say as much. Even Thursday seemed ill at ease as we waited for a rig to be gotten ready for our return to the authoress's home. And, uncharitably, I thought for a moment that he had brought all this on; after all, it had been his hand that carved the macabre tableaux. Then I began to wonder if it had been Thursday's doing in fact. Rather: of course it was his hand—but what if it had not been his design? That is to say, what if some other force had been directing poor Thursday? Had been using him as a kind of familiar against his knowledge?

Rubbish! I scolded myself, and my imagination! Still, during the carriage ride to Mrs. Haeley's—and an interminable ride it was—I could not prevent myself from stealing glances at the authoress's mild-mannered fellow, wondering what he was about. Moreover, I seemed to catch Miss Edith doing likewise. I wanted to speak up on the subject of the jack-o'-lanterns but instead held my tongue, perhaps afraid of what I would learn.

Nineteen

~

T HE HOUSE WAS QUIET WHEN WE RETURNED. IT TOOK MISS
Edith and me a few minutes to settle Thursday in his room; I
swear the poor, exhausted fellow was snoring before I shut his door.
Then, without exchanging a word, we set about searching for Mrs.
Haeley. Miss Edith looked in her room upstairs whilst I canvassed
the music-room, kitchen, washroom, and finally her beloved yard.
There was no trace of the authoress—not a used teacup, not a dented
sofa pillow. I had been unmindful of the house's transformation,
and its cleanliness and orderliness at first surprised me—I felt that
I had somehow stepped backward in chronology, to a time before
Stephen Haeley's death, though I'm not certain that the house had
ever been so clean and orderly when the gypsy-like Haeleys were
its chief occupants. Miss Edith and I met in the kitchen and knew
precisely where the lady of the house must be.

I lit a candle and opened the cellar door. It was still daytime but
very little light would leach into the cellar's gloom. I led our search
party of two down the narrow stairs, where Thursday had once
fallen, and understandably so. The cellar was indeed benighted, but
I was confident of our path and went directly to the theatrical curtain
that cordoned off Mrs. Haeley's den, which I realized I'd begun to
regard as a projection, or extension, of the authoress's mind. Yes,
somehow entering Margaret Haeley's private writing space felt like
a violate exploration of her inner being—dare I say, her soul. And
though she had asked me to call her by the familiar name of "Mae,"
and though I felt myself in love with her, Margaret T. Haeley in many
ways remained quite a stranger to me.

As I pulled back the heavy black curtain, the image from Thursday's carving—the image of Mrs. Haeley upon her deathbed—came to me in full measure, and my hand actually trembled as it gripped the ebon velvet. My other hand shook as well, and candlelight wavered weirdly within its small sphere of influence in the cellar gloom. Miss Edith, whose presence had nearly slipped from my mind, took hold of my arm to steady the candle, but she too lacked the solid hand of a jeweler, and hence let loose after a brief moment. The cellar was as still as a mausoleum, and besides my own pounding heart the only sound I detected was the clicking of tiny rodent claws in some lightless corner.

With the curtain withdrawn, I stepped forward. The high back of Mrs. Haeley's queenly writing chair obscured my view, but then the candlelight, weak though it was, shone upon a ghostly pale hand lying limp upon the carved arm of the chair. It appeared for an instant to be a severed hand—its extreme pallor certainly supported such wild speculation—but of course it was merely that the authoress wore a long black sleeve. She lay slumped upon her table. I feared the worst but soon determined she was breathing, though she was profoundly insensible, cataleptic even. I put my hand upon her shoulder, and felt its skeletal nature through her dress and coarse shawl.

"Mrs. Haeley," I said gently, then with more force: "Mae."

She did not respond. Meanwhile, Miss Edith had moved to the other side of the authoress and felt her left hand, which rested upon the table. I realized a quill—a cheap raven quill—was still betwixt her ink-stained fingers.

"She is formed of ice," said Miss Edith. "We must remove her to her room."

"Agreed."

Miss Edith took the quill from Mrs. Haeley's frigid fingers and placed it in a cup alongside several others. It must have been habit that caused her to use such a quaint means of inditement. I pulled back her chair, which itself was heavy though Mrs. Haeley's weight added but little. Together we lifted the authoress from her chair. Her head lulled back on her shoulders, exposing the cheek that had been resting against the final page of her manuscript, and there was a black mark upon her pale skin, a dark hieroglyph without meaning;

and I thought, just as darkly, what if Mrs. Haeley's manuscript is nonsensical? . . . the way a dreamt idea can seem perfectly lucid while we're still in the state of the dream, but when fully awake, its sense is shed like a cold-blooded reptile does its skin.

After an awkward attempt or two by Miss Edith and me to transport the authoress in unison, it was decided that the most practical approach was for me to carry Mrs. Haeley myself. Miss Edith took up the candle and led our ascent from the cellar. Halfway, the governess inquired if I were doing all right, and I assured her that Mrs. Haeley weighed nothing. In fact, it seemed almost a literal statement of fact—and I knew the phenomenon was not effected due to my overdeveloped physique.

I carried Mrs. Haeley through the house and toward the stairs. Her eyes seemed to open briefly but otherwise her insensibility persisted. The mark of ink on her cheek remained a meaningless blur until, passing a mirror in the foyer, I caught a glimpse of it in reverse—that is to say, reflected in proper order—and it appeared to be a word, *Ende* . . . German, I recalled, for "The End." Upstairs, as soon as I placed the authoress upon her neatly made bed, Miss Edith thanked me, which was a polite dismissal from the lady's room. I suggested that we send for Dr. Carter, but Miss Edith wasn't certain it was necessary and wanted to settle Mrs. Haeley first. I went to the parlor and waited, though not patiently. I listened to the shuffling of feet in the room above me while the generous-hearted governess cared for a woman she barely knew, at least other than by literary reputation—and from that source I daresay no one knew the true Margaret T. Haeley at all.

I debated within myself whether I should send for Carter in spite of Miss Edith's inclination to see to Mrs. Haeley herself first. Before I could quite decide the better course, however, Miss Edith came to the foot of the stairs and called to me if I would be kind enough to heat a kettle for tea.

She was returning up the stairs when I came into the foyer. "How is she?" I called.

"We must warm her, and get something in her stomach," said the retreating form of the governess.

I went to the kitchen and discovered the kettle was nearly full, so

I merely stoked the flames in the stove, directing the bulk of the coals beneath the kettle's burner. They were hot, thus the water should be ready in due haste. I readied the tea leaves and set a cup and saucer and what remained of the honey on the tray, along with a somewhat tarnished spoon and the wooden honey-dipper. Still, there was time to wait, so I sat at the table. It was then that I noticed the cellar door was yet open, which led to my thinking about Mrs. Haeley's, apparently, finished manuscript. Was it a new novel, finally, after all these years since the sensation of *Dunkelraum*? Perhaps another book of poetry, though her first went all but unnoticed by readers? The reviewers and the public at large wondered what Mrs. Haeley would do to properly follow her famous, and infamous, debut, until they had no choice but to conclude . . . *nothing*—fanning the naysayers' fires that Stephen Haeley was more the author of *Dunkelraum* than Margaret Haeley was its authoress, and with Haeley's untimely death his widow's fancy was struck dumb forever, some said. I had to admit that I deemed the hypothesis plausible, though I never wanted to believe it.

Proof, one way or the other, now lay at the bottom of those cellar steps. I could be the first person on earth to solve a riddle the literary world had pondered before its own cruelly impartial sphinx for more than a decade. I could walk down those stairs, retrieve the manuscript pages, bring them into the light of the kitchen, and learn the truth. The entire operation could be completed in less than two minutes' time. . . . I realized I was a bit afraid to know, perhaps I'd been more dubious of Mrs. Haeley's authorship than I'd allowed myself to acknowledge—

The kettle began hissing on the stove, reprieving me from making a decision, for the present anyway. By the time I reached the stove, the water was whistling. Using the heavy rag designated for the purpose, I wrapped it around the bottom of the kettle, then placed it on the tray and began carefully making my way upstairs. Miss Edith met me at Mrs. Haeley's door and relieved me of the weighty tray. I gained a glance of the authoress more or less propped up in bed, but I couldn't tell if she possessed any further wits.

Miss Edith thanked me, but it was clear she didn't want my meddling in Mrs. Haeley's recovery. She shut the bedroom door with her foot.

I returned to the parlor. A cup of tea suddenly sounded very good, but alas all the things were in Mrs. Haeley's room. I noticed the secrétaire, where the proof-pages for *Andersen's Romance* had been, and it further impressed upon my mind the awareness of Mrs. Haeley's completed manuscript in the cellar. I felt myself drawn toward it but also repelled, out of trepidation that it would reveal Mrs. Haeley to be a literary charlatan, and also out of a sense of its violating the authoress's privacy, like eavesdropping through the wall on someone's involuntary sleep-confessions, their most private somnilocutions.

I checked the time and it was but midafternoon. I took up the book of Scottish and Welsh folktales, hoping to divert my mind, but I couldn't prevent myself from thinking about Mrs. Haeley's manuscript. I even theorized that I should retrieve it for its own sake, as if it may catch a cold in the dank air of the cellar.

This is ludicrous, I scolded. Mrs. Haeley would not object to my reading her work—which, after all, is its purpose: to be read. In fact, she must intend to read from it herself at tomorrow evening's literary soirée. Resolved, I put aside the book of folktales and began toward the cellar. However, in the foyer I encountered Miss Edith, just returning from the authoress's bedroom.

"She appears to be all right," she said from the first step, so that she was just a trifle taller than me. "She took some tea and is a good deal warmed beneath her quilts. She's sleeping soundly, and I'll check on her in a few minutes."

"That's very good—thank you for seeing to her." I may have sounded a shade guilty for I felt as though I'd been caught with my hand poised just above the cookie tin.

"What are you about?" She stepped down to the floor. It was a provocative question, but she spoke it innocently.

"I was just going out," I lied, without premeditation.

"Out?"

"Yes—we need to be resupplied," I said as lightly as I could manage. "Tea and honey and such—you know, our staples."

Miss Edith smiled. "That seems a sound idea."

I realized I was coatless and hatless, and faced in the wrong direction. "Yes, well, since Mrs. Haeley appears quite all right. . . ."

I turned about and returned to the parlor. It was best to leave the house for a time, though I was feeling rather drained, as some distraction may rid me of my anxiety regarding Mrs. Haeley's book. As I was donning my coat and hat—it's truly astonishing how one recollection can spark another—I recalled my battered hat, the one kicked about during the Heiress Presumptive's celebration riot, the riot that interrupted the puppet-show—the one about the Princess whose betrothed has been kidnapped. . . . Of course these connections were all made in the flash of an instant, like lightning traveling down to Mr. Franklin's key; and my anxiety over Mrs. Haeley's manuscript was replaced by my anxiety over the Princess and her little dog being in the cave with the wounded man, who may or may not be her lost beloved. . . . The question mark had been lodged in my half-awareness for some time, and now it seemed vitally important.

And, moreover, there seemed but one way to solve the enigma: I must find the waif, for surely she knew the end of the story.

Nearly every time I had sallied forth into the City I had run across Miss Organdy. Perhaps this time locating her would be just as simple, like finding due north—one must merely look and in time the workings of the heavens would reveal all.

I exited 261½ Wicker's Lane through the front door. Long shadows stretched across the street and boardwalk at obtuse angles to the homes and places of business that generated them. Being in an older section of the City, the lane was quite full of various edifices, all pushed close together—in marked contrast to Thursday's weird rendering in which Mrs. Haeley's house stood solitary on some plane of its own. From the curb, I looked back at the house. In spite of the truth of my description of the neighborhood, somehow Thursday's depiction seemed true too: there was a singleness about Mrs. Haeley's home, as if it had absorbed its mistress's isolation, her loneliness. Would I sense the house's singularity if I were ignorant as to its occupant? I believed I would.

Now, where to find Miss Organdy? Twice I'd seen her near the Museum of Natural History—perhaps, then, that would be a logical place to search. I felt my trouser pocket where I kept my wallet; there were sufficient funds for the moment, there was also no questioning my shrinking wherewithal. I had to fight the urge toward self-pity and remind myself that the Wheelwright family was fortunate in that only its fortune had been lost and we Wheelwrights ourselves were alive and well.

I walked in the general direction of the Museum until I was able to secure a cab, which was shortly. The streets were moderately populated, while the cabbies were turned out in their full force. After informing the large-boned fellow of our destination, I settled into the seat and attempted to put aside my anxieties. I should have been anxious in regards to my fast-approaching reading. Besides the fact I had not selected which pages to read, no matter what I read, A. B. C. Murry would finally discover that I had totally reconceived *Andersen's Romance*—and there was no way to predict his reaction. However, given the time and capital he'd already invested in the original tale, one did not need to be gifted with a fertile imagination to guess at it.

I peered out the carriage windows hoping to spy the street waif, though the odds were nil at best. I was trying too hard, and nearly every teenage boy and tomboy looked at first like Miss Organdy. The momentary exhilaration at finding her and subsequent disappointment, time and again, were too much, and I quitted the process, directing my gaze instead at the filthy floor of the cab. Then I began thinking of the waif herself: what sort of life must she be leading, living, it would seem, on the streets of London, living by her ingenuity and natural showmanship (show*woman*ship)? Perhaps then the stage was her future. If not—the streets, but peddling herself rather than someone's show?

The cab seat was thinly upholstered, and when I shifted my position I discovered I'd been partially sitting upon a folded newspaper, *The City Standard*. Delighted for the distraction, I opened the rag and began reading. There were some articles about goings-on in Parliament—it all meant little to me and as such did not hold my interest. Anchoring the forward page, however, was a report on measures the City was taking to curb a recent rash of street crime which had been principally perpetrated by the legion of children who appeared to "live on the charted byways like packs of dogs foraging for their next easy meal." I was struck by the fact that the City was only initiating punitive measures, and not taking any steps directed at the heart of the matter. That is to say, there was no mention in the article of efforts to find shelter for the street urchins and to redirect their energies toward schooling or work which could earn them honest wages.

Somewhat disgusted with the City leaders and their myopia, I flipped the newspaper to the backpage and immediately spied a theatrical notice for a performance of the Bard's *The Tragedy of Romeo and Juliet*. Reading on, I discovered it wasn't being staged at a theater but rather at a pub called Lizzie I's—and, what was more, it was an all-feminine cast! Surely that would account for the camera obscura's unusual scene: it was a sort of advertisement for the play. Miss Organdy must be one of the company's principal actresses. I checked the dates and times of the performances—it was true serendipity. The play was to be performed on this very day in . . . I fumbled for my watch . . . in just more than an hour's time!

I knocked on the roof of the cab and called out the tavern's address. The cabby immediately began directing his pair of mismatched mares about the corner. Consumed with incredulity, I reread the play's notice again and again, tolled the days over in my mind, and studied my watch to be sure it was recording the time properly—but it all continued to be true.

It was a longer ride than I was wanting, and by the time we arrived at the tavern, in an especially ancient district of the City, the sun had sunk so low evening was all but upon us. I decided some pennypinching was in order and paid my fare with a humble gratuity, to put it generously. I suppose, given the cut of my suit, the cabman felt he'd been gypsyed by the most avaricious of old misers. He snapped the reins sharply and his rig rattled off with his barely audible grunt of "G'evenin."

I stood before Lizzie I's (said "Lizzie First's," I suspected), an ancient establishment of chipped brick and cracking plaster, and it seemed possible that the foundation, at least, may have indeed dated from the glorious reign of the Virgin Queen, Spenser's celebrated Faerie Queene.

There was a heavy door with a boar-head knocker in such condition it didn't appear that anyone had had to knock for admittance in quite some time. As such, I let myself into the tavern, which, inside, seemed to already be well into an hour of night: the dark, smoky air was cut periodically by coruscating lantern flames along the walls. Besides the requisite tobacco smell there was mixed with it something unusual—not the greasy scent of frying fat that was common in such establishments—but rather something . . . floral, like jasmine or violet, or even a touch rosy. A long brass-edged bar stood to one side, the lanternlight glowing weakly in the metal. Tables and chairs and even some benches were set up here and there on the plank floor in a haphazard scheme. At the far end of the tavern I could see that floor space was left clear (for a staging area, I gathered). Perhaps two dozen patrons, mostly seated, took up only a fraction of capacity.

"Have a seat, love—what can I bring ya?" rasped a salty-looking barmaid as she whisked by in a red flowing skirt and a peasant-style blouse. "The show'll begin presently."

"Ale of some sort," I said to her departing back.

It was not difficult to secure a table near the staging area, so close I would be able to hear the actresses take breaths betwixt soliloquies. I placed my hat upon the table and waited for my ale. I noted that the stage, such as it was, was void of any theatrical tropes, like a backdrop or set furniture or props . . . not even a curtain by which the thespians could make dramatic entrances and exits. I was used to American productions, which, by comparison especially, seemed as much concerned with the theatrical trappings as with the guts and bones of the play itself. I thought for a moment, recalling the last play I'd attended back home . . . ah yes, I'd escorted my mother and sister to see *Mr. Washington and His Fair Lady*, about the general and his Martha before the needs of the nation-to-be interrupted their, apparently, idyllic lives at Mount Vernon. It was all a grand affair; and every action was underscored by a string quartet, plus fife and drum, in the pit. Mother and Claire loved the production and wept energetically when heroic Mr. Washington—that is, General Washington—donned his powdered wig and his impressive uniform of American blue and blood red, and strode off stage, larger than life, to take command of the ramshackle army of youthful patriots.

When I recalled the play's sticky sweet storyline, of the

romanticized rendering of the protagonists' marriage, I wondered if it had influenced my writing of *Andersen's Romance*, which I had only just begun at the time, and had barely a glimmering of a notion what the story would be. The theory stands up, I thought, as it's the novel's sweetness that I'd been exorcising from it, as if a demon that'd been possessing its narrative soul.

Perhaps it was unfair to blame the book's flaws on *Mr. Washington*: there certainly was a healthy vein of sweetness in *Sketches of Old New Yorkers* as well, but it tended toward nostalgia and not romance, strictly speaking—though nostalgia is a sort of romance: a sticky sweet love of the past, and most probably a past that never existed. I realized then that in Kathy—let's say, the concept of *kathy*—I had succeeded in both: I recollected a past romance whose intensity, as I recalled it, in all likelihood did not exist. Fabricator and fancifier that I am, I fabricated and fancified (hence falsified!) our time together.

Of course I did, of course I did.

After all, how easy it was to drop elements of fault into the soup of Katherine's character—that's Andersen's Katherine—her dependence on the bottle (though my Kathy did not drink), and her machinations to transform Andersen into her father, or rather a woodcarver's copy of her father (though my Kathy had no such designs, as far as I could say). So I had not assigned my Kathy's shortcomings to Andersen's Katherine, but I accepted the reality that my Kathy had faults, that she was not a paragon of the feminine.

I began to ruminate on Kathy's imperfections, and then it came to me (nothing short of an epiphany!): Finding specific fault was unnecessary to clear away the false fog of nostalgia; simply accepting that there were faults was quite enough to liberate me from that romanticized past, to unshackle my heart from it and leave it quite behind. . . .

I noticed my glass of ale sitting before me. I was so deep into my reverie I hadn't noticed the salty barmaid set it there. Had I paid her too and couldn't recall it? There was no time to ponder the mystery further as the players began assembling into the staging area. They seemed to come from all points in Lizzie I's, each carrying a chair and placing it (then herself in it) along the walls—some twenty or so players in all, each female, seemingly, though in some instances the pinned away hair, and theatrical mustaches and vandykes made it difficult to be certain. They were costumed in Elizabethan-style garb, though not elaborately so: ruffs, doublets, peascods and short cloaks on the male personae; for the females, gowns with hooped skirts, longer cloaks, and ruffs as well.

I of course recognized Miss Organdy—Romeo; "he" and his Juliet, a truly lovely young woman with long chestnut hair, sat at the back of the stage, perfectly centered; flanked by a waiting gentlewoman (next to Juliet) and a player in brown monk's habit (by Miss Organdy). Then by these two, couples made to look older and costumed somewhat more grandly (gaudy necklaces and rings of fake stones caught the lanternlight as they took their places): Lords and Ladies Capulet and Montague no doubt. And then I realized the pattern: the Capulet clan and the Montague clan were seated against opposing walls, and the line of each group ended with Juliet and Romeo, together at the center of the U-shaped assembly. Though they had taken their places more or less together, I realized that the principals had not spoken, nor for that matter even looked at one another.

Once assembled, the players stared straight on, silent as stones, for what seemed an odd stretch of time. I wondered if perhaps they awaited a signal to begin. I sipped my ale, a touch too warm for my taste but good nevertheless, and I waited. . . . Then with such suddenness it startled me, the players, all save for Romeo and Juliet, began speaking in well-rehearsed monotonic unison:

"Two households, both alike in dignity, in fair Verona, where we lay our scene, from ancient grudge break to new mutiny, where civil blood makes civil hands unclean...." They spoke of the "star-crossed lovers" and requested our "patient ears attend" the "two hours' traffic" on their stage.

The instant the choral recitation ceased, a pair from the Capulet clan began speaking, still in their chairs, and I wondered that the entire play would be acted from their seats . . . for two hours! Though I wanted very much to speak with Miss Organdy, I doubted that I could tolerate such a performance.

One of the Capulets started speaking lustily about "thrusting" the Montague maids "to the wall" and "cutting off their heads"—

the lines being delivered in this odd way, via feminine voices, had a strange effect upon the words, somehow amplifying the male violence replete in the dialogue. Continuing in this vein, the Capulet partisans spotted some Montagues coming toward them, and the one Capulet informed the other to "draw thy tool," to which he responded, still seated, "My naked weapon is out."

Perhaps I was a mere innocent when I had seen the play years before, but I did not recall this sort of dialogue, steeped in masculine violence.

From their chairs on the opposing side of the stage, the Montagues commenced their taunting; it went back and forth thus until one of the Capulets challenged his enemy to draw his sword or be counted unmanly—at which the four players leapt from their chairs, weapons drawn, and a fray began on the stage. Not realistic, I suppose, but with much clanking of opposing blades, and overall an uncommon grace about their movements. This dance was broken up before any blood was let, and the Prince of Verona, in brocaded jacket and not seated on the stage but rather among the spectators at the tables, came forward to pronounce that any more feuding would result in a death sentence for the participants. He referred to their long-bladed swords as "cankered."

Though the acting was well accomplished, I waited with growing impatience for Miss Organdy to rise from her chair and enter the play in earnest. I listened to Lord Montague say of his son Romeo that "private in his chamber pens himself, shuts up his windows, locks fair daylight out and makes himself an artificial light"—and I could not but help thinking of Mrs. Haeley, whom I realized I missed on this solitary ramble of mine. I supposed I must eventually leave Wicker's Lane and make my way to Belgium, to my old friends, and survive on their generosity until the Wheelwright fortunes were resuscitated enough to bring me home. The ale had perhaps an ironically sobering effect on my constitution, and I realized it may be years before I had the wherewithal to return to America. Perhaps my brother, in suggesting that I go to the Blackwoods, was telling me that I was an inhabitant of Europe—of the Blackwoods' home—for the indefinite future.

At last Miss Organdy's entrance came, and she rose from her

chair the despondent youth Romeo, rejected by the fair Rosaline, who "hath forsworn to love," and as such he asserted, "I have lost myself; I am not here; this is not Romeo, he's some other where." I must commend Miss Organdy on her performance: she was a convincing Romeo. Her cockney accent, that I heard at the puppet-show, was shed for something more City proper. She returned to her seat, continuing her air of discontent while the Capulets planned their ball and their daughter's betrothal to Count Paris.

Finally, chestnut-haired Juliet enacted her part. The young actress was older than Juliet's thirteen years but not by far. Our Juliet was lovely, moving about the stage with the sort of innocent elegance that only beautiful girls can effect. In that I was reminded of Miss Chamberlain, though I do not know that the actress could match Miss Hilary's radiance, and then I wondered if Miss Hilary's radiant quality was effected by being the daughter of a very wealthy man, so that she didn't so much radiate beauty but rather wealth, or the possibilities that wealth allowed. Perhaps it was unfair of me. I tried to imagine Miss Hilary dressed in the rags of a common charwoman, and I could not induce the image to solidly form: it seemed quite impossible that Miss Hilary could be anything other in this world than a rich man's beautiful daughter, indeed his only child.

I drifted back from my contemplation at the point where Romeo's compatriot (Mercutio?) was describing the dreamworld of Queen Mab, whose "chariot is an empty hazelnut made by the joiner, squirrel or old grub—time out of mind the fairies' coachmakers. . . ." After further fancifying, Romeo halted his speech: "Peace! Thou talk of nothing." I considered my own fancifying—and Mrs. Haeley's, and Edmund Holland's—was it all indeed *nothing*, as downtrodden Romeo suggests, or does it *mean* something? Another Montague, taking up the simile that made-up tales are as thin as the wind, declared: "This wind, you talk of, blows us from ourselves." In the context of the play it seems a negative declaration, but I wondered: is that not, in fact, its value—that when tales blow us from ourselves, we can look back from a new perspective, seeing ourselves as a stranger might, unprejudiced by too-close knowledge—and then we come to understand ourselves anew? . . .

In due course, the youngsters met, fell in love, realized each other's heritage, and Romeo scaled the Capulets' orchard wall (really a bench that another actor had placed on the stage, and Miss Organdy hopped over it, spry as a wily tomcat: "Can I go forward when my heart is here?"). For this rash action, his friend, left behind on the other side of the orchard "wall," called him a "madman!"

Romeo darted about the stage, as if from tree to tree, before spotting chestnut-headed Juliet at her bedroom window (in fact standing on the very bench which had been the orchard wall only moments earlier). Juliet spoke her thoughts aloud, wishing that her Romeo would "refuse thy name," and from the darkened orchard Romeo spoke out: "Call me but love, and I'll be new baptized— henceforth I never will be Romeo."

Then came a familiar-sounding exchange, the one Thursday and his sister recited in the camera obscura: "By name," said Romeo, "I know not how to tell thee who I am."

How could I help myself? But I had begun to see Romeo and Juliet as metaphorical for me and Mrs. Haeley, though our narrative was little like the star-crossed teens'. As such, I felt that the waif spoke for my heart when she said, "Were thou as far as the vast shore, washed with the farthest sea, I would adventure for such a sacred place." My passions for the authoress were being heated by the antique play; then I felt a stab of pain at recalling my doubt of her and her completed manuscript—of course she was the sole authoress of her work! Who was I to doubt? My pain was amplified when Juliet spoke the line "O, swear not by the moon, the inconstant moon, that monthly changes in her circled orb. . . ."

I literally gripped my sides with the blow, and held tighter with "I have no joy at this contract tonight; it is too rash, too unadvised, too sudden—too like the lightning, which does cease to be ere one can say, 'It lightens.'" Clearheaded, wise-beyond-her-years Juliet was eviscerating my very soul. On the one hand, I wanted to return to Mrs. Haeley's home—it was unfathomable that I should have left her, even in Miss Edith's compassionate care, given the condition in which she lay—but I also felt it imperative to speak with the waif, and only after the curtain fell, metaphorically at least, would that be possible.

Young Juliet was speaking of opening the cave where poor Echo lay when some fellows behind me, having grown impatient, began hissing at the thespians. One called out: "'Nough's enough—let's see some titties—din't come for no po'try!'"

Said another beery voice: "That's a fact, girlies—time to lift your skirts . . . an'drop your drawers."

Apparently the drunk ruffs thought the all-feminine cast was performing a burlesque of the Bard's great love tragedy, or they thought it ought to be. Miss Organdy and the chestnut-haired actress noticed the rude calls but acted onward, undaunted.

The unruly pair were about to hiss further insults—and I thought I should do something to prevent it (it would be, after all, the gallant thing)—but, like that, the salty barmaid was at their table and had them by their ears. Over my shoulder I saw her speak into the ears that she twisted as if she meant to remove them from their overwide heads. Whatever she said was immediately effective, and the louts sat there drinking their pints as docile as repentant acolytes when she at last let them loose.

Though I had no expectation of the show turning bawdy, and though it was competently acted—I found myself growing more and more restless, pulled between my desire to return to the authoress's side and my need to speak with Miss Organdy, who was on stage now as the lovesick youth, being patronized by his companion: "Now is he in the numbers that Petrarch flowed in—Laura to his lady was but a kitchen-wench; marry, she had a better love to be-rhyme her; Dido a dowdy; Cleopatra a gypsy; Helen and Hero hildings and harlots; Thisbe a gray eye or so. . . ." The list of infamous literary ladies only magnified my conundrum.

At last the rash youths enacted their wedding plans. Center-stage, Miss Organdy shifted her gaze from Romeo's monkish mentor and seemed to speak directly to me (I was but a few feet away): "Do though but close our hands with holy words," recited the waif, "then love-devouring death do what he dare. . . ." It was unsettling to be the direct recipient of the actress's declamation. I could not be certain, but Miss Organdy at that moment seemed to recognize me—perhaps as the American author Jefferson Wheelwright, or at least as the fellow who kept popping up . . . at the puppet-show, on the Velociquad, in the audience of *Romeo and Juliet*. I feared she'd viewed me as some sort of threat to her personal well-being. After all, happening into one another twice could be believable coincidence, even in the Old City with its teeming masses some two million strong—but a third encounter in such a brief period . . . well, such circumstances must have been by design, for only in literature could mere luck bring characters together with such opportune frequency.

"Romeo" finished her lines and turned her attention elsewhere. The drama proceeded to the couples' off-stage marriage (that is, with their sitting mutely in their original chairs, but now clasping hands and staring into each other's love-drenched orbs), and thus, in proper Shakespearean form, began the series of deaths. Juliet, upon learning of the first death, Tybalt's, and her new husband's banishment, cried out: "O serpent heart, hid with a flowering face! Did ever dragon keep so fair a cave?" Then she tearfully listed a host of ironic opposites—beautiful tyrant, fiend angelical, dove-feathered raven, wolvish-ravening lamb—whose images so transfixed me that I but half noticed the climactic unfolding of the play: before I knew it Juliet's dead form was lithely draped over Miss Organdy, also dead upon the floor, and their stunned parents looked on in horror.

The prince of the realm concluded the most woeful tale, and the cast, including all the resurrected, held hands for a deep bow in acknowledgment of the audience's appreciation. Persons must have been trickling in throughout the performance as I was surprised at the number when I glanced behind me. Even the reformed ruffs were clapping and whistling with enthusiasm.

After a second bow, the players began going to friends and relations in the audience to be hugged and congratulated. I was struck by the fact that Miss Organdy and the chestnut-haired actress seemed to have no interest in one another once the performance was concluded; I wondered even if the two young women were on speaking terms. I suppose I wanted Romeo and Juliet to be in love and hand-in-hand beyond the temporal confines of Mr. Shakespeare's tragedy.

I drank my ale keeping a close watch on Miss Organdy as she moved from congratulatory handclasp to congratulatory embrace. She appeared to be navigating the room with a purpose, with a specific destination in mind, and I suspected there was an "unrough youth," some admiring, moon-eyed teenage boy, to whom she was making her way. Instead however she sought out an old man with a great shock of pure white hair. Miss Organdy spoke to him, he smiled and enfolded her in a great, bearish hug. As he held her, she almost disappearing from view altogether, I noticed he had a cane in hand, black and hard-used, I could detect even from across the room.

I finished my ale and began making my way toward them. As I went past various performers I smiled and offered my sincere congratulations and kudos. But I rushed a bit as I did not want to lose sight of the waif. She noticed my approaching and did not seem surprised. At last I reached the pair and said, "How do you do; my name is Jefferson Wheelwright—"

"The American author," said the old man, who had not bothered to shift his gaze toward me but rather stared into space somewhere beyond Miss Organdy's head. I realized the fellow was blind.

"Yes, that's right. . . ."

"I have had your *Sketches* read to me several times."

"*Several* times," said the girl, teasing the old man.

"Mr. Wheelwright, may I introduce my niece, truly, or should I say 'Romeo'?" He placed a gentle hand on his niece's shortly cropped, sand-colored hair.

It took me a moment to realize he meant that her name was "Truly" and he wasn't employing an oddly placed adverb. "Perhaps you should—it was a delightful performance, truly . . . Truly."

The waif and I bowed to one another.

"I am Terrace," said the old man, extending his hand, with the cane hooked over his wrist.

"It's a pleasure, sir," taking his hand.

"I've seen you before," said Truly, "haven't I, Mr. Wheelwright?" Her accent was neither cockney nor City proper; in fact she sounded much like Miss Edith and Thursday, so perhaps hailed from the same corner of England.

"Yes; we keep bumping into each other. In fact, I wanted to ask you something in particular, regarding our first meeting—"

"At the puppet-show."

"Yes—quite."

Her uncle's lips formed a slight smile.

"You've found the ideal time to inquire," said Truly. "Uncle Terrace is the puppet-master."

The old fellow's smile now revealed a straight row of teeth as angelically white as his hair.

I said, "It was during the street fair. . . ."

"For the Heiress Presumptive's celebration," said the girl.

Her uncle added, "And there was the riot, a demonstration of some sort."

"Yes, which interrupted your show."

"It will be recorded as a memorable performance," said Truly—and I realized that that day the responsibility of saving the puppet-show materials fell almost entirely on her small shoulders, not to mention also getting her blind uncle to a place of safety. I'd thought of the waif as resourceful from the first instant I saw her, and now even more so.

I said, "When the performance was cut short, the puppet Princess had found a fellow in a dark cave—well, it may seem silly, but all this time it's been weighing on me—had she found her Prince? That is, how does the story end?"

"Do you mind if we sit, Mr. Wheelwright? My legs are old."

"Of course," and we all three sat. I offered to order him and his niece drinks but they declined.

The puppet-master rested both hands on the top of his cane; in the lanternlight they seemed the size of bear paws. "That show is based on an old tale, an old Bavarian folktale that was told to me many, many years ago. In that folktale, the young princess finds her love in the cave, but he is mortally wounded. Before he perishes, however, he discovers that his young fiancée has come to him against all odds, and they exchange their pledges of eternal affection and devotion. His breathing becomes labored, and when daylight at last creeps into the cave, she learns that the prince has died during the long, dark night. According to legend, to this day, if you go into the cave and extinguish your light, you can hear the whispering vows of the young lovers. When I was a young man, I visited the mountain cave and heard their voices as plainly as yours and Truly's, but my companions, who were wary of extinguishing their torches, heard nothing."

"That is a marvelous legend," I said.

"But that story would be too depressing for children," said Truly.

"Quite so," said her uncle, "thus in our revision the Prince lives and the following morning he and the Princess and their two dogs are rescued by the palace guard, the Black Prince is imprisoned, a cannonade from the combined armies destroys the Black Castle, and the Prince and Princess live happily thereafter." Then he added, "Children deserve happy endings if it's possible to provide them," and he reached out and put his great hand on Truly's head for a moment.

"Quite so," I repeated.

"Tell me, Mr. Wheelwright, are you planning a trip to Germany?"

"Germany? That remains to be seen; I intend to visit friends in Belgium eventually, with a sojourn in Paris along the route perhaps. Why do you ask?"

"It's just that no lover of tales should bypass a tour of old Germany," he said.

I had been thinking of something, and said, "I have an invitation for you, for both of you—tomorrow evening there is to be a private reading, at 261½ Wicker's Lane, near Saint Ursula's Church, and I would be most honored if you should attend."

"Will you be reading, sir?" asked Terrace, not quite looking my way.

"Yes, from a new book I've been working on—and also the poet Biron Swinford."

Truly recited, "'Hummingbird hover'd about its floral house, hover'd there where bees too had been before, supping nectar and vigorous of wing—enigmatical as creatures of lore.'"

"Wonderful," I said: somehow Swinford's sometimes too-sweet verse seemed just right when spoken by the young thespian. Perhaps I was overly critical of his work. "And," I continued, "there will be some surprises too—allow me to tease you with that to assure your attendance."

"We must, Uncle—it would be rude considering how much trouble Mr. Wheelwright went to to watch our little play."

I wasn't certain if she meant the puppet-play or *Romeo and Juliet*, but her uncle concurred.

"Perfect—I will bid you adieu until tomorrow evening, seven o'clock." I took up my hat and bowed to uncle and niece; then I went out of the tavern in search of a cab to employ. I was gratified that I'd met Truly and learned for certain the end of the interrupted show, but now all my thoughts shifted to the authoress and I was most anxious to return to her.

Twenty

I T WAS FULLY NIGHT, AND THE LANTERN-LIGHTERS WERE ABOUT
their business. One such dark-whiskered fellow walked past me
with his stepladder and pail of embers. He nodded and I returned
a tip of my hat. Lantern-lighters but no cabbies it seemed. No
matter—I had a general knowledge of direction so I began walking.
No doubt a cabby would come along sooner than later. I overtook
the lanterneer, who was stopping to perform his duty. As I was then
in advance of him, the street I crossed into was quite dark. Not even
a candleflame could be seen in an unshuttered window. In fact the
whole district appeared deserted. I listened intently for a sound that
may imply a cab was in the neighborhood, but I heard nothing, save
for my own shoeheels.

I glanced behind me just for the comfort of seeing the light of
the lantern, though it was now a few blocks distant, but the street
must've angled in such a way that my view was blocked—and behind
was just as dark and desolate as before me. It didn't seem possible
that the Old City could be so vacant of life, only in early evening at
that.

There was nothing to do except keep moving in the direction I
hoped was more accurate than less. The Old City's loneliness was
palpable. As a child I used to go with my family to visit a maiden
aunt who'd grown old in a cottage on a plateau above the Hudson.
She was bland, as I recollected her, with never much to say other
than to report the progress of her faltering health. The cottage had a
pungent and unique scent, something of a mixture of furniture wax
and garden mold. But more potent than that was an aura of loneliness

that seemed to surround the old girl, in her layers of black muslin. The aunt died when I was yet a boy, and I had not thought of her in years—however, the Old City evoked the memory of her, having outlived her immediate family and the friends of her girlhood, to sit quite alone in the world on a bluff overlooking the ancient river.

London was like that, on this night anyway, in this out-of-the-way district.

I passed an alley, pitched in an even darker shade of night, and a rustling noise caught my attention—perhaps a street-cat prowling for a meal or a mate; yet the sound seemed too subdued, too accidental, to support that assertion very far. I tried to concoct other explanations, as I hastened my pace along the dark walk, but each was more menacing than the one previous.

The odd desolation persisted, and, absurdly, I began to doubt I was in the Old City at all—but rather some other metropolis, in America or in Europe, that is, from my past or from my future. I began to feel the same sort of foreboding I'd felt when viewing Thursday's bizarre jack-o'-lanterns. It was as if they were windows into some other world, or into a facet of this one that normally remained hidden from our perception. I felt a bit dizzy and would've blamed the ale except that I'd only drunk a single glass. Was that true? I hadn't recollected the salty barmaid's bringing the ale in the first place; perhaps I'd sat there finishing off a whole congius of the stuff, lost in the play and in my own thoughts, unaware of my steady drinking. I remembered the silencing of the rude ruffs, and I questioned my perceptions of that as well: Could I have been the one who quieted them? Or might I have been among their number and called out lewd comments of my own?

It seemed a flimsy partition of truth that separated me from the actual events and a host of alternative scenarios—and remaining on the truth-side of that divider felt more a matter of chance and less a consequence of personal will. I shifted my focus for the sound of a cab, or for any fellow pedestrians, but the streets were utterly abandoned, as if the populace had received reports of an invading army of barbarians on their doorstep, and every citizen absconded with a tablecloth bundle of family valuables. I hoped to encounter another lantern-lighter, or at least the fruit of his labor, but it seemed the Old City was desperately short of them. I sensed the need for a more northerly direction and crossed a dark street, accordingly, then turned a corner. . . .

I was quite surprised (and relieved!) to see a couple strolling only a few blocks ahead—at least the beshadowed figures seemed to be a tall-hatted man and a hoopskirted woman: the meager starlight that filtered down to the street, through a gauzy cloud cover, allowed for only the vaguest of identifications. Nevertheless my spirits were gladdened to see them, and I quickened my pace in hopes of overtaking them, and perhaps asking direction, or if nothing else, at least wishing them a good evening and thereby soliciting the sound of a human voice in this evacuated metropolis.

On this night perhaps *necropolis* would be more fitting. Indeed the couple moved like shades along the shadowed walk. More than once I thought they were an illusion, a trick of the darkness, as they seemed to disappear altogether. Each time, after a moment or two, they would show themselves again, though no more distinctly than before. I was tempted to run but didn't want to startle them, so I maintained my steady yet speedy gait.

As I gradually gained ground, I realized they were speaking to one another, and in a rather animated tone: they were having a disagreement, a somewhat heated one in fact. Now I was especially reluctant to overtake them. We all three were locomoting in essentially the correct direction for my needs (so I believed); thus I was not damaging my purpose by following their path, though we had long since been in a part of the City that was totally foreign to me. Yet I sensed a familiarity in my surroundings, in spite of knowing full well that such a familiarity was impossible. The French have a phrase for it: déjà vu. Perhaps it was merely a matter of its being a darkened city and was in that regard like any darkened city in the world, New York, for instance, or Boston, or even Albany.

My ears—the ones that earned me the nickname "Chimp" among my cleverest school chums—began picking up specific words hissed (yes, hissed is not too strong) between the man and woman. I was too far back and their speech was too subdued for me to hear their exact dialogue, but individual words and phrases could be discerned: your father, the office, drink, shameful. . . . My sense was that one of them—the man surely—had effected a display of public drunkenness, which was "shameful," and this had led to certain embarrassment among his colleagues at "the office." How "father," or for that matter *whose* "father," fit into the trigonometry was unclear from my eavesdropping. I was careful to remain far enough behind that I wouldn't be detected—how quickly I had reversed my objective, one-hundred-eighty degrees, to tap into this juicy narrative. I heard something about "nuptials" and "mother" and "the scandal." Could it be that this episode of inebriation had led the couple to break their engagement?

Though the street remained quite dark (and silent and utterly abandoned except for the three of us), figurative lights began to flicker on for me and my comprehending. It seemed that it was the young lady who'd been drunk . . . at some sort of social gathering connected to the gentleman's place of business. Now I was filling in the narrative gaps as much by invention as by actual hearing, but it appeared the gentleman worked for his father's firm, thus magnifying the ignominy of the incident; and could it be that the young lady was demonstrating behaviors of her mother, who was well acquainted with drink? . . .

I had managed to match their pace so that I remained the ideal distance behind, about a city block, in order to half hear their conversation without my being detected—but I quite suddenly halted, dead in my tracks as it were, as the scene the young couple depicted was eerily familiar: it was from Chapter Twenty of *Andersen's Romance*, when Katherine's thirst for the bottle is unceremoniously revealed at a holiday party for the office staff of the senior Andersen's firm. I had written that new scene not thirty-six hours earlier.

It must've been some incredible coincidence—or, more logically, the scene was still fresh in my fancy, and in an effort to infer the missing parts of the couple's dialogue, I'd supplied details from the revised storyline of my book. Yes, that made sound sense. Satisfied, I hurried to catch the young couple. They once again had disappeared in the strange darkness, darkness that was a patchwork in degrees of black: what the eye mistook for feeble starlight was merely a less intense black, a tone moving in the scale toward gray. I was not concerned at first with the discordant couple's disappearing—they had done so before several times—but on this occasion their absence from view lingered . . . and was becoming worrisome. I thought, This must be how a loving parent feels when his child has become lost in a crowd, and he begins to fret if he will ever again see their freckled features or hear their lisping laugh.

My heart began to drum in my chest.

The emptiness of the London streets had been strikingly odd all along; now though with the dematerialization of the quarrelsome couple the absence of all light and sound and, especially, human fellowship was dispiriting and oppressive. In the whole of the world there was only I, and my ringing footsteps, and the percussive pulse of my heart. I thought of the chapter in *Dunkelraum* in which the Professor goes for a stroll in the mountains to clear his head and becomes hopelessly disoriented for a time. He begins to imagine that there'd been an especially virulent plague and humanity was exterminated save for him. In a densely wooded pass, Dunkelraum becomes momentarily panic-stricken and imagines the trunks of the aspen trees closing in upon him like a cage. . . .

I began to panic that I would become panic-stricken like the Professor. I assured myself it was all quite silly, as I asserted effort to bring my respiration under control. Meanwhile I strained to see in the dark street, to catch sight or sound of the couple . . . but it seemed a doomed cause, as the more effort I exerted, the more recalcitrant the darkness was to coalesce into any intelligible design.

In spite of myself, I quickened my pace. Surely if the couple were no longer on the street, that meant they entered a building, except I'd heard no sounds to indicate it: no creaking hinge, no turning knob, no clicking key, nor tinkling bell, clanging knock . . . indeed, nothing of the sort. Moreover, none of the building fronts implied any sort of activity; they were as static and as sterile as the back of a painted stage.

Taking a sudden chance, I came to a corner and turned right, placing my fortunes on pure luck. I strained to see into the unknowable distance—!

The couple was standing, stock-still, right in front of me. Had I taken one more harried step I would've run into them. They were facing me, I determined after a brief moment—the darkness was so complete it was not an easy conclusion to reach.

"Hello . . . I hope I haven't startled you," though it was my voice that slightly caught with the racing of my respiration.

The couple did not speak. In fact, I was tempted to reach out and touch an arm or a shoulder to prove to myself they were there at all, and not more optical trickery. I also thought of the ancient Greeks and their underworld shades: I listened for Charon's splashing pole in the inky water of the Styx.

I tried again: "I'm a visitor to the City and have lost my way. . . ."

I thought the gentleman's head moved, the brim of his hat bobbing ever so slightly, as if he may have been glancing about him, reckoning his location in the wide world. Then, "We are out of place as well."

"You are American—I'd heard your voices before, on the street, and I thought—"

The young lady spoke: "Why wouldn't we be American?" There was a subtle slurring in her words, a remnant of the evening's overdrinking no doubt.

"Well, you know, it's a large city, yes, but what are the odds, really? . . ."

My stammering query solicited only more silence. We stood there facing one another on the dark street, not speaking, for what seemed a long moment. All the while, I tried to discern the couple's features—yes, all right: I attempted to discern their identities. Their earlier dialogue, which so well matched my Andersen and Katherine's, had quite unnerved me, and I wanted to prove the notion utterly preposterous. Yet nothing in our brief exchange had accomplished the unmasking; far from it in fact.

"Where are you from?" I said.

Somehow the question prompted silence of even deeper profundity, a silence that delved beneath normal earthly quiet, a silence that was the other side of echo, the sudden silence of a cave when the last shade of echo has perished in the dark . . . the silence that surrounds the soul in the loneliest hour of wakeful night. . . .

"Not here," said the fellow, and I thought I heard a touch of trepidation in his voice as well, as if my uneasiness had infected him, like Dr. Carter's notion of the tiny sickness-bearing creatures that fly through the air from one person to another. . . .

It is difficult to say which came first, but our conversation was broken by a fourth voice: "Looking for a ride, gov'ner?" and the couple was gone. Had they somehow slipped away in the dark while I'd been happily distracted by the cabby? It was the only explanation: people do not simply evaporate before one's eyes—granted, one's tired, overstrained eyes—like a morning mist before the sudden sun. I took no time to ponder it as I hurried to accept the cabby's offer before he too vanished: the lanterns on either side of his cockseat were the first points of light I'd seen in a long while, and they were welcome indeed.

I told the fellow Mrs. Haeley's number as I climbed into the carriage. As we clattered off—and I wondered vaguely why I hadn't heard the cab's noisy approach—I looked for the American couple on the walk. Pedestrians began to emerge, and I noticed a lighted lantern at a street corner, but the gentleman and his young lady were not to be seen.

In a moment the Old City—the world!—was quite itself again; yet the feeling of strangeness lingered, like the fractured memory of a bad dream, like the scent of woodsmoke on one's clothes and in one's hair the morning after a campfire. It was an unfortunate simile as it recalled the Wheelwright family's warehouse fire and our lost fortune, which in turn recalled the grand beginning to my Continental tour. The loss of it all saddened me, to be sure, but there was no question that it'd led to my time with the authoress, an experience, no matter how it was destined to play itself out, that I would not have traded for all the furs in North America.

I sat quietly for a time; even my mind was quiet in its way. The cab-wheels clattered on the unevenly paved streets. Outside, voices called to each other, some hawking wares, others hawking themselves, and customers of either variety calling back in response. At one especially spirited exchange I looked from the cab window and saw an enormous black shadow upon a brick wall. It must've been a trick of the light, making a normal-size fellow appear a giant against the building. As I watched, looking backward from the steadily advancing cab, the shadow appeared to move from the wall as if it were intent upon following me. I looked out the opposite window for a light source and a lean fellow who'd been made to look a giant, but neither showed themselves on the walk, which had grown busy with pedestrians and peddlers.

I returned my view to the original window and of course observed no shadow in pursuit of me, striding along from wall to wall, as if an ourang-outang that could only move from limb to limb in the jungle canopy. Nevertheless I was once again unsettled and very much desired to be at Mrs. Haeley's home. The cab-wheels continued bouncing, jostling my brains, and perhaps this had a volatile effect, like it does to shake combinations of chemical materials to make them react, and thus form new, even unanticipated, substances. All of these most recent events brought to my recollection an event from the evening I wandered the streets in a fog of despair induced by too much port wine—my memory of the episode was equally befogged. Yet now, with the chemical materials of my brains being shaken as if in an apothecary's jar, the incident with the woman in black, who believed something terrible was trailing her—of all things, I most vividly remembered the touch of her hands on my chest—that woman must've been the authoress herself, on her own mad rumble. Could she have believed her own literary creation, her own monster, was following her? Intent on doing her harm? I tried to recall the precise details of our encounter, our precise dialogue, but it remained a cloudy muddle, perhaps even a confusion almost entirely of my own invention. . . .

I looked out the cab window—and perhaps saw the giant shadow again . . . or perhaps not, perhaps only an oddly angled corner of a building, suddenly appeared in then disappeared from my advancing view. In any event, I felt my heart step up its percussive rhythm, and my mouth was quite dry, and my tongue detected a queer taste, not unlike blood when one bites a lip or staunches a cut by putting one's finger to one's mouth. . . .

I saw in my mind's eye horrid wolf teeth, bared and caked in dried blood, fangs of sanguine sharp death—and it seemed a memory though it could not possibly be. There were of course the puppeteer's ferocious wolves, the ones that attacked the Princess—but surely they, bouncing herky-jerkily on their strings, could not evoke such terrifying rememberings, could not evoke the scent of death on their lupine lips. . . .

There it was again, the giant shadow on a brick façade, plain as day, well, plain as night. Again I went to the opposite window, this time with feline reflex, but again saw no one or nothing that could account for the shadow. I looked back and witnessed it move from the façade with its own feline felicity.

The cab came to a stop, and I suspected at first the cab-man was playing a trick, that he somehow knew of my state of agitation over the giant shadow which pursued me—however, it was simply that we had reached the authoress's house.

"Here's the number, gov," called the fellow from his seat when I was slower to exit than his usual fare.

I unlatched the door and stepped down to the curb. I took the wallet from my trouser pocket and fished about for the proper remuneration, about a tuppence, but I was especially clumsy as I was distracted by also keeping watch for the giant shadow. At last I handed the fellow up a shilling, which was too much by far, but he thanked me with a tip of his battered derby and shook the reins to start his grays moving. As the cab pulled away from the curb, I was afforded a view directly across Wicker's Lane—and there it was, against the brown-brick opposite Mrs. Haeley's house. It—he! . . . yes, the shadow was gendered in my mind and he was a he—he stood facing me—yes the shadow possessed a countenance, and he stood facing me—I was certain of it. . . .

We looked at one another across the empty street, transfixed, and stayed thus for a length of time that defied counting—not that the length was so long that it perplexed one's ability to count it; rather the nature of the mutual watching fell outside the bounds of normal time: Does the dragonfly perceive time as the tortoise does? The toadstool as the oak? Thus was the queerness of our watching, the shadow's and mine. It occurred to me that he stood essentially where I had stood the first time I came to call upon the authoress—that his point of view was what mine had been when I first gazed at Mrs. Haeley's house, and spied Thursday come along with his load of broken furniture. In fact . . . could the shadow be me, or some remnant of me, following my self since my (*our*) arrival in England? Somehow separated at sea, as we chaotically crossed the great expanse between New World and Old? Come to think of it, standing there, staring, I had smelt something that reminded me of the ocean, something brackish, though we were too far from any docks to account for it. I realized then that my cheeks were damp with my own tears, my own salt-tears. . . .

"Mr. Wheelwright?"

The voice startled me, to put it mildly, even though I recognized it at once: I turned toward Miss Edith, who had opened the door, no doubt having heard the cab and expecting my prompt entrance.

"Is everything quite all right?"

"Yes," I managed. I looked for the giant shadow but he was of course gone, back into the night, or the light, to wherever such shades return. I tried to surreptitiously dry the tears from my cheeks.

I waved to Miss Edith as I walked toward her, wanting to reassure her I was perfectly fine, though the gesture did little to convince myself.

Twenty-one

~

M ISS EDITH WAITED FOR ME AT THE DOOR THEN SHUT IT BEHIND me. I listened to her latch two of the four locks and I planned to do the others when she wasn't paying attention: I was more anxious and unsettled than before I left. It suddenly came to me that I had departed under the pretext of resupplying our slender larder, and here I stood emptyhanded. In fact Miss Edith seemed to be taking note of my emptyhandedness—she may have even detected the odd floral scent of Lizzie I's still on me: I felt like a wayward husband returned to a suspicious wife. Given the circumstances Miss Edith may have even speculated that I'd snuck out of the house to patronize a brothel—London appeared rich in them even by New York City standards. I considered defending myself, and explaining that I'd sought to learn the conclusion of a children's puppet-show and had gotten side-channeled into watching an all-female production of *Romeo and Juliet*; then I couldn't find a cab—or virtually any people—in one of the most populated metropolises in the world; then I perhaps encountered my own literary creations. . . .

Let her believe in the brothel.

She said, "Mrs. Haeley awoke and was asking to speak with you—it seemed important to her—but that was some time ago. I shall see if she is still alert." Perhaps it was my heightened anxiety but there seemed a healthy degree of accusation woven throughout Miss Edith's statement.

While I waited for her return, I went to the parlor and hung up my hat and coat. Then I lighted the lamp next to the sofa. Momentarily Miss Edith was at the parlor doorway:

"She is sleeping again, but I know she wanted you to read this —" Miss Edith held the authoress's manuscript. "—and assist her in deciding what to read tomorrow evening."

It is a cliché to say that one's heart came instantly to one's throat, but it was quite an apt description for myself at that moment. I went to the governess and reached out trembling hands. I would have been embarrassed to be so overwrought by a mere sheaf of papers, except I knew that Edith understood; and perhaps her own hands trembled a touch too as she handed me the manuscript, as if it were the newborn prince of the realm, born to a queen whose people had come to believe her barren.

"Thank you" was all I managed to say.

Edith, in full awareness of the moment's solemnity, nodded to me slightly then left me alone with the authoress's words. I kept even one hand upon them as I changed from my shoes to my calfskin slippers, which I'd left there in the parlor. Then I went to a sofa, propped my tired feet on an Ottoman, and began reading. . . .

<u>Young Germany</u>
:
<u>A Memoir of a Life Shared</u>

By Margaret T. Haeley

It was on a boat, the river-man navigating the Rhine's swift and icy channels, when she looked up and saw Wolfsburg Castle : a lonely sentinel overlooking the storied waterway – – it sat there as lonesome as the final wolf of a perished pack – – : It was then that the full weight of what they were doing came upon her. Though she did not yet show the gentle bulge beneath her layers of clothes – – all the clothing that she owned in the world – – she involuntarily reached down and felt her living womb and thought in a real manner about the baby that would be Haeley's and hers – – she knows now, as a woman, that it was too soon to feel the baby's movements, but there, passing lonely Wolfsburg, Haeley at her side but not thinking of her or their child – – instead composing, forever

composing verse in his mind (a thing for which she loved
him) : there she seemed to feel the baby, almost reaching out
to its mother, wanting to know – – <u>needing</u> to know if he
would be as lonely in this world as that castle upon the hill, if
he would be a kind of wolf-last-standing ~~aching~~ hurting for
the harmony of companion howls on moonlit nights : Now,
as a woman, she knows she was painting her own thoughts
onto the baby's, her own worries, a seventeen-year-old girl on
the run, as one journalist back in England was to phrase it – –
on the run with a married man, himself fleeing an unloved
wife but a loved child, too, risking his fortune and reputation
for her : she hardly felt worthy of the honor – – though she
did hurt for that fatherless boy, she, a motherless girl who felt
<u>her</u> absence every day of her life as a one-eyed fellow must
be reminded every waking moment of what he is missing ~~in the world~~.

Our boat neared a small dock, which looked as ancient
as the forested hills themselves, and Haeley suddenly ordered
the river-man to halt there. The hale German, a Lower Saxon,
with brown hair and the fairest of skin, protested that this was
not our stop, that our village of destination was some distance
downriver. When Haeley adamantly declared that he knew
all of that but to dock nonetheless – – Haeley and the river-
man managed surprisingly well in their broken English and
German, each employing a French word or phrase now and
then to support clarity : she had read Goethe, of course, and
Kant, and Wolff – – but their formal styles had not prepared
her to cluck along in workaday Deutsch like a Bavarian
busy-body. As the river-man began steering toward the
dock – – not a difficult feat as the current intended the path
of its own ancient accord – – the German fellow matched
Haeley's adamancy to be sure they were clear that they were
not receiving in return any part of their fare : the price had
been quite agreed upon. Haeley dismissed the matter as if
he already had his family inheritance – – a prospect that was
still years in the future, and now quite in jeopardy altogether
due to his rash actions with her. She considered trying to

convince the German to return a small portion of their fare : though just a girl she understood poverty in a way that her Haeley never would – – but had she tried to retrieve a pfennig or two, though sorely needed, it would have injured Haeley's pride : or so she believed : in truth they barely knew each other – – only that to the furthest depth of their souls they loved each other and quite intended never to be apart until the end of time. – – Romantics as they were it never occurred to either of them that their end-times would be so much different.

(Later, she would come to learn that Haeley had considered haggling for the refunded fare himself, but he did not think she understood their dire financial predicament, and he did not want her to worry if it could be helped.)

They were unceremoniously deposited on the old dock with all their worldly belongings : a canvas bag with their few personal items and a small oaken chest crammed full of books – – it was their treasure chest, stolen, or merely borrowed they told themselves, from her father's library before they departed, absconding in the night quite like common ~~thieves~~ burglars with the family silver. She took up the bag and Haeley shouldered the chest, his narrow frame barely broad enough for the feat – – had she not been pregnant she would have been quite better suited for transporting the heavy collection of books. Haeley, reckoning their course by pure instinct, led them to a path which appeared to wind through the woods on the landward side of Wolfsburg Castle : apparently their destination though Haley had said nothing to that effect – – in fact barely anything at all. That was his way : a practitioner of taciturnity in everyday life, saving his words for his poet's pen, as if one had but so very few to use in a lifetime, and he did not want to squander his allotment in idle chatter. They talked of books, of ideas, of political principles, of childrearing (in the abstract, not the rearing of their coming child) – – but common news, 'gossip' Haeley would term it, held no interest for him. She was so grateful that someone of learning – – and Stephen Haeley had received the finest English education – – that someone of learning sought and cared for her opinions : on things other than how much salt should be shaken into the soup stock, or the quantity of lye to lay upon the laundry : – – well, it was heady for an unschooled girl; and she loved him for it, as she loved his glacial blue eyes, and flaxen curls, and the fine cut of his cheekbones : sharper than any village beauty's who can enchant the farm-boys with a toss of her tresses. In a word, Haeley was <u>beautiful</u>. And he loved <u>her</u>, who could count on one hand the number of boys' heads she'd turned and leave her thumb free to put alongside her nose for all those who hadn't given her the hour of the day.

Haeley led them along the path, with new-fallen snow crunching beneath their shoes, and a carpet of old-fallen leaves beneath the snow. Soon the way became steeper and the snow deeper; in fact <u>the way</u> was no longer clear at all. Haeley, perhaps to reassure her, his expectant adolescent ~~lover~~ sweetheart – – he removed a pen-knife from his pocket, managed to extend its blade without depositing the chest of books on the ground; and he hastily carved his initials, SBH, into a tree trunk – – a marker in case they lost their way : she understood, though she glanced behind her at the heavily trampled path and thought there was little chance of their not being able to find their way in reverse. Bless him : practical matters were not her Haeley's strongest suit. He repositioned the chest and they continued their snowy ascent. . . .

Miss Edith knocked on the doorframe with the side of her shoe, then entered with a tray. "I have just made tea, Mr. Wheelwright, and thought you may like some." Her tone had returned to its normal congenial manner—I was forgiven my wayward ways. In addition to the teapot and cup, there were two biscuits with butter and honey on a small plate.

"Thank you, Miss Edith; it is very kind of you." As if on cue, my stomach growled noisily in the quiet parlor, and we both had to smile at the timing.

She placed the tray on the Ottoman seat and exited. I set the manuscript aside to pour a cup and to quite devour the biscuits, being far hungrier than I'd realized. While I washed the biscuits down with the good, strong English tea, I considered Mrs. Haeley's memoir. It seemed the authoress's style was unique: her use of punctuation was unusual (no doubt the result of her being, as she phrased it, "unschooled"); and her syntax was almost . . . geometric, as if written by someone whose true calling in life should have been arithmetician. Before publication, the punctuation of *Dunkelraum* had been brought into convention—perhaps by Haeley, or by the novel's editor—and someone must have filed the sharpest edges from Mrs. Haeley's geometric prose, but nevertheless the authoress of *Dunkelraum* was clearly here on the leafs of this memoir: there was no doubt, and I felt relief at this inarguable conclusion.

More than all of that, the memoir itself was enthralling. Here was an intimate look at quite possibly the most famous literary couple of the century—no question the most infamous—and the raw honesty with which Mrs. Haeley was telling their story . . . well, only a few pages into the narrative, and I knew I was holding in my unworthy hands a landmark book, a manuscript of pure gold. It was not a novel, but it read as one, in large part due to Mrs. Haeley's writing of herself in the third-person point of view—not in itself a wholly original approach, but normally its function is to provide a cold formality to the writing, but here it is quite the opposite effect: we are not just wafted along beside Margaret Haeley, but alongside her very soul.

Time escaped me as I continued reading the authoress's memoir. She and Haeley completed their ascent to Wolfsburg Castle, where there was a shrine to a long-ago occupant's long-dead mother— Haeley had read of the shrine's existence, in the castle's ruined courtyard, and thought his young mistress would appreciate seeing it: on the one hand, a thoughtful gesture, since certainly she had erected a sort of mental shrine to her own long-deceased mother, and hence could appreciate the sentiment; but considering the terror that Mae was feeling at the idea of herself giving birth, the dead-mother shrine only deepened her fears—which she did not share with Haeley until much later. Readers of *Dunkelraum* (and who is not?) will of course recognize the shrine scene from the novel, the impetus for the Professor's creating his monster. In the memoir, the couple eventually spent a cold, damp and uninvited night in a barn some distance from the castle, only to be run off at daybreak by a peevish dairy farmer.

I read of the loss of her baby, a little girl, born at seven months . . . of Haeley's wife's suicide back home in England . . . of the authoress's half-sister's death in childbirth . . . of the couple's profound money troubles . . . of a second pregnancy and eventual stillbirth. But also through it all there were Haeley and she, whose love for one another was of a depth and profundity I could only begin to comprehend. I had thought the concept of a "soul-mate" to be romantic claptrap, but here in the neatly quilled pages of this manuscript, its existence was demonstrated: Stephen Haeley and Margaret Townsend were soul-mates, and they knew it from the moment they met in her father's study, the young poet having come to pay his respects to the well-known philosopher, William Townsend. And from that moment they had no choice but to be together. Though he was an atheist, Haeley believed in a higher authority than mere man's—something intrinsic in the soul, but not the soul as Christians perceive it, something more like one's inner mind, one's true being. The authoress discussed it at some length in her memoir's third chapter via a dialogue between Haeley and her: "Religion, as it has come to be in the modern world," said Stephen Haeley, "is a corruption of our true souls – – and the corruption is so systematical and so complete, we no longer are able to understand, leave be speak, the language of the soul : That, Mae, is the genuine Hell – – Hell as a deadly fen betwixt our waking minds and our true souls : in essence separating us from our Selves."

Then the young couple departed for Europe, man and wife in spirit, if not in law. The only reason that they married at all, after Haeley's wife's suicide, was that Haeley's solicitor advised them that a legal marriage would smooth the way for his regaining custodianship of his abandoned child: "They set aside their principles for the sake of that little dear one, who needed his 'Pop-pop,' as his childish tongue called him." That all happened very quickly—the suicide, the loss the authoress's baby, their return to England and marriage, the reunion of father and son, and the beginning of the writing of *Dunkelraum*—all in just over a year's time.

I must say that it was this section of the manuscript, the composition of *Dunkelraum*, in which I was most interested. It came about midway through Mrs. Haeley's manuscript, a tome of nearly six-hundred pages in length. The genesis of the novel is famous in itself of course: Haeley and she had made their way to Geneva to spend a few weeks in the Alps with poet friends. The visit was in general a disaster—uncongenial weather that kept them indoors, and often equally uncongenial temperaments. It did not assist Mae's pleasure that she was pregnant—with the child who would be born prematurely and not survive. Someone among them was reading the book of German ghost stories, *Fantasmagorie*, translated into French, and eventually they all read from it; hence it was suggested that each of them, including Mae, who had barely written anything besides personal correspondence, that each of them try his hand at writing an original tale of horror. It was this challenge, which became at times . . . meanly spirited (ha!), that led to Margaret Townsend's nightmare—the unholy Professor Dunkelraum figure poised over his stitched-together monster: the beginning of the writing of *Dunkelraum*.

Chapter Twelve of the memoir detailed this ill-fated yet fateful Genevan holiday in full measure.

After reading approximately half the manuscript what I'd learned most poignantly was that I was even more deeply in love with Margaret Haeley—my old adolescent crush was renewed with increased ardor by reading about the audacious young woman who both dazzled and enraged the literary establishment with her shockingly bold novel; but also my more mature self sympathized with the painful losses, and profound fears of the unknowable future, which she expressed with such unvarnished eloquence. At the same moment I was slowly being crushed by the realization that no matter how much love and protective affection I felt for the authoress it would never come close to the impassioned connection that Stephen Haeley and she shared with every bit of their soul-mated beings. It was no wonder the authoress had never remarried—not even this cherished friend, Mundie, who died of typhus in Venice. . . .

I was deep into these reveries, probably sitting a trifle slack-jawed even, when Miss Edith came into the parlor again. "Mr.

Wheelwright," she pressed my attention, from her position by the doorway, "Mrs. Haeley is awake and asking for you again."

I crisscrossed the stack of manuscript pages I'd read with the ones I hadn't to keep my place, and stood and stretched. "Thank you . . . what hour has it become, if you please?"

"Nearly midnight," said Miss Edith, who looked very tired: the natural gleam of her gray eyes shone somewhat dully, and her dark hair, always arranged in an attractive bun, was slightly disheveled, with a few strands come free. I spoke what I was thinking: "You appear tired, Miss Edith; you need your rest too."

She smiled. "Soon, Mr. Wheelwright—I'll retire soon." Even her gray frock appeared to hang on her form a trifle wearily.

Not wishing to let go of the manuscript, I carried it upstairs for my interview with the authoress. Reading the work had been an emotional experience—at the conclusion of a day and evening that had been fraught with the entire spectrum of moods and feelings, from epiphanic joy of an almost religious nature to primal childish fear . . . add to it all the anguished pangs of a secret suitor en route to a beloved who has no awareness of his affections, and from whom there is no hope of their return. . . .

Well, let us say, I was in a rare state as I climbed the staircase toward Mrs. Haeley's chamber. I reached the top as if the summit of Mount Pisgah, but a dense fog lay upon the land, obscuring whether it be a land of Promise or a land of Waste. Miss Edith had left a candle burning on a small table in the hall. With supreme deliberation I tightened my grip on the authoress's manuscript and walked to her door. I tapped, and she must've been listening for me as she beckoned me inside immediately. Her room was better lighted than I thought it may be. A lamp was on her dressing-table, opposite the foot of her bed, and a candle burned on a small side-stand, allowing her enough light by which to read. The authoress was beneath the bedclothes, on top of which was a diamond-pattern quilt; yet I saw she wore a white sleeping-gown and a robe of black or dark gray wool. Her face seemed more wan than usual, but she wore a cheerful expression that warmed an otherwise sickly hue. A glass vase on the dressing-table held the sprigs of some herb that gave the room a somewhat minty aroma—but instead of freshening it, the smell reminded me of the hospital I'd visited with Dr. Carter, and the ineffectual scent that was used to try to mask a plethora of vile odors. Nevertheless, the room was more agreeable than perhaps I'd anticipated it to be.

She must have guessed my instinct, as a gentleman, was to leave the door ajar, for she instructed me to close it—my first thought was that Miss Edith would not approve. Mrs. Haeley of course saw the manuscript in my hand: "You've been reading it," she said, pleased, her voice a bit feeble. She nodded toward a chair by the side-stand, inviting me to sit, which I did.

I rested the heavy manuscript on my lap. "Yes, it's . . . it's incredible, Mae . . . it's astonishing, truly. . . ."

The authoress smiled, and in it there was perhaps a touch of relief at my good opinion. "I did not ask you up here so you would sing its praises—though, I must say, you have a lovely voice. . . ." This was the charming girl with whom Stephen Haeley fell in love, and now I loved her too. "I do want to speak with you about the book, but in a few moments I must broach a far weightier subject, one that may test the breaking-point of our new friendship. I don't mean to tease you, Jeff, but it really is best to speak regarding the book first."

I was of course intrigued by this "weightier subject"—one that caused a shadow to pass over Mae's otherwise cheerful countenance at only a mere allusion to it. In fact, my gut became filled with rollicking wasps in anticipation; nevertheless I had no choice but to trust her judgment in the matter.

She continued: "Edith has communicated to you my seeking your opinion as to which section to read . . . tonight, at the soirée?"

"Yes—now, I have had only time to read the first half or so, but I'm thinking possibly something from the Genevan section, regarding the conception of *Dunkelraum*, or even the opening scene and your improvised excursion to Wolfsburg Castle—in truth, Mae, it's all quite wonderful, so it is all but impossible for me to advocate one section at the expense of others."

It was difficult to say for certain because of the quality of the lighting, but Mrs. Haeley seemed to color at my lush praise. Perhaps tears even glistened in her eyes. "Thank you, Jeff, for your kind words—they mean more to me than you can know."

The authoress reached out and took my hand, and our clasped hands rested on the sheaf of her manuscript. Her hand was cold, so I placed my other hand on top of hers to warm it. Our sudden intimacy quickened my heart.

She said, "I was thinking similarly as to my reading—I will consider of it further. Now . . . there are other matters we must discuss." The authoress squeezed my hand, though her grip was weak. "Your arrival here, at my doorstep, has been quite a fortuitous event, from my perspective . . . I am going to make two requests of you—*enormous* requests, far larger than I have a right—"

"Mae, you may ask of me anything—anything at all. . . ." I wanted to confess my feelings for her but I could not find the words—the heartrending irony!—and she went on.

"I . . ." Her voice faltered for a moment. "I have not been well. Before your arrival, I was—how to put it?—out of touch with my own mind. I cannot say for how long, and I don't know why your coming here so much improved me . . . why I was able to reclaim myself. I wanted to believe that my reclamation was permanent, but I know now it is not—"

"Mae—"

"Please, Jeff, let me just lay it all out; then we can sort through it as much as you wish." There was a suggestion of desperation in her voice. She had been holding a book in her hand, and now set it aside without marking her place. It was Edmund Holland's *Things in Mist*.

"I don't know that anyone will be interested in my book—in Haeley's and my story—but I entrust the manuscript to your care. I know it needs polishing, some 'filing down of the sharp edges,' as Haeley used to say." The recollection brought a smile to her colorless lips. "And my punctuation, well, it cannot be helped—my country is determined that I should be uneducated." The smile gave way to a bitter note. "In any event, do with it what you're able . . . if you generously accept the task, that is."

"Of course, of course. I am humbled and honored. . . ." I considered protesting, saying that she should oversee its publication herself, but I knew there was no point to my protestation, and my heart grew leaden. Mae sensed my mood and squeezed my hand; I realized the irony of *her* comforting *me*.

"Even though taking on the book is no mean task," she said, "the one I am about to ask is far greater—and you must feel at liberty to decline, otherwise I shan't ask."

"Yes, all right." Becoming choked with emotion, I could barely give voice to the reply.

She removed her hand from my grasp and took up Mr. Holland's book again; not to read, however—more out of nervousness, more for support. "That silver urn," said the authoress, motioning with the book toward a corner of the room, largely in shadow; but I saw the obelisk-shaped urn, lamplight glinting dimly along one edge. It sat upon a diminutive table, near the room's single window, and it had some sort of dark-colored cloth spread beneath it, lending it an air of religiosity, of sacredness. I had not noticed the urn previously. "That is what remains of my Haeley—ashes to ashes, as it were."

I was still looking at the urn as she spoke, and the knowledge of its contents transformed it into something holy indeed: the glint along its edge seemed to instantly shine more sharply, as if in fact the light source were *inside* the urn—Stephen Haeley's poetic soul beaming forth, la flamme éternelle.

"You know my Haeley's story, how he died."

The way she said it implied to me that she wanted to recount the tale: "Perhaps not all of it," I said.

The authoress spoke into the space before her, into the chilly air of her room, but, as it seemed, not to me: "Haeley went to Italy to sail with friends, a yachting regatta. I remained in England, pregnant again. The newspapers at the time made it sound like he had callously abandoned his pregnant wife—as he had abandoned his first wife, they insinuated—but that is not how it was. I encouraged him to go. I knew his spirit, and he needed to go, to be with nature for a time. He did not intend to make the trip—he understood his duty to me—but I in turn understood my duty to him and convinced him. I was only a few weeks pregnant, and he would be returned to England long before the birth."

In fact I did not know this part of the story; my recollection was that Stephen Haeley, the egoist, had left his wife at home, thoughtlessly, while he went yachting. I didn't know of the pregnancy, which must have ended as tragically as the previous two, nor of Mrs. Haeley's insistence that he make the trip—that is, her insistence he make what became his fatal trip.

"I received a letter from Mundie, who'd accompanied Haeley to Italy but was a devout hydrophobe and hence luckily remained on dry-land during the regatta—Mundie informed me that a freak storm had arisen, Haeley's yacht was capsized, all were lost." Mae paused, continuing to stare into the space before her. I realized that though the accident had occurred eleven years before, this accounting may have been the first time she had shared her tale with anyone—having no family and, it would seem, no friends except Agamemnon Mundie, who already'd been privy to the particulars. I assumed she discussed the accident in her memoir, but I had not read that far.

She went on, "In the letter, Mundie reported that they were planning an open-air cremation, according to Haeley's wishes, but had had to petition the Italian government for permission. Once everything was completed, he would return the remains to me in England. You can imagine my devastation." She turned her head toward me; tears had gathered in her eyes.

"On the contrary, Mae, I cannot imagine it, not fully."

"Nearly three weeks later, Mundie arrived here bearing that silver urn and all that remains of my Haeley: two handfuls of ashes, impurely combined with the ashes from the funeral scaffold." She was staring at the obelisk, blotting her eyes with the bedsheet. "Actually, Jeff, there is one thing more, besides Haeley's poetry of course, which will survive us all."

"One thing more," I repeated.

She undid the top button of her sleeping gown, reached beneath it and pulled out a locket that she kept on a chain around her neck. "There is this. I do not mention it in the book; it seems too macabre to most, I suppose, and the public already prefers to think of Haeley and me as godless, wanton ghouls." She held the locket in her ghostly white fingers. "I have opened this but once in eleven years, and that was to confirm its contents. Mundie gave me it along with the urn: it contains a tiny sliver of Haeley's heart, a sort of representation of the poet's soul. His friends retrieved the organ from his body, after the funereal flame had rent it. Mundie wore a similar locket and when he succumbed to typhus, also in Italy—a country to avoid it would seem—I was hoping to retrieve it, but no one had any knowledge of it; and I was loath to inquire too fervidly."

Mae let go of the locket and took my hand again. The locket remained on the outside of her gown. "I always intended to return to Germany, where we were happiest, and spread Haeley's ashes there, but time and means get away from us, and I have not honored my intention; I have not honored Haeley and his memory." She hesitated but only a moment. "This is my request, Jeff: Would you be kind enough to escort me to Germany, to deposit my Haeley's ashes in the place that seems most fitting?"

"Yes, of course, Mae, of course—I am honored." I was attempting to perform the calculations to determine if I had sufficient wherewithal for us to travel to the Rhine Valley, when the authoress spoke to the very subject:

"I am hopeful that a publisher will pay me enough for that stack of paper to cover the expenses of the journey."

That should not be a problem, I thought, and began to feel relief regarding the pecuniary aspects of the trip, which allowed my mind to turn to other matters. For example, when did Mae think we would take this journey? I planned for nearly a year's time before embarking on my Continental tour—for all the good it did me. Also, it was with difficulty that I imagined the authoress having the strength to last during tonight's literary soirée—in fact, I entertained the notion of postponing it—leave be travel to Germany and deliver Stephen Haeley's ashes to a suitable resting place. Then again, I recollected all this frail-looking woman had survived—all the losses of family and friends—and knew that I was underestimating her.

I said, "I will assist you any way that I'm able. I. . . ." I considered adding *love you*, or something to that effect, but my confession of adoration seemed as feeble to me as Mrs. Haeley herself appeared now. The authoress's eyes and mine met at that moment, and I realized there was no need to state it: Mae knew, and she squeezed my hand as if to say *Had there been another time, another place. . . .*

"May I get you anything?" My voice broke somewhat.

She released my hand and smiled. "No thank you, Jeff; but thank you for your generosity—you have put my mind at ease, more at ease than in a long while."

I rose from the chair, and she added, "Please leave the manuscript. I am going to rest for a while then think about the reading. You have a reading to prepare for as well—it is in fact your night."

In the hall I closed the door behind me. One would think my mind would be racing with all that had just transpired, but in truth I was suddenly exhausted and felt I barely had the energy to make it to my bed just two rooms away. I figured I would get a brief sleep, then I could look at *Andersen's* afresh and prepare for the reading. Passing the candle on the small table, I noticed *my* shadow upon the opposite wall, except it seemed to me not my shadow at all but rather the alien shadow that had followed me to Mrs. Haeley's house—an absurd idea and unquestionably the product of my exhausted senses. Nevertheless, I was quick to enter my bedroom and shut out the lurking shade.

Twenty-two

INSIDE THE CAMERA OBSCURA . HOT . OPPRESSIVELY CLOSE
. someone is smoking . a child coughs . no image has
materialized on the white circle . not a circle precisely . i look
closely . the shape of a human eye . but all white . no iris . nor
pupil . we stand around the eyeshape . in thrall to its blankness .
 . the child coughs
again . or is it a woman . my cravat is tight at my swollen
neck . i hear a growling . lupine . seemingly from inside the
dark chamber . again . no one seems to be troubled by it . but
me . i look around me . a circle of strangers . all their faces
cast down . staring at the blank eyeshape . i feel i should say
something . but my cravat is strangling me . preventing me
from voicing my concern . i cast my eyes down again . and the
shape is no longer blank . its entirety is filled with a moving
scene . wolves stalking along . a trio . they growl peevishly
at one another . their growls are heard inside the camera
obscura . though i do not understand how this is possible
. i am relieved that the wolves are outside . not inside . the
cough again . now sounding something like a growl . lupine
. the tobacco smoke is odd . the smell . sweet like tinged
with blood . i believe then the camera obscura is filled with
voracious wolves . i fear to look left or right . or anywhere
except the eyeshape . which somehow follows the trio of
wolves . though the camera obscura lens is fixed . the wolves
trot over snowdusted ground . harbinger of winter . frost
upon the greengray grass . the wolves menace one another

. bloodstained teeth bared in corpsebone grins . i hear their threatening growls within the chamber . as if the packleader has moved closer to the lens . his bloody grin becomes large on the eyeshape . i watch as his crimson tongue licks at the blood . i hear the lick of crimson tongues within . as i watch the eyeshape . transfixed . a leaf of paper . blown by the wind . sticks to the wolf . in his bloody muzzle . and another . he seems not to notice . or care . another . the eyeshape view moves back . all three wolves are being papered over . as they stalk across the snowdusted ground . menacing the world . the eyeshape draws back farther . i see the leafs of paper . blown from an unknown source . yet i feel i know it . or should know it . the eyeshape draws back farther . the wolves are all but covered in the leafs . they are wolfshapes made of paper . within i hear the rustle of pages . and smell the black smell of ink . still moist . yes . i see . the wolfshapes are covered in glossy black script . I know it is the memoir . that covers them . leaf upon leaf . a memoir page misses its mark . covers the eyeshape . i read the words . greatly magnified .

her haeley lay his
head upon her swollen womb
and whispered words to their growing
baby ode to a meadowlark
written only minutes

before . I assume . the words flutter . then the memoir page blows . from the eyeshape . revealing a new scene . an acting company . upon the snowdusted graygreen grass. shakespearean . with neither stage nor props . i hear their words . within the dark chamber . the capulets. as they approach the capulet vault . memoir leafs blow among the players . they seem not to notice . or care . the horror that awaits them . inside the imaginary vault . causes me to tremble . on the eyeshape . the capulets continue . toward the vault . i look at the chamber door . invisible in the dark . i expect it to open . to flood the chamber . with moonlight . to reveal the bodies on the floor . juliet draped upon romeo . both still warm to the touch . i try to see them in the blackness

. but cannot . i am alone . except for the eyeshape . on which
i see memoir leafs cling . to lord capulet . his stockinged legs
. he moves strangely . as if on strings . and it is quite simple .
the players are puppets . controlled by a master . out of view
. how could i have not noticed . before . capulet continues
to be covered . by pages that strike him . a thigh . a hip . the
small of the back . i stare into the eyeshape . on the floor . but
do not see the puppeteer strings . a signet ring flashes . as his
hand moves . mechanically . another leaf of memoir blocks
the view .

she held the quill in her

hand trying to create life on the

blank page but all she could think of was the

life no longer inside her body

always and forever

dead . i smell the ink within . then the leaf is blown free .
the machine is rolling away from the eyeshape view . yet at
an angle . by which to see two female figures . one in black .
one in gray . the wheels turn in perfect unison . the figures
pedal . at a steady pace . the eyeshape follows them . on their
machine . so that the view does not change . in spite of their
movement . the female figures ride and ride . covering a great
distance . yet the field appears boundless . i hear the click
of gears . within the dark chamber . and the sour smell of
lubrication oil . the figures alter their course . angling right .
instead of left . when the alteration is complete . they appear
two male figures . one still in black . one still in gray . the
male figures pedal . steadily . i of course recognize their hats
. the high round crowns . within the dark chamber . a child
coughs . or a woman . on the eyeshape something appears .
on the horizon . a row of hedges . the figures pedal faster . the
hedge row looms . quickly . not a hedge row . not precisely .
a labyrinth . the figures steer . into its entrance . the view of
the eyeshape changes . now the view of the lead figure . the
foremost wheels . gloved hands . upon the steeringbar . the
hedge walls . of the labyrinth . the speed is reckless . given
the closeness . of the turns . yet each turn is managed . within

the camera obscura . a child coughs . or sobs . yes . sobs .
i glance up from the eyeshape . perhaps there are figures .
around me . but if so . they wear dark colors . black . gray .
and are quite invisible . again the child sobs . a girl . i look to
the eyeshape . in time to see a small foot . and leg . disappear
around a corner . the figures on the machine . are quite on
her heels . a little girl . the whip of a skirt . at the top of her
high shoe . surely the figures . are not . attempting to overtake
her . to overrun her . on their fast machine . they appear to
be . gaining ground . on the little girl . running . the sobs
increase . in volume . a corner is turned . practically on her
heel . unexpectedly there is a long . straight . section of the
labyrinth . the little girl . dark hair flying . dress skirt whipping
. runs . it seems . for her young life . she glances over . her
shoulder . panicstricken . the figures . on the machine . are
nearly upon her . more sobbing within . the straight section .
of the labyrinth . stretches out . interminably . a leaf of paper
. blows from somewhere . passing by . her feet . another .
this one sticking . to her leg . and another . another memoir
page . blows upward . disappears from view . suggesting it
has adhered . to the figure in the black suit . another to the
running leg . of the girl . another leaf rises .

> haeley was opposed to
> burial only cremation made sense to
> him but she needed little mary to be someplace if
> only a sad plot of earth in a sad
> cemetery and insisted upon

it . the memoir leaf flutters away . the eyeshape is dark .
remains dark . a child coughs . remains dark . i grow anxious
. with the waiting . then a light falls across . the eyeshape .
and on the eyeshape . someone has opened . the door . of the
camera obscura . the eyeshape offers . the same perspective
. as my eye . for a moment . i remain stock still . while the
eyeshape view . follows a pair of figures . out into the bright
day . thursday . miss edith . the door closes . yet i watch them
still . the eyeshape view . is from behind . as they walk . toward
a fountain . the orphic fountain . their pace is steady . they

reach the fountain . and begin circumambulating it . opposite
clockwise . their left hands . trail in the water . within i hear
the cascading stream . the eyeshape pulls back . the figures
. orpheus and euridice . are pathos itself . in the shining
day . a memoir leaf   ·   suddenly . covers the
eyeshape. but   ·   ·   the   reverse
side   .   .   ·   .   only bled
through   jots   ·   of ink . just
as suddenly . it flutters   ·   away . euridice and her
look of despondency . the instant before . being drawn back
. to the underworld . the eyeshape is the view of orpheus .
reaching out . with bronze hands . within a child . or woman
. sobs . i stare at it . the eyeshape . at euridice . beyond the face
of despondency . three figures . stand . peering back . to the
orphic pair . thursday . miss edith . in front . behind . a figure
in black . Mourningwoman . free of her paper mummification
. a starkly dark figure . in the shining day .

Twenty-three

~

I HAD BEEN LYING ABED FOR SOME TIME SENSING THE GENERAL hubbub in the house without being awake enough to realize its cause, which dawned on me quite gradually—along with the understanding that rosy-fingered dawn herself had passed a considerable time ago: the tumult had to do with preparations for the evening's literary soirée. I rose with a start—I had not bothered with my nightshirt, and was still in my underclothing and (now) severely wrinkled shirt—and I checked my watch, which I located in the pocket of my vest hanging upon one of the bed's foot-posters. My word! It was getting to be one o'clock of the afternoon! I had not slept so late, when in sound health, since my early teen years.

I used the basin and pitcher—kindly refilled by Miss Edith no doubt—to freshen myself before dressing. At first I was in a near panic as I had not decided upon a selection for the reading, but as I wetted and combed my hair it became clear to me that I should read the first revised scene with both Andersen and Katherine. From that scene it would be clear to Murry precisely how drastic my revisions have been: the Rubicon will have been crossed.

My resolution, to be out with it, felt a great relief, and I was light of heart . . . but only for a moment as I immediately recollected my interview with the authoress, and the promise I'd made, which in the brightness of day took on an herculean aspect, a thirteenth labor as it were. I went downstairs, a bit sheepish due to my late rising. The house was bustling with servants I did not know. I received a polite nod of acknowledgement as each would pass, but otherwise my presence was of no more significance than a shadow's—and, yes, the comparison, which came to mind spontaneously, struck me as unsettling. It seemed that much of the commotion had to do with preparing food and drink for the soirée—the house was filled with pleasant aromas from things baking and boiling and broiling. Plus serving women were carrying in baskets and trays of rolls and cookies—I noticed a batch of Lord Chamberlain's beloved raspberry cakes pass by. I was standing in the foyer, in awe of the preparations.

The front door had been left open to accommodate the comings and goings, but I was turned away from it, watching the tray of raspberry pastries, and thus didn't notice the fellow with a pair of straight-back chairs, and as such he had to request my pardon. Startled, I stepped aside, and he continued into the music-room. I followed and discovered it had been quite transformed. The old damask draperies, which had probably hung before the windows for twenty years, since prior to the Haeleys' taking possession even, had been replaced with velvet panels in vibrant crimson and trimmed in gold. Tables, covered in fine embroidered cloth, had been set along the walls, to be used for service. The room had been arranged so that the focal point was a delicate-looking podium with a fluted trunk. The usual furniture—now with dust-free upholstery and polished arms and legs—had been angled toward the podium, and the servants were adding chairs brought in, most certainly, from the Chamberlain estate. In fact, I imagined Lord and Lady Chamberlain, along with their lovely daughter, were at the root of this miraculous transformation.

Without thinking of doing so in advance, I went to the pianoforte, which was more or less in its accustomed place. "Junges Deutschland" was still on the cabinet's music-desk. The keys had been cleaned, I could see, and I wondered if a tuner had been at work. I looked about me. A servant had just deposited two more chairs and was exiting through the doorway. I assumed he or another servant would return presently, but nonetheless I sat upon the upholstered bench and placed my fingertips at the keys. I read the music and took a moment or two to gather my bearings . . . then I began playing. Even my metallic ear could detect immediately that someone had in fact tuned the old Broadwood. The strains of "Young Germany" no longer echoed in the room, now so full of furnishings, but they retained a haunting quality, even in their pitch-perfect crispness.

My playing was far from magical—I had no illusion to the contrary. My technique was just as rigidly rusted as the first time I'd played the score, yet I seemed to simply know it more thoroughly, which was manifested in smoother transitions from one chord structure to the next. Perhaps it was this smoothness, this fluidity of musical phrasing, or perhaps the improvements rendered by the tightened and tuned wires—but whatever the precise cause, I found myself being transported by the song. At first my mental destination was indefinite; then the images before my mind's eye were clarified: I was seeing scenes of Haeley and Margaret Townsend as they tramped across Europe—scenes as my fancy had constructed them based on Mrs. Haeley's writing. As I turned from one musical phrase to the next, I was struck by the scenes' vividness. I felt that I'd been there, a silent observer, hiking beside them, sitting in the corner of a borrowed parlor, loitering at their bedroom door.

"Junges Deutschland" was the ideal accompaniment to the episodes of young Margaret Townsend's life. I played on and recollected the authoress's memoir, like images passing across the eye-shape in the camera obscura—I suddenly recalled my bizarre dream—except these images, from Mrs. Haeley's turbulent life, were sharper, richer, more evocative. Each shift in tone brought on a new episode: their hike up to Wolfsburg Castle, their discussing Rousseau over sweetened coffees, their argument brought on by their finances, their making up in a coach bound for Geneva, Margaret's terrifying dream of the mad professor, the loss of their first child, Haeley's insistence that she transform her nightmare into a fully rendered story. . . . Each scene completely experienced under the song's spell but yet also displayed as if a painting in a panoramic gallery of the authoress's youth.

I must have turned the sheet of music, but I had no recollection of it, only a semi-acknowledged awareness that it'd been done. The song ended, on the music sheet, but I continued to play, repeating the final phrases again and again, watching the scenes of Mrs. Haeley's life—each new, and building in poignancy like chapters of a manuscript adding upward, layer upon layer.

I seemed to recount it all, to the point I'd stopped reading, and it was only then that my fingers ceased their seeking of the keys, as if experiencing a sort of possession of their own.

I was staring into the space above the sheets of music; in fact just beyond the sheets, where the notes of the song would have risen up from the body of the pianoforte, undetectable to the eye of course, but it was as if the memoir scenes had taken shape upon those invisible sharps and flats, like lanternlight casting shadowed images upon the thick rolling smoke of a bonfire.

All of this came into my mind in a second or two as the final chord wasted away upon the sweet-smelling air, and then I was interrupted from my reverie by clapping hands.

"Bravo, Mr. Wheelwright, bravo." Miss Edith was standing just inside the doorway. She wore the lavender dress, which seemed to be her favorite, and over that her accustomed apron. I noted that the music-room preparations were complete as as many extra chairs had been added as was reasonable, and china plates, cups, saucers, and silverware had been nicely lain out on the service tables. The room must have been quite busy during my impromptu recital, yet I hadn't noticed the workers at all.

I sat dumbly for several moments, feeling as though I'd spent a considerable length of time swimming underwater and had now broken the surface—only to find that my old natural world seemed strange, even alien. "Thank you," I finally managed. "You are kind … I am certain my performance does not warrant such enthusiastic accolades." My head was slow to clear.

"We are at work in the parlor and have done all that can be without touching your belongings."

It required a bit before I realized what she was implying. "Ah, so you would like me to remove my things."

"If you please."

"It is quite all right." I leaned upon the pianoforte to assist myself in standing. I felt an odd possessiveness regarding the sheets of music for "Junges Deutschland," as if the slender leafs contained Mrs. Haeley's memoir—no, more than that . . . as if they held those turbulent years of her life themselves, or at least their very essence—but it was a mad notion and I resisted the urge to bring them from the instrument's music-desk.

On my way out of the room I stopped and stood beside Miss Edith, both of us surveying the space. It hardly seemed the dusty, cobwebbed room I'd first encountered with the authoress and Thursday, ghostly covers here and there over the furniture or heaped upon the unpolished floor. Now it was entirely changed into a place of liveliness and light. In addition to the new drapery panels, podium, chairs, and the fact everything shone with a fresh cleaning and polishing—there were also paintings upon the walls, portraits of fine folks, vibrant landscapes, and one that engaged my view most arrestingly: a rustic tableau with a brick farmhouse in the background and an unkempt pumpkin patch in the fore. I could not help but think of Thursday's weird jack-o'-lanterns.

In the parlor I had a pair of heavy trunks that I'd been loath to transport myself, but it was a simple matter to find some stout workmen to manage the task.

A few minutes later, sitting at the little desk in the corner of my bedroom, a desk and chair made more for a child or petite woman, I located the section of the proof-pages I wanted to read. I was disinclined to separate them entirely from the stack of pages for fear that something would happen to them, that they'd be destroyed or simply lost; and, besides, they would be difficult from which to read, they were such a mess of deletions and emendations, arrows and asterisks—thus I resolved to copy the passage afresh, and use that as my script for the soirée. It took some effort at times to decipher my own designs for revision, and I had sympathy for the copyists and compositors who would be given the responsibility to reset my pages—that is, assuming Murry did not simply reject this new version out of hand.

It took some time to copy the pages, but I was pleased with the story. To my thinking, it was tenfold better than the original version of *Andersen's*, and I was cautiously optimistic any reader worth his salt could see the truth of that immediately. I was in the throes of copying when there was a knock upon the door. I called for the visitor to enter, assuming rather absentmindedly that it was either Mrs. Haeley or, more likely, Miss Edith, but it was a chestnut-headed serving girl who entered with a tray: "Scuse me, sir," she cockneyed, revealing a twisted front tooth, "but they thought you to be hungry."

She placed the tray on the nightstand, after moving the lamp aside. I realized then that I *was* quite hungry, and when she shut the door behind her, I finished the sentence I was copying and then inspected the tray: a china pot of black coffee and a cup, toasted bread with gooseberry jam, and a sliced red apple sprinkled with cinnamon. I felt for a moment that I was returned to my luxurious accommodations at The Saint Georges.

I gobbled down the repast, more famished than I'd realized; then I returned to my copying. Instead of being rejuvenated by the wholesome meal, however, I became sluggish. Nevertheless I completed my task. I knew it'd be prudent to read the pages aloud— to rehearse, and ideally at a volume appropriate for the site—but it seemed impractical. So I did read aloud but barely above a whisper. It took between a half and three-quarters of an hour. I liked it; in fact, I liked it very much. There was no question in my mind the revision was positively the correct course. Without fully realizing it, I'd been worrying all the while that I was merely mucking up a sound piece of writing, and I would accomplish nothing more than an unpublishable mess of words. My revision was not complete; now, however, I was confident of my path. I said a silent word of thanks to the enigmatic Edmund Holland for inspiring me in this aesthetic direction.

My post-repast sluggishness combined with the peace of mind gained by knowing with confidence my book was on the correct trail, and it all made me quite sleepy, in spite of my late rising. I put my proof-pages and copy script aside, and went to the bed, where I then laid atop the quilt. I crossed my hands over my calmly beating breast and was instantly asleep: the last/first sound I heard was the growling of wolves. . . .

mr wheelwright . mr wheelwright . knocking . mr wheelwright . are you all right . mr wheelwright . . . .

"Mr. Wheelwright. . . ."

"Yes, just a moment. . . ." I rose from the bed, disoriented. The character of light seeping into the room from the edges of the shade told me it was twilight.

"Guests are beginning to arrive," said Miss Edith from the hallway.

"I will be down presently," I said to the door. I was surprised that I was not in a blind panic; on the contrary, I felt as calm as a boy's summer afternoon. I freshened myself, again, then donned my dove-gray suit of clothes, even putting on a newly laundered white shirt. I had a cravat of purple and crème diagonal stripes—very smart—that I'd been saving for a special occasion; and I inserted my favorite opal stud to hold the cravat in place. I combed my hair in the mirror. I had not had it cut since I'd left New York City, and its rare length seemed to pin back my chimpish ears. I stood back and primped for a moment: I was pleased.

I took up my script and placed them inside the pages of Edmund Holland's *Verses & Vignettes*, which was on the desk as well. Along with everything else that would transpire this evening, I hoped to also get to the bottom of the Edmund Holland enigma. Then I went to meet the earliest arrivals. While passing through the foyer, I saw that a pair of maids, in pressed gray and white uniform dresses and ruffled caps, were tending the door—which happened to be open and thus afforded me a view down to the curb, where white-wigged footmen, in French-blue coats and holding lanterns, were assisting guests from their coaches. It was a grand operation, all compliments of the Chamberlains I was quite certain.

I continued through the foyer into the parlor, whose transformation was not quite as miraculous as the music-room's but remarkable nonetheless. Several comfortable seats had been added, along with a half dozen or more side tables. Near one of the room's two windows, where a sofa had stood, there was a lace-covered table with a crystal punchbowl, matching cups, and cut-crystal saucers holding candies and nuts; a pretty young woman, in the uniform dress, was serving the guests, of whom six were standing or sitting, talking and drinking red punch. I immediately recognized one fine fellow who was seated in profile and had not noticed my entrance:

"Carter, how do you do?" I said approaching the doctor, in his accustomed brown suit and pince-nez.

He rose, an excited smile brightening his vandyke. "Jefferson, there you are—was beginning to think the fashionable thing in New York City was for a writer not to appear at his own reading."

"I couldn't say, as the fashionable is not my area." We shook hands, and he introduced me to the other gentlemen, each of whom was a member of the King James.

We chatted for some time about nothing in particular. Several fellows joined in our convivial conversation. It seemed the parlor had emerged as the meeting place for the men, while the ladies congregated elsewhere, presumably in the music-room. To my knowledge the authoress had not come from her room yet, but for all I knew Mrs. Haeley was holding court in the music-room just as I was in the parlor.

Carter was in midsentence regarding some new medical procedure he'd read of when he stopped and spoke to a new arrival: "Now there's a fine-looking fellow—how's the leg holding up?"

Thursday had entered the room. He was on his crutches of course, but he was wearing a dark-blue jacket of the newest cut, a white ruffled shirt, and gray trousers that someone (his sister in all likelihood) had neatly cuffed just at the top of the cast. It was quite a contrast from the workaday clothing he'd been in since my arrival. Thursday looked as if *he* may have been a man of letters himself . . . then I recalled the mystery of Edmund Holland . . . Thursday's real name was Edward Hill—no, it was mere coincidence, I told myself. Edward Hill was a common enough name; there probably were a thousand Edward Hills just in London. . . .

"It seems well enough, Doctor—itches some."

"Unavoidable I'm afraid; another month or so and you can be freed from your sarcophagus."

Thursday had taken a comfortable seat, and he propped his crutches against an adjacent wall. "The mummy awakens," he said.

"I say, Carter, is that one of your *French* techniques? Entombing some poor soul in plaster?" I'd already forgotten the gentleman's name, one of Carter's fellow club members, wearing an olive-green coat and black tie. He held a silk handkerchief in one hand and continually dabbed at his moist, bald brow. He went to where Thursday had put up his leg on an Ottoman seat, and he gave the cast a firm rap with his knuckles. "Quite like a brick. A good firm splint served well enough for me when I was thrown during the King's charity steeplechase as a young buck." He patted his right leg as he returned to our coterie.

"No doubt," said Carter, "why you have that subtle limp." And he was right: the gentleman did appear to favor his right leg. "Thursday here should lose no length in the leg as the bone knits itself together."

"Still, the French," and he clearly intended that to be the final word on the subject.

The serving girl had taken Thursday a cup of punch.

The conversation continued; I, however, listened as a matter of politeness. In truth only half-listened. More and more my mind was on the reading and on Mrs. Haeley—her frail health, and the request she made of me, and *her* reading: which I would follow, and simply from a theatrical standpoint that promised to be a poor idea: the great authoress emerges from obscure seclusion to read from her long-awaited manuscript; and it is shockingly beautiful. Would anyone even pay attention to me? Other than as a matter of politeness? Half-listen, as I was doing just now?

My musing was broken by the commencement of the pianoforte in the music-room. At the first opportunity I excused myself and went to look in on the musician. Carter came with me. I recognized the song as Beethoven, his "Tempest" sonata. The foyer was a hullabaloo of activity. A gentleman and his wife were just arriving—I wasn't paying particular attention to them, engrossed in following the Beethoven, but I recognized the hat that the servant had taken in hand, or at least I recognized the design, with its unusually high crown. I turned to speak with Lord and Lady Chamberlain . . . but it was not they. Then I watched as the servant took the hat to a long bench in the hall and placed it with some others of the same odd design.

"We're calling it 'the Wheelwright.'" I knew the portly little fellow as another member of the King James Club. Indeed, I thought: my hatter called it "the Londoner." We shook hands as Carter greeted him by name, Eddington.

The doctor and I continued into the music-room, which was even more bustling than the parlor and foyer.

"It's becoming a splendid crowd," observed Carter. "Your publisher should be pleased."

I nodded in affirmation, but thought, Yes, at first . . . and then mortified.

I was surprised to see that the pianoforteist was in fact Miss

Hilary Chamberlain. The lovely girl sat upon the bench in a gorgeous gown of crimson silks. Even more than the music, Miss Hilary seemed to radiate light; her playing was most accomplished. She must have brought her own music sheets as I had not noticed the Beethoven piece previously. I wondered that she might play "Junges Deutschland" and I hoped not—it seemed to possess a kind of magic, and I did not want it to cast some dark spell on the authoress.

We stood for a few minutes while Miss Hilary finished the piece. Some guests chatted while the beautiful young woman played beautifully, but most knew to enjoy the moment by listening closely. She had made up her hair in a very modern style, gathered off her lovely neck and with a pair of strands curled and framing her flawless face. The curls coiled and bounced with the rhythm of her head as she worked her way through the difficult chord structures with what appeared genuine emotion. She completed the "Tempest" sonata with its final flurry, a true thunderstorm of penetrating notes; then sat as if dazed for a moment while the music settled upon the guests like a finely wrought silken web.

We all applauded politely but enthusiastically. Miss Hilary smiled to acknowledge our appreciation as she looked about the room. Her deep-brown orbs fell upon us and instantly her whole being was beaming. Egoist that I can be, I thought at first that seeing I had arrived—the famous American author—accounted for her overjoyed expression; I soon realized however that her joy was directed at Carter. Miss Hilary nodded to me warmly, but it was Dr. Carter's presence that sent a shock of happiness through her pristine heart.

Well, I'll be, I thought. I was about to suggest that Carter go say hello, except Miss Hilary, blushing now, hastily found another piece of music and began playing. It was another Beethoven, in fact the German composer's best-known piece, "Pathetique."

I turned to Carter nevertheless, expecting some sort of blissful expression on his countenance as well, but instead there was perched a most woeful look. It was fleeting and vanished in an instant, only its shadow remained on the doctor's usual mild demeanor. For a moment I was perplexed as to its cause—possessing the eye, and heart it would seem, of the beautiful and talented daughter of a wealthy and powerful man—but just as quickly I came to suspect the true nature of the situation: Miss Hilary had taken a fancy to a mere city physician—and he to her no doubt—but there was no path to Lord Chamberlain's approving the match, which perhaps in turn accounted for the conspicuous absence of Miss Hilary's suitors. The strong-willed young woman would have nothing to do with them as long as her heart was set on another, whose worthiness was plain save for his purse and worldly prospects.

Maybe it all wasn't true; however, it was a narrative into which the pieces fit as if finely tailored for them.

Miss Hilary, whose lovely face I could observe in perfect profile, played the piece by looking above the sheets of music, and I wondered if she too watched flickering images on the invisible webwork of Beethovanal notes rising up from the Broadwood: scenes of Carter and her in their first shy encounters . . . or scenes of imagined bliss, painful in their firmly fixed impossibility. I could not tell which in her unreadable concentration.

Things began to happen quite quickly as more and more guests arrived in a steady stream. I found myself greeting them as they entered the music-room as if I was at the head of a receiving line, and in effect I was. Lord and Lady Chamberlain arrived, he in stately charcoal black, she in a high-style lavender gown, her silver mane expertly coiffed. They must have come with A. B. C. Murry, who followed Lady Penelope. My English publisher appeared the same as he did upon our first meeting, in Lord Chamberlain's carriage, in his suit of bleakest mourning black and of course those unusual spectacles with the rectangular lenses. We shook hands. He smiled sanguinely and glanced at the book and manuscript pages I held in the other.

"A lovely event," said Murry.

"Indeed." I wanted to be cleverer but nothing came to me, and he moved on, along with the Chamberlains.

More guests came through the doorway; meanwhile Miss Hilary continued her recital. Miss Edith had just brought me a punch, which I drank down thirstily, when the waif and her uncle entered. Truly, "Miss Organdy," was almost unrecognizable in a proper dress of turquoise-dyed silk, with a subtly exotic Persian styling;

she wore a matching band on her head of close-shorn, sandy locks. The turquoise color highlighted the oceanic blue of her eyes, and I thought for the first time that she was a lovely girl. Terrace, her blind uncle, whose arm she held firmly but naturally, was in a well-worn yet still quite appropriate gray coat and white trousers. His sightless eyes roamed the crowded room.

Miss Edith was still there, taking back the empty punch cup, so I introduced the puppetmaster and his niece as my special guests and wondered if Miss Edith could find them a good place to sit. The governess smiled and took Truly by the hand.

In a moment the poet Biron Swinford arrived, a touch rattled as he was afraid he was tardy. He wore a long purple coat that magnified his height and leanly lank frame. I assured him all was well, and said that he should relax and have some punch. I also wondered that he should comb his wild hair, but, no, he fit the bill of Muse-flogged poet perfectly.

By then the arrival of guests had slowed considerably, which was a good thing as the music-room was filled. Chairs had been squeezed together and several pieces brought in from the parlor; yet still it would be standing space only, and several young gentlemen were standing. The servants had had their hands full delivering cups of tea and coffee and rum punch, and also plates of any manner of meats and cheeses and sweet-treats galore: cookies, cakes, puddings, tarts. It all looked exquisitely delicious, but I resisted offers of bringing me something as I had become a trifle nervous—not so much about my own reading per se. Yes, it was true that I couldn't know for certain how Murry would react to my revisions, but I knew that if he rejected the book after all, some house would take it; perhaps not one with the prestige of Murry's, but *Andersen's Romance* would find its way into the world by hook or by crook.

My nervousness was more due to the authoress . . . why she had not come down from her room . . . how the reclusive woman would respond to a house full of guests, almost none of whom she knew ... then there was the question of her health and of her losing hold of reality . . . and our impending trip to Germany. . . .

And what of Edmund Holland, another of Murry's authors? I felt certain he was here—in this very room! Perhaps my sensing of him was another product of my overcharged imagination. Still, I surveyed the room from time to time, thinking I might somehow spot him, that he would reveal himself to me in some manner. I would have been satisfied with a secret sign of a sort, some signal passed surreptitiously between him and me: it did not have to be a public discovery, using the term in a theatrical sense; it would have been enough for me to know—I would keep the author's anonymity in place, as sacred to me as much as to him.

I was discharged from my reverie by a sort of Galvonic energy sweeping through the assembled guests, and I instantly knew its cause: the authoress had come down from her chamber. The wave of energy swept before her just as ripples of meteorological disturbance precede a thunderstorm. All became hushed; even the disciplined musician Miss Hilary ceased her sonata in mid measure. I'm certain it's quite impossible—the story-stuff of myths—but my sense was that even the pendulum of the upright clock, moved into a corner of the music-room, halted in its swinging once the wave had overtaken it. For myself I can attest that I held my breath—I presume my heart continued its uninterrupted beating but I would not take an oath to it.

Mrs. Haeley entered the room, on the arm of Miss Edith, only pausing for a half moment to take in the scene of the room, perhaps as one stands before a Flemish oil upon first entering a well-plotted gallery. The music-room was dazzlingly illuminated by a hundred candles in single holders or candelabras, plus at least a dozen lamps. After a moment they moved on to a pair of chairs that had been left vacant near the podium—I hadn't even noticed them beforehand— and the authoress settled into one of the winged chairs, open-armed Gomms in plush mohair, while Miss Edith left her side, to perhaps retrieve her a punch. Miss Edith had been holding Mrs. Haeley's reading script but placed it in her hands before stepping away. The authoress wore a dress of charcoal gray with a flower of purple silk pinned at the left breast. A decade or more ago the outfit might have been quite smart, but now it only reinforced the narrative that Margaret Haeley was of a different age . . . and here she was, risen from her own past, a revenant of her own turbulent life.

Seated, she smiled briefly to no one in particular and in that way acknowledged everyone. She was pale, in spite of a touch of rouge at each sharp-edged cheekbone, applied, I suspected, at Miss Edith's well-meant suggestion; however, it merely emphasized the authoress's cadaverous pallor. But it was the look that hovered about her eyes, also a leaden hue, a look that held a mixture of wonder and fear and anticipation. I might have writ it off as a kind of stage-fright, but knowing what I knew about her tenuous grasp of the present, I interpreted the look as that of someone who was struggling to comprehend her surroundings . . . and who was tempted to withdraw to the familiar environs of the past.

The governess brought Mrs. Haeley a punch and placed it on the little table between her chair and the still vacant one that was intended for me. Miss Hilary continued her sonata, one I did not recognize, and guests returned to their chattering.

I came to the realization that there was no one left to greet just as I felt a hand on my shoulder. It was Biron Swinford, who bent to speak in my ear:

"If you are quite ready, Jefferson, we shall commence with the program."

"Of course." I went to the seat left for me; it and the chair occupied by the authoress were facing the podium but angled so that most of the guests could observe us to varying degrees in profile. Though, in fact, the room was so packed with humanity that we were being viewed from nearly every angle. The podium was essentially in the corner of the music-room, diagonal from the door. At first chairs had been arranged in an orderly fashion facing the podium, with narrow but neat aisles in between; however, so many seats had been added from the parlor and elsewhere (I noticed Mrs. Haeley's old kitchen chairs standing in a sort of picket around the pianoforte) and guests had rearranged things so liberally to their own needs that in final form the music-room was simply a chaotic sea of chairs in all manner of shapes and sizes, and humanity (in all manner of shapes and sizes as well).

It was becoming quite warm; Mrs. Haeley from time to time fanned herself with her manuscript pages, which I could see were, like mine, copied sheets from the original, done in a neat feminine script: the handiwork of Miss Edith no doubt. It seemed that the

governess had replaced her brother as Mrs. Haeley's right-hand—
perhaps she would be called "Wednesday" . . . like Thursday, but one
better.

I wasn't certain who would be the master of ceremonies, but it
was Lord Chamberlain who rose from his seat and stepped toward
the podium just as his lovely daughter was drawing a Schumann
piece to a well-timed close. His lordship stood at the podium, with
its fluted trunk, and smiled out at the hushed gathering. There was
no question that he was a distinguished-looking figure with his neatly
trimmed beard and mustaches, still mostly ebon, except accented
here and there with streaks of white.

"Welcome," he said, employing a moment's dramatic pause, "to
a special meeting of the King James Club. We the members, and I
as secretary, are most pleased to share this unique evening with you,
ladies and gentleman, and honored guests—" He looked to Mrs.
Haeley and me. "—and a sincere thank-you to Mrs. Stephen Haeley
for opening her home to us all." He clapped in appreciation, as did
we all, and the authoress smiled and nodded in response. I realized
she hadn't uttered a word since entering the music-room.

"As we are all quite aware we will be privileged to hear three
very special presentations—three original works of literature by two
distinguished authors and one distinguished authoress: Mr. Biron
Swinford, who will read from a new collection of poems titled 'The
Wolfsburg Sonnets'; then our hostess Mrs. Margaret Haeley will be
reading from her recently completed memoir, 'Young Germany'; and
finally, our featured speaker, Mr. Jefferson Wheelwright, shall favor
us with selections from his forthcoming novel *Andersen's Romance*."

Polite applause filled the space of the music-room. I glanced at
Murry, seated next to Lady Penelope, and he wore the same placid
expression to which I was becoming accustomed. I wondered if it
would change when he heard my reborn tale.

Lord Chamberlain introduced Biron Swinford more fully, author
of *Avians of the Garden* and *Sisyphus from on High* . . . American poet
. . . whom *The Sun* of Baltimore called "the Republic's most original
voice" . . .

At last Mr. Swinford, in his lavender coat, was allowed to take
the podium. He had in hand some sheets which had been folded

inside his coat pocket, and they were heavily and precisely creased. He took a moment to look at the topmost sheet, reading as if they were words written by another; then he tossed back his unruly mane, gazed out at the audience, meeting eyes (I imagined) with no one in particular, and began:

"The river ran for you, wild and uncheck'd;
As your whetted words, you of slender neck,
Sliced popular convention to be free—
Casting aside birth-name and rank, blood fleck'd
And downcast for all of England to see.
Cut off from friend and fam'ly unfairly—
A wide and capricious sea viewed on deck,
Roiling, boiling like your spirit to lee.
 Yet you had a sustaining jewel within;
 Whose title was held in the chamber dark,
 And for whose very life, bold you'd striven.
 Tossed tempestuously in your bare bark.
The tiny jewel was to be paid dear,
And thus in doing pleased England's ear.'"

I was stunned by Swinford's poem: its subject must have been the authoress in her youth—yet having only *heard* it . . . perhaps I'd misunderstood. I wanted to step up to the podium and relieve the sonneteer of his script and read it for myself. I glanced toward Mrs. Haeley and she appeared to wear the unaltered mask of fragile calm. I looked from face to face in the audience, and no one seemed to sense anything unusual in Swinford's topic.

The audience, accustomed to such soirées, knew not to applaud after each poem but to wait until the poet was finished altogether. Without any sort of gloss, Biron Swinford began his next sonnet, and I listened eagerly for its subject matter: this sonnet's central image was the River Rhine—undoubtedly "the river" of the previous sonnet—and it involved a young couple on an excursion who feel tension between themselves in spite of "a love" that is "luminescent."

I was quite certain now that the poet's Wolfsburg sonnets were about Margaret Townsend and Stephen Haeley, but, still, I appeared to be alone in that awareness. I searched the gathering of candle- and lamplit faces for Thursday's or Miss Edith's—surely they would recognize Swinford's subject. I spotted Thursday in the far corner of the room, in a chair more or less behind Miss Hilary, who had remained on the pianoforte bench. I searched the extremities of the music-room for Miss Edith and thought for a second that she was not present; then I saw her, in the thick of things, a row behind and just to the right of A. B. C. Murry. Thursday was too distant, and there were too many faces between us; so I attempted to make eye contact with Miss Edith, to somehow communicate my wonderment at Swinford's poetry and to see if the governess shared in it. But I could not draw her attention before Swinford began again.

He spoke of a hike up a mountain trail, and of the "howl of wolves" coming it seemed "from nearby Wolfsburg." I studied the poet's thin face, with his long, slender nose, his side whiskers, and his black mustaches that curled down to his cleft chin. I wanted to see some sign of his own recognition of the oddity of his selections, given the circumstances of the soirée—but he was as difficult to read as Miss Hilary had been over her Beethoven.

Stubbornly, I studied the poet's eyes, tempestuous gray beneath angry black brows—brows that belied his usual phlegmatic nature. In fact, the more I studied his eyes, like a detail of a highly romanticized portrait, the more I sensed a turbulent anger beneath the calm surface of his verse, which he recited with a determined precision that was itself a kind of passion. At first the listener may brand Swinford a middling reader, that is, performer, of his own work; but in time the listener's lackluster opinion would be overcome by the stylized accuracy of the poet's spoken phrases, by his practiced articulation, by the nuances of stress he gave well-selected syllables.

As I studied his eyes with a sort of ferocity of my own, and Swinford moved from one sonnet to the next—each an intimate biography of our hostess, to my ear at least—I became aware of another presence, though how I became aware was not quite clear. To the right of the podium was a silver candelabra ablaze with six tall candles, providing the primary light by which to read. But their brilliance cast the left side of Swinford's face in a dramatic shadow, a sort of animated mask of darkness, fluctuating with the movements of his mouth and the candle-flames when caught by a capricious draft. As such, the dark mask, or rather dark patches of mask, seemed to move of their own accord—and my awareness of the mask became my awareness of the shadow behind the poet.

It lurked in the corner—and, yes, it lurked precisely where the physical laws, given the positions of the candelabra and of Mr. Swinford, dictated it should be—yet, still, there was something unnatural about it: the shadow was too large for one, even with the poet's taller-than-average frame; and the shadow was too, well, shadowy, that is, too dark, almost a blackness upon the walls (I glanced about to see if anyone else was casting such an impenetrable shadow, and there was none); but by far its strangest aspect was that the shadow seemed to move independently of Mr. Swinford. Or rather: it did not move, and thus was independent from the poet, who moved his head of course, glancing now and then at his audience, and down to his creased pages, and who would shuffle one page behind another as he progressed through his program, and who from time to time shifted his weight standing at the fluted podium.

The shadow however was still, as if waiting, watching, listening. Perhaps there was a perceptible, though profoundly subtle, alteration along its ebon edge, which fell across portions of two walls and a newly draperied window—or it may have simply been a trick of my straining and twitching eyes, which I blinked and rubbed to clear.

I would look down at Mr. Holland's *Verses & Vignettes* and my script copy—and tell myself that the weird shadow was a product of my overcharged imagination. Then I would look back to the speaker and beyond him to the dark presence . . . waiting there against the walls like a disquieting stranger . . . like heartbreak . . . like disaster . . .

Polite applause roused me: the poet had concluded and was leaving the podium. The shadow did appear to move, but Lord Chamberlain was there so speedily it may have been that their going and coming threw normal shadows atop the abnormal one. I was apprehensive about Mae taking the podium and reached out for her hand, which was icy in spite of the closeness of the room. The authoress perhaps took my gesture as wishing her luck in her reading, and she squeezed my hand back with her skeletal fingers. The black lace at the end of her sleeve fell across my knuckles and it was too much the texture of a shroud, so that a chill ran up my spine there in the warm music-room.

His lordship began his introduction: authoress of *Dunkelraum* . . . book known around the world . . . *Blackwood's* called it "the most original work of the century" . . . editoress and caretakeress of Stephen Haeley's poetry . . . reading from her long-awaited new work. . . .

He at last invited Mrs. Haeley to the podium. She let go of my hand, giving it a final pat, and rose from her chair. She appeared a bit unsteady but nevertheless completed her journey amid steady applause. I looked out at the faces in the audience and there was a wide mixture of expressions: from genuine pleasure to wonderment to, well, let us say, superiority. For many, Margaret Haeley's novel and the authoress herself represented immorality and impropriety . . . I'd even read somewhere that *Dunkelraum* was "the death-knell of the Empire."

Margaret T. Haeley, authoress, stood at the podium while this uncertain reception faded to completion. She gazed out at the audience members without speaking for longer than seemed appropriate, and I began to question whether she were up to reading after all: she appeared a raw widow at the podium, about to deliver a heartwrenching eulogy, though there lingered a subtle smile on her gaunt face.

The audience was beginning to fidget in their awkwardness when Mrs. Haeley at last spoke: "Thank you so much for coming tonight, and indulging me to read. I shall be brief, for like you I am most interested in the words of our guest of honor. . . ." She looked over to me, and I had the impression that she meant to conclude her sentence with my name but couldn't just then recall it. She continued, "I wish to read this evening from a work I've been writing for a very long time—a work entitled, in German, *Junges Deutschland*."

With that the authoress's leaden irises turned downward to her script and she began her reading. Her voice had been clear but weak—not the gravel-tongue of the elderly or infirm, but without strength, as if you heard someone speaking on the opposite side of a thin partition. Once she began in earnest, however, her voice immediately gathered force, and by the second paragraph Mrs.

Haeley was reading as a young Puritan maiden may have read Bible verses on Virtue at Sunday morning worship: with conviction and clarity and the assumed goodwill of the congregation.

She read, "'Her Haeley shouldered the box of books—"the library" as they called it—relieving her, and they continued making their way along the narrow Wolfsburg road, cut through the ancient wood and barely wide enough for opposing wagons to pass abreast...'"

I glanced at Biron Swinford, who'd taken his seat near Murry, expecting a flash of . . . of what? . . . surprise at the coincidence? . . . confusion? . . . or perhaps the conspirator's self-assured gaze— but I saw nothing save for interested composure, a devotee of the *Dunkelraum* authoress in thrall. Indeed, as I surveyed the room, nearly everyone wore the same captivated countenance, even Mrs. Haeley's moral critics it seemed. They were spellbound by the intimate tone of her memoir; by the authoress's revealing details of her time with Stephen Haeley that had been unknown previously. I of course shared in that curiosity, though its satisfaction also pricked painfully at my heart; and my love for Margaret Haeley bled in drops from those pinpricks. Even if we were to go to Germany, as she'd requested of me, she and I would never share a single soul as she and her beloved Haeley had. If that sort of profound closeness was truly what was meant by *intimacy*, then the authoress and I would forever strangers be: hearing her memoir, beautiful though it was, made that point achingly clear.

And what of the shadow?

It was there behind Mrs. Haeley, unaltered even though the authoress was shorter than Biron Swinford by a foot, and thinner than he still. I watched it closely as she read—and I couldn't help but listen: the authoress read her words with a captivating rhythm—not rhythm as poetry has (not, for instance, the rhythm of Swinford's unsettling Wolfsburg sonnets); rather, it could be called a rhythm only in that the drumbeats of the words were consistent within themselves. That is to say, Mrs. Haeley's sentences constructed a pattern but one that was too complex to be adequately described in the language of poetry (not meters and feet and the schemata of rhyme). The pattern had less to do with the sounds of the words— though that was certainly part of its structure—and more to do, I came to realize, with the images, and the nuanced moods the images evoked.

At first I believed the notes of music—of "Young Germany"—were only playing in my head, that Mrs. Haeley's reading had conjured them: they were so soft they seemed a product of my imagination. But the song grew in strength, and it seemed not to echo only in my mind; rather, the somber chords came from my left, that is, from the opposite side of the music-room. Miss Hilary was accompanying the authoress, softly but clearly playing "Junges Deutschland," matching the rhythm and tempo of the authoress's voice. It was a spontaneous accompaniment, an invention of the clever young woman, who understood the connection—or at least sensed that there was a connection—between the Schlözer composition and Mrs. Haeley's composition.

Rather than distracting from the authoress's reading, the music, perfectly timed, added to it—or more accurately, amplified it: when Mrs. Haeley described Haeley's eyes as blue, the music made them bluer; when she said the Rhine was turbulent, "Junges Deustchland" made the waters roll more vehemently; when she spoke of the lonesomeness of the forest, the chord structures made one nearly weep; and on and on.

It was perhaps my moist eyes which blurred everything in the blazingly illuminated room that prevented me from immediately realizing the shadow behind the authoress was moving, and not only slightly, not only along its ebon edge. The shadow moved right, it moved left, its dark shoulders hunched and seesawed across the walls and draperies, its black head bobbed. In spite of the two-dimensionality of its space, the shadow seemed even to "step" forward and "step" back. I watched its strange dance as Mrs. Haeley read her memoir and Miss Hilary played the pianoforte—and I realized it was precisely that: a dance. The shadow moved to the complex rhythms of the authoress's narrative. Not a popular dance, mind you, not a waltz or a reel, but instead something interpretive, something like ballet.

I looked to the faces in the crowded room, especially to those that I knew . . . Carter, the Chamberlains, Miss Organdy, her uncle, Swinford, Murry, Thursday, Miss Edith . . . could they not see the

dancing shadow behind the authoress? Were they not alarmed by
it? Surely Miss Hilary, who played the spell-casting composition,
surely she saw the shadow moving to the rhythms she accented with
her nimble fingers upon the keys of dark and light . . . yes? No—
she too appeared bewitched by the story and the song, and nothing
penetrated her senses beyond that potent pairing.

I perspired and attempted to loosen my cravated collar for some
air.

Mrs. Haeley spoke of her expected child and how desperately
she wanted it. From her memoir, one understood that even as a
moonstruck girl, in love for the first time, she knew that Haeley
would be difficult at times—not blackhearted, but driven so far
within himself, to commune with his poetic soul, that she would
often be alone, even in his presence: "'She longed for the dawning
of that comfort and companionship, more precious than the rarest
Egyptian jewel.'" This section of the memoir, in retrospective, was
profoundly lugubrious, as nearly everybody in the music-room
recalled that the little girl was not long for this world.

With a keen sense of the dramatic, Mrs. Haeley concluded
her reading at that point, just as the final chord of Miss Hilary's
accompaniment rose up from the Broadwood. Returning to her
quiet voice, she said, "Thank you," and left the podium. Slightly
stunned, it took a moment for the audience to begin their applause,
and the authoress was already at her seat.

It required another moment for Lord Chamberlain to react, but
he did push himself up from his seat to deliver the final introduction
of the evening: mine of course. At the podium, he cleared his throat
in an effort to fully regain his composure. I understood his effort.
To clear the moisture, I pinched the inside corners of my eyes with
my finger and thumb. I glanced at the authoress, who also appeared
misty-eyed, but otherwise had returned to her delicate calm. I
touched her hand and whispered, "Nicely done"; she however didn't
respond, not even to my touch, as if our hand-holding was a thing of
the distant past, or had never occurred at all. I put my fingers back
on Edmund Holland's book.

". . . our final reader," Lord Chamberlain was saying, "quickly
becoming a distinguished literary figure on both sides of the ocean."

He went on to enumerate my books and even some of my lesser-known tales that appeared in the literary papers. In spite of my lingering discomposure, I was flattered when he namedropped to mention my visitations to his home. At last he said the magic phrase—"Please join me in welcoming . . ."—and it was my turn at the fluted podium.

Twenty-four

I MADE A DELIBERATE EFFORT TO SMILE AS I STEPPED TOWARD THE podium. The audience applauded warmly—I could detect that Carter, seated only a few feet from my chair, clapped with special vigor. I watched Lord Chamberlain move away from the dais, still applauding, and the instant he departed the speaker's position, with its sextet candelabra, the shadow disappeared. Golden light fell upon the vellum-colored walls. My instinct was to turn right and left for its whereabouts, but I forced myself to keep a levelhead.

I placed Mr. Holland's book on the podium desk and removed my copy script. I looked around the music-room at the various faces, most of which wore a welcoming, even if insincere, smile. "Thank you," I said. "Those are difficult acts to follow. Thank you, Mr. Swinford and Mrs. Haeley, for being a part of this evening, and also of course, Mrs. Haeley, for allowing us into your lovely home. Finally, Lord and Lady Chamberlain, and Miss Chamberlain, and members of the King James Club, I offer my sincerest appreciation for making tonight possible." I applauded, and others joined in, rather lacking in enthusiasm however. "This evening I shall read from my novel *Andersen's Romance*, which will be brought out early next year by Mr. Murry's distinguished house." Or so I hoped as I nodded to Murry, whose pacific expression remained unaltered. I wanted to check behind me, to determine if the shadow had rematerialized, but resisted the urge and instead began my reading.

In the original version of the novel—the version that A. B. C. Murry purchased—Katherine's and Andersen's parents orchestrated their match from an early age. Indeed the powerful New York City families had all but arranged their marriage for the families' mutual gains. Thus they had known each other since childhood. The third scene in the novel had been the society gala at which Katherine's father announced the official engagement. In the new version, Katherine and Andersen meet on a busy New York City street, quite by accident, when Katherine becomes separated from her mother amidst a throng of pedestrians. Andersen, still a young member of the bar in the revision, has left his firm for a midday meal when he spies the lovely young woman who is clearly out of sorts. Andersen's first instinct is to pass her by, perhaps with a tip of his hat if she's paying any attention—after all, the City was rife with pretty young women—but something about *this* young woman arrested him.

I glanced up at Murry, and there was an added element to his pacific features, something situated behind the oddly rectangular lenses of his spectacles, or perhaps hovering on the edge of his upper lip. Something, but impossible to say just what in a second's glance. I also sensed that the audience was interested in the story of Andersen and Katherine's meeting. I did not have an especially theatrical voice, nor a commandingly bass one; nevertheless it was naturally resonating and could hold an audience's attention, assuming the material were worthy.

After the briefest of pauses to check Murry's demeanor, I returned to Andersen and Katherine on the street, and the titular character's surreptitious watching of the increasingly agitated girl. It isn't shyness that prevents his approaching and speaking with her. Rather, he enjoys watching her, unnoticed, "'as if a shadow upon the wall' ..." and my voice faltered reading the suddenly ironic words. It seemed to me then that the shadow had disappeared from the music-room walls because it had managed to migrate to the text of my novel. My eyes and my mind effected a bizarre change of perspective, and I began to see my words on the page not as swoops and swirls and t-crosses and i-dots of black ink, but as shadows of words fallen on the paper—where were the *real* letters? And where was the light source? . . . I couldn't begin to ponder. . . .

I had mechanically continued my reading even as these strange and unsettling ideas ran through my mind like lightning streams of ink from a tipped table-top. I was nearing the end of a page and nearly believed when I turned to the next one only the same shadowed projection would remain, leaving me lost in my own text and unable to continue my reading. My heartbeat beat harder; my collar constricted; my own spoken words thundered in my ears like menacing Algonquin drums. I read down the page, my eyes straining at the shadow-words. I put my finger and thumb upon the corner of the page, preparing to turn the leaf. My hand trembled and the words seemed to dance on the page, as the shade had danced on the walls, convincing me that my story had become merely a shadowed projection.

Swallowing back what could only be called fear, I turned the paper—with great relief I saw the inked words turn over as well, and a new page of the script showed itself. I read of Andersen and Katherine's first conversation, wherein the attraction for one another is lain but some of the obstacles begin to reveal themselves as well, like Katherine's strong-willed father already having matrimonial plans for his lovely daughter. I involuntarily glanced up at Carter, concerned that my words may have bitten him, and maybe there was a trace of something akin to pain on his neatly bearded countenance. I glanced toward Miss Hilary as well but hadn't the time to search her face for signs of hurt. Then it seemed to me there was always a trace of hurt—of painful longing—mixed with the young woman's perfected features, something that added a depth to her umber eyes, a sincerity to her smile. Moreover, I realized Mrs. Haeley wore it too, except that the authoress had worn it so long that it had begun to usurp her fine features. She wore the pain of missing Haeley like a reveler wears an ornately beaded mask. Her pain had become exquisite in its intensity—so finely wrought that at first it didn't resemble pain at all, but rather a kind of tragic beauty.

As Andersen and Katherine part on the busy City boardwalk, he watches her become obscured, piece by piece, in the crowd until only her blond plaits beneath the lavender hat can be discerned; then she disappears altogether, "like a moon that wanes through its phases during a single brief viewing."

I replaced the other sheets atop the final one and said, "Thank you" as the applause began. I knew I had not left them stunned as the authoress had, but I'd read well in spite of my distractedness, and

I found I cared not a jot for Murry's opinion: I was pleased with it, and that was all that must matter. I stood at the fluted podium while the audience applauded warmly. I made no movement to leave the speaker's place, the heat from the sextet candelabra warm on my cheek. Perhaps the audience believed I was merely soaking in the long-missed adulation. In truth I had another purpose, though it be only partially formed in my mind. As the applause slowly receded and as I considered this half-made idea, I looked across the music-room of faces—but it was not the faces that I saw: upon the walls and the carpeted floors—and upon one another—their shadows fell: an entire soirée of shades having a sort of alternate reading . . . a reading of shadow texts by shadow authors shared with a shadow audience. . . . It was an insane thought, yet I couldn't help thinking it.

The applause died out completely—it seemed Carter's and Miss Hilary's were the final hands—and Lord Chamberlain began to stir from his chair. I had not moved, and I stayed his lordship with a raised index finger.

"Thank you," I said, "for your generous appreciation. I know you have been seated for some time, but I feel the evening would be incomplete unless we were to hear one final reader. . . ." A sort of energy of nerves ran through the audience, each member speculating as to my intention. I looked to the authoress and she also was watching me, rather blankly however. "There is a writer among us, I'm quite certain, whose time is come to step forward into the sunlight and be known for his great works. . . ." Another wave of nerves vibrated through the room like the sound of discordant keys struck upon the pianoforte.

I held up *Verses & Vignettes*. "The author of this and other magnificent works must come forward . . . Mr. Edmund Holland, if you please. . . ."

People looked from one to another and back to me, no doubt wondering if I were quite in earnest; and I believed I was. Guests in the front of the gathering, like Carter and the Chamberlains, twisted in their chairs to see if anyone in the rear of the music-room was stepping forth. Truly looked about her, curiosity on her waifish face, and her uncle Terrace even appeared to scan the audience for the mysterious Mr. Holland. The moment seemed to stretch out like confectioner's taffy, longer and longer until it surely must break. Yet even in my agitated state I was enjoying the pregnant drama. I noticed however that Mr. Murry was immune to the excitement. He sat as calmly as ever, looking at me through his rectangular lenses— bemused was one way one may describe his state. Excitement was starting to ebb into irritation and disappointment (in fact I was feeling them too) when A. B. C. Murry stood and walked toward me at the podium. He was old enough to be my father and I thought he was going to paternally take charge of the awkward moment, perhaps explain that I'd been under a lot of stress working to prepare the book for publication, something like that, and then guide me to my seat. . . . I did step aside when he stood squarely at the podium desk.

He looked out upon the gathering. "As most of you know, I am Babylon Murry, Mr. Wheelwright's London publisher—and am very pleased to be bringing out his newest work." He turned to me and said in a low voice, "In fact I'm anxious to read it." Those near at hand must have heard the comment but knew not what to make of it. He continued to all, "I believe Mr. Wheelwright is correct to say that Edmund Holland should come forth into the light. However—" He reached out for *Verses & Vignettes*, and I handed it to him. "— as lovely as this debut work is, I think in the spirit of the evening, Edmund Holland's brand-new writing should provide the text." He worked his hand into his inside coat pocket and removed several pages that had been folded lengthwise. "Entrusted to me not ninety minutes ago by the very hand which authored them. Mr. Holland, if you please. . . ."

I tried to determine where Murry was looking, but it was difficult to say with his odd lenses and upon them the glare of golden light. Once again members of the audience looked about themselves anxiously. Murry stood at the podium with the manuscript pages extended toward the audience but to no one in particular. Mrs. Haeley shifted in her chair and I thought for a second that she was Edmund Holland. She gazed out upon her guests, only aping their anxious gestures, however, for she continued to wear the face of fragile calm.

My heart resumed its drumming, and I seemed to feel dark hands slip over my shoulders from a figure behind me: there was no one there, I knew, without bothering to look.

Though it seemed longer, only seconds passed before a guest rose from a chair. Perhaps because the sextet was directly before me, dazzling my eyes, but at first I could not identify the person who stood; that is to say, this person's form would not take shape as if Mr. Holland were determined to remain an enigma, to me at least. I held my hand to block the light, feeling the heat upon my palm, and my blinking and straining eyes discovered it was Miss Edith who was stepping forward. At first, a lone person applauded her, in the back of the room, her brother—up from his chair, balanced on his good leg, clapping and smiling, his teeth whiter than Miss Hilary's ivory keys. Then a few others joined in, including me finally, but most guests were too stunned or baffled, and merely stared.

Miss Edith, somewhat bewildered herself, took the manuscript sheets proffered by Murry; then he had to gently direct her to take her place at the podium. He added certainty to the otherwise uncertain applause before starting for his chair. Miss Edith looked over her shoulder at me and smiled, almost apologetically—at the deception? . . . at stealing my limelight?

I returned her smile and touched her elbow, intended as a sort of gesture of welcome or of congratulations, something reassuring; I returned then to my seat next to Mrs. Haeley.

The governess—rather the *authoress*—looked upon the gathering, sharing in the guests' uncertainty, almost commiserating with them. She absentmindedly unfolded the manuscript pages and her hands worked at smoothing the crease that ran down the center. Noises to my left made me turn: a few guests were leaving, and what I could see of their faces told the tale: they had no intention of listening to a Negress, or perhaps they couldn't accept that she was indeed Edmund Holland. I, on the other hand, felt that I'd always known, or at least that I should've known.

The departure of some of the guests steeled the authoress to her task, it would seem. "I am not certain, Mr. Wheelwright, whether to thank you or curse you. One can be burned in the intensity of sunlight, especially one who has been raised in beclouded England. The courteous thing of course is to thank you, so I thank you, for your high praise especially. And, Mr. Murry, for all your kindness and support these last few years. Well . . . I suppose there's no turning back. . . ." Miss Edith looked to her manuscript and began:

"'The London streets confounded me. I had the address of her residence, obtained via my London publisher—how difficult could it be to find, 261½ Wicker's Lane? How difficult indeed! The cut of my suit was like a giant flame for the moth-like streetpeople, hawking their wares directly in my face, so that I smelled their rotting teeth and breakfasts of spoiled turnips and onions. And solicitous women . . . at ten in the morning? Even Old New Yorkers waited until after a proper luncheon for such engagements, I would think.

'In spite of the distractions I found the inauspicious house on Wicker's Lane. I stood across from it and gazed somewhat in awe: here was the residence of Margaret T. Haeley, authoress of so many of my fretful nights. For months after reading *Dunkelraum*, before I could settle into sleep, I would check under my bed and in the wardrobe for Mrs. Haeley's monster—ridiculous, I knew even then, for a giant to be lurking in such small places. But if it were possible at all for her monster to exist, my still childish mind must have reasoned, then it was equally possible for him to break the physical laws of space.

'My wonder at Mrs. Haeley's monster contributed in no mean part to my wanting to take up the pen myself. Which reminded me, I still needed to finish the proof-sheets for *Andersen's Romance*; Murry—that was Mr. A. B. C. Murry of Claxton House—was, I imagined, growing impatient as he wanted to capitalize on the renewed interest in America in *Sunnydale*, my second book and first full-length novel; there was a stage play in the works, rumored to be starring none other than Mr. Junius Booth. Murry had had the proof-sheets delivered to the hotel and the stack was waiting in my room upon my arrival. No rest for the weary, they say.

'The thought of the house's occupant quickened my pulse but the narrow-shouldered structure itself was remarkably unremarkable: brown-stained boards, in need of fresh stain, which led one's eye to black-shuttered windows that were too small for the house's two and a half stories; the windows gave the impression the old house was squinting. I recalled the boyhood trick of squinting at an object until the act of only partial seeing—of shutting out more and more light—transformed the object into something altogether of another world. I was tempted to narrow my eyes at the old structure.

'Church-bells' peeling in the neighborhood broke my reverie. I was readying myself to cross the lane and call on Mrs. Haeley when I noticed a slightly built black fellow approach the house with a leather tote of wood—wood, yes, I realized, but not split logs or kindling as such—rather broken pieces of furniture: a severed table leg protruded conspicuously from the tote, which the fellow balanced quite easily on his narrow shoulder. He bypassed Mrs. Haeley's front steps and instead went to an alternate door to the side, below street level, that I had not observed at all. A moment to fiddle with the lock and the black fellow with his sticks of furniture disappeared from view.

'I waited for a dray to pass; the malnourished beast pulling it deposited a fresh dollop of manure in the lane. Then, dodging the droppings, I went to Mrs. Haeley's front door. There was a bell-key positioned beneath a pane of stained glass, glass which was too smudged and greasy for me to make out its figures. I turned the key and heard the rattling chime within. I imagined its echoing in the empty foyer of a haunted and abandoned house. Thinking of Mrs. Haeley's monster had worked its old spell on my fancy."

Edmund Holland's new story was of course unmistakable. To hear my own story—my *life*—rendered in fictional prose was, well, disorienting. As I listened I began to question which was real: Miss Edith's somewhat fanciful version, or the one I recollected, which, like the fictive version, no doubt obscured certain facts while also embellishing others. I gripped the chair's armrest, testing its corporality; unable to prevent myself, I reached out and took Mrs. Haeley's hand: the thin flesh, the hard bones, the cold—all presented as real to me.

Miss Edith/Mr. Holland read on. The guests who'd remained seemed quite engrossed by the tale, which gave me an odd sense of accomplishment—proud I suppose that my life could be turned into narrative worth reading (hearing) and proud that an artist would choose me for her subject . . . perhaps, more accurately, the authoress was her subject and I merely the conduit, the lens of the camera obscura, the occultist's familiar. At first Miss Edith's voice had been somewhat thin but quickly she felt at ease with her audience, and her tone became more resonant, her pacing more dramatic. There was a shadow behind her but it was obviously her own, a perfectly sized gray figure moving in perfect unison on the vellum walls.

She concluded with "my" wondering about the authoress's recent literary output and hoping that "I" may become one of her dearest friends; and she let the pages angled for reading go flat on the podium-desk. Everyone began applauding all at once, though Thursday's ovation could be heard above the rest. Miss Edith smiled wanly, unsure of the brave new world she had just entered—her anonymity shattered, and with it, I understood, the persona of Edmund Holland. She could continue to use the nom de plume but no one would ever again look for Edmund Holland browsing, say, in Bookman & Sons; no one would wonder if that fellow having boiled cod in the corner of the tavern was Edmund Holland; or if it were he stepping from the carriage with *The Times* under his arm. Edmund Holland was dead, and that too was in the mixture of Miss Edith's emotions: the heavy mantle of mourning.

I realized quite suddenly that Mrs. Haeley was not applauding. Instantly—and unkindly—I conjectured that she was jealous of the attention another authoress was garnering . . . *and in her own home!* When I looked at her, however, I thought she had somehow fallen asleep, except her eyes were very slightly open, the left more so than the right. I touched her frigid hand: "Mae . . . Mae, are you all right?" and there was no response whatsoever. By then others had noticed the authoress slumped in her chair, and they too knew something was amiss. The realization spread across the room in harmony with the dying applause.

I started to motion for Carter, but the good doctor was already coming to Mrs. Haeley. Kneeling before her, he felt the pulse of her left wrist as I was still holding her right hand, and he lifted her eyelids, one at a time . . . only the bloodshot whites were visible. "Her breathing is shallow," Carter said almost to himself, "and her pulse is irregular." He turned and spoke to Miss Edith, who was still at the fluted podium: "We must get her to her room."

Miss Edith left her manuscript at the podium and came to the authoress; then she and a stout maidservant gently lifted Mrs. Haeley from her chair and began transporting her upstairs, with Miss Edith supporting her shoulders and head, and the maid her legs. The authoress was as listless as a ragdoll. Miss Hilary sprang from the pianoforte bench to go ahead of them, no doubt to make way and to open Mrs. Haeley's bedroom door. Carter followed behind.

I was left in the music-room with the Chamberlains, and Thursday, and anxious guests, including Truly and her uncle, and A. B. C. Murry, who discreetly stepped to the podium to retrieve the manuscript pages and return them to his coat pocket.

Standing near my chair, I spoke in general to the group: "I am certain it is sheer exhaustion; Mrs. Haeley has been driving herself to complete her book—it is harder work than most realize." The latter was meant as a sort of joke, to somewhat lessen the tension, but had no such effect. Lord Chamberlain encouraged everyone to partake of more food and drink, and a few did perfunctorily—but in short order the guests departed (I played the host, thanking them for coming and bidding them adieu).

All the while, my mind was revolving with the evening's strange events: Mrs. Haeley's collapse of course but also the discovery of Edmund Holland's identity. I was bodily exhausted by the time the guests were completely gone. Lord and Lady Chamberlain were among the last, making me promise to send word of Mrs. Haeley's condition just as soon as anything concrete was known. Miss Hilary had come downstairs only moments after the authoress had been settled in her room. The magnanimous young woman took charge of the servants to supervise the ordering of the house after the soirée.

I was grateful and returned to the parlor to await any word from Carter or Miss Edith. As the uniformly dressed maids were bustling to and fro, I requested a cup of punch, with an additional shot of rum for my nerves. I was on the sofa just beginning to partake of the drink when Carter came into the room and sat in an adjacent chair. I could tell by his grave expression the diagnosis was not optimistic.

He took a handkerchief from his coat pocket and polished the lenses of his pince-nez as he spoke: "It is not good, Jefferson. I am quite certain of a brain tumor. Her right eye is not dilating and I believe is blind, and she has lost all sense of her left arm and leg. I would suppose a simple stroke if not for the mental acuity issues of recent months—confusion about people and places, and the disordering of time—I presume a tumor of the right hemisphere, which in turn, either directly or indirectly, is applying pressure to the optic nerve."

"She appeared to be improving . . . she'd been confused when I arrived but became quite lucid for days. . . ."

"I'm afraid I can't account for it. The brain is an enigmatic organ, the mind an obscure and unknowable space. Perhaps the tumor shifted position temporarily, allowing cerebral blood flow to key lobes . . . there's no way to say with certainty."

"Will it shift again? Might she return to us for a time? She wants me to accompany her to Germany."

"Again, nothing may be said in absolute terms in such cases, but I believe it highly unlikely, Jeff." Carter let the news penetrate for a moment then asked, "Does she have family? Anyone who should be notified?"

"No one whom I know. Perhaps Thursday could say better."

"I shall go look him up then." Before departing, Carter squeezed my arm and said, "I'm sorry."

He was away before I could respond but there was nothing of worth to be said anyhow. I stared into space and sipped the strong punch. A maid had come into the parlor and was extinguishing lamps and candles; thus about me darkness was gathering. She left but a single lamp glowing on the side-table nearest me. I said not a word to her while she took care of her business, and then she left me alone there in the nearly dark room. I was tempted to lean over and extinguish the remaining lamp myself, rendering the darkness complete.

In a few moments there was a gentle tapping at the door, and it was Miss Edith who came into the weak sphere of light. She sat in the same chair Carter had. "You know of her condition?"

"Yes, Dr. Carter informed me."

"She's resting as comfortably as can be managed. The doctor administered black-drop."

"Good. Has she awakened?"

"Not fully, and the poor dear doesn't seem to know anyone."

We sat quietly for a minute or two, I sipping the punch, Miss Edith settling into the chair and straightening the skirt of her dress.

I felt I was half occupying a kind of netherworld when I said, "So, you are Edmund Holland."

"For a while now. Mr. Murry assisted in selecting the pen-name. Edith, Edmund of course, in addition to my being an ardent admirer of the poet Edmund Spenser; and I have a great affinity for Holland—I received my training to become a governess in Rotterdam."

"Well, your writing is . . . remarkable, truly."

"Thank you—that means so much coming from a writer I greatly admire as well." She waited a moment: "Do you mind being the subject of my newest project?"

"Not at all—it is a compliment—but I am curious about some of the details you've altered. There are those, like my name, which I understand—though I assure you I would not litigate—but, say, the color of the authoress's house, and for that matter its number, 261½ . . ."

"It is difficult to say . . . I felt the green of the green clapboard brought with it too many symbolic connotations—like springtime and rebirth or renewal—which did not seem right to me. And I added the half to the house-number to assert the impression of transition, of moving from one sort of life to another, or from life to death perhaps—" Miss Edith checked herself, thoughtlessly calling up the grim specter.

"I understand," I said, "but why then brown for the house color? Why not, say, dark wood turned black with age?" But then, catching onto the authoress's tracks, I answered myself: "We are shortly introduced to brown-skinned Thursday, which in turn makes the house seem almost a living thing, I suppose, with its 'squinting' windows."

Edith smiled serenely in the feeble light.

"Speaking of 'Thursday,' you've certainly demoted your brother, to mere servant. Is he not insulted?"

"He knows his presence here makes more sense in that capacity, in outward appearance at least."

"So might you reveal later his doctoral candidacy in belles lettres?"

"Perhaps . . . though it may be best to leave 'Eddie' a mysterious figure himself, the fact that there is more to him than meets the eye deepening his shadow upon the page, without revealing so much that it complicates and muddies more than it clarifies."

I thought her wise, and there was much more that I could learn. "How will your story end, 'Mr. Holland'? Like this—" I motioned around me. "—with Mrs. 'Haeley' collapsing after the reading? Surely the American author and the widowed English authoress will not fall in love, marry, and return to his sun-dappled New York estate to living happily thereafter."

"It is too distant in the narrative future to see clearly, but, no, that ending isn't to be—not in an artistic work . . . maybe in a penny novel or a puppet-show."

"I suspect I know the ending, in general at least: this 'Jefferson Wheelwright' will end up as he began: alone. What could be more artistic than that? It would be perfect aesthetic symmetry."

"Perhaps," said Miss Edith, enjoying the conversation in spite of her obvious exhaustion, "but you've read my work; you know I do not find perfect symmetry especially artful. . . . Perhaps 'Mr. Wheelwright' will not end up alone, or I may return to the beginning and rewrite it so that you, that is, Mr. Wheelwright, is not a solitary figure watching Mrs. Haeley's house across the street."

"But would that not be straying too far from the truth of the matter? It is one thing to recolor a house or to tack a half onto a number, but . . ."

"We are writers, sir—we create our own truths."

"Indeed, madam." I sat there pondering what "Mr. Holland" had said, curious about what was to become of the fictional American author, feeling a strong, but I suppose understandable, kinship with him. I asked, "Do you have a title for your project, madam?"

"I've been thinking of it simply as 'The Authoress,' but there is a line from *Romeo and Juliet*, a line by Juliet's father. . . ." Miss Edith hesitated but saw that I wanted her to go on. ". . . that's been repeating itself in my mind—'Death lies on her like an untimely frost'—and it could yield . . . an evocative title."

I finished my punch and placed the cup on the side-table. "Even though she may be incoherent, I would like to look in on the authoress."

"Of course. A servant is with her. Take the lamp; I am quite content to sit in the dark for a while."

"Thank you." I gripped the lamp by its warm font as I rose from the sofa. At the parlor doorway I paused and looked back at Miss Edith: she'd dissolved into nothingness in the pitch-black room. Even the scent of her fragrant French soap was overcome by the lamp's burning oil.

Twenty-five

$\sim$

I N THE FOYER I DISCOVERED MORE WORK HAD BEEN ACCOMPLISHED
than I'd realized. The house was quiet except for low voices
coming from the music-room, now dark save for the glow of maybe
one candle. I believed the voices belonged to Carter and Miss Hilary.
Nothing seemed certain: the voices may have been Thursday and
one of the remaining maids . . . or, for that matter, Katherine and
Andersen . . . a memory of Romeo and Juliet . . . or perhaps the
authoress had already passed, and the shades of Stephen Haeley
and Margaret Townsend haunted the old house in long overdue
reunion...

Another weak light showed from the kitchen but it seemed to be
extinguished even as I glanced down the hall.

I began climbing the stair to the authoress's chamber. On only
the second step, however, the lamp's untrimmed wick failed me
and the light went out: no matter—I knew the way in what had
become utter darkness. I kept climbing. In another step or two I
felt something odd underfoot, like a small stone. Then I felt another.
In fact, the stair-steps felt altogether strange—not like steps at all,
but rather unlevel ground. I stood still with my hand on the rail
considering my position. In my left hand the lamp had already
grown cold, and in truth felt not like a lamp . . . more like metal . . .
an obelisk-shape. . . . Of course, it was the silver urn. My right hand
gripped the tree trunk that supported my climb up the mountain
path. The river-man, in his broken French, had been correct: the
sun set more quickly than I imagined, and I should've waited until
morning to accomplish my task. There was nothing to do now,

however, but keep moving forward. Once I reached the castle steps
and cleared the wood, moonlight should show my way. I continued
on. The smell of juniper was heavy in the crisp air. There seemed
to be something accompanying me in the woods—a trio of things.
I vaguely recalled hearing the howls of mountain wolves earlier;
perhaps a small pack was marking my progress up the trail. They
did not menace me, and I found that the thought of them did not
cause me fear; in fact, the idea of their shadowy presence among the
black trees was, if anything, comforting. I continued to reach out,
groping and taking hold of tree trunks for support. I thought that I
must be nearing the castle that was my goal. I was becoming tired
and decided on a brief rest. A nightingale sang somewhere deep in
the wood. Holding onto a trunk, I had an idea. I fished the camping
knife from my pocket and opened its blade. Working blindly I carved
initials into the tree: first a pair, then farther down another set. I
tried to carve carefully, but when I went back over my work with my
fingers, the letters didn't feel right. I put the knife away and struck a
match, whose light was weak and alien in the dark wood, accounting
perhaps for the strange look of the letters: sh + mt, and below jw—
not at all what I'd intended. I trusted that in the morninglight they
would read correctly. I snapped out the flame and tossed the spent
match onto the damp forest floor, soon to be covered in hoarfrost. I
looked up the path and noticed the phantasmagorical moon breaking
through the black limbs. I was close after all and imagined for a final
time what I would do: I watched myself complete the ascent; then
locate the castle wall overlooking the river, turbulent and ebon far
below, truly like Hellenic Chaos renewed. I would open the silver
urn, lunarlight bright on its sharp edges, and release their combined
ashes upon the Bavarian wind, returning them to where they'd been
young and happy, full of promise and hope. Then I would pack the
obelisk away for posterity and begin my long trek to Belgium, to
waiting friends, and on the journey I would often touch the locket at
my breast that held the two thin slivers.

Researching the Rhythms of Voice

by Ted Morrissey

(The following first appeared in Glimmer Train Press's *Writers Ask* #54.)

Like the vast majority of writers who have come out of a university creative writing program, I was taught to write contemporary literary fiction. However, for over a decade now, I've been mainly attracted to historically based narrative, both as a reader and as a writer. When we think of writers tackling a story or novel set in another time and another place, we imagine them doing extensive research on things like people, on the chronology of events, on various aspects of the material world they are attempting to fabricate—and we tend to imagine rightly. For me, though, there is another sort of research that must go on as well, the results of which are not as easy to spot in a story as, say, an infamous assassination or an obsolete gadget; and that is researching the structure of language itself. It can be a nebulous term, but what I'm most interested in is a setting's *voice.*

Voice should contribute to the ring of authenticity, to be sure, but, more than that, voice can actually compel the movement of the narrative; voice can shape its structure. William H. Gass (recipient of the American Book Award for *The Tunnel,* and copious other awards and honors) spoke to this phenomenon in a 1976 interview for *The Paris Review,* saying that "word resemblance leads you on [as a writer], not form. So you've really got a musical problem, certain paragraphs you are arranging, and you imagine you are orchestrating the *flow* of feelings from one thing to another." Gass summed up by saying, "Once you get your key signature, the theme inherent in the notes begins to emerge: the relationship between art and life and all that." Gass, author of some of the most admired books in the

English language, suggests that the physical structure of the words on the page—and the meanings, feelings, moods that they convey—help guide the writer to, essentially, everything else in the narrative: plot development, characterization, theme, setting. . . .

The importance of this sort of research in historically based fiction is nicely illustrated in Charles Frazier's highly acclaimed novel *Cold Mountain*, which is set in Civil War-era Appalachia. In an interview available online, Frazier said, "I wanted the language of the book to create a sense of otherness, of another world, one that the reader doesn't entirely know." Frazier did library research regarding the material world he was creating, finding "words for tools and processes and kitchen implements that are almost lost words." Beyond that, however, he was interested in "getting a sense of the particular use of language in that region, the rhythm of it." Frazier culled period letters and diaries for much of his information, but he also had the benefit of having actually heard "that authentic Appalachian accent" when he was a child.

For my own writing I've been attracted to more distant times and places, and as such have not had the benefit of *hearing* period speakers so printed examples of voice have been my guideposts. Nevertheless, the feel and rhythm of the language can filter into one's writing by paying attention to the linguistic structures. For my current project [*An Untimely Frost*] I've been creating a first-person narrator based on the American author Washington Irving. It isn't a fictionalized biography. It's more that Irving's persona has been the primary inspiration for my protagonist. When I first became interested in the project, I tracked down an obscure collection of Irving's letters that he wrote between 1821 and 1828.* The book has been invaluable to me in my effort to develop an effective narrative voice.

Simply put, in Irving's day a well-read New Englander structured the language in ways that sound quite foreign—quite exotic even—to us now. Take, for example, this letter written at "Beycheville," France, October 17, 1825:

> I have had something of a dull bilious affection of the system which has clung to me for more than two weeks past. . . .
> The greater part of Mrs Guestiers household, who have lately

removed here, are unwell—I have tried to shake off my own morbid fit by exercise—I have been out repeatedly hunting, as there were two packs of hounds in the neighborhood, but though I have taken violent exercise I do not feel yet reinstated by it. . . .

The terms are spectacular, yes—heaven help anyone who contracts "a dull bilious affection" and Irving's reference to "violent exercise" makes me think of junior high P.E. class—but even more meaningful to my eye and ear are the syntactic rhythms. Today one might say, "I've been feeling sick for a couple of weeks," but for Irving the "affection of the system" has "clung" to him "for more than two weeks past." The structure implies that his sense of unwell-being is a sort pernicious companion of whom he can't quite rid himself, in spite of his taking "violent exercise"—giving the act of exercise a physicality, as if it were an item from the apothecary's pantry.

Yet I have no particular interest in my protagonist's contracting a bilious affection or partaking of violent exercise. Rather I want the *structure* of the language. I want to tell my own tale, but I want to form the sentences as Irving might have had he written of the same events nearly two centuries ago. I normally keep the book of Irving's letters on my nightstand, and every so often I open to a random page and read awhile, perhaps a few pages but often as little as a sentence or two, because I'm not searching for information: I want to keep retracing the sentence rhythms in my brain, like wagon wheels along a worn track, so that when I sit down to write, the words flow as naturally in the direction of his prose style as if he (or someone like him) were composing them himself. (I must go now—I feel the onset of a bilious affection.)

* *Washington Irving and the Storrows: Letters from England and the Continent, 1821-1828.* Ed. Stanley T. Williams (Harvard University Press, 1933).

Discussion Questions

1. The issue of narrator reliability is always worth considering when you have a first-person point of view ("I"). Does Jefferson Wheelwright strike you as a reliable narrator? If so, why? And if not, why not?

2. Thursday seems an enigmatic character from the start. What character details or plot developments add to his mysteriousness in the novel?

3. Though long dead, Stephen Haeley's presence is felt, especially by Jefferson, throughout the book. How is Haeley's presence felt by the narrator? And how does the long-dead poet influence the novel's plot? Does Haeley influence other elements in the story?

4. Jefferson often has to fight against dissolving into the awestruck teen who developed a crush on Margaret Haeley. Is he always successful? If not, what are some examples of his behaving like a moonstruck adolescent?

5. There are numerous stories within the novel's overall story: the puppet-play, the burlesque version of *Dunkelraum*, *Romeo and Juliet*, and even Jefferson's on-going revisions of *Andersen's Romance*, among others. How do these other narratives function in the novel? Do they seem to support certain themes, or contradict them?

6. The novel seems to be concerned with both sexism and racism. How is each issue treated? Jefferson is perhaps rather forward-thinking on these issues, given the novel's setting of approximately 1830, but does he at times seem a product of his time period?

7. The secondary title of the novel is *The Authoress*. To whom does that title refer, Mrs. Haeley or Miss Edith, or both? The term "the authoress" would be considered a sexist term today. Does our modern sense of sexism affect how we respond to that term, which is used frequently in the book?

8. The mystery of Edmund Holland's identity is introduced early in the

novel and ultimately figures into the plot's climax. Why does Jefferson become so obsessed with Mr. Holland? Did you anticipate Edmund Holland's identity, or were you surprised at the conclusion of the literary soiree?

9. The book makes numerous references to chaos, and it ends with an allusion to the Greek notion of Chaos. Research Hellenic Chaos. Does a deeper understanding of it affect your reading of the novel?

10. The shadow becomes an important character by the end of the novel. What or who is it? What may it represent in the novel?

11. Identities become unstable by the end. What do you think has happened by the end of the book? Are there other elements in the story, perhaps even going back to some of the earliest chapters, that contribute to this narrative instability?

12. Margaret Haeley appears to live in both the past and the present—or to migrate between the two. How so? Do other characters experience a similar phenomenon?

13. In "Researching the Rhythms of Voice," the author talks about his efforts to recreate the voice of somone like Washington Irving. Is he successful in his efforts?

14. Research the biographies and the works of Washington Irving and Mary Shelley, and discuss what real-life elements appear in *An Untimely Frost*, and what seems wholly made up.

The author invites you to respond to these questions, or anything else you care to comment on, at his website: tedmorrissey.com/comments.